ASKING FOR A SECOND CHANCE

"What can I do to convince you I'm sincere?" Andrew asked.

"I want to fix this, but I'm not sure how to get past it."

Andrew covered her hand. "I'm truly sorry. We must overcome this."

"I have no doubt your apology is sincere. I'm miserable letting you go. But I vowed not to marry another man who didn't treat me as a partner. You should've trusted me enough to know te 's story wouldn't have mattered."

"I do trust you. you love me?" Andre much hope."

"Yes. I love you. . Love isn't enough. I learned this lesson whe Gerald. You had me convinced we'd built a firm foundation for a marriage and future, until this. Please give me time."

"I'll leave, but I urge you to reconsider your decision. We grew a friendship, which blossomed into a long-lasting love and respect for each other. I promise you we can have the future you desire." He walked to the door and glanced over his shoulder. "I love you, Maryann. I always will . . ."

Books by Molly Jebber

The Keepsake Pocket Quilt series
CHANGE OF HEART
GRACE'S FORGIVENESS
TWO SUITORS FOR ANNA

The Amish Charm Bakery series
LIZA'S SECOND CHANCE
ELLIE'S REDEMPTION
HANNAH'S COURAGE
MARYANN'S HOPE

Collections

THE AMISH CHRISTMAS SLEIGH
(with Kelly Long and Amy Lillard)

AMISH BRIDES
(with Jennifer Beckstrand and Amy Lillard)

Published by Kensington Publishing Corp.

Maryann's Hope

MOLLY JEBBER

ZEBRA BOOKS
KENSINGTON PUBLISHING CORP.
www.kensingtonbooks.com

ZEBRA BOOKS are published by

Kensington Publishing Corp.
119 West 40th Street
New York, NY 10018

Copyright © 2021 by Molly Jebber

All Kensington titles, imprints, and distributed lines are available at special quantity discounts for bulk purchases for sales promotion, premiums, fund-raising, educational, or institutional use.

Special book excerpts or customized printings can also be created to fit specific needs. For details, write or phone the office of the Kensington Sales Manager: Attn.: Sales Department. Kensington Publishing Corp., 119 West 40th Street, New York, NY 10018. Phone: 1-800-221-2647.

Zebra and the Z logo Reg. U.S. Pat. & TM Off.
BOUQUET Reg. U.S. Pat. & TM Off.

First Printing: February 2021
ISBN-13: 978-1-4201-5067-4
ISBN-10: 1-4201-5067-7

ISBN-13: 978-1-4201-5068-1 (eBook)
ISBN-10: 1-4201-5068-5 (eBook)

10 9 8 7 6 5 4 3 2 1

Printed in the United States of America

Ed, my loving husband and best encourager
Sue Morris, my beautiful and loving mother

ACKNOWLEDGMENTS

Thank you to:

Dawn Dowdle, agent, and John Scognamiglio, editor-in-chief, for their support, kindness, and guidance. I'm grateful for you both.

Misty, my beautiful, talented, and smart daughter who lights up my life and helps me in so many ways.

Mitch Morris, the best brother, friend, encourager, and someone I admire.

To Debbie Bugezia, Lee Granza, Margie Saenz, Mary Byrnes, Connie Melaik, Elaine Saltsgaver, Kelly Hildreth, Barbara Visto, Mary Salan, Lynn Smith, Linda Schultz, Beverly Hancock, Georgia Bulson, Margie Doerr, Donna Snyder, Melanie Fogel, Ginny Gilmore, Cyndee Perkins, Darla Landren, Ann Wright, Sigrid Davies, Shirley Madden, Doris Kerr, Diane Winters, Marcia Appel, my Southbridge, Quilt, and Church friends. You know who you are and how much you mean to me.

Aunt Sharon Sanders, Beth Sanders, and Aunt Sheila Walters for their support, love, and memories.

Patricia Campbell, Diana (DJ) Welker, Marie Coutu, and Southwest Florida Romance Writers group for your advice, love, and friendship.

To Connie Lynch, you are such a blessing in my life. I appreciate you so much.

To Marilyn Ridgway and Carolyn Ridgway—You have lifted me up more times than I can count! You're such a blessing!

To Sandra and Denise Barela—Celebrate Lit Publicists. Thank you for your friendship, advice, and encouragement!

To the Keeping Up with the Amish Group—I appreciate your support and encouragement so much! I appreciate you.

To my readers—I couldn't do this without your encouragement. Thank you so much.

Chapter One

Charm, Ohio
December 1, 1913

Maryann gazed across the cozy corner table into Andrew Wittmer's light brown eyes. He was twenty-two. They were out of their teens, the same age, and had plenty of time to learn if they were meant to have a future together. She hoped she wouldn't let her past get in the way of trusting another man. "Danki for inviting me to supper." He'd captured her heart in such a short time. How fast time had gone since she'd fled Massillon, Ohio, and returned to Charm after her late husband, Gerald's, murder. Could she trust her judgment about men?

His eyes twinkled as he chuckled. "I wondered how many socials and after-church meals you would insist we attend together before you'd accept my invitation to supper where we could talk and not be interrupted every five seconds by our friends."

She'd been cautious about him. His patience and irresistible kind heart impressed her. She doubted many men would've waited as long as he had until she was ready to

have supper at the corner restaurant by themselves tonight.
He had attended his fair share of family and community
social events with her before now. "I hope you don't
mind."

"I'm teasing you. I'd have waited for as long as it took
for you to be comfortable kumming to supper with me."

She gave him a lopsided grin. "We've been having conversations and sitting together at social events and after-
church meals for several months, and it seems like we've
been acquainted much longer." She liked the waitress's
choice for the table in the small restaurant, near the beautiful orange hue of the flames in the fireplace. A wilkom
change from the cold wintry snow falling outside the
window. Andrew made her laugh, listened, and cared about
what she had to say. She bit her lower lip. She should be
careful. She had much to learn about her new suitor. She
wondered if he'd be spending the holiday alone. She didn't
like the thought. "I can't believe this is December first.
You're invited to join my family for Christmas."

"Danki. I'll look forward to it." Andrew pushed his
empty plate to the side and he leaned forward. "Maryann,
I haven't had a strong connection with any woman like I
have with you. I'm amazed you're a mamm and manage a
bakery, unlike most Amish women. I admire you for it."

"Most Amish men may not approve of my working at
the bakery. I'm glad you do. I was surprised when Ellie
and Hannah quit after they married. I could understand
Ellie leaving, since she's with child, but I expected Hannah
would stay after she wed and wait to cut ties with the
bakery until she had a boppli. I miss them, but I'm glad
they're happy staying home. I've learned a lot managing
the bakery, and I love it."

Who wouldn't like a man who supported your dream?

Not to mention his tall frame, broad shoulders, and handsome face. His easygoing nature and quick wit were attractive, and he was quite talented. "Enough about me. The handcrafted hardwood desk and chair you gave Mr. Kline to sell for you in his small store is beautiful. Did your daed teach you how to build things?"

"Danki. Yes, Daed and Uncle Luke. I have the best memories of Daed and me in his woodshop. He kept his tools and wood organized. We designed pieces and worked on them together. He was a good teacher, and he was inspiring. We visited Uncle Luke and Aunt Dora, or they came to our haus. He's Daed's bruder, and he has a furniture store with a workshop in back of it to build things. The three of us worked together whenever we visited them in Millersburg. Uncle Luke and Aunt Dora and I exchange letters to keep in touch." He shrugged. "It's never been a chore to create things." He grinned and his eyes widened. "I've been saving money to buy a furniture store."

"Andrew, what a wonderful idea."

He should open a store. His attention to detail in the kitchen table and chairs he'd made to sell had been exquisite. She could understand why Mr. Kline had set it in the big display window.

He shrugged. "I'm saving money to open a store in Charm, but I may have to relocate based on the right location and price."

Her stomach churned. She didn't want to leave Charm. She'd left once, and it had been a mistake. She'd missed precious memories with her family and friends. Her daed and bruder told her Mamm had turned difficult and temperamental after she left. She cringed when they told her how hard life had been with Mamm during her absence. She didn't know if she could leave and cause Mamm to sink into her sullen and dark moods again. But she wouldn't worry about this now. He said he'd consider Charm. She'd face this if it became a problem. She didn't want to discuss this anymore tonight. "Do you miss Shipshewana, Indiana?"

The young waitress approached their table. "Are you finished? Would you like dessert? We have sugar cream or butterscotch pie." She laughed. "Since we buy them from your bakery, Maryann, you know they'll be good."

"We can't pass up dessert. We'll each take a piece of butterscotch pie. Danki." Andrew handed the girl his and Maryann's empty plates.

"You didn't have to order dessert. You've been generous to buy supper." Maryann's face heated.

"You love butterscotch pie, and having dessert gives me more time with you." He gave her an endearing smile.

"The waitress interrupted us when I asked if you missed Shipshewana. Do you?"

He must've had family memories and friends he'd left behind.

"Before Mamm and Daed passed from bad health, I liked growing up and enjoying life there. I was seventeen when Daed died, a year after Mamm. He was lost without her, and his health declined. He had trouble breathing and was too weak to get out of bed about three months before he took his last breath. Afterward, the place held sad and lonely memories for me. I pictured Mamm and Daed in their favorite chairs, as I sat on the settee, and Daed whistling on his old weathered stool when I was in his woodshop. I needed a fresh start, and I'm happy I moved to Charm and met you."

Her cheeks warmed. "I'm glad too." She gave him an impish grin. "You're a charmer."

"I assure you, I'm sincere." He locked his gaze with hers.

She wanted to reach over and cover his hand to let him know she cared about him, but it wouldn't be proper. "I'm sorry. I shouldn't have teased you. I didn't mean to imply you weren't sincere. I enjoy your compliments." She liked not having to guess if she was special to him. He didn't mince words. "Tell me more about your family."

"You can tease me. I like how comfortable we are with each other. It was the perfect opportunity for me to tell you I'm serious about you." He smiled. "I've told you about Uncle Luke and Aunt Dora and my parents passing away. There's not much more to tell. I'm looking forward to having a family of my own one day." He raised his brows and grinned.

Her face heated. "I'm surprised you didn't move to Millersburg from Shipshewana and work with him at his store." She was curious to find out why.

"Uncle Luke has a best friend, Clyde, who's his right-hand man. He didn't need me, and he likes being the sole owner. Clyde is younger than Uncle Luke. I'm sure he'll pass the store on to him when he can no longer manage it."

"He and your aunt don't have kinner?"

He shook his head. "They would've made wonderful parents. It's unfortunate. Speaking of kinner, Betsy is such a sweetheart. She's a mirror image of you with her blond hair and sky-blue eyes. She made my day when I first met her and she reached her arms to me."

The waitress returned and provided them with clean forks and their pie. "Enjoy." She smiled and walked away.

Maryann finished a small bite of butterscotch pie. "Betsy warmed up to you fast. Danki for the wooden blocks you brought her. She loves them. My parents and family like you, and that's not an easy approval to gain. Mamm and my schweschder-in-law, Ellie, are hard to win over. They're the most hardheaded and opinionated women in all of Charm, in my opinion. And they have a fierce love for their friends and family. I treasure them."

He exaggerated a swipe with his hand across his forehead. "I'm relieved I met with their approval." He cocked his head. "How is it you're available? I'm sure you've had lots of suitors interested in you."

"I had one interested widower, but he wanted an arranged marriage. A fraa to take care of his six kinner. I want to marry for love. Most Amish men don't approve of my past marriage to an Englischer, nor do they want to raise another man's boppli. As I mentioned earlier, I'm sure my job at the bakery doesn't thrill them either. They may not trust me to stay in Charm or to remain faithful to the Amish life. You recognized my last name, Harding, is not Amish the first time we met, and you still asked me to supper. I was shocked and pleased."

"You caught my attention right away the day I walked into the bakery. I couldn't leave without knowing we would meet again. You're as beautiful inside as you are on the outside, and I can't resist those sky-blue eyes." He leaned forward. "It's not your fault your husband passed. You chose to return to Amish life. I assumed you'd asked forgiveness for leaving to live in the outside world, once you returned. It's obvious you've committed your life to God and the Amish traditions. Do you mind telling me how you were able to leave your family and Amish life behind?"

She didn't want secrets between them. That was what ruined her first marriage. She hoped their courtship would lead them to a future together. She was smitten with him. She set her fork on the plate beside her half-eaten pie. "I was young, immature, and curious about the outside world.

Mamm smothered me, wanting us to remain close. Gerald offered me a life of freedom with him. He was fun-loving and handsome and had a good job at a bank to provide for us."

"How did you meet him? It must've been hard to escape your mamm if she had a close eye on you."

"I ran to town for anything she or Daed or Joel needed, and met Gerald. They were happy to have me fetch things in the stores for them. I feel terrible for what I put them through. I was a selfish and thoughtless girl. I'm thankful God has forgiven me, but I'm not sure I've forgiven myself. Daed and Joel told me Mamm's mood changes were difficult on them. She's different from other women in this way. She's not right in the head. We are aware her drastic mood changes aren't normal. I knew this, and I left. She smothered me and wanted me with her all the time. I couldn't take it anymore. Gerald offered me a way out, and I took it. I'm guilt-stricken over it. They're relieved I'm back, and she's better."

"It's shocking and sad about your mamm. I'm also relieved she's better." He forked another piece of pie. "Did you love Gerald? Were you happy in your marriage? If I'm asking too many questions, tell me. We can change the subject."

She shook her head. "Since we're courting, it's best you know everything. I fell for Gerald the minute he approached me and introduced himself. He was handsome, had a zest for life, and made me feel like the most beautiful girl in the world. I told him I needed an escape from Amish life and my hovering mamm. He told me about the beautiful music, clothes, conveniences, and things he'd provide for us."

"How long did you court before you married him?"

Maryann gave him a crooked smile. "In six weeks, he asked me to marry him. He was tired of sneaking around. He was in town to train a manager as a favor for his daed's friend who owned the bank. He had to return to his job in Massillon, and I went with him. He found a judge the day we arrived, and we got married. My infatuation with him turned into love until he put our lives in jeopardy and kept secrets."

The waitress glanced at their empty plates. "Would you like me to remove these?"

They nodded.

The waitress gestured to their cups. "Would you like more hot chocolate?"

"Yes, please." Andrew thanked her. "I'm not ready to leave. Are you?"

She shook her head. She would tell him her story. She hoped he wouldn't change his mind about her. If he did, she wouldn't blame him. "We were happy at first. He had dark hair and eyes, and he was tall and confident. I was attracted to him the first time we met. He lied about working at the bank after hours. A man approached me, saying my husband owed him money from a gambling debt. I told him I'd speak to my husband about it. He stomped away. I confronted Gerald, and he admitted he had been playing cards for money."

"Did he say he'd stop?"

"No. He insisted he made enough money to take proper care of us and for me not to complain. He grew short-tempered and tired from staying out late, and lied about where he went at night. I begged him to quit."

"What about Betsy? Was he happy when you told him you were with child?"

"He said he was happy, but this news put more pressure

on him. We lost our haus and had to rent it from the owner for about a month and then sell our furniture to pay his gambling debts. We had to move to the boarding haus. Then he got into a dispute over a debt he owed a man, and the man killed him. He put himself and us in danger."

"Was the murderer caught?"

"Yes. The sheriff caught the murderer. I was devastated and homesick for my family. I was afraid the men he gambled with would think I had their money. I wrote Joel, and he and Ellie came and brought me back to Charm." She folded her trembling hands on the table. "I can't blame Gerald for everything. I was young and selfish leaving my family instead of staying to take care of Mamm. I was in love and made the decision to go with him. He didn't force me."

"Didn't his family take you and Betsy into their home?"

"His mamm had passed, and his daed wanted nothing to do with me. He had no love for the Amish. His father did love Gerald, and he kept him employed. He wouldn't acknowledge me or Betsy after Gerald passed. At this point, I asked God to forgive me, and I longed for Amish life and my family again."

His eyes widened. "What a tragic story."

Maryann kept her head down and stayed silent. Her heart hurt. She had loved Gerald, and as difficult as he was, she mourned his death. She resented him for the secrets he kept that ruined their once-happy marriage. She'd been given a second chance to return to her family and Amish life. She'd attended an Englischer church and never abandoned her faith in God. Reliving this story tonight made her feel guilty all over again. She rolled her shoulders back and sighed. "I'm trying to put it all behind me."

"We all make mistakes. God forgives us, and we should

forgive each other. I care for you and for Betsy. I'm hoping our courtship grows more serious as we learn more about each other. I'm sure it wasn't easy for you to tell me about your past. Danki for being open and honest with me."

She relaxed her tense shoulders. He hadn't withdrawn or held anything she'd done against her. She half expected him to pay the check and drop her off at home as fast as possible, but he'd listened and not judged her. Andrew Wittmer was a keeper. She'd be heartbroken if there was something they couldn't overcome that severed their courtship. "Danki for your understanding. It means more to me than you know."

The waitress returned with their hot chocolate. "I apologize. I got distracted and took too long bringing your drinks out. If you don't want them, I'll take them off your bill." She sucked in her bottom lip and waited.

Andrew patted the table. "No need to apologize. We've been enjoying our conversation and didn't notice. Leave them. It's all right. Danki."

Maryann admired him for his kindness to the waitress. Not all men would be as patient or forgiving. She scanned the restaurant. They didn't have anyone seated around them, except for a couple in the far opposite corner not paying attention to them. This had been the perfect evening to tell him what he needed to know about her before they moved further along in this courtship. She pressed a hand to her chest. He'd be a good partner to communicate with and resolve problems together.

She was amazed he wasn't already married. "Were there any available women who caught your attention before you moved to Charm?"

"A couple, but neither worked out."

"You must tell me more. I told you everything." Maryann

swallowed around the trepidation in her throat. She hoped both these women wouldn't show up or pursue him. He was handsome and humorous and had ambition. What could've happened to deter him from courting them?

Andrew traced the top of his hot chocolate cup. "Natalie and I went to school together. She lived one farm over from ours. We were childhood friends and our friendship blossomed into a courtship when we were sixteen. She developed a terrible cough, became weak and bedridden, and died within six months. I mourned her death for over a year."

Maryann's eyes widened. "How tragic." She shook her head. "It's difficult to lose someone you love. I'm sorry." She toyed with her red and white checkered cotton napkin. "You didn't open your heart to anyone after Natalie?" She couldn't imagine girls had left him alone. He had everything to offer them. He'd inherited his parents' farm and he could handcraft beautiful furniture. He was handsome, kind, and courteous. Those traits were enough to entice any woman.

He rolled his eyes and sighed. "Then there was Maggie. She was a redheaded spitfire. She wanted to get married much sooner than I was ready, and she broke off our courtship. Four months later, she met and married Nathaniel. I went to their wedding and wished them well. And there's the end of my courting stories. I believe I've met the last woman I'll need in my life." He grinned. "I should take you home. You have to get up early tomorrow." He paid the check, helped her on with her gray wool hooded cape, and escorted her outside.

She slipped her mittens on her hands, held one out, and watched the snowflakes melt. "I like having snow for

Christmas. Maybe we can work in some time for ice skating together soon."

He slid onto the bench beside her, and rolled the brown broadcloth curtains to the buggy floor to shut out the cold wind and moisture. The curtains were used instead of doors on the enclosed buggy to save money, and they made the opening easier to get in and out. But he wondered if they might be a good investment. He then guided the mare to head to her home not far from town. "Good idea. We'll check the ice pond near your property and go when it's safe." He reached back and covered her with a dark green wool blanket he kept on the back bench.

She held the lantern to light the way. This night couldn't have gone any better, aside from the news he may have to search for a store site outside of Charm. Mamm was older, and Maryann had been the only one who could pull her out of her gloomy moods. Betsy had brought much joy to Mamm's life. Daed and Joel thanked her often for being there for Mamm and them. She couldn't leave Mamm again and have her suffer, bringing hardship to her family. Andrew was in Charm now, and there was a good possibility he'd stay. She'd ignore his suggestion that he might have to move in the future. "This is a good packing snow. We might get an extra two inches on top of the two already on the ground."

He pulled close to her haus where her parents had set out lanterns on the porch to provide light for them. He stepped out and helped her down. Then he set the lantern on the snow on the ground. He bent, pushed snow together to form a ball, and ran with it making a larger ball for a snowman.

She laughed and made one herself and ran with it to make a medium-sized ball for the snowman's middle.

"Stop!" He ran to her, hoisted hers, and set it on top of his big one. "We need one for the snowman's head." He rolled another one and set it on top of the middle snowball. "This is for Betsy. She'll be tickled and amazed when she wakes up and peeks out the window." He reached up and pulled a thin branch off a small tree. He broke it in half and stuck them on either side of the snowman for arms.

"She will love having a snowman in our yard! I've made little ones when we've played outside. She loves the snow, and her cheeks turn bright red in the cold. She cries when I take her in, even though she must be freezing."

"Are you looking forward to more kinner?" He escorted her to the door.

"Yes, I do want more. Do you?"

"Yes, as many as the woman I marry will agree to. I'd have a houseful." He rubbed his gloves together and shivered. "We can continue this conversation later. I don't want to keep you out too long. You'll resent me when you're having trouble staying awake tomorrow."

She could've enjoyed his company the rest of the night. She didn't want to leave him. He made her heart soar. She wanted to know every little thing about this man. But she was a mamm and she did have a job. "I do have to be at the bakery by five. You must get up early too."

"I do, but I can take my time doing my chores. You have hungry mouths to feed and bread to bake. Good night, Maryann. I'll stop by the bakery and we'll make more plans together."

"I look forward to it, and danki again for tonight." She went inside. She was thankful to have a minute alone in the living room. Her parents must be in the sitting room. Betsy would be asleep. Happy butterflies fluttered in her stomach. She closed her eyes and whispered,

"Dear Heavenly Father, please don't let anything kumme between Andrew and me. Danki for putting him in my life. I love you, Father. Amen."

She opened the door to Betsy's bedroom and peeked in at her. Betsy, lay flat on her back, fast asleep, and with her tiny lips parted. Peaceful and precious, she was comfortable. She opened the door to the sitting room.

Mamm threw her knitting needles and ball of yarn in the basket and strode to her. "Are you all right? I was worried. The snow and ice can be treacherous."

Maryann rubbed the back of her neck. Mamm was overreacting. She didn't want to confront her. It was easier to ignore Mamm's anxiety. "Where's Daed?"

"He's gone to bed. I couldn't sleep until you were home. I was sure you were in an accident." Mamm wiped a tear.

She gazed into Mamm's worried eyes. Her resolve wavered. She should be more compassionate. Mamm couldn't help her over-the-top possessiveness of her. Maryann held her. "Mamm, I'm fine. Andrew took good care of me. Everything's all right."

Mamm calmed and she released Maryann. "If you marry Andrew, I'm happy his property is close and one over from ours." Mamm gripped her sleeve. "And you'll visit me, and I can kumme to your haus. You and Betsy mean the world to me." Mamm's eyes filled with tears. "I'm blessed and happy you're with us. I missed you when you were gone."

"You don't need to worry. Please, Mamm. Please relax." She held Mamm's hand, kissed it, and watched Mamm go into her bedroom before entering hers. Maryann's chest tightened. She was relieved Mamm had not been frustrated and argumentative. Mamm's obsession over her, and now

Betsy, was abnormal. It always had been, but what could she do but reassure her?

She couldn't imagine how awful it had been for Joel and Daed when she was away. She and Betsy had proved to be the best medicine for keeping Mamm even tempered and happy. She loved her, and she would take care of her. It was her duty as her dochder. Joel and Daed needed her to take on this role, and she owed it to them and to Mamm. She prayed Andrew would stay in Charm.

Andrew had a good time with Maryann this evening. On his way home from her haus, he grimaced and drove under a large hanging branch. *Thud.* His heart beat fast as he glanced over his shoulder. He shuddered. The large limb had just missed him. He shook off the scare and pictured Maryann's big blue eyes. He was falling in love with her. Her story about her late husband and Betsy touched his heart. He'd heard part of it before today. She'd been open and shared the details. He respected her for being forthcoming.

Her having a child wouldn't turn him away. He loved kinner. Maryann was strong and courageous to return to Charm and Amish life. Most Amish would wilkom her with open arms, but each community had their share of gossips and not all of them would accept her without judgment and ridicule.

A buggy passed with an Amish couple in it. "Good evening."

He nodded and tipped his hat to them. Charm was a friendly community. He'd made a good choice moving here. Maryann had been a wilkom find. He got the impression her mamm's illness was unusual. Not the kind of sickness he'd ever encountered. Her closeness to Maryann sounded overly possessive, unlike most Amish mamms. He could tell Maryann felt her mamm was her responsibility. It was a lot for Maryann to have on her back.

He should've told her his secret, but maybe it wasn't necessary. He was doing the right thing keeping the information to himself. It might keep her from giving him a chance. Maybe he'd tell her someday, but not for a long time. It was the Amish way not to discuss such things. He had done nothing wrong, but his association with this particular man might upset her. She'd put her past behind her, and he wanted to leave it there. He pushed this man out of his mind. She had enough responsibility with Betsy, her mamm, and the bakery. He wanted to show his support and encouragement and learn all he could about her.

Andrew threw on his coat and headed for the woodshop. This Tuesday morning had flown by. He slid on the long patch of ice, regained his footing, and stomped through the inches of snow on the way to the woodshop not far from his barn. He scrutinized different pieces of maple, pine, hardwood, and cedar. He could work for hours and make beautiful furniture, toys, and gifts. A property manager was what he needed.

He'd ask Maryann for her recommendation, since she knew a lot of the Amish. He valued Maryann's opinion, and it was good to ask her advice and discuss what was on his mind. She didn't shy away from the hard questions he'd asked her.

He sanded four maple table legs and then closed his doors. He hitched the horse to the buggy and headed for the bakery. He'd had such a good time with her last night, and this was a good excuse to meet with her again.

He drove five minutes to the bakery, parked in front of it, entered and shut the door against the crisp and cold wind. He gazed into her beautiful blue eyes. Two customers came in and walked past him to the counter. "Maryann, you're busy. I'll kumme back."

She waved him over to a stool at the side counter. "Nonsense. Have a seat." She poured him a cup of coffee and greeted her customers. She filled their orders and then served him a warm maple sugar cookie.

"Danki." He watched her with the two Englisch women.

She treated them as if they were her friends. She satisfied their orders, packaged them, and accepted their money fast. Liza, the owner of the store, was blessed to have such an efficient and friendly manager.

"I came to ask a favor."

"I'll be happy to help." She quirked a brow.

"I'd like to hire a property manager who can also construct furniture. I wouldn't expect him to build during the busier planting and growing months. But having a property manager in that period would free me to build and consign pieces to sell to Mr. Kline, and it's what I love to do."

Maryann tapped her nails on the counter. "Would you be willing to train someone on wood crafting?"

He nodded. "Do you have a man in mind?"

"Rachael's bruder, Toby. He's a hard worker, and he has taken the role of man of the haus and provided for the family since their daed's illness. They have a small garden, and he works odd jobs to make ends meet. He's quiet, and I don't know him well. I trust Rachael's opinion. She's been a blessing to us in the bakery. Let's talk to her. Just a minute." She stuck her head in the open doorway to the kitchen. "Rachael, will you join me for a minute?"

Rachael limped to the counter and stood next to her. "Good morning, Andrew. Maryann, what can I do for you?"

"Andrew needs help at his place. What about Toby? It would be steady employment."

Rachael cupped her cheeks. "What a marvelous idea. Toby needs dependable work. He tires of traveling from one farm to the next for small jobs two and three times a day. He doesn't say, but I suspect he worries if the work will be available ongoing to pay our bills. He's proud and doesn't like to ask for handouts."

Andrew sipped his coffee. "I'd like to speak with him. Where's your place?"

Rachael met his gaze. "We live a mile out of town. We're the second haus on the left on Mill Road. Danki for considering Toby."

"You're doing me a favor. I look forward to discussing the job with him." Andrew finished his coffee. "I shouldn't keep you both any longer." He stood.

"Goodbye, Andrew." Rachael limped to the kitchen.

"Danki for stopping by. Don't be a stranger." Maryann smiled.

"We'll get together soon." Andrew winked at her and left to visit Toby. He drove the short distance, parked his buggy in front of the small haus, and knocked on the door. A tall man about his same height and a few years younger than himself answered the door.

"How can I help you?" Toby held the door open halfway.

"I assume you're Toby?"

Toby tilted his head. "Yes. Have we met?"

Andrew held out his hand. "I'm Andrew Wittmer, and

I live on this same road about four farms past yours. I am courting Maryann Harding. I spoke with her and your schweschder, Rachael, at the bakery this morning and she recommended I speak to you about the property manager job I have open. They hoped you might be interested."

Toby's eyes widened, and he shook Andrew's hand. "Yes, I'm Toby. Please kumme in. I am interested."

The haus was sparsely furnished. He sat on one of three maple chairs with worn cushions. The logs in the small fireplace fed a little fire to keep the room warm. He breathed in the scent of liniment. He eyed a basket of bandages and a jar of liniment next to a chair with a tattered patchwork quilt bunched on the seat about three feet from him. He rose as a tall, thin woman with tired eyes entered the room.

"I'm Toby's mamm, Eleanor Schlabach. Please call me Eleanor. I recognize you from Sunday services, but we've not been introduced."

"A pleasure to meet you. I'm a friend of Maryann Harding's. She works with your dochder, Rachael, at the bakery. Maryann and your dochder recommended Toby for the job I have open to oversee my property. They praised him and thought he'd be a good hire."

Toby blushed and stayed silent.

"I would agree. Please sit and make yourself comfortable. Would you like coffee?" Mrs. Schlabach's smile broadened.

Andrew shook his head. "No, danki."

"I'll leave you men to talk." Eleanor left the room.

Andrew sat across from Toby. "I'm surprised we haven't met before today."

"I stay home with my daed, Vernon, to allow Rachael

and Mamm to attend the services and outings. He's sick, and he has good and bad days. He's asleep in his bedroom. The doctor suspects it's his heart. He's not sure. Daed refuses to go to the hospital. He's a selfless man who doesn't want to cost his family money, no matter how much we tell him we care and want the best for him. He insists God will heal him or take him home, and he's content with whatever the outcome. I also take care of our small property and do repair and farm work for friends during the week and Saturdays." Toby settled back in the chair.

"I'm sorry your daed is in bad health. If there's anything I can do for you or your family, I'd be happy to." Andrew liked Toby on sight. The man had compassion and love for his family. He didn't indicate in any way that he was resentful or wished things were different.

"Maybe you can. I'm interested in the job you mentioned. Please tell me more about what the work would entail."

"I need a man to manage my livestock and farm. I like to build furniture and sell my pieces in stores more than I like to farm. I plan to buy a store when I have the proper funds saved. Do you have experience managing a farm and livestock?"

Toby nodded. "We had an eighty-acre place before moving to Charm and before Daed's health went downhill. Daed and I had no problem keeping up with the farm and livestock. Mamm and Rachael did their part, but not much was needed from them outside the home. I'm handy with tools and can fix about anything. I'd be thankful for a permanent job rather than depending on odd jobs like I've been doing."

Andrew discussed salary, job duties, and the schedule

with Toby. "Is all of this agreeable to you? Do you have any questions?"

Toby hadn't moved a muscle, and he'd not stopped smiling. "Your offer is generous, and no, I don't have any questions. You've covered about everything."

Andrew held out his hand. "You're hired."

Toby sat on the edge of his chair and shook Andrew's hand. "Danki. I won't let you down, Mr. Wittmer." Toby's eyes creased, as he grinned.

"Call me Andrew. Don't bring your dinner. Treat my kitchen as yours. You're wilkom to what I have in the cupboards or on the counter. There are always fresh eggs, and you can make them scrambled, fried, or the way you'd like on the cookstove if I'm short on groceries."

"No, I don't want to take advantage of you. I'll have breakfast before I leave and pack a dinner." Toby stared at his worn black shoes.

"I insist." He sensed from the small haus and property size, the family struggled to make ends meet. He was sure the family depended on the monies Rachael and Toby made to keep them afloat. He'd do what he could to make their lives easier and provide meals for Toby and cut down on the groceries needed for them. He hoped he and Toby would grow a close friendship. He liked Toby's quiet demeanor, but he wanted to lighten his new friend's mood and make his life better. He stood. "I won't keep you any longer. Please give your parents my regards."

"I'll be at your place at five thirty in the morning. And danki again." Toby opened the door for him.

"Remember, don't bring food. I've got plenty, and I wouldn't mind the company at the table." He gave him a curt nod. "And, Toby, you're doing me a favor." Andrew tipped his hat and headed home. He pulled close to the barn, unharnessed his horse, and led him into the barn to the stall. He tromped across the snow to his haus and went inside to start a fire in the fireplace. Stomach growling, he took off his coat, opened a container of leftover stew he'd kept in the icebox, and poured it in an iron kettle he hung on the hook over the small fire.

Andrew plopped into his favorite chair, grabbed the patchwork quilt Mamm had made him years ago, and covered himself as he waited for the stew to heat. He hoped he and Maryann didn't encounter any differences they couldn't mend. He could foresee her having a problem with moving from Charm. She'd reunited with her family and friends, and Betsy was a big part of her parents' lives. Would she contemplate ending their courtship if he asked her to leave Charm to open a store in the future?

Chapter Two

Maryann peered out the window of the bakery at the wintry mix of sleet and snow flurries. She loved the white fluff nestled on branches and untouched by boot prints out in the fields as she drove to work this cold Wednesday morning. A contrast to the dirty slush on the road and walkways in town. Buster, her horse, plowed through the cold weather on the way to the bakery without hesitation.

She couldn't be happier in Charm with her family and her courtship with Andrew. She prayed he'd open a store in Charm when the time was right. His excitement showed on his face when he talked about it. She was sure he would, for her and Betsy's sakes, if they were meant to marry in the future.

Rachael came up behind her. "What are you day-dreaming about? Andrew? I am rooting for the two of you." She beamed. "I no sooner had my coat off when Toby burst in the living room and jabbered about Andrew's job offer and the details. It did my heart good to have him so enthusiastic about working for Andrew. He's devoted to us, and he never complains. I'm happy for him. Toby wore a big smile early this morning, gulped down his breakfast, and flew out the door with a lilt in his step. He won't take time to do anything with friends, but maybe he and Andrew will form a friendship."

"I'm pleased it worked out for Andrew and Toby. And yes, I did have my mind on Andrew. He walked into my life when I least expected it, and he's handsome, attentive, and responsible. I'm like a silly schoolgirl and giddy about him. He's made a big impression on me. I'm already praying we have a future together. He's everything I want in a man. He accepts Betsy and my past. He doesn't dwell on negative things about me or anyone. It's refreshing." She frowned. "I've overheard gossips whisper they can't understand why any Amish man would consider me a proper fraa." She blew out a breath. "I'm glad they don't dissuade him."

Magdelena joined them. "Those women are a nuisance when they wag their tongues saying upsetting things about us or our friends. They need to listen closer to Bishop Fisher's messages on how we are not to gossip and we are to love each other. Ignore them. I admire Andrew for his forgiving nature and kind heart. I'm thrilled for Toby. It's like God is blessing Toby by bringing Andrew into his life and offering him this opportunity."

"Toby doesn't ask for anything. He gives without taking. I'm thrilled for him."

Maryann wrinkled her forehead. "How is your daed?"

Rachael frowned. "He's keeping a small amount of food in his stomach, which is a plus, but he's weak and his persistent cough isn't any better. Sores are on his arms and legs, and his skin is paper thin. The sores heal, and then new ones form. He has days where they are better and less in number than others. He doesn't complain, but I've caught him wincing in pain when we dress him or bandage them. Dr. Harrison said the best thing we can do is to keep him as comfortable as possible." She stopped and put a finger to her lips. "The back door slammed."

Maryann narrowed her eyes and lifted her chin. "No one but us kummes through the back door. Who could it be?"

Rachael and Magdelena went with her to the back.

Maryann threw open the door to the storage room and the door leading out to the back. She rushed outside and ran after the chubby Englisch boy with light red hair. He had on a nice heavy gray wool coat, a hat, and new boots. Why would he need to steal? "You kumme back right now!"

"Maryann, kumme back," Magdelena called. "We'll alert the sheriff. Let the lawman find and talk to the boy."

The boy ran out of the alley and onto the main road.

Maryann chased after him.

Andrew halted his buggy as the boy passed him. "Maryann, what's happening?" He jumped out, sprinted to the boy, and caught the boy's arm. "Why are you running from Maryann?"

The boy scowled and fidgeted, but Andrew's grasp held him tight.

Maryann reached them, stopped, bent over, and caught her breath. "You came along at the right time. The girls and I were in the front room and the back door slammed. We went to find out who came in and found this boy escaping with a sack I suspect contains things he stole from us." She rubbed her arms and her teeth chattered.

"Let's go inside the bakery. Maryann, you're going to get a cold if we don't warm you up. You shouldn't be out without a coat." He stared at the boy. "Stop fighting to get away from me, or I'll take you to the sheriff." He gripped the boy's arm tighter and dragged the young Englischer inside the shop, walking alongside Maryann.

Magdelena and Rachael stood with the back door open. They stepped aside for Maryann, Andrew, and the culprit to enter.

Rachael glared at the boy as Andrew held his grip on him. "You scared us, you naughty boy. Your clothes and boots look new. You don't appear to need to steal. Why did you?" She shook her head and crossed her arms.

Magdelena said, "Andrew, your timing couldn't have been better. Maryann wouldn't listen to us. She was determined to catch him."

"We should get the sheriff. He's not remorseful. He's upset he got caught. Maybe he needs to learn a lesson." Rachael stared at the young robber. "What's your name?"

The young boy stuck his hands in his pockets and snarled. "Wally."

Andrew stared down at him. "Wally what?"

"Ferguson." His angry eyes fell on Maryann. "The sheriff isn't going to punish me. I'm a kid! I'm only eleven."

Andrew shook his head. "You're wrong. You stole from a store. It's a crime."

The boy's face softened. His mouth gaped open. He held out the bag. "Please, don't tell the sheriff. Here's everything I took." He held the bag out to her.

Maryann grabbed it from him and looked inside. "Why did you take a hammer, nails, and a screwdriver? How did you know we had these things in our backroom? Why didn't you borrow them from your daed or a friend?"

He shoved his hands in his pockets again. "Mom brought me here, and when you and she weren't paying attention, I snuck back there to nose around. I didn't want to borrow tools. I wanted my own. Girls don't need tools." He puffed out his chest. "Men do repairs, not women. I figured you wouldn't miss what I took."

"Do you want to alert the sheriff, Maryann?" Andrew shrugged. "Or I don't mind taking the boy home and having a talk with his daed."

"Don't tell my father. He'll tan my hide. He says I'm too young to build things. He won't let me near his tools." The boy jerked his head to Andrew. "Please don't tell him."

Maryann was relieved Andrew had arrived when he did. She didn't want to deal with this small Englischer. She wasn't sure what to do, and she was happy to hand the lad over to him. "I'd appreciate you taking the boy to his parents. He's young. I don't want to get the sheriff involved. I hope he's learned his lesson. Have you, Wally? I don't want to learn of you breaking into our shop or any other store again, or I will alert the sheriff. Understood?"

Wally bobbed his head and gazed at Maryann with worried eyes. "Thank you. I won't steal again. I promise."

Four ladies entered the bakery and sat at one of the tables in the café area of the bakery in front of the display case. Rachael and Magdelena greeted them.

Andrew whispered, "Maryann, I came to ask you to supper tonight. May I pick you up at six this evening at your haus?"

"I'll look forward to it." She blushed. "Danki for taking care of how to handle Wally and his bad behavior."

"I'm glad I could help." He grinned. He walked with her to the front of the store.

Rachael waved to Andrew. "Danki for hiring Toby."

"We had a good conversation about his schedule for

the day this morning. I'm sure the arrangement will work out well for both of us." He didn't let go of Wally's arm. "Let's go have a conversation with your daed."

"I'm sorry for the trouble I caused you." Wally met Maryann's gaze.

"I hope you've learned your lesson." Maybe he would appreciate her generosity, and the scare of being caught would change his mind about attempting to steal again.

Andrew tipped his hat and dragged Wally outside to his buggy.

Maryann watched Andrew and Wally get in the buggy. She pressed a hand to her heart. He'd make a good daed. Maybe to their kinner in the future. He respected her, asked her opinion, and communicated with her. She hadn't had that with Gerald.

She couldn't explain how it had happened so fast. She just knew it was true. She had fallen in love with him, and he was the right man for her and Betsy.

Andrew covered Wally's legs with a wool blanket. "Are you warm enough?"

Wally nodded his head.

"Where do you live?"

Wally gave Andrew directions and stared straight ahead.

Andrew was glad he'd been there to relieve Maryann from having to contend with this child's bad behavior. He'd do anything for her. He also wanted to give this boy another chance to learn a valuable lesson before he got older and made decisions that could ruin his life. "Is it this haus or the next one?"

Wally pointed to a two-story white haus with a large red

barn off to the side. The land had to stretch out over about 180 acres. The property was beautiful, with big trees and a large frozen pond. "My father will be real mad at me. Please drop me off and leave. I'll tell him you offered me a ride and I accepted."

"No. Your actions have consequences. It's important you understand how wrong this is at your age, so you don't do this again. Stealing is a serious offense. If you were an adult, you would've been thrown in jail with scary men who had committed worse crimes. Do you realize this?"

Wally kept his chin to his chest. "No." He sighed. "I should warn you. My father doesn't like the Amish."

"Why?" Andrew stiffened. He hadn't considered the Fergusons' prejudice. Maybe this wasn't the best idea.

"My father thinks you're strange. You wear odd clothes, talk funny, and don't go to school past the eighth grade."

Confrontation wasn't the Amish way to handle differences with Englischers. He had assumed Mr. Ferguson would be grateful he'd brought his son home without reporting him to the lawman. He hadn't encountered prejudice for being Amish for a while. "Do you have the same opinion?" Andrew glanced at him.

Wally shrugged. "You don't seem any different from me or my family."

Andrew halted his mare a couple of feet from where Mr. Ferguson stood in front of the haus. He got out and offered his hand to the man. He didn't want any trouble. "I'm Andrew Wittmer."

"What are you doing with my boy in your buggy?" The man jutted his square chin and ignored Andrew's offer of a handshake. He wore a fancy brown hat matching his wool overcoat and stood tall, with broad shoulders.

Andrew dropped his hand to his side. The man wasn't going to make this introduction easy. He opened his mouth to answer.

Mr. Ferguson balled fists, tightened his jaw, and interrupted him. "I asked you a question."

He braced himself for a punch to the face. "Wally, please tell your daed what happened at the bakery."

Wally stood a yard away from his daed. "Mr. Wittmer offered me a ride. Said it was cold outside. I accepted."

He gave Wally a hard gaze. "Wally, tell your daed the truth."

"Are you calling my boy a liar?" Mr. Ferguson took a step closer to Andrew.

Andrew stepped back. This may have been the worst idea he'd had in a long time. "Wally dashed into the bakery's storage room and stole tools. I came upon him and the bakery's manager, Maryann. She told me what happened, and Wally had the tools in hand. I offered to bring him home and inform you instead of taking your boy to the sheriff."

"Is this true, Wally?"

Wally nodded and hung his head.

The man pointed to the haus. "Get inside and go to your bedroom. I'll deal with you in a minute."

Wally dragged his feet inside the impressive haus.

Hands on hips, Mr. Ferguson squinted. "Thank you for not reporting my son to the sheriff."

"You're wilkom." Andrew relaxed, nodded, and hurried to his buggy. He didn't want to leave room in the conversation for an argument or the Englischer's reasons for not being fond of the Amish. He'd end things on a decent note.

He hoped Mr. Ferguson would be better accepting of the Amish after their encounter.

From Mr. Ferguson's strong reaction to the news, Andrew was sure he would talk to Wally and help him understand the error of his ways.

He looked forward to having kinner, and he couldn't wait to become a daed someday.

His face cold against the slight wind, Andrew arrived home. He unharnessed his horse and walked the animal inside the barn. "Toby, you've whipped this barn into great shape. I've been meaning to put the tools, ropes, pails, and metal bins in a better order, and I never got around to it. This is great. Danki."

Toby rested his hands on his hips. "I enjoyed putting everything in order."

Andrew clapped him on the shoulder. "Would you like to kumme with me to the woodshop?"

Toby nodded, followed him, and stepped inside the large space. "You have this shop outfitted with anything a person would need for handcrafting pieces. Do you have time to teach me how to build a chair or table? I haven't built any furniture, but I'm interested in learning the craft."

He was encouraged by Toby's enthusiasm. "Since the farm equipment is in good shape, winter is the best time for us to work together on building pieces. You can consign what you make with Mr. Kline, and I'll take half the profit for the materials."

Toby rubbed his hands together. "You don't have to. The training you give me is payment enough."

"No, I insist. It will make the craft more fun for you." Andrew showed him how to construct a simple crate. "Draw your design for size and then select the scrap lumber to do your project. After you have managed to construct a good solid crate, then I'll teach you how to do something harder."

"I'm eager to start." Toby picked up a sharpened pencil and drew his design, chose his wood, and explained to Andrew what he understood he was to do to accomplish his task.

Andrew sanded and smoothed the edges of the hardwood shelf he'd constructed a couple of days ago and then lifted his brush to paint it.

Toby worked for the next hour and then lifted his small crate. "What do you think?"

Andrew took the crate from him and studied the angles. "Excellent work." He checked the clock. "Time for you to head home. Would you like to take the crate with you?"

Toby grinned. "Danki. I need one." He accepted his creation from Andrew. "Is there anything more you'd like me to do before I leave?"

Andrew shook his head. "No. You've done a good job today. I made the right decision hiring you. I'll show you how to build a small table tomorrow. Do you have a friend who might like to join us? Someone you know who may be interested in handcrafting furniture?"

"No. I haven't had time for friends between taking care of Daed and chores. But I don't mind. My family is my first priority, and I like taking care of them. I'd love to stay and talk, but I've got to go. Goodbye, Andrew." Toby strolled to the door.

"Goodbye. Danki for your help today." He liked Toby's eagerness to learn and his taking initiative to organize the barn. Toby wasn't much younger than himself, and he enjoyed his company.

He locked the woodshop and hurried to the haus to change his clothes for his supper with Maryann and then drove to her haus. There was the love of his life waiting on him outside. He jumped out and helped her into the buggy. His heart beat faster sitting next to her. "I would've kumme in and spoken with your parents and held Betsy for a couple of minutes. You didn't have to wait in the cold."

"I fed Betsy, and Mamm was rocking her to sleep." She sighed. "I can't believe she's thirteen months already. Daed is snoring in his chair." She chuckled.

"I can't understand how you do it. You work all day, kumme home and take care of little Betsy, and look beautiful no matter what time of day it is." He covered her lap with the wool blanket, and Maryann tucked the edges under her legs.

She rolled down the heavy curtain and tied it closed to keep the wind out of the buggy. "You flatter me, Andrew. And I don't mind." She grinned. "How was your meeting with the Fergusons?"

"I found out some disturbing news on the way there. Wally told me his daed isn't fond of the Amish. I was surprised and prepared myself for the worst."

"Did we make a mistake? Should we have alerted the sheriff?" Maryann gripped the blanket.

He shook his head. "No. We did the right thing."

"Did Wally lie about what he did?"

"He did, but I insisted he tell his daed the truth. He was reluctant, but then he confessed what he had done to his daed. His daed was upset Wally fibbed and thanked me for not reporting him to the sheriff. We parted without dissention. Our meeting may have him reconsider his negative attitude about us. You have more exposure to the

Englischers, working at the bakery, than I do. I hadn't considered being Amish might be a problem."

"We've been fortunate. Wally is the first one to give me any trouble since Hannah and Ellie have stopped working at the bakery. They told me stories about dealing with some rude customers. But Wally or their stories didn't put me off about working at the bakery. I enjoy it. The sheriff is a friend, and he would be happy to help. I trust him. He came to the bakery at his usual time after you left, but I didn't mention the incident to him. I would prefer to handle these situations like you did with the Fergusons."

"Bishop Fisher likes us to settle our differences among ourselves, and I agree with him when we can and not put ourselves in danger. I would rather you had told the sheriff if I had not kumme along. I don't want you to take any chances."

"I like your being protective of me." She blushed.

"Good. I plan to protect you for a long time." He drove to the restaurant. "Danki for recommending Toby to me. He's doing a good job. He organized my barn, and we worked together in the woodshop. I enjoy his company."

"Rachael's thankful he'll have you as a friend. She said she wishes he'd take time to cultivate friendships with other men and find time to choose and court a woman."

"He's in a rough spot with his father being ill, and he wants to spend his free time with him. I'm sure he's afraid he might not have much longer with his daed." Andrew parked the buggy and hopped out to assist Maryann.

He followed Maryann inside the restaurant and the waitress seated them at a table not far from the crackling fireplace. Andrew pulled out Maryann's chair for her. He turned to the waitress. "Danki. This is perfect."

The bubbly young Englischer held her small pad of

paper and a pencil. "This is our best table. It's away from the other tables and provides warmth from the fire. I'm glad you're pleased. We have meatloaf and whipped potatoes; ham, beans, and cornbread; or chicken and stuffing with mixed vegetables. What would you like to drink?"

"I'll have hot tea, danki. Maryann, would you like some?"

She nodded. "Yes, please."

"I'll get your hot teas while you ponder what you'd like for supper." She left them and went to the kitchen. She returned a short time later with the cups of hot tea, a cup of cream, and a small bowl of sugar, and served them. "What are you having this evening?"

Andrew gazed into Maryann's eyes. "I'm having the meatloaf and whipped potatoes. What about you?"

She grinned. "The same. Danki."

He sat back. He'd fallen in love with her a short time after they met. He'd been captivated by her beauty and kindness. "Maryann, in the couple of months we've been talking, I've fallen in love with you. I hope my revealing this to you won't scare you off."

"Scare me off? No, just the opposite. I love you, Andrew. The first time you came into the bakery and persisted in making sure we'd meet again, you captured my interest."

He stretched his hand out to cover hers and then retracted it. This wouldn't be proper or the Amish way. He let go of his inhibitions when he was around her. She was captivating. His heart danced in his chest, and he didn't want to wait much longer to call her his fraa. "I would've waited if you had not felt the same. I'm glad you didn't allow your unhappy marriage with Gerald to taint your view on finding love again. After what you've been through, I admire you for opening your heart to me."

"I wanted to fall in love and marry again and find a suitable daed for Betsy. I'm happy we found each other."

The waitress delivered their food and moved to the next table.

Andrew and Maryann bowed their heads. Andrew offered a prayer to God for the food. He inhaled the aroma of the large slice of meatloaf. He dipped his spoon in the rich brown gravy on top of the heap of whipped potatoes. He took a bite. "This is delicious."

She wiped her lips with the red checkered cloth napkin. "This is scrumptious."

Andrew sensed her family liked him. He didn't expect they'd have any misgivings about him, but he didn't want to assume. "I've talked and gotten closer to your parents, and also Joel and Ellie after the services and at socials. Do they have any reservations about you and me?"

She shook her head. "They like you. Before Ellie got acquainted with you, she was skeptical and had questions. She loves us, and she's overprotective. She lived in the outside world, where she met Englischers who brought trouble to her life. She also met caring Englischers who became her friends. She's put her past behind her and is a wonderful fraa to Joel, and she'll be an excellent mamm to their kinner. She's given us her stamp of approval, and she's the toughest one to win over."

He chuckled. "She is inquisitive. But I could tell she loves you, and you're blessed to have a schweschder-in-law who cares about you. I've had friends say they tolerate their in-laws."

"She's a blessing. I'm not sure Joel would've answered my letter by kumming to get me if it hadn't been for Ellie's prompting. She and I connected at our first meeting. We became fast friends." Maryann sipped her tea.

Andrew told her about building projects he had in mind, and Maryann told him about her day at the bakery while they finished their supper. He liked discussing their work with each other. He couldn't be happier with her. He checked the clocks for sale on a shelf on the wall. It was almost seven thirty. He should take her home. She had to get up earlier than he did in the morning. Andrew paid the bill, escorted her to his buggy, and covered her legs with the wool blanket. He got in and headed to her haus. "Looks like we'll get another inch of snow."

Maryann pulled her cape closer. "I worry about my parents in this weather. Mamm catches chills and fevers more often than the rest of us. She frets about the smallest things. She can go from sad to angry and jump to happy in a matter of minutes. I love her, and I regret the time I spent away from her. She's wonderful for Betsy, and I'm looking forward to having Mamm around to help me teach Betsy how to quilt and make dresses. She's better at those things than me."

Andrew drove about eight minutes out of town and pulled to a stop in front of her haus. He'd known from the minute he laid eyes on her she was the one for him. She might need more courting time. He'd take the chance and find out. "Do you mind if I kumme in? I won't stay long. I'd like to speak to your daed about an important matter."

"What is it?"

"I'll tell you after I speak with him." Andrew got out, and she accepted his hand to exit the buggy. "Ellie and Joel are here. Their mare is hard to miss with its unusual brown and white spots."

"Ellie likes to bring them supper. She's like a hen taking care of her chicks. She's always doing things for us."

Her parents sat next to the fire. Joel had on his coat and Ellie had on her heavy black cape. Ellie cocked her head. "We stayed as long as we could to try and catch Maryann. Andrew, we're glad you're here, too. How was supper at the corner restaurant?"

Maryann grinned. "It was magnificent. Meatloaf and whipped potatoes. I'm glad you're here. Your cheeks are rosy, and you're chipper. Are you nauseous in the mornings?"

Ellie beamed. "Nope. I need to put the fork down. I'm hungry most of the time." She grinned. "I can't wait to hold this little one." She rubbed her protruding stomach.

Mamm grinned. "She and Joel didn't leave any chicken and dumplings on their plates. And Ellie had two pieces of vanilla cake. But I'm not complaining. I told her to enjoy it."

Daed patted his stomach. "I enjoyed two pieces."

Mamm raised her brows. "I didn't notice you had another piece."

"When you stepped out of the kitchen, I cut another piece and put it on top of the one I had, and then I didn't waste any time devouring them both." He chuckled.

They laughed.

Joel put his hand on Ellie's back. "With this unpredictable weather, we'd better head home. Wilkom." He shook Andrew's hand.

Ellie smiled at Andrew. "Take good care of my schweschder-in-law."

"I plan to." Andrew gestured them to stay. Ellie and Joel would appreciate what he had to say. "Can you wait a minute?"

Her parents and Joel and Ellie stared at him. He cleared his throat. "I'd like Maryann's family's permission to ask her to marry me."

Daed put his hand on Andrew's shoulder. "I approve, Andrew. She's been cheerful all the time since she's met you."

"Yes, I'll marry you!" Maryann bounced on her toes.

Her mamm had happy tears. She clapped hands to her cheeks. "Wilkom to the family, Andrew."

Ellie narrowed her eyes. "It's kind of soon. You've only been seeing each other several months."

Andrew froze.

Joel frowned at her. "Ellie, what more does this man have to do to prove to you he loves Maryann? He's answered your one thousand questions, and you can't find anything wrong with him."

Andrew, Maryann, and her family laughed.

Ellie winced. "Sorry, Andrew. They're right. I'm delighted for you both. Planning a wedding will be fun." Ellie squeezed Maryann's hand.

Joel ushered his fraa to the door. "Ellie, you'll have plenty of time to plan this wedding with Maryann. Right now, I've got to take you and our unborn boppli home."

Joel and Ellie hugged his parents, then Maryann and Andrew, and advanced outside to their buggy.

"Andrew, I had no idea you'd propose tonight. I'm shocked and ecstatic you did." Maryann beamed.

His heart thumped with joy. He couldn't wait to have her as a partner. He loved her family. He'd been alone, and being accepted by them gave him a sense of belonging. "Ellie had me worried for a moment."

"She had me holding my breath. I'm relieved Joel set

her straight. If he hadn't, I would have. I don't want anything or anyone to stand in our way." She gazed at him with loving eyes.

"I'm glad your family approved. I would've been embarrassed and speechless if they hadn't. More importantly, I'm happy you were ready. I was afraid I might be asking you to marry me too soon."

"I'm ready." Maryann held clasped hands under her chin.

Her daed stood and beckoned her mamm. "We approve. Kumme on, fraa of mine, we should let this young couple have some privacy. I could use a cup of hot chocolate."

Naomi Wenger moved to stand beside him. "So happy for you both."

Andrew watched them head for the kitchen. "Maryann, I'm the happiest man on earth right now. Do you have a calendar?" He didn't want to wait another minute to get plans rolling and arrive at their wedding date. Each day they'd talked, laughed, and discussed serious matters, he'd fallen deeper in love with her. He wished they could exchange their vows tomorrow.

She crossed the room, pulled open a drawer, and removed a calendar. She joined him and pointed to May fourteenth. "What do you think of this date?"

He wrinkled his nose. "Why not April second?"

"You and our friends and family will be busy with planting. I'd like for as many as possible from the community to attend." She cocked her head. "Don't misunderstand. I'm as anxious as you are for us to wed. I'm considering the best time for everyone."

He tapped a finger to his chin in deep thought. "I'll settle for May fourteenth."

"Are you sure? What about planting?" She tilted her head.

Andrew grimaced. "Amish are always busy. I'm for a May wedding."

Maryann marked the calendar. "You win. May fourteenth is the date, as long as the bishop has it open on his calendar."

"I'm not sure if I can wait that long to call you my fraa." Andrew reached for her hand. "I'll ask the bishop tomorrow to mark the date on his calendar, and I'll kumme to the bakery and let you know if it's confirmed." He would move the date up if Bishop Fisher didn't have May fourteenth available, even if it was planting season. "I should head home and let you get to bed." He pulled her close and gently kissed her lips. "I love you, Maryann." He opened the door, hurried to his buggy, and headed home, shivering under the wool blanket. He was glad to have his kerosene lanterns to provide light on his way home, and he was thankful his home wasn't too far from Maryann's parents' place.

Andrew poured Toby a cup of hot coffee and carried it to the barn Thursday morning. "You're earlier than usual."

Toby was almost an hour before his regular starting time. He handed Toby the mug.

"Danki. It's a relief to have a regular job, and I like taking care of your place and livestock."

"I proposed to Maryann last night, and she agreed to marry me. I'm sure she's told your schweschder and Magdelena this morning at the bakery."

Toby grinned. "Congratulations, Andrew." He cocked

his head. "I'm surprised. You and Maryann have had a short courtship. How did you know she was the one for you?"

"The moment I saw her in the bakery the day we met, I was drawn to her. We had a strong connection. And we didn't waste time with small talk. We discussed our pasts and our likes and dislikes early on. She's smart, kind, funny, stubborn, and a sweetheart. I can't imagine my life without her. Believe me, when you know, you just know."

"I can tell the way you talk about her that you're in love. I wish you both the best." Toby gave him an approving smile.

"Danki. I'll visit Bishop Fisher a little later and then go to the bakery to tell Maryann what he says about the date we chose."

"When is the wedding?"

"Thursday, May fourteenth. Mark your calendar. I expect you there."

"I wouldn't miss it."

Andrew clamped his hand on Toby's shoulder. "How old are you? You can't be much younger than me. I'm twenty-two. You should consider a woman to court. Don't you want to find the right girl and get married?"

Toby shook his head. "I'm twenty, and I've still got time to get married. I'm not ready to consider courtship. I choose to concentrate on my daed and work for you. My schedule doesn't leave time for much else. My family needs my labor and the money you pay me. And I don't begrudge the position I'm in. I can put a little money away, but it will take a while for it to build before I can consider courting a girl."

"Toby, together, we can build you a haus, and I would loan you the money."

"I appreciate your offer, but I'm content with the way

things are right now. I'm unsure how much time I have left with Daed, and I want to take advantage of every minute I can. Mamm and Rachael have become dependent on me, and I want for them to have the assurance I will take care of them."

Andrew stared at Toby in disbelief. His friend had gone from responsible to stubborn. "You can take care of them and have a fraa. Your fraa would be a help to you and your family."

"I'm in no rush. I'll know when it's the right time."

Andrew raised his palms. "I won't pester you about it. You're doing all the right things. You make it hard to argue the point. I admire your dedication to your family. Be aware things will never be perfect."

"Danki for the advice." He adjusted his hat on his head. "Are you building anything today in the woodshop?"

He got the message. Toby didn't want to discuss this topic any longer. He'd concede and talk handcrafting.

"Yes, would you like to join me?" Andrew noticed the glint of happiness in Toby's eyes when he offered. He liked teaching Toby how to build things, and his new friend was good at it.

Andrew drew designs and examples, discussed processes, and demonstrated ways to sand, finish, and build chairs, tables, and other furniture for the rest of the afternoon. He glanced at the antique clock he'd kept from his parents' belongings. He remembered them each time he looked at it. "Time for me to go to the bishop's. I'll be back soon."

Toby set the hammer in his hand on the worktable. "Hope you get the date you want."

Andrew departed and drove to the bishop's haus. He knocked on the door.

"What brings you by? Kumme on in." Bishop Fisher ushered him inside and to a chair.

"I'm excited to inform you Maryann Harding has agreed to marry me."

The bishop slapped his own leg. "Why, I'm tickled for you both. What date did you have in mind?" He yanked his calendar off the oak end table next to him.

"We'd like to schedule May fourteenth with you, if you have it free."

The bishop flipped the pages to May. "I will mark the date. You sure? It's planting season."

"I'm patient where most things are concerned, but not about marrying Maryann. I'm ready today. May is too far, but I must be reasonable." He chuckled.

Bishop Fisher penciled in their names. "Women like to have a lot of time to sew their dresses and make arrangements."

"Yes. I want her to enjoy the time leading up to, and the actual day of, our wedding."

"I miss Faith. My sweet fraa wasn't on earth with me long enough before she took ill and died. It's been five years, and I still expect to find her at the stove in the mornings. Cherish each day."

Andrew's heart went out to the man. He didn't want to think about losing Maryann for any reason. He chatted with him a couple of minutes and then bid him farewell.

He got in his buggy and drove to the bakery. They had firm plans in place for their wedding. She'd be pleased he'd taken care of this. He parked his buggy in front of the bakery and stopped at the post office to collect his mail. He glanced at each envelope and opened the letter from his uncle Luke. Guilt settled in his stomach. He'd owed them a letter.

Dear Andrew,

I pray this letter finds you in good health and enjoying life and home in Charm. I hope you haven't grown roots there, as I have a job offer for you. How would you like to work with me for the next couple of months, and then I'll hand the store over to you to manage? When I'm gone, it's yours. All I ask is for you to take care of your aunt Dora. Clyde had been my partner for twenty-five years, and he died in his sleep November twentieth. He was seven years younger than me. I never expected he'd leave this earth before I did.

I'm not well, and I'm not sure what's wrong. It doesn't matter. I'm ready when God chooses to take me home. I have a young man overseeing the store, but he's not interested in staying. He's doing me a favor. I need you to kumme as soon as you can. It won't take long to tell you all you need to know about the store to run it. I can put the store up for sale, but I'd rather keep it in the family. The farm next to me is for sale. The haus is in decent shape and the land is one hundred acres. I've got farmhands taking care of my property. We can hire additional men to take care of your land next door if you want to buy it. I've asked the owner to wait until I hear from you before announcing it's for sale. He's a friend.

I'm excited about having you close. You've always been like a son to me and Dora. Write and tell me how soon we can expect you in Millersburg to talk this over.

Love, Uncle Luke.

Andrew groaned and shook his head. "What am I going to do?" He had a lot to consider before he spoke with Maryann. He'd promised to tell her about their confirmed wedding date, but he couldn't think straight. He'd tell her what Bishop Fisher said tonight. He got in his buggy and headed home. Maryann had her unstable mamm who needed her. He wasn't sure she would leave Charm. This was the opportunity of a lifetime for him. How would Maryann react to this news?

Chapter Three

Maryann poured coffee in Dr. Harrison's and Sheriff Williams's mugs early the next day. "May I offer you another custard pastry?"

The sheriff split the newspaper with Dr. Harrison. "I'll take another one, danki, Maryann."

Dr. Harrison patted his flat stomach. "Not me. I'm full." He stared at the paper. "Says Denver, Colorado, may reach forty-five inches of snow by the end of today. A record for them. Article says roofs are collapsing, the roads aren't passable, and the railroad is at a standstill. What a mess. I wouldn't want to live there."

The sheriff huffed. "I'm sick of the snow, and it's just started. January and February are usually the worst for us. Says the First Lady, Ellen Wilson, is about ready to decorate the White House for Christmas. Were you aware President Benjamin Harrison was the first president to put a Christmas tree inside the White House?"

"Interesting tidbit of information. Why, I couldn't have gone another day without being told such an important fact. How impressive." Dr. Harrison chuckled.

The sheriff harrumphed. "You'll go home tonight and

tell the wife about it for interesting conversation. You don't fool me."

"You're right. I can't fool you. You've got me pegged, old friend." He laughed.

Maryann stifled a chuckle threatening to escape. She enjoyed the two best friends' banter at the same time each morning. It was endearing that the bakery was their meeting place and time for discussing the latest news. She didn't mind learning what was going on in the world, even though she wasn't supposed to care, according to the bishop. "I like the change of seasons, and I like to ice-skate, so I don't mind the snow."

"The wife and I ice-skated when we were younger. Now we're older and not as flexible. I'd for sure end up on my rump or break a bone. The older I get, the more I like summer."

The two men chatted, drank their coffee, and departed twenty minutes later. Maryann cleared their dirty plates and mugs.

She wilkomed the two Englischers entering the bakery. "What can I do for you ladies?"

The two women ignored her greeting and sat at the far table in the corner. The older woman lifted her chin. "Get us two cups of hot chocolate and two oatmeal cookies each."

Maryann whirled around, selected the cookies and set them on two plates, and then poured hot chocolate in two mugs and served them. "Would you like anything more?"

The older woman glared at her. "No. Please leave us. We're trying to have a conversation."

Maryann left them and returned to the counter. She heated water on the small stove behind her for coffee. These two women could use some manners.

The woman's friend rolled her eyes. "I hope she'll leave us alone. I find the Amish odd. Look at her dress. No buttons. How ridiculous." She sipped her hot chocolate and then set her mug down. "Enough about them. I've got important news. My niece Glena made a terrible mistake by moving to Canton and marrying Norman."

"Why would you say such a thing, Minnie? You told me they were meant for each other."

Minnie sat on the edge of her chair. "Her family needs her. Her mamm's not well, and she's worse without her. Her father and brothers are taking care of her, but it's not the same as having her daughter close."

Minnie's friend cocked her head. "Why did they move? Her husband had a good job at the bank."

Minnie smacked her hand on the table. "Nancy, you won't believe this. A friend wrote and surprised him with the position and increase in pay at a larger bank. My niece intended to visit often. Weather, distance, and responsibilities keep her from it. I do what I can, but she's in a dark mood now Glena's left."

Nancy splayed her fingers on the table and huffed. "Family should come first. He made enough money in Charm. Young couples can be selfish and greedy."

Minnie heaved a big sigh. "I agree. Selfish is right. Family should always come first." She finished her last cookie. "Let's pay our bills and head home. I'd like to finish the dress I'm making."

"For yourself?"

"Yes, I pin-tucked pleats in the blouse. You'll love it." Minnie paid Maryann.

Nancy dug in her reticule and lifted out her coin purse. She dropped her coins in Maryann's palm and followed

Minnie to the door. "I want you to make me one, sight unseen! The blouse sounds lovely."

Rude Englischers. Maryann grimaced. They could've said danki. Most of the Englischers she encountered were pleasant. Maybe they were passing through Charm and she wouldn't have to serve them again. What a difficult spot Minnie's niece's husband put her in. She wouldn't want to make the same decision.

Hannah and Ellie strolled in.

Ellie furrowed her brows. "We bumped into two women kumming out of the bakery on our way in, and they told us to watch where we were going and bustled away. They could use a lesson in manners. Did you have any trouble with them?"

"Minnie and Nancy were their names. I overheard their conversation while they sat at a table not far from the counter. They need to learn to say *danki* and *please*. A *goodbye* might be nice. I was invisible to them. The two women judged Minnie's niece for relocating and leaving her mamm, who has a tendency to sulk when she's not around."

"Why did she leave?" Hannah perused the baked goods.

"Her husband was offered a better job."

Ellie whistled. "That's a hard one. I value family. I would hope Joel would pass up an opportunity and choose to stay in Charm."

Maryann didn't want to discuss this with Ellie. She wasn't sure how she felt about it. Andrew's comment about possible relocation pricked her mind. "Enough about those women. Let's change the subject."

Ellie lifted the lid above the plate on top of the counter containing butter cookies. "I love these." She lifted one to her nose. "My favorite scent. We miss you and working at the bakery. We thought we'd stop in and visit."

Maryann pointed to Ellie's stomach. "How are you feeling? Are you sticking with the name Emma for a girl and Amos for a boy?" The names were precious. She'd consider them if she had kinner in the future, if Ellie chose not to use them.

"The nausea has passed, and I can't get enough food. I'll be bigger than a barn if I don't stop eating. Yes, we love the names and haven't changed them. We're both excited for this little one to appear. I'm guessing the boppli should arrive sometime in June." Ellie pointed to the molasses cookies. "I'll have one of those, please. We came to have cookies and discuss your upcoming wedding. I hope this boppli doesn't arrive until after your marriage to Andrew."

Maryann handed her the cookie. "We're planning a May fourteenth wedding, depending on the bishop's schedule. He's supposed to let me know if he got the date confirmed, but he hasn't kumme in yet. I love the way he asked you and the family. He didn't hint at supper about a proposal. I was shocked and thrilled."

Ellie brushed crumbs from her lips. "Are you sure you're ready to marry him?"

Maryann walked around the counter and crossed her arms. "I thought you liked him." Ellie had been skeptical of Andrew at first, but her schweschder-in-law had been in favor of him soon after. The hairs on the back of her neck prickled. Why would she say this?

"I do like him. You and he have courted such a short time. I'm asking the question to make sure you aren't rushing into this." Ellie gently squeezed Maryann's arm.

Hannah gazed at her. "We love and trust you. If you're

ready, we'll support you. There's no question Andrew adores you. It takes more than love to have a firm foundation for marriage. I have no doubt you both are committed to God and the Amish life. Are you agreeing on finances, kinner, and those types of decisions?"

Maryann shook her head. "I appreciate your concern. But rest assured, I am ready to marry Andrew. I'm confident we agree on what is necessary for us to marry."

Rachael and Magdelena strolled in from the kitchen.

Magdelena hugged Hannah and Ellie. "I recognized your voices. Rachael and I had our hands in dough and couldn't kumme out right away. We always love it when you both visit. Ellie, you are glowing."

Ellie beamed and patted her stomach. "I'm great. Danki. I'm twenty and consider myself young and having plenty of time to have more kinner. Joel is twenty-four and worried he's getting too old. I teased him and said maybe we'll have twins. He choked on his milk."

They all laughed.

Maryann said, "He's got plenty of time to have more kinner."

They all nodded in agreement.

Rachael squeezed Hannah and Ellie's hands. "We miss you."

Hannah grinned. "Ellie and I miss you, too. Sunny keeps me company while I bake and that sweet husband of mine, Timothy, is working. The dog loves to snuggle and is pleasant to have around, until I find where my furry friend has gotten into the trash looking for bones and made a mess."

"Speaking of misbehavior, I've got a story to tell you."

Maryann shared with them the encounter with Wally Ferguson.

"The little imp was fortunate Andrew didn't march him to the sheriff." Ellie shook her head.

Hannah said, "Andrew is brave and kind to take Wally to his daed. Mr. Ferguson could've tried to pick a fight with him since you said he found the Amish strange. His act of kindness may have given Mr. Ferguson a reason to reconsider his prejudice about the Amish."

Ellie scowled. "I'd have taken Wally by the ear, loaded him in the buggy, and hauled him home. I'd have told his daed he should teach the boy manners, gotten in my buggy, and left them both standing there."

Maryann covered her open mouth. "Ellie, you wouldn't dare. It wouldn't be proper for an Amish woman or any woman to confront a strange man."

"I would, and then you, Hannah, and the girls would've told me what a mistake I'd made." She held her stomach and laughed. "The old Ellie would've done it, but not the new Ellie. I had you going. You all believed me."

The girls laughed with her.

Maryann put a hand on Ellie's shoulder. "You know how to get a rise out of all of us, you tease."

Hannah circled her arm around Ellie's waist. "She does keep us laughing. I love her for it." She nodded to Ellie. "We should go and let them get back to work."

Maryann packed some goodies for them.

Ellie peeked in her bag and closed it. "Danki for the extra butter cookies. And tell Andrew we are sorry we missed him. He was leaving town when we came in the bakery." She and Hannah hugged the girls.

Why hadn't he stopped in the bakery? Maryann hugged them. "I will."

Hannah and Ellie left, and Maryann closed the door behind them.

"It's always good to chat with Hannah and Ellie." Magdelena clasped her hands in front of her.

Rachael glanced out the window at them getting in the buggy. "I love them. They're special. Now let's get back to work. We've got pies to bake." She gave Magdelena a playful push to the kitchen.

Maryann took care of the customers ambling in. Her thoughts flashed to Andrew as she filled their orders. *What has kept Andrew from visiting today?*

Andrew urged his horse to go faster on the snow-covered roads.

He had assumed his uncle would sell his store to his longtime friend and partner. He'd planned to stay in Charm, save enough money to open a large store, or approach Mr. Kline when his finances were in order. Now everything had changed. Would Maryann understand he'd had the best intentions to honor her wishes to stay in Charm, but his uncle had changed this plan and he had to consider it? Ellie and Joel would be close by for her parents. Everything would be all right, or would it? His stomach churned as he turned down his lane. He'd told her he'd stop in the bakery. He felt bad for not doing so. What would he have said?

Toby met him outside the barn. "I'll take care of your horse. How was your trip to town?"

He wasn't sure how to answer his friend's question. Toby would be affected by the move. He shouldn't discuss his uncle's offer with anyone until he'd told Maryann. He held the letter to his side. "I got what I needed. When you're finished in the barn, join me in the woodshop."

"I'll be in right after I unharness and put your horse in the barn." Toby followed him.

Andrew crossed the snow-covered ground between the barn and the haus. The clouds moved in and covered the sun. The sky was a blanket of gray. Much like his mood. He carried the letter to the shop, lifted the latch to a small wooden box he kept on the shelf, and dropped the envelope inside. He chose the hardwood and sawed it into four sections for table legs. He lifted one and sanded it.

Toby joined him. "What would you like me to do?"

Andrew nodded to a section of wood. "Sand one of the three sections of wood left for use as a table leg. We'll try and finish all four before you leave." They worked for the next two hours until all four were complete. Andrew studied them. "Two need a little more sanding. You take one and I'll take the other. The last two are fine."

Toby sat on the stool and balanced his piece on his legs. "You've changed my life, Andrew. We've become friends, and you've given me a love for building furniture, toys, and more. I want to learn it all."

"You've got talent, Toby. I enjoy training you. You take care of your family and work hard. You need something to look forward to. I'm pleased it's handcrafting." He didn't want to disappoint Toby. He'd have to find him a full-time position with a steady income.

"Sometimes, the weight of the responsibility and worrying if Daed will be with us much longer gets to me. Please keep this between us. I wouldn't have it any other way. I love my family. But being at your place takes my mind off things."

"We're friends. You can talk to me about anything. I've had to get things off my chest about Maryann, and you've listened to me. I've benefited from your friendship, too."

Toby reminded him of a close friend he'd had in the past. He pushed the painful thought away.

Andrew patted his gloves together to release the wood dust. "Our fire in the stove is dimming. I'll go outside for more small logs."

Toby stood. "I'll get it."

Andrew pushed the door open. "You stay put. I'll be right back." He walked out and a black dog wagged his tail and stared at him. "Kumme to me, boy. You're a puppy. Do you belong to anyone? You're scrawny, and you must be hungry." He gathered some wood and the dog followed him inside.

"Who's your friend?" Toby patted his leg, and the dog ran to him. He scratched the dog's ears. "I haven't noticed this dog in town before today. Do you think his owner abandoned him?"

Andrew watched Toby and the dog. The animal ran to Toby and wagged his tail. His friend couldn't hide his excitement. The last thing he needed was a pet. Maybe Toby could take the dog home. That might not be a good idea with his daed sick. His daed needed quiet.

"I'm sure the owner dropped him off. We're both familiar with our Amish community's pets, and this one is new to both of us. Do you want to take him home?"

Toby's cheeks reddened. "I can't take the chance it might disturb Daed. If you keep him, I'll take care of him while I'm at your haus. What should we call him?" He snapped his fingers. "His fur is pitch-black. How about Pepper?"

"Pepper is a great name." He would tell Toby about his

possible move to Millersburg tomorrow after he spoke with Maryann. He'd figure out what to do about the dog later. "Sure, I can keep him." What was he saying? He should tell him no and why. *Not now.*

"Someone's rapping on the door." Toby got up and opened it. "Bishop, kumme in and get warm by the fire." Toby stepped aside and unfolded a wooden chair for him.

Bishop Fisher sat close to the stove and held his hands near its warmth. "We didn't settle dates for your counseling sessions when you secured the wedding day with me, Andrew. We can start them in April. Are Tuesdays at six in the evening agreeable to you and Maryann?"

Andrew cleared his throat. This was getting more complicated by the minute. He had to speak with Maryann this evening. Would they move the wedding up? Marry in Millersburg? Maybe he could find someone in Millersburg to run the store so he could return to Charm for April and go to the counseling meetings. His head started to ache. "Sure. Please mark your calendar. If Maryann needs a different day and time, I'll discuss it with you. Danki for stopping by. Would you like coffee? We have some on the stove inside the haus."

"No, I've got errands to run." He stood. "Toby, how is your father? I'll visit him today."

Toby's eyes saddened. "He's not any worse. He has been eating better, but he's weak."

"Let's say a prayer for him." The bishop prayed with them. "Toby, you're doing a good job taking care of your family." He scanned the woodshop. "I'm glad you're working with Andrew. Have you always wanted to craft furniture?"

Toby nodded and held up the table leg. "Yes, but I've not had the opportunity until now with Andrew. I like the hobby much better than I'd anticipated." He held up a near-completed table leg. "This is my project for today."

Bishop Fisher whistled. "Looks good."

"He's caught on fast." Guilt ran through Andrew. He wouldn't have much time to teach Toby everything he'd planned. He'd hoped to have Toby make and sell furniture of his own. At least Toby had the skills now to make potato boxes and small things.

The bishop bid them farewell and left.

Hours later, Andrew finished the last of the four legs and glanced at the clock on the shelf in the woodshop. "It's almost time for you to go home. I'm going to head over to Maryann's. I'll catch up with you in the morning. You did a good job on the table legs. We'll put it together tomorrow."

"Danki, Andrew."

Andrew went to the haus, freshened up, and left for Maryann's haus. His stomach churned. He was concerned about his uncle's health. His uncle had helped out his family and later himself when his parents died. He'd stayed with him for a few months after his parents passed. He loved him, and they'd been close.

Andrew turned into her place, and Maryann was walking from the barn to the haus. He parked and jumped out. "I hope this isn't a bad time."

"It's never a bad time for you." She shivered and pulled her cape closer. "Let's go inside where it's warm. Did you talk with Bishop Fisher? I missed you kumming to the bakery today. Ellie came in to the bakery, and she mentioned she noticed you leaving town. Why didn't you stop in?"

"I'm sorry. I had errands to run. I planned on telling you what the bishop said tonight. The bishop marked his calendar. May fourteenth is the day we'll wed." He grinned and followed her inside. He should've visited her at the bakery. He hadn't considered a friend or family member might've noticed him in town and told Maryann. She'd accepted his explanation without hesitation. He wasn't sorry he'd taken the time to think things through. He was ready to tell her tonight what they were facing. Her mamm sat in a chair, with Betsy on a blanket at her feet playing with a small wooden duck, cow, and pig.

"Andrew, I hope you'll stay for supper. We're having ham and beans and cornbread." Naomi stood.

He inhaled the aroma of fresh cornbread. "I'd love to. Danki." Andrew stooped to Betsy.

Betsy raised her arms.

He picked her up. His heart thumped with joy. "She came to me!"

"She took to you the second time we talked at an after-church meal." Maryann beamed.

Shem joined them in the living room. "I thought I recognized your voice, Andrew. You must stay and have supper with us."

Naomi smiled at her husband. "I invited him, and he said yes. It will be a pleasure to have him." She tilted her head and grinned. "I'm working on Maryann's dress for the wedding. I'm relieved you're not taking my girls away. We're fortunate you'll only be a short distance from our place."

Shem chuckled. "She'll cook your favorite meals to entice you to supper every night. You may wish you lived far away." He chuckled and winked at his fraa.

"You stop your teasing, Shem Wenger." She gave him a playful grin.

Maryann rubbed her mamm's back. "We may not make

it every night, but we'll be happy to oblige often. We both love Mamm's cooking."

Andrew bit his bottom lip. His news would break Naomi's heart. He didn't relish this. He cared about her. But he didn't have a choice. He'd wait until after supper. "Naomi, you are an excellent cook."

Naomi beamed. "It's about ready. I've had it on the stove, and the cornbread should be golden brown in about five minutes."

Maryann took Betsy from Andrew. "I'll go change her diaper and be right back."

Shem gestured for Andrew to sit. "Danki for making Maryann happy. I have no doubt you'll be a good daed to Betsy. She's been through a rough time, and we're grateful she's kumme home and then found you. Naomi's a new person with Maryann and Betsy around, which makes our family's lives much easier."

Andrew shifted in his seat. He rubbed the back of his neck. He couldn't get comfortable. He'd have to tell Maryann alone and let her and Shem tell Naomi after he left. They would know how to calm her. Maybe he should tell Shem first. "Shem, I have—"

Naomi held a dish towel to her chest. "Kumme and sit. The food's on the table."

Shem gazed at Andrew. "Did you have something you wanted to tell me?"

"It can wait." He followed the family to the kitchen.

Maryann put Betsy in her high chair. She dipped a small serving of beans and ham chunks and mashed it to make it easier for Betsy to chew. Betsy clapped her hands and held her little spoon.

Naomi had the table set with food already on their plates.

She had provided full glasses of water for each of them. "Shem, say the blessing before everything gets cold."

They bowed their heads, and Shem prayed for the food and raised his head. "Maryann, will you work at the bakery after you and Andrew marry?"

"Yes. I'd like to. Do you mind continuing to care for Betsy for me? I love the customers and working with Magdelena and Rachael. I'd be heartsick to leave." Maryann poured half her water into a smaller tin cup for Betsy.

"I had hoped you would keep your position at the bakery. Betsy and I have a good time together. I would've been sad to change our routine." Naomi grinned at Betsy.

Betsy picked up her cup with both hands and drank half of the water. "Firsty." She grinned.

They laughed.

Naomi slathered apple butter on her cornbread. "Andrew, do you mind Maryann working?"

He shook his head. "I don't mind. It's her decision. I'm agreeable with whatever she desires." She'd miss her friends and the bakery. They both had family responsibilities. How was this going to work?

Maryann beamed. "I've got to get your measurements. I need to stitch a new shirt and pants for you for the wedding."

"I'll be happy to help with them. I'll make the pants. They are your least favorite thing to stitch." Naomi took a bite of her cornbread.

"Mamm, how sweet of you. I'll take you up on it. Danki."

"Yes. Danki." Andrew scooped up a spoonful of food.

Shem raised a finger. "Several of the men have mentioned to me how kind of you it is to employ Toby. The community is doing what they can for the family. Mr. Schlabach's illness is such a mystery. He has good and bad days, but he'll never work again. It can't be easy on Toby, his mamm, and his schweschder."

"He's been a good find. I've had him in the woodshop making small projects. He's observant and pays attention to detail. He'll be ready to sell what he's made in Mr. Kline's store soon. They do their best for Mr. Schlabach, but it is difficult for them to watch him struggle to move and not be the strong man they remember. Toby says his daed doesn't complain and he asks for little." A pang of guilt pricked him. Toby. He'd made the man's life easier, and everything would change if he moved away. He was disappointing a lot of people with this move. He needed to talk about a happier subject. "We have a new pet."

Maryann's eyes widened. "What?"

"A black dog showed up, and Toby took to him right away. I must say the dog is easy to like." He couldn't tell if Maryann liked him taking in the dog or not.

Shem held his water glass. "Is your pet a girl or a boy?"

"Pepper is a male, medium-sized, good-looking dog. Friendly and loving. Pepper made it hard to refuse him food and a new home." Maybe Maryann's family would want the dog when he had to leave to go to his uncle Luke's and aunt Dora's. He didn't want to take a dog without asking for their permission first.

Maryann grinned. "I love dogs, but I didn't want the responsibility. I'm considering a puppy for Betsy when she is older and can take care of it. When can I meet Pepper?"

"You're wilkom anytime, or I can bring him for a visit." Having Maryann take the dog wasn't going to work. She didn't think it was the right time for Betsy. He'd leave Pepper at his haus and ask Toby to take care of the dog for now and figure out what to do about the pet later.

"We aren't ready for a dog full-time, but Betsy would love to pet it. Mamm and Daed, do you mind if Andrew brings Pepper over for a visit?"

Naomi set her napkin on the table. "I'd enjoy it."

"Me too." Shem drank the rest of his water.

Betsy rubbed her dirty hands on her mouth and laughed. "Done."

Maryann wiped her dochder's hands and mouth and removed her bib. "You did a good job cleaning your plate, little one." She lifted her out of the high chair. "I'll change her into her gown, read her a story, and put her to bed."

"I'll help clear the dishes." Andrew carried over the dirty plates.

Shem poured warm water from the pot on the stove. "I'll help wash."

Naomi shooed him away. "Andrew and I will clear the table and wash and dry the dishes. You go relax in your favorite chair."

Andrew dried while Naomi washed the dishes. "Your meal was delicious." He studied her. Her face had become ashen white.

Naomi moaned, lifted her hands out of the water, and grabbed her head. She dropped to the floor and rocked back and forth. "The pain is excruciating. I can't stand it." She closed her eyes and groaned.

Andrew knelt beside her, his heart thumping fast in his chest. "Naomi, what can I do for you?" He felt helpless. From her pallor, he was afraid she'd pass out. "Shem, please kumme quick! Naomi's in pain and holding her head."

Shem hurried to the kitchen from the living room and supported her as she stood. He circled his arm around her waist and held her arm. "It's all right, Naomi. Let me take you to bed. I'll get the aspirin powder."

"Would you like me to help you, Shem?" Andrew's heart thumped fast. "Or should I summon Dr. Harrison?"

"Dr. Harrison says there's nothing he can do for her. She needs darkness and quiet. Danki, Andrew."

He watched Shem and Naomi leave the kitchen. The woman had scared him. She had been in serious pain. He washed and dried the last of the dirty dishes and wiped his hands. How often did Naomi have these severe headaches? Maryann hadn't mentioned them.

Maryann walked into the kitchen almost ten minutes later. "I finally got Betsy to sleep after reading her a story. I thought I heard you call for Daed. Is everything all right? Where are my parents?"

"Naomi has a terrible headache. Shem took her to lie down. Does she have headaches often?"

Maryann fidgeted her hands. "She's had headaches, and she says these are more painful than any she's had before. Maybe we should ask Dr. Harrison to kumme, or take her to him."

He gazed into her worried eyes. "I offered to ask Dr. Harrison to kumme, and Shem said no and he'd give her aspirin powder."

She paced. "I should go talk to him and check on Mamm."

Andrew put his hand on her shoulder. "Give them time together. I'm sure he'll join us in a few minutes. Then you can find out why he chose not to alert the doctor."

Shem had been calm, as if he'd gone through this with his fraa more than once. He'd wait for Shem and let Maryann ask her questions. This night was turning out worse than he'd expected.

Shem padded into the kitchen. "Andrew, danki for taking care of the dishes."

"I'm happy to do it."

"Daed, what should we do about Mamm? We have to get her help."

Shem motioned for them to go to the sitting room. "Kumme sit, and I'll explain. Your mother didn't want you to know how bad her headaches have gotten, but you should know."

They sat, and Shem cleared his throat. "She had her first bad headache two weeks ago. She couldn't stand light or noise. She has intense pressure on the right side of her head, and she becomes nauseated and loses any food in her stomach. Some are more painful than others.

"She told me tonight's occurrence was the most agonizing. I had Dr. Harrison to the haus after the first episode. He said they don't have much information about these kinds of things. He suggested we could try and find a more knowledgeable doctor. Your mamm refused." He sighed. "Dr. Harrison offered the aspirin powder and said a dark room and rest is best when they happen. A cool cloth over her eyes is comforting. Her mood changes are challenging, and now this happening worries me. I suspect the two go hand-in-hand."

Maryann blinked back tears. "Didn't Grossmudder complain of severe headaches, and then she died after one of them?"

Shem nodded. "Yes. Your grossmudder did have severe headaches, and she did pass after having a severe one. I'm thankful your mamm has recovered after having each one. The doctors don't know much more than they did when your grossmudder passed. We just have to put Naomi in God's hands."

Maryann dried her tears with the corner of her apron. "Why didn't you tell me?" She pressed a hand to her chest. "My heart hurts for her. I want to do something to help her."

"You've been working at the bakery when she's had them. She said not to tell you. And there's nothing you can do. I've taken care of Betsy when she's had headaches."

Andrew swallowed hard. Maryann's grossmudder passing with the same symptoms worried him. He wouldn't add the possibility of moving away to the shock Maryann had already endured tonight. Maybe he'd wait until the end of the week to mention it. How serious was his uncle's condition? Did he have time to wait another day before setting things in motion? He had no choice. Maryann needed time to digest this shock about her mamm. "I'm sorry she's suffering with this. I'll pray for her."

"Danki, Andrew. It's all we can do for now, and make her as comfortable as possible when they do occur. She's had headaches now and then since we've been married, but not like this. They were bearable. They didn't stop her from her daily activities. These are more severe. Now I wonder if they had anything to do with her mood changes while you were away."

"I didn't consider her headaches serious when she first had them. We've all had them a time or two. These are different. Scary painful. I'm sure my running away from Charm and marrying Gerald added to her agitation and worry and spurred on these severe headaches and mood changes." Maryann heaved a big sigh.

"Your being home has removed her worry. She's ecstatic you and Betsy are living with us. But the headaches are increasing in intensity each time."

Maryann slipped a handkerchief from under her cuff

and dabbed her eyes. "Maybe I should quit the bakery and stay home with her."

Shem shook his head. "Dear dochder, please don't fret. You heard your mamm earlier. She'd be devastated if you left the bakery. She loves her time with Betsy, and she likes helping you by doing it. It's the highlight of her days. Betsy isn't in danger. Your mamm has put her in the playpen and fetched me when she's needed help. She would never put Betsy in jeopardy. She fights through the pain when she needs to."

"Should I stay home Monday?" Maryann crumpled the handkerchief and held it tight.

"No. Naomi will be better after she's had a good night's rest."

Maryann let tears drip onto her cheeks. "I couldn't stand to lose her."

Andrew struggled not to take her in his arms and soothe her. He ached watching her being worried and afraid. He'd respect this was Shem's place to comfort her.

"Maryann, let's not assume anything. We'll take this one day at a time." Shem reached over and held her hand.

"All right. But promise me you'll tell me if you need me to stay home."

"I promise. The best thing you can do is go to work and treat your mamm like normal." Shem gave her a reassuring smile. "Enough about this unpleasant topic. Let's talk about your wedding. Is there anything I can do?"

Maryann shook her head. "Not until a couple of days prior. Then we'll need to borrow benches and tables used for the Sunday services. Mamm wants the wedding in Charm. I like the idea, as long as it's not too much work for her."

Shem grinned. "You and she will have more ladies to pitch in than you'll want, offering their services."

Maryann chuckled. "You're right. But we'll be glad to take them up on all their offers."

Andrew stood. "The wedding date is too far away. I'm ready to marry you tomorrow. But I'll be patient. I should say good night. Please tell Naomi I wish her well."

Shem crossed the room and opened the door. "I will."

"I'll put my cape on and walk you out." Maryann grabbed her gray wool cape.

"It's freezing out. You stay inside. We don't have Sunday service. You spend it with your mamm."

"That's sweet of you." Maryann gazed into his eyes.

"Sleep well." Andrew left and drove home. His lantern lighted the way. He wouldn't rest until he'd told Maryann he must leave for Millersburg. They wouldn't have to make any rash decisions until he found out what was going on with his uncle.

Chapter Four

Maryann fretted as she waited on customers Friday morning. Where had Andrew been this past week? He must be busy finishing up projects. He might have stayed away to give her more time with Mamm in the evenings, but why not kumme to the bakery? Mamm hadn't had any more headaches this past week, even though she seemed more tired and weaker than usual. Her family and friends had been praying for her and increased their visits with her.

Rachael slid a butterscotch pie onto the shelf. "What's heavy on your mind? You've been quiet all morning. Is it your mamm? Did she have another bad headache? I've been praying for her."

Magdelena arranged loaves of bread on the shelves. "Yes, how is your mamm?"

"Danki. She's been fine this week. But the severe ones give no warning. She's gone a week without one before, and then she has another one." She held the rag to her chest. "It's Andrew. Something's wrong. He's not been to the bakery all week. He usually stops in every other day."

"Toby said Andrew's not been his cheerful self this past week. He's sure something isn't right." Rachael limped to her. "I told Toby to ask him if anything is wrong. He said he did and Andrew said no. Maybe if you go to him and ask him, he'll tell you. Did you have an argument?"

Maryann shook her head. "No, we don't have disagreements. We communicate and discuss anything on our minds. It's why I'm drawn to him. There are no secrets. This is the first time I've suspected he's holding back something from me. I can't imagine why he would, but I'm concerned he's having second thoughts about marrying me." She loved him with all her heart. It would break her heart if he chose not to marry her. She had to get to the bottom of why Andrew seemed different, or it would drive her mad.

Rachael went to the kitchen doorway and stopped. "The man loves you. I'm sure he'll stop in the bakery or at your haus soon. I doubt it's anything to do with your wedding."

Magdelena moved next to Maryann. She patted her back. "I agree with Rachael. I'm sure Andrew will stop in and talk to you soon."

Rachael covered her open mouth and pointed to the window. "Two men are in a serious argument! One's clutching a bag. The sheriff's kumming to the door."

Sheriff Williams shoved the bakery door open. "You girls stay inside. Lock the door!"

Maryann locked the door, and they crowded to the open window where the men were fighting several feet away.

"Give me my half of the money, Butch!" A burly man with a rugged face punched a man about his same size who they assumed was Butch.

"No, Lionel!" Butch threw a punch at Lionel, and Lionel ducked.

"Sheriff, arrest them! They robbed me!" Across the street, Mr. Sanders shook his fist. He held a rifle.

"Get inside your store and lock the door, Mr. Sanders! Take the rifle with you."

The two men scuffled on the ground.

The sheriff and his deputy approached them not far from in front of the bakery. The sheriff raised his Browning pistol, aimed it at the sky, and pulled the trigger. "Stop fighting!"

The men separated, wavered, and stood.

"Hands up in the air." The sheriff demanded.

His deputy grabbed one man, and the sheriff snatched the other.

The sheriff shoved his pistol back in the holster under his coat. He had ahold of one thief, and he handcuffed him. He headed for the door.

"Those men are scary." Maryann unlocked the door.

"We're fortunate they didn't rob us." Rachael gripped her apron.

Magdelena hugged herself. "We might have been next."

Maryann lifted her shoulders and pressed her arms to her sides. "I hope not!"

Rachael dragged Magdelena to the kitchen. "Let's bake and take our minds off those bad men!"

Maryann greeted the two women kumming into the bakery. She served customers and kept the coffeepot filled for the next hour.

The sheriff came inside and stomped the snow off his boots. "Maryann, I'd like some hot tea, if you have it, instead of coffee this morning."

"I have it ready." She served him a cup. "Danki for alerting us to the trouble this morning. You take good care of us. We appreciate it."

The sheriff batted the air. "It's my job, and I have to take care of you girls. This is my favorite place for breakfast."

Dr. Harrison rushed in a couple minutes later and sat next to the sheriff. "What happened this morning? Fred Sanders said his general store got robbed, but you caught the culprits."

"They were the dumbest robbers. Fred said their hands shook as they pointed guns at him, and they argued while they ordered him to hand over the money. They are brothers from Canton, Ohio. They begged me to let them go. They aren't right in the head. I'll let the judge decide what to do with them."

Dr. Harrison slapped his friend on the back. "Good job, buddy. I take for granted the danger associated with your job. Thanks for keeping us safe."

The sheriff blushed. "It's my job. We have a peaceful town. I've not had to deal with their kind often. Thank goodness."

"I'm chilled to the bone. Should have figured we'd have a colder winter when I noticed the wooly worm had a full fur coat in the fall. Got some hot coffee, Maryann?"

Sheriff Williams set his paper on the counter and swiveled on his stool to face his friend. He frowned. "I need advice. I'm in big trouble with Gladys."

Dr. Harrison turned his gaze from the paper to the sheriff. "What did you do this time?"

"Told Gladys her dresses looked a little tighter and my shirts were snug. Suggested we should lay off the desserts for a while. Hands on hips, her mouth pinched, and cheeks red, she stomped out of the room. She won't talk to me. I don't care if she's thin or round. I worry about her health and not what she looks like. What should I do? She's furious with me."

"You are one to talk. You love sweets. You wouldn't last a day without them." The doctor gave the sheriff a stern eye. "Friend, I've told you this before, when you've gotten in trouble with Gladys over hinting about her having too many sweets. You never mention a woman's weight. Ever. She may never make you another dessert. You better buy her something she would love and write her a romantic note to go along with it. Assure her you think she's beautiful."

Maryann put a hand to her mouth. She had to hide her smile or the sheriff might take offense. He had done it this time. She wouldn't like it if Andrew had said anything about her weight.

"Maryann, any suggestions?"

"The Inn has all kinds of pretty things. They have a variety of beautiful reticules, jewelry, and dishware. The gift shop has a shelf dedicated to Amish-made dolls, tea towels, and aprons some of my friends take to sell there. I suggest you consider buying her a bracelet. I noticed she wears them often, and she said she can't have enough of them."

He slapped his leg and smiled. "You're a lifesaver, Maryann. She would love a bracelet."

"Don't forget the note." Dr. Harrison turned the page of his paper.

"Got it." Sheriff Williams popped the last of his bread in his mouth.

* * *

Andrew had avoided Bishop Fisher and Maryann this week. He couldn't believe it was December twelfth and so close to Christmas. Had he done the right thing, taking this week to make decisions? He wanted to give Maryann time to adjust to her mamm's illness. He should tell her what was on his mind today.

He'd taught Toby to build potato boxes, and then they'd finished assembling the table. He drew sketches for Toby to refer to when building a table and chairs. He'd shown him different ways to cut and sand the wood for different projects. Toby had jotted notes.

"Toby, you're a fast learner. I'm amazed at how well you've done with each piece. You should approach Mr. Kline about selling your potato boxes in his store."

"Do you think so?"

"Yes. I wouldn't have said it if I didn't mean it. You're a skilled craftsman."

Toby grinned. "I'd like to surprise Mamm and Rachael by making sewing boxes with drawers for Christmas."

"You design what you envision, and I'll show you how to build them." He had to tell Maryann this evening. It also wasn't fair to Toby to keep his leaving from him. They'd become good friends, and he didn't want to lose Toby's trust. He was sure Maryann would appreciate him waiting to share his news after learning about her mamm's headaches.

He and Toby worked on the desk he'd designed to sell in his uncle's store. Four o'clock struck on the clock, and Andrew nodded to Toby as his friend left to go home. He locked the woodshop door, went inside the haus, and changed clothes. He threw on his wool black coat and went to Maryann's.

Maryann answered the door. "Andrew! I've missed you this week. What has kept you so busy?"

"I've been teaching Toby how to handcraft furniture. I wanted to give you time with your mamm." He grimaced. "How is Naomi?"

"She's not had another headache since you were here, but she's weaker and more tired than usual. I'm concerned she'll have more." She hung his coat on the knotty-pine coat tree.

Shem motioned for him to sit. "Take the chill off and have a seat close to the fire. Stay for supper?"

"I will. Danki." Andrew liked Maryann sitting next to him. He'd missed their conversations this week. His stomach was in a knot. He didn't want anything to change between them. He was sure she'd be upset if he asked her to leave Charm.

Naomi poked her head around the open doorway from the kitchen. "Andrew, what a nice surprise. I insist you have chicken and dumplings with us. I'll try not to stick you with the dishes."

"I'm happy to do the dishes if it means I can stay for supper. I love your cooking, Naomi."

"You know how to win my heart. Kumme. The food is on the table." Naomi motioned for them to join her.

Shem asked them to bow their heads, and he prayed and thanked God for the food.

Naomi smiled. "Betsy is happy in her high chair, rolling some leftover peas we had for supper last night. She'd rather play with them than eat them. I've been letting a small dish of mashed chicken and dumplings cool. Maybe she'll like what we're having for supper better."

Andrew tousled Betsy's hair, and she bounced in her

chair and grinned. She handed him a pea, then snatched it back.

Shem passed the buttered rolls. "Naomi, why are you pressing fingers to your temple?"

Naomi cleared her throat and clasped her water glass. "I have a slight ache. Nothing to worry about." She dropped two small amounts of food on her plate.

"Mamm, you're not spooning enough supper on your plate. You need more to keep up your strength." Maryann patted her mamm's arm.

"I don't have much of an appetite. This will be plenty." Naomi passed a small bowl of peach jam to her dochder.

Andrew had lost his appetite. He had to have the conversation with Maryann about his news, no matter what happened tonight. He'd waited too long. The hairs on the back of his neck prickled. What would be her reaction?

Betsy dug her fist into her bowl and tried to stuff soft dumplings into her little mouth. Food dripped from her bib onto her lap. She giggled and clapped and splattered the food on her hands.

Maryann jumped up and wiped Betsy's mouth and hands. She removed the bib. "Enough for you, little girl. You are a mess."

"She did better than I expected. Half her bowl is empty. She drank her half cup of milk." Naomi squinted and rubbed her head. "Let me take her. You finish your supper."

"I'm full, Mamm. Rest and keep these men in line." Maryann chuckled. "It won't take me long. She's ready to go to bed." Maryann left the room with Betsy holding on to her neck.

Andrew discussed the cold weather and the types of wood he had in mind for his next two projects. Shem kept darting his gaze from him to Naomi. He read the concern in Shem's eyes.

"Naomi, why don't you lie down? I insist on doing the dishes. I wash and dry them at my haus. Please. You're always feeding me. It's the least I can do."

"Danki, Andrew. The pain is worse than last time. I'm sorry to have this happen again with you here."

"You can't help it, and I'm happy to help." Andrew carried the dishes to the counter. He poured warm water from the large pot heating on the stove for washing the dishes.

Shem rose and clasped Naomi's hand. "Andrew, I'll be back."

"Take your time and then relax. I'll have these dishes washed, dried, and back in the cupboards in no time."

"You fit right in with our family. I appreciate your understanding. I'm looking forward to having you for a son-in-law." Shem and Naomi left the kitchen.

Andrew swallowed the dread in his throat as he gathered the dishes, scraped the remains in a bowl for Pepper, and washed and dried them. Maryann's mamm's illness could prevent her from leaving Charm. He frowned as he stacked plates and glasses in the cabinets. Moving would be difficult for her, but he didn't want to lose her. He had no idea how she'd take uprooting her and Betsy from Charm and settling in Millersburg.

Maryann joined him as he placed the large serving bowl in the cupboard. She plopped in one of the kitchen chairs, and he sat next to her. "I peeked in on Mamm. Her pain has grown more intense with this attack since she went to bed. Regular headaches are painful enough. I can't imagine what she's going through. The aspirin powder might help a little, but it seems as if it has to run its course. She's always weak the next day. The more she has them, I can't help wonder if there will be permanent damage to her brain. Dr. Harrison told us there's not enough known about this type of illness."

"I'm sorry for you and your family. We're praying for her. We don't always understand why these things happen. We have to trust God and leave her in His hands."

"You're right. She wouldn't like it if she heard me fretting about her. Let's sit and talk. Tell me more about your week."

He reached across the table and took her hand in his. "Maryann, my uncle wrote me. He's ill, and his friend, who he thought would take over his furniture store, has died. He needs me to kumme right away. He'd like me to take over for him."

Maryann gasped and pressed her hand to her throat. "He's in Millersburg. The town's about nine and a half miles from here, which would be two and a half to three hours by buggy, depending on stops or no stops." She rambled and paced the floor. "What about the wedding? My job at the bakery? And Mamm? Taking Betsy away from my parents?" She crossed her arms and plopped in the chair. Worry lines creased her lovely face. "I'm sorry. I'm being selfish thinking of my side of things. You care about your uncle like I care about Mamm. I understand your uncle needs you. You must go, and then we'll have more information." She gazed at him with concerned eyes. "There's much to ponder, discuss, and overcome."

Andrew reached for her hand. "Maryann, please relax. It hurts me to have you upset. I waited this week to allow you to digest what's going on with your mamm before revealing my uncle's need. Like you, I'm unsettled about this. I've asked the same questions, and I don't have answers." He gently squeezed her fingers. "I'll visit my aunt and uncle, find out what they're facing, and find out how I can help. They've been there for my family and were there for me when my parents passed. My uncle is like another daed to me. His offer to give his store to me is like a dream kumme true. I'll keep my place in Charm and have Toby manage it. I need to assess my uncle's health and the store first before I buy a place in Millersburg and sell my property here."

Maryann gripped her apron. "I didn't plan on leaving Charm ever again. This is quite a shock. I love you, Andrew, and I want to marry you. Betsy adores you, and I have no doubt you'd be a wonderful daed to her. But there's much to consider. Mamm's severe headaches give me pause. Daed and Joel depend on me. Ellie is about to have a boppli, and Mamm isn't right in the head with her mood swings, and now she has this new development. I've put them through so much. I'm torn." She held her cheeks.

Andrew gently removed her hands from her face and held them. "Please, Maryann. Let's not fret. We'll take things one step at a time."

"When will you leave?" She wiped a tear.

"I've been preparing to leave this week. I'll go in the next two days." His stomach knotted. It hurt to upset her. "I might not be back for Christmas. It may take longer to get things in order for him. I'll ask Toby to drop off gifts from me for you and your family."

Maryann slapped her skirt. "I almost forgot to give you the presents I have for you and your aunt and uncle. I'll be right back." She left and returned with three packages.

"Danki. I won't peek at mine until Christmas." He winked and hoped he'd lightened her mood.

"You mentioned Toby would drop off our gifts. He must be disappointed about you moving to Millersburg.

You and he have made a good team." She gasped. "Does Toby have Pepper?"

"He does have Pepper. We've become close friends. I do plan to find him work when my place sells. I'll pay him to oversee my property while I'm away and to care for Pepper, so his routine won't change for a while."

"Will Toby keep Pepper and take care of him at your place when he's there during the day?"

"Yes. This arrangement works out best for everyone. I don't want to add any more stress to your family."

"Betsy would be tickled to have a pet, but you're wise. The timing isn't right for us to have a dog."

"Maryann, we need to pray and be patient. I believe it is God's will for us to work out. We'll keep our wedding date." He brushed her cheek with the back of his hand.

"Your uncle and Mamm's illnesses complicate our having a life together. We're both needed by our families." She held his hand. "Andrew, what are we going to do? I don't want to lose you."

"We must have faith. I'll miss you while I'm away. I'll return as soon as I can. It may take weeks or months, depending on my uncle's health." He gazed into her eyes. "Let's pray together." Andrew prayed for Naomi and his uncle's health and for God's intervention to give them direction in what to do. They opened their eyes and gazed at each other. Andrew said, "Let's tell your daed while your mamm is resting."

Andrew and Maryann found Shem in the living room sitting by the fire reading his Holy Bible.

Andrew sat across from him. "Shem, I have to leave Charm to check on my uncle, who is ill. He has offered me his large store in Millersburg. I hadn't considered the store, since he had a partner. But his partner died. I'm leaving Sunday. It would mean Maryann and I would live in Millersburg after the wedding."

Shem shut his Bible and set it on the end table beside him. "The timing isn't good with Naomi's bad health. Could you open a store in our town?"

"Millersburg is a larger town than Charm, and my uncle has a big store with established customers. He and my aunt need my help due to his failing health. Mr. Kline has a store not as big, and it's not for sale. Charm is a small town. I don't want to open another furniture store and compete with him here. It wouldn't work." He sighed. "I'm concerned for Naomi, and I realize it will be a hardship for your family if Maryann chooses to move with me. She can visit, but I realize that's not the same as having her living close by."

Maryann knelt beside her daed. "What am I going to do?"

Shem patted her hand. "Your wedding isn't until May. Maybe your mamm's health will improve. Your moving would make things worse for her condition. It's a hard decision for you, dochder. Let's pray on this."

Andrew pressed his elbows to his sides. He'd hoped to have Shem's support and encouragement. He didn't blame the man. Naomi's mental state and severe headaches would be too much for him to handle. He had a farm to run. Ellie and Joel couldn't take over her care. They would soon have a child to raise and a farm to manage. His marriage to Maryann was looking bleak. "Your daed's right. We've got until our wedding date to assess how Naomi and my uncle are doing."

Her lips trembling, she rose and nodded.

He winced and stood. "I wish I didn't have to leave, but I've got a lot to do tomorrow to get ready to leave the next day. I'll tell Toby what has transpired and ask him to stay on to manage the property and care for the dog."

Shem shook his hand. "I pray God intervenes and you and Maryann can stay in Charm and open a store in town. As I get older, I realize how much it means to us to have Joel, Maryann, and Betsy close."

"I've prayed for a store, and God has answered my prayer. And my uncle needs me. I hope you understand my point of view if we still need to relocate to Millersburg." Andrew liked Shem, and he enjoyed a good relationship with him. It was important Maryann's daed understood why he'd ask Maryann to live in Millersburg.

"Don't misunderstand. I like you, Andrew. You're an excellent choice for a husband for Maryann and daed for Betsy. I wish the circumstances were different. Travel safe and write when you have time. We'll look forward to your return."

Andrew nodded.

Maryann threw her cape around her shoulders and handed him his coat. "I'll walk you out."

Andrew followed her outside and they stood on the porch. The cold temperature turned Maryann's nose and cheeks red. His face grew cold. He wouldn't keep her outside long. He put his hands on her shoulders. "I love you, and I'll miss you every day."

Tears trickled down her cheeks. "I can't imagine my life without you in it. I'm afraid I may have to if our circumstances don't change."

"I love you, and I believe we'll be together in the end of this." He'd written down his aunt and uncle's address on a slip of paper and pressed it in her palm. "Write when you have time, and I'll do the same." He kissed her gently on the lips, held her gaze for a moment, and left. Why must life be so difficult?

The next morning, Andrew tightened the scarf around his neck, crunched the icy snow beneath his boots, and met Toby's wagon next to the tall white barn. "Toby, kumme inside before you get started on chores. I've got eggs, bacon, and fresh biscuits on the table. Even if you've grabbed something at home this morning, join me anyway."

Pepper stood beside Andrew and wagged his tail as Toby patted the dog's head.

Toby straightened and patted his stomach. "Sounds delicious. Danki. Rachael and I both left without breakfast this morning. Mamm usually has eggs or pancakes for us, but she stayed up most of the night with Daed."

"Trouble with his breathing?"

Toby nodded.

Andrew and Pepper hustled with Toby into the haus and to the kitchen.

Toby took a seat. "He had a persistent cough last night. He finally got to sleep after Mamm gave him some tea with honey and rubbed his chest with Vicks Croup and Pneumonia Salve."

Pepper sat between Andrew and Toby's chairs.

Andrew served Toby and himself breakfast and hot coffee. He and Toby bowed their heads, and Andrew prayed to God and thanked Him for the food. He tore open his biscuit and offered Pepper half. "I'm glad he got some rest. Maybe today will be better for him." He slathered it with honey. "I received a letter from my uncle who lives in Millersburg. He's ill and would like me to manage his store for him. I'll leave this morning. I'm not sure when I'll return to Charm."

Toby cleared his throat. "I'll pray for your uncle." He traced the rim of his coffee cup. "Will you sell your place? Will you and Maryann wed in Charm or Millersburg?"

"It's been a shock for me and Maryann, and I'm sure it is for you. My uncle had a partner who died. I had never considered my uncle's store as an option for me, but his partner's death changes things. Maryann isn't happy about leaving her family again. Don't worry. I won't sell this property right away. I'll discuss the offer with my uncle, ask about his health, and then make a decision."

"Are you close to him?"

"Yes. He and my aunt were close with my family and stayed in touch with me after my parents passed." He set his fork on the plate. "Do you mind managing the place alone while I'm gone? Without my help, it will make more work for you. If at any time you're needed at home more, I can hire someone to help you."

"I can manage, and I'm happy to do it. Since it's December and I only have the animals to take care of, I'll have time to help with Daed if I need to. Rachael and I help in the evenings to give Mamm a break. Will you miss Christmas in Charm?"

"Yes. I have gifts in the barn for Maryann, her family, and Betsy. Do you mind delivering them right before Christmas if I'm not back? I constructed a desk and chair for Naomi and Shem, a hope chest for Maryann, a potato box for Joel and Ellie, and I bought puzzles and small wooden animals for Betsy from Mr. Kline's store. There will be an envelope addressed to you tied to a new settee with cushions, for your family."

Toby's cheeks pinked. "The settee you had in the shop?

It's beautiful. My family will love it. Danki, Andrew." He forked a small portion of scrambled eggs. "I'll deliver them for you, and danki for the envelope and settee in advance."

"I'm glad you and your family will enjoy the settee. I had hoped to have more time to teach you about building, but you're catching on fast with the projects we've done together. It's been a pleasure getting acquainted with you. I'm relieved you'll be taking care of things for me while I'm away. Danki."

"Are you certain about moving to Millersburg? You have such a nice place, and you've said Maryann is the one for you." Toby squinted.

Andrew raked his fingers through his hair. "I'm not sure about anything at the moment. I'll be better informed when I return." Andrew carried his plate to the washbasin.

Pepper followed him.

Andrew put an extra pancake and biscuit in a bowl and placed it on the floor. He poured water from a pitcher into a second bowl for him.

Pepper put his nose in the food.

Toby glanced at the dog. "Pepper will be company for me while you're gone. I'm blessed he came when he did. I'll take him to visit my family. Mamm and Rachael love animals. He might lift Daed's mood." He headed for the door and glanced over his shoulder. "I pray you get clarity about what you need to do. It would be a shame for you and Maryann not to have a future together."

"I've faced trials, but this is the hardest." He poured himself more coffee. "I plan to find you other work if I move to Millersburg. I would take you with me when I move and hire you for the furniture store there, but I realize you wouldn't want to leave your family."

Toby nodded. "I appreciate it. And you're right. I could never leave my family. I can't imagine being in your position right now."

"I pray you never have to experience this." He poured hot water from the pot on the stove into his basin. "I'll take care of the kitchen, gather my belongings, and be on my way soon. You can go ahead and tend to the animals if you'd like."

"Danki for breakfast, and I'll harness your horse to the buggy."

"I'd appreciate it." Andrew glanced over his shoulder and watched Toby leave. He cared about his friend and he would miss him. He cleaned the dishes and put them away. Maryann and her family had succeeded in making him a part of their circle. He'd miss them, too. And he liked this haus, the friends he'd made, and Bishop Fisher and Sunday services. His heart heavy, he packed two more shirts in his bag to take to his uncle's place. He had spent the week in the barn, workshop, and haus to get things in order, and to eliminate some repairs for Toby. He had his buggy ready, said goodbye to Toby, and headed to the bishop's haus. He arrived and knocked on the door.

Bishop Fisher rubbed his eyes and held a cup of coffee as he opened the door. "Andrew, is everything all right?"

Andrew entered the haus and took off his hat. "I won't be at Sunday service for a while, and I'm not sure how long I'll be gone. My uncle is ill, and he's asked me to kumme to his home in Millersburg as soon as possible. Please pray for Maryann and me as we face the dilemma of her mamm and my uncle's bad health."

"Yes. I will. It will be a tough decision for Maryann to

relocate. Naomi was a handful for Shem and Joel when Maryann left the first time."

Andrew gripped his hat. Anxiety skipped in his stomach. He'd thought nonstop about Naomi's health and how it might be the reason Maryann wouldn't marry him. He wouldn't move if it wasn't for his uncle's health and the opportunity he was offering him. "I'm concerned about Naomi's and my uncle's health. Maryann and I are torn about what to do. We're leaving it in God's hands and keeping our wedding date. If we can't find a way to be together, we'll cancel it. I hope that doesn't happen."

"Neither do I." He gazed at Andrew. "Will you oversee your uncle's farm for him?"

Andrew folded his hands. "He has a manager for his farm. He's offering me his furniture store located downtown near the general store. His partner passed away, and his shop is the size I was saving to buy. I'd be there to help my aunt and uncle at their home and manage the store. I'll stay with them and keep my place in Charm for now. I'll eventually sell it and buy a haus there."

The bishop nodded and held up his cup. "I'm sorry. I should've offered you coffee. Would you like a cup?"

"No. Danki. I'm on my way to Millersburg. I respect you, Bishop Fisher. I wanted to tell you what was going on with me before I left town." He walked to the door and held the knob. "I've appreciated getting to know you since moving to Charm."

"It's been a pleasure to get acquainted with you, Andrew. You and Maryann have a difficult decision to make. Before you leave, let's pray together. Dear Heavenly Father, please protect Andrew as he travels and visits Millersburg. Be with his uncle, during this difficult time with his health.

Help Andrew find the right employees for the store. Give him and Maryann the wisdom to make the right decisions as they plan to marry and relocate. Amen." The bishop followed him to the door. "You've got close to a three-hour trip if you stop along the way. Do you have enough water and food? I've got some ham slices and jars I can send with you."

"Yes. I wish I was traveling in warmer temperatures, but I'll be all right. And yes. I do have plenty of nourishment. Danki, Bishop, for your offer. But I'm all set." Andrew pushed his hat on and left.

His teeth chattered as he covered his legs with his wool blanket to help keep him warm against the bitter cold temperature. He was ready for sunshine to melt the snow. The dirty slush on the roads wasn't his favorite. It might take him longer than anticipated to arrive in Millersburg with these conditions. He scanned the farms along the way. The blanket of untouched white land appeared bright and clean. Icicles hung on tree branches and patches of snow decorated them. He passed through an old covered bridge and enjoyed the short reprieve from the wind batting against his broadcloth buggy curtains. He drove into Millersburg, and then found his aunt and uncle's haus about three hours later.

A tall man with a wrinkled face and a patch of gray hair poking out from under his hat wore a big smile and approached him. He offered his hand. "I'm Levi. I manage this property for Luke Wittmer. What brings you by?"

Andrew exited the buggy and shook Levi's hand. "I'm his nephew, Andrew. He's expecting me."

Levi accepted the reins. "He told me he was looking forward to your visit. A pleasure to meet you. I'll take your horse and put him in the barn and I'll unload your things and bring them inside. You go on in the haus. You'll freeze standing out in this cold weather too long."

Andrew held up his bag. "Danki, but this is all I brought." He held on to his hat against a gust of wind. "How's Uncle Luke doing?"

Levi shook his head. "His health has declined each week since he took ill. The doctor isn't sure what's wrong with him. His legs ache, and he grabs his chest when he coughs. Some days aren't as bad as others. He uses a cane most of the time. You being with us will perk him up."

"Danki for taking care of my horse." He handed Levi the reins and stepped onto the porch.

Aunt Dora threw open the door and wrapped her thin arms around him. "Luke, Andrew has arrived!" She dropped her arms and ushered him into the living room. "Take a seat close to the stove. I'll get you warm cocoa. You must be frozen half solid with the long three-hour drive."

Uncle Luke sat on a thick navy cushion in his oak chair and raised a shaking, frail hand. "I'm glad you arrived safe. I've been looking forward to your visit."

Andrew blinked away the tears filling his eyes. His uncle had lost his once-round stomach, and he looked much older than his age of fifty. His thick brown hair once there was gone, and now he was bald.

He crossed the room to his loved one's chair and held his hand. "It's been too long since our last visit together. I'm sorry you're sick."

"Your arrival has taken a load of worry from me. I'm in great need of your assistance at the store. I'm not over Clyde's passing. He was such a good friend and business partner." He motioned to the settee. "Take a seat and get comfortable."

Aunt Dora carried in a tray with sugar cookies, embroidered napkins, and three mugs of warm cocoa. She set it on the oak coffee table. "Help yourself." She set her husband's cookies and mug on the end table next to him. "I've got a bedroom ready for you. Treat this home like it's yours."

He lifted the mug and sipped the cocoa and then set it back on the tray. "Aunt Dora, danki, this hits the spot. You've always been gracious to me." He scanned the room. He remembered the green and white patchwork quilt Dora had made when he was a boy that was folded and draped over the settee. His uncle's worn Bible sat on the end table. The familiar maple desk and chair he used to sit at and draw pictures on paper was nestled in the corner of the room. He'd made a couple of marks in the wood by accident. His daed wanted to tan his hide, but Uncle Luke insisted it gave the desk character and forbid it.

"The haus next door is for sale. You'll have to drive over and get a closer look at everything to appreciate it. You'd be close to us and just a mile from the furniture store in town." Uncle Luke broke off a piece of cookie.

"I'd rather your neighbor not wait on me to sell his haus. I need to take one thing at a time." Studying his uncle, he caught a glimpse of what Toby was going through with his daed. The once robust man he'd known was now thin and frail. He was glad he'd kumme to help and spend time with him. He should've visited them before now. They'd aged, and he'd missed them.

"Do you have your haus advertised for sale?" Luke folded his hands in his lap.

"Not yet. I have a friend, Toby, taking care of the livestock while I'm with you. He'll advertise and sell it when I write and tell him I'm ready. If you don't mind, I'll stay with you for a while." Andrew didn't want his uncle to push him into considering the haus next door. He would change the subject. "How is the store doing?" Andrew reached for a cookie.

Luke adjusted the dark blue blanket to better cover his legs. "You're wilkom to stay with us as long as you like." He shook his head. "The business has suffered under Zeke Miller's management. The young man is forty, and he's the only one I trusted to take over when Clyde passed. Zeke's a farmer, and he has no interest in selling furniture nor is he any good at it. He's running the business as a favor to me. He isn't a salesman or a craftsman."

"Do you have enough merchandise since he isn't making furniture?" He wouldn't have time to build anything until he learned the store, studied the accounts, and hired a craftsman.

Luke shifted in the chair and winced. "We're low on merchandise. Two other handcrafters consign with us and their pieces have kept the store afloat. Clyde and I worked in the back of the store crafting products and furniture when we didn't have customers. One of us was in the back at all times. We've built a stellar reputation and customers travel from all over to buy furniture from us. The store provided an abundant living for us until I became ill and Clyde left this earth. The crops and cattle have been good, too."

Andrew admired his uncle. His mind was sharp, and he would be a much needed resource to bring him up-to-date and turn things around fast. "Do you have any suggestions as to who to hire as a salesman? Craftsmen I could approach to sell their pieces in the store? We could use a couple more." Andrew would have to enlist a partner right away. He'd like to fill the store with other builders' pieces until he had time to handcraft furniture. Customers wouldn't return if the store was half empty, and word would spread it wasn't worth the trip to shop there.

His uncle shook his head. "The men I've had work for me during peak times have taken other jobs or moved out of town. You could advertise at the general and hardware stores. Dora has taken over the accounting, and we've managed to pay our bills. I'd like you to take over the accounting. I'd like to get back to making extra money so we don't have to worry each month about our living and store expenses. After you have the store making a good profit again, we can work out an agreeable percentage of money for Dora and me. We don't need much. When I die, the store is yours."

Andrew leaned back. "You're being generous in not having me buy the store."

"You've done us a great service to save the store."

Andrew's heart swelled with gratitude. "I can't thank you enough. Danki." He smiled at Dora. She was as patient as he remembered. She'd let them talk and hadn't interrupted.

Dora shifted in her seat to look at Andrew. "I'm glad you're staying with us. I'll rest easier knowing you are living in the haus to help me if I need you."

"Anything you need, don't hesitate to ask." Andrew excused himself and went to his room. His heart plummeted. He'd have to move to Millersburg. He wouldn't let his aunt and uncle down. They didn't have any alternatives.

His uncle's illness and store put him in an unattainable position with Maryann but his choice was clear, although it ripped his heart from his chest thinking of her not wanting to leave Charm. He understood why. She was loyal to her family, and her mamm's illness made it a no-win situation for her. What would this mean for him and Maryann? Her ending their courtship seemed inevitable, given the circumstances. He prayed Maryann would choose him, but his heart told him otherwise.

Chapter Five

Maryann helped Mamm unload the basket of dishes that she'd taken to church earlier once full of meat spread sandwiches, slaw, and a custard pie that now were empty. "I'll set these dirty dishes in water to soak, and then we can wash and dry them in the morning."

Hands on her hips, Mamm cocked her head. "You've been quieter than usual today. Are you all right? Have you and Andrew had a spat? Why wasn't Andrew at the service this morning?"

Maryann tensed. She should've told her family and friends Andrew was leaving town last night. The words wouldn't kumme out of her mouth. She would have to let Andrew go. The realization sickened her, but she had no choice. Mamm had had another severe headache last night. Her father had slept in her bed, while she slept with Mamm. He'd been exhausted and needed his rest. Her mamm had cried with pain, and it had been hard to watch. Mamm was drained but woke without pain. This would be a good time to tell them. "I have something important to tell you and Daed."

Mamm cupped her ear and raised her chin. "The door

creaked open. Joel and Ellie must be here." She called to them. "We're in the kitchen." She covered Maryann's hand and looked at her with sunken eyes. "What were you going to tell me, dear?"

"Let me tell everyone at once." She had dreaded having to go to Joel and Ellie's and repeat her latest news about Andrew leaving Charm. This way she would have to tell them about the latest development only once. She followed Mamm to the living room and hugged Ellie and Joel. "What a pleasant surprise." She glanced at Ellie's stomach. Soon she'd have a niece or nephew. She'd looked forward to being close by for the birth and being a part of the little one's life. Betsy would have a cousin to befriend.

Daed grinned and gestured for Joel and Ellie to sit. "I love having my family together."

"I've got pie for us. I'll be right back." Mamm went to the kitchen and returned carrying a tray of pie plates filled with large slices of butterscotch pie and glasses of water.

"I'm always ready for dessert, Naomi." Daed sat next to Joel in his favorite high-backed chair.

Maryann rushed to distribute the plates and glasses. Mamm shouldn't be doing this heavy work after last night. She held her plate, and her stomach clenched. She didn't expect this to go well. "When you all asked why Andrew wasn't at Sunday service, I told you he had something kumme up he had to take care of. I should've told you the whole story earlier, but it's been hard for me to find the right time and words."

"Spit it out. You're making me nervous." Ellie sat on the edge of her chair.

"He's gone to visit his aunt and uncle in Millersburg. His uncle wrote a letter explaining he'd taken ill and needed Andrew to run his furniture store."

Ellie wrinkled her nose. "Didn't his uncle have a partner or friend who could step in for him?"

Maryann shook her head. "His partner passed away. He has a man taking over temporarily until Andrew's arrival. His uncle was aware of Andrew's dream to own a store, and he was sure this would be ideal for him."

"What!" Mamm fisted her hands and paced. "You can't be thinking of leaving. We need you. Why can't he open a store in Charm? We have some extra money. We'll lend it to him. Please, Shem. Say something."

Maryann rushed to Mamm's side. "Please, Mamm. Sit and calm down. I don't want you to get a headache." She squeezed her eyes shut, sucked in a deep breath, and squelched the cutting pain in her heart. "I'm not going to leave you."

"You're engaged to marry Andrew. You'll have to leave if you marry him." Mamm shook her head. "His uncle needs him. But I need you more. I can't take it. Please don't leave us again." Tears rolled onto her cheeks.

Maryann's throat ached. The all-too-familiar childlike outburst from Mamm had appeared again. She'd pushed down the strong opposing reaction she'd anticipated from Mamm. She hadn't wanted to face the inevitable canceling of the wedding. Mamm was irrational. She couldn't leave her, knowing she wasn't right in the head, and with her illness. "I realize now I must cancel the wedding, and I'll stay in Charm."

Daed set his half-eaten pie back on the tray. "Maryann, I'm sorry you and Andrew have such difficult circumstances."

Joel gave Maryann a steady stare. "I hope you won't change your mind. We all need you."

"I'm not going to change my mind." Maryann gazed

at Mamm. "Maybe you should lie down." She worried this conversation would erupt into a severe and painful headache for Mamm. She hoped Mamm lying down would prevent this.

Mamm whimpered and went to her bedroom.

Joel paced the room. "Maryann, I mean it. Mamm has been manageable and her moods lighter since your return. It's selfish of me to ask, but I must. You've got to stay in Charm."

Maryann pinched her eyes shut and then opened them. She stared at her bruder. "Joel, I said I'm not leaving." Maryann struggled to remain calm. She'd returned to Charm and proven to her family she regretted the way she'd left the first time. This was different. Gerald was an Englischer. A man they forbade her to marry. Andrew, an Amish man committed to God and Amish life, had won their hearts and approval. It wasn't out of the question why she'd want to consider relocating to have a life with him or to expect they'd understand. But she wouldn't abandon Mamm. This was a sacrifice she'd have to make.

Daed cleared his throat. "Let's not be too hard on Maryann. Andrew's the love of her life, and we're asking a lot of her."

Maryann sat across from Daed, Ellie, and Joel. "I love Andrew for his devotion to his family, and he will respect my decision and love me for my devotion to mine. But it's tragic our future together must end because of it."

Joel sighed. "These headaches Mamm is having are serious. I'm certain they'll get worse if her mood darkens, like last time you left. Otherwise, we'd understand you starting a new life in Millersburg."

Ellie rubbed her stomach. "This boppli will be an adjustment for us, and your mamm doesn't consider me an adequate substitute for you. I agree with Joel. She'll be in a bad way without you. I'm not sure any of us can be an adequate substitute for you with her."

Daed gazed at Maryann. "Please talk to Andrew. Surely he can build furniture in Charm and find a buyer for his uncle's store. This decision, to choose between your mamm and Andrew, is tearing me up inside. I don't want to make your life miserable. You've suffered much in your young life, but I am extremely worried what will happen to your mamm if you leave."

"Danki for your concern, Daed. I understand. I'm not willing to shoulder the burden of her getting worse because of me. I'll write and tell him we should call off the wedding soon, considering our responsibilities to our families. But not today. I need time to think about how I'll word the news to him." Maryann pressed a hand to her broken heart, as tears dripped onto her white cotton blouse. Andrew was the love of her life. He was wise, kind, and patient. She'd miss him every day.

"It's been a long day. Ellie, we should let Maryann and Daed get some rest." Joel stood and motioned for Ellie and headed for the door.

Ellie glanced over her shoulder at Maryann. "Please bring Betsy to me this week. I'd love to take care of her while you work at the bakery." Ellie squeezed her hand. "I'm sorry, Maryann. I realize this is a trying time for you. We'll talk later." Ellie followed Joel outside.

Daed patted her back. "Joel reacts without thinking. He's concerned about reliving what he went through with your mamm when you first left. He shouldn't have spouted off to you. He missed you, and he loves having you back, as we all do. Mamm's attachment to you has made life better for us. Your promise to stay hasn't sunk in with him yet."

Maryann buried her face in his shoulder and wept. She raised her head and wiped her eyes. "I'm heartbroken, Daed. Andrew's my soul mate. He and I agree on most everything. There are no secrets. We're open and honest with each other about all things. I doubt I'd find a man like him again in my lifetime."

He embraced her and prayed for guidance for her, to protect Andrew while he was away, and for healing for Naomi. He raised his head. "God will intervene if it's His will you two should be together." Shem kissed her forehead. "Go get some rest."

Maryann went to her bedroom and fell onto her bed. She stared at the ceiling. Was there a reason God didn't want her to marry Andrew? She didn't understand why they had met and fallen in love if they weren't supposed to be together. This devastating decision was worse than when Gerald had been killed. She loved Andrew with all of her heart, and she was certain he would have been a devoted daed for Betsy.

She dabbed her eyes with her handkerchief. She'd left Daed and Joel to care for Mamm, knowing it would be difficult for them considering Mamm's unusual attachment to her. And also Mamm's anxiousness and brooding when things didn't go her way. She wouldn't abandon her family again. She had to show them she was loyal, dependable, and truly cared. Her staying by Mamm's side would prove her love and devotion to them, and she knew her presence might help her mamm calm down and help the severity of her painful and serious headaches. Her family had to kumme first.

* * *

Maryann scooped sugar into a measuring cup and dropped it in the bowl. She'd arrived at the bakery earlier than usual on this blustery and snowy Monday morning and started to bake. She had her third pie crust in the oven. She had the wood-burning stove in the corner going with a warm fire to heat the room.

Rachael and Magdelena appeared at the doorway of the kitchen. Rachael took off her heavy black cape and shook the snow off. "I am chilled to the bone." She shook her shoulders. "My goodness, Maryann, what are you doing at the bakery's worktable so early?"

Magdelena hung her gray cape on the metal wall hook. She removed her mittens and held her hands close to the stove. "Is it summer yet? I'm ready." She tied her apron behind her neck and at her waist. "I would've kumme in early to help if you needed me to."

Maryann stirred her ingredients for butter cookies. She heaved a big sigh. She didn't want to ruin their day, but she had to tell them. She intended to devour a couple of these cookies to comfort herself. She tended to use food to calm her nerves. She'd better be careful or she'd be as round as she was tall. The older she got, the harder it was to lose these extra pounds. She looked up from the bowl to her friends. She shared Andrew's news and the decision she'd made to end their courtship. "I would've told you at church yesterday, but I hadn't told my parents or Joel and Ellie. I told them after we got home."

Rachael's mouth gaped open. "I wondered why Andrew wasn't at the service, but I kept forgetting to ask you. When I asked Toby, he shrugged his shoulders. He's been quieter than usual, and he didn't tell me Andrew left. He tends to keep things inside for a while before he's ready to talk. Now I understand." She moved closer to Maryann. "You must be heartbroken."

Magdelena's hands flew to her cheeks. "I'm shocked!" She put her hands on Maryann's shoulders. "You and Andrew can't cancel your wedding. Your family has to accept they'll have to take care of your mamm. Your place is with your husband once you're married."

Hannah rushed into the kitchen and surprised them. "Good morning, girls. I'm glad the door was unlocked. I'm freezing. I'll keep my coat on for a while. Maryann, I had to kumme before you served customers. Ellie and Joel stopped over last night. I take it from Rachael and Magdelena's concerned faces, you've told them your plans have changed."

Maryann nodded and tears pooled in her eyes. Telling her family and friends had been heartbreaking. "I don't want to cancel our wedding. I love Andrew, but I'm frightened and concerned for Mamm. She's not right in the head, and now, she's having more episodes. I must do this."

Hannah and the girls huddled close to her. Hannah put her hands on Maryann's shoulders. "Are you sure you want to let Andrew go? This is a crucial sacrifice you're making for your family. It's selfish and unfair. Don't make a hasty decision without thinking of Betsy and you. Joel and Ellie shouldn't put the burden of your mamm on your shoulders. It's wrong of them to think only of themselves. Joel and Ellie tend to speak without thinking when they're frustrated. Your family will adjust without you, like they did the first time you left."

Magdelena rubbed her chin and glanced at the ceiling in deep thought. "If Liza is in agreement, I'll manage the store and take the burden off you. You've taught me how, and who to order supplies from, and your accounting method, and I can manage the front when needed."

Maryann managed a weak grin. "I have no doubt you'd be an excellent manager, but I must put Mamm first and stay in Charm."

Rachael leaned against the counter. "I can kumme in earlier and stay later to bake if necessary. We always have desserts and loaves of bread left over each day. We can manage with the two of us."

Hannah beamed. "I'll hire or fill in when you need a baker until we find a permanent replacement."

"We'll manage, Hannah. And I promise we'll ask you for help if we need it." Magdelena smiled.

"Wonderful!" Hannah clapped her hands and grinned. "Maryann, we've solved the problem of you leaving the bakery. Your family will take care of your mamm. Now wipe those worrisome thoughts out of your mind and look forward to marrying Andrew. We'll miss you each day, but we'll visit you. And you can visit us."

"I appreciate your support and encouragement, but I can't ignore my family's valid concerns about Mamm. Her condition could worsen. I'd never forgive myself if I was the reason she suffered more frequent episodes. I've made my choice." Maryann's lips quivered.

Hannah waved a finger. "I don't appreciate the position Ellie and Joel have put you in. When they stopped over last night after leaving your haus, I reminded them what it was like when Joel's mamm disapproved of Ellie, and how distraught they were thinking they might never win her approval. Ellie said it tore her heart in two to think she and Joel may not get married. Both of them expressed regret they'd been selfish and thoughtless about your love for Andrew. Do I expect them to apologize? No, they're still afraid of what your mamm will do without you. But listen, they'll adjust to you being gone."

Maryann reached for Hannah's hand and squeezed it. "I love you, Hannah, and danki for your discussion with Ellie and Joel. But this time, they're right. For whatever reason, Mamm is attached to me more than anyone else. It isn't fair, or a healthy mamm-and-dochder relationship. It's something I have to acknowledge and accept. I have to put Mamm first in this situation."

"I'm heartbroken for you." Hannah pressed a hand to her heart.

Rachael limped to the cupboard and chose a big metal bowl. "Toby hasn't said a word. Andrew must've hinted to him about your mamm's and his uncle's bad health being a problem for the both of you. I wonder why he's been quiet about it."

"Toby is in a precarious position. He cares about all of us. Maybe he wanted me to have a chance to tell you when I was ready. Our obligation to our families is complicated. Andrew and me didn't want to face we may have to make the ultimate sacrifice of giving up each other."

"When did you make the decision?" Rachael picked up the salt shaker.

"I made the decision yesterday." Maryann put a hand on Rachael's shoulder.

"You're right. Toby would want to give you the opportunity to tell me first. He's considerate and puts others' needs before his. I suspect he's upset and trying not to show it. He and Andrew formed a bond, and he looks forward to going to work at Andrew's each day." Rachael sighed.

Hannah hugged the girls. "I'm sorry you have to go through this, Maryann. I can't imagine how painful it must be for you. I respect your decision. The sacrifice you're making kummes with a hefty price. If you need to talk more, please kumme to me." Hannah gave her an endearing smile. "I love you, dear friend."

"Danki, Hannah." Maryann gazed at Hannah and watched her leave. She was thankful her friends were compassionate and sometimes more understanding than her family.

Maryann baked molasses cookies, custard pies, and sugar milk pies with Magdelena and Rachael until time to open the bakery. She turned her sign and made a mental note to lock the front door when she came in early tomorrow. She hadn't been thinking straight. Her mind swirled with thoughts of Andrew. What was he doing? Was he excited about his uncle's store? How was his uncle's health? She hoped to receive a letter from him soon. She dreaded the day he would get her letter.

Toby opened the door and walked in. "Good morning, Maryann. Is Rachael in the kitchen?"

"Yes. Did your daed's condition worsen?"

"No, he's the same. It's hard to find time to talk to Rachael without my parents present. I'd like to discuss a family matter with her if you can spare her for a couple of minutes."

"I'll get her for you." She stepped to the open doorway. "Rachael, Toby would like to talk to you." Maryann pointed to the coffeepot. "Would you like a cup?"

He shook his head. "No. Danki. I won't be long."

Rachael held a rag to her chest. "Has something bad happened?"

"No. Can you sit with me? Maryann said I can steal you for a couple of minutes." Toby moved to the back table in the corner.

"What is it?" Rachael sat across from him.

Toby whispered, "Has Maryann said anything about Andrew leaving town?"

"She told us about his ill uncle offering him the furniture store in Millersburg. She said she can't leave her mamm. I feel terrible for them. She's writing him today to tell him they must cancel the wedding. Their high moral standards to care for their loved ones leave them no choice but to give up their life together." She sat back in the chair and crossed her arms. "How long have you known Andrew had to leave for Millersburg? Why didn't you tell me before now?"

Toby motioned to keep her voice low. "I wanted to give Maryann time to tell you. I'm not surprised Maryann is choosing to stay in Charm. I couldn't leave our family with Daed being sick." He folded his hands on the table. "Andrew asked me to manage his property while he's away. I suppose he'll ask me to advertise his place for sale soon."

"What will you do for an income?" Rachael twisted the rag in her hands.

Maryann rearranged loaves of bread and desserts on the shelves. She overheard their conversation. Her heart sank. She didn't want Andrew's decision to bring hardship on Rachael's family.

"I'll find odd jobs like I did before Andrew hired me. God will provide." Toby managed a weak grin. "Don't worry. I'm thankful for the time I've had doing this job, and for the friendship I've made with Andrew."

Rachael stood. "You're the best bruder. I can always count on you." She grinned. "And you can count on me. I also like my job at the bakery. It's more like a hobby than a job."

"I can relate. I like to build things to sell, and I enjoy it.

I don't consider it work." He straightened his shoulders. "No matter what happens, I'll always take care of our family." He stood. "I should head back to Andrew's. I thought it best to discuss this away from Mamm and Daed. I don't want them or you to worry when my job ends with Andrew." He crossed the room.

Maryann read disappointment in Toby's eyes. He had a positive attitude, but Andrew's change of plans had definitely put a strain on him. She handed him a bag. "Cookies to nibble on." She admired the relationship Rachael had with Toby. She had a similar closeness with Joel during their childhood. Her leaving to marry Gerald had damaged their relationship. He loved her, but they weren't as close since she'd returned to Charm. She prayed in time they would be again. Rachael's bruder had such a burden to carry. She'd placed that same burden on Joel with Mamm when she'd left the first time.

She doubted Toby got much sleep, and she didn't know how he accomplished all he did in a day. Joel had gone through the same before she returned. She was sorry she'd put Joel through so much turmoil. She wanted to cheer Toby before he left. Pepper would be a pleasant subject. She grinned. "How's Pepper?"

Toby's frown turned to a grin. "I love the dog. He's good company, and he's obedient. Pepper loves food. He'll finish a bowl as if he's starving and then beg for another."

Maryann smiled. "I'm glad you're taking care of Pepper. I would've taken him, but I worry about Mamm with her headaches."

"Toby, bring Pepper home from Andrew's tonight." Rachael smiled and nudged her bruder's arm. "He might be a wilkom addition to our family."

"I will, and I pray Daed will enjoy Pepper. I'll do

anything to make Daed happy." He held up the bag. "Danki." He opened the door and stepped outside.

Rachael closed the door behind him. "I'm relieved Toby told me about Andrew's relocation to Millersburg. We're close, and I want him to share with me whatever is on his heart. He's taken this new development in stride. When Andrew sells his place, I'm sure Mamm would agree to take Pepper into our haus. She'd do anything to make Toby happy after all he does for us."

Maryann sighed. "He sets a good example for me. He's taking care of his family, and I need to take care of mine." She pressed a hand to her throat. The loss of Andrew in her life hurt more than she cared to admit.

Rachael circled her arm around Maryann's shoulders. "I understand this will be a trying time for you, and I wish you didn't have to carry this burden. If you need time off, Magdelena and I can manage. Or if you need a shoulder to cry on, I'm here for you."

Maryann hugged her. "Danki. Having friends like you, Hannah, and Magdelena will make it bearable." She kissed Rachael's cheek.

"I better help Magdelena bake or she'll be asking for a new baker!" Rachael bustled to the kitchen.

Maryann watched Rachael scamper to the back room. The girls knew how to cheer her up.

Dr. Harrison and Sheriff Williams caught her attention, taking their seats at the counter.

"Good morning, gentlemen." She poured them coffee. "Warm cinnamon rolls with maple butter frosting, or apple fry pies?"

The sheriff sniffed the air and grinned. "Cinnamon rolls. Thank you."

"Me too, Maryann."

She served them the rolls. They had their noses in their papers as usual. She smiled. They were so predictable.

"Wonder what is going on with President Wilson today. Were you aware his father, Joseph, was a Presbyterian minister and his mother, Janet, was a minister's daughter and originally from England?" Dr. Harrison opened his half of the paper he shared with the sheriff.

"I did not. Interesting." The sheriff cut the roll into four sections, licked his fingers, and picked up his paper.

Maryann glanced at the men. She learned tidbits about what was going on in the world from them each time they talked about their articles. Bishop Fisher wouldn't have been too happy about her interest in world events. She'd be careful who she told any of the information she found out from Dr. Harrison and the sheriff's conversations.

Dr. Harrison was quiet and had his nose in the paper. He huffed. "Listen to this. The actor and comedian Charlie Chaplin will start his film career today and make one hundred and fifty dollars a week. Do you believe it?"

The sheriff choked on his coffee. "What! I'm in the wrong profession. I should've been a comedian."

Dr. Harrison set his paper on the counter. "You'd have a hard time being a comedian. Although you do make me laugh when you don't mean to. But you're not one-hundred-and-fifty-dollars funny." He resumed reading his paper.

"You're as humorous as a doorknob. Good thing you're a doctor." The sheriff lifted his chin and grinned.

"I've made you laugh a time or two," Dr. Harrison huffed.

Maryann couldn't believe a man would be paid one hundred and fifty dollars a week to make people laugh. The bakery brought in good money, and Liza was generous to pay them a good wage. She rubbed her stiff neck. The sheriff and Dr. Harrison had taken her mind off her troubles for a couple of minutes. But the ache in her heart returned, and she wondered if it would ever leave.

Andrew sat at the table. "Where's Uncle Luke?"

"He's in the bedroom. He's moving slow this morning. I expect he'll join us in a couple of minutes."

Andrew had slept in a little and then woke and sniffed the aroma of bacon. He hoped Maryann was having a good start to her Monday. "I remember your breakfasts are the best. Can't wait to have cheesy eggs and bacon."

His aunt stood over an iron skillet. She flipped the bacon strips. "I've got grits and biscuits and sausage gravy the way you like it, too." She filled his plate and set it on the table and then placed a basket of biscuits in front of him.

"You're spoiling me. I'll have to have bigger clothes if I finish meals like this each day." Andrew slathered the warm biscuit with butter and raspberry jam. He moved to the coffeepot and poured himself a cup and sat down.

She grinned. "I'll make you bigger clothes. You have all the food you want." She swatted him with her dish towel. "I would've poured you a cup if you'd waited a moment."

He gave her a loving smile. "My arm's not broken. I intend to help you and Luke while I'm here."

The cozy kitchen had the same maple hutch with white porcelain platters, bowls, and larger dishes in it. The hardwood table and chairs had been re-varnished. He recognized the embroidered tea towel hanging from a hook by the sink as one his mamm had given Aunt Dora years ago. It was faded and thin. He wondered if she'd left it out on purpose to remind him of his loving parents. It would be like her to do so.

She patted his back. "We're pleased you're with us. I hope you're happy about his offer of the store."

"I am grateful." He met her gaze. "How is Uncle Luke?"

She dragged a chair back and sat across from him. "He's not good. The doctor can't understand why he's losing weight and tired most of the time. But he can take care of himself for now. Having you to manage the store will relieve his mind."

Luke used his cane as he shuffled to his seat. "Are you bragging about me again?" He winked at Andrew and kissed her on the cheek. "I hope you find a good fraa like my Dora."

"I have found a sweet and lovely woman like Dora. I met her in Charm a while back. Her name is Maryann Harding. Our wedding will be May fourteenth in Charm. I'd love for you to kumme to the wedding. Maybe Uncle Luke will be better by then. You'll like her." Andrew snatched another biscuit. He hoped they'd have a chance to meet her. He pushed that thought out of his head.

Dora slapped her hand on the table. "Congratulations! What exciting news! Why didn't you tell us about her yesterday?" She moved to the stove and filled a plate for Luke and set it in front of him.

Luke grinned. "I'm happy for you."

Andrew cast his eyes on his coffee. "I'm not sure we'll end up together."

Aunt Dora swiveled to him. "Why?"

"It's a hard decision for her to move. Maryann's mamm isn't well. She may need to remain in Charm to take care of her. I'm hoping she won't call off the wedding, although I'd understand, given the circumstances." Andrew gripped his napkin. He'd be heartbroken if she stayed in Charm, but the Amish took care of their families. Her mamm's illness was unusual, and she was dependent on Maryann.

Dora spooned sugar in her coffee. "I wouldn't have left my family if I'd been in her shoes. I pray her mamm gets better."

"Yes. I do, too."

Luke's hand shook as he lifted his mug. "I'm not strong enough to make the trip. But we'll think of you on your special day, and we wish you the best. When will you return to Charm? I expect you'll have marital counsel from the bishop before your marriage."

"You're correct. I plan to leave sometime the first week of April."

"You must be excited. I can't wait to meet her. I'm sure we'll love her." Dora folded her hands against her chest.

Andrew stood. "Danki. I hope you get the opportunity." He patted his middle. "That was a delicious breakfast." He wasn't sure there would be a wedding, and he didn't want to say any more about it right now. "I should go to the shop. I can bring back groceries or anything you need from town." Going to the shop to assess the sales, inventory, and management of the furniture store would be a good way to take his mind off worrying about his predicament with Maryann.

Dora rose. "Danki for the offer, but nothing for us. You enjoy your trip to town. I'm sure you'll be delighted to visit the store again. It's been a long time since you've been there."

"I'll be anxious for your report at the end of the day.

Danki for taking over for me, Andrew. I can rest easier now."

"Happy to oblige, and I'm thankful for your generosity. I've always loved your store." He tipped his hat, shrugged into his coat, and exited the haus. His boots crunched the snow on his way to the barn. "Levi, danki for harnessing my horse to the buggy. I'm off to the store. Do you need anything from town?"

Levi grinned and handed him the reins. "Wouldn't mind some lemon drops from the general store."

"I'll buy lemon drops for both of us." Andrew smiled as he drove to the shop just five minutes away. Amish and Englischers came in and out of the shops carrying packages and crates full of groceries. Buggies and wagons filled the parking spots along the road. Millersburg was a thriving community. A good place to own a business and start a family. He prayed it would be Maryann's choice to relocate. He left his horse at the livery and dodged the buggies, crossing the street. The town was larger and busier than Charm. He watched a Model T automobile park in front of the hardware store. They were sparse in these parts. He entered Wittmer's Amish Furniture Store.

A short, round man approached him. "I'm Zeke. How can I help you today?"

The man exhibited a cheerful smile and rosy red cheeks. Andrew liked him on the spot. "I'm Andrew Wittmer."

"You're Luke's nephew. I've been anxious for you to arrive. Luke's my friend, and I owed him a favor. When he asked me to manage the store, I wouldn't let him down, but this isn't my cup of tea. He's done many things for me and my family. I didn't have the nerve to refuse. I'm a farmer, not a salesman or builder."

"It was kind of you to help." He faced the man. "Will you

recommend a man to work with me? I'll need a salesman. It would be great to find a man who has your pleasant disposition."

"I've asked friends for names, and they haven't kumme up with any. They're farmers or owners of businesses who have loyal employees who've worked with them for years. I posted an advertisement in the general store, but I haven't had anyone apply." Zeke shrugged. "I'm at a loss as to what to do. I'm glad Luke asked me to mind the store in the winter months. If it had been planting season, I couldn't have done it. My sons are performing maintenance on our equipment. I'm anxious to join them." Zeke squinted at Andrew. "I'm not partial to indoor work."

"Aunt Dora showed me the accounting journal. I need to catch up on our suppliers and what we have in stock. Then you can leave and I'll take over." Andrew had hoped Zeke would stay on and assist him for a couple of days. He could tell Zeke had no intention of offering this. He didn't blame him. He'd done enough.

"The store opens at eight and closes at five." Zeke reached for the journal and flipped the pages. "The shop's profit has declined in the last couple of months, but we have two handcrafters who bring in their products to sell, keeping it afloat. Our inventory is a little better since the consignors dropped off their pieces last week. We've got a lot of space for more things to sell."

"Is the workshop in the back stocked?" Andrew scanned the large shop. The man hadn't arranged the furniture in order. Headboards and kitchen tables and chairs filled the space in one corner, and desks and potato boxes were together. It was a confusing mess. The floor hadn't been swept, and it was damp and slick from the snow their boots tracked in. The furniture hadn't been dusted, and the counter had food stains on it.

He followed Zeke to the back room. There were some half-finished projects but no pieces ready to put on the sales floor. He picked up a piece of maple and then pine. He'd have enough to make some decent chairs, bread boxes, and a desk to bump the profits to 100 percent on what he'd construct. He noticed the journal showed a drop in income since Clyde had passed. His uncle had depended on consignors to keep the store stocked. "I have to hire a clerk soon. I'd prefer they liked to handcraft, to help me before and after the store opens. Then one of us can be handcrafting while the other waits on customers. Are you sure you can't think of someone?"

Zeke rubbed the stubble on his chin. "Matt Yoder is a man about your age who is a talented handcrafter. You might ask him, since you're desperate."

Andrew furrowed his brows. "Why haven't you or my uncle hired him?"

"He jilted a sweet Amish girl, Annalynn Burkholder, on their wedding day. There have been hard feelings over his decision. The Burkholders are close friends of mine and Luke's. Matt left Millersburg, and then he returned five months later. The gossips say he remained true to God and Amish life while he was in Sugarcreek, Ohio. He might be a good choice. I'm skeptical about him since I don't know him well." Zeke dropped a ring of keys in Andrew's hand.

Andrew sighed. It wasn't any of his business why Matt chose not to marry Annalynn. He didn't have a problem giving the man a chance. He wouldn't hold what happened against him. He hadn't told Luke and Dora about Maryann's background. He didn't want any prejudice against her. He wouldn't tell them unless it came up, for some reason. "Where does Yoder live?"

"A mile north of town. Take the main road and their place is the large farm with the corn silo. Third haus on the left. You might want to talk to your uncle first. He's not too keen on him. Care if I leave? If you get in a bind, I'll fill in. But I'm not your man for the long haul."

"Danki, Zeke. Yes, you can leave." Why was Zeke shuffling his feet and glancing at him? He snapped his fingers. "You want to be paid." He flipped the journal until he found the payroll information. He removed the money he owed Zeke from the metal cash box and handed it to him.

Zeke shrugged into his coat and pushed his hat on his head. "Tell your uncle I'm praying for him."

"Will do." Andrew watched the door shut behind Zeke. The place was quiet. For the next three hours, he dragged furniture to arrange it in appropriate sections like he wanted it. He rubbed the ache in his back. The pieces were arranged by bedroom, kitchen, sitting room, office, and smaller products. He grabbed a rag and scrubbed the counter, dusted the furniture, and mopped the floor.

A distinguished gentleman and elegant woman entered. "Why, Helen, Luke must be back. This place is rid of the chaos we found it in last week."

Andrew crossed the room to them. "I'm Andrew Wittmer, Luke's nephew. I'll be managing the store. Danki for your compliment."

Helen grinned. "We're Christopher and Helen Redding. We love this furniture store. We miss Luke. Zeke said he was ill. I hope he'll recover and return soon."

"My uncle has retired. Due to his failing health, he's chosen to hand over the store to me." He held out his hands. "Are you wanting a particular piece of furniture?"

"Please give your uncle our best wishes." Mr. Redding scanned the store. "I need a chair for our bedroom. I'd like one with fancy spindles in the back and wider than most in the seat. Maybe maple."

A woman entered wearing a red velvet coat and hat. She tapped her fingernail on the counter. "Sir, can you help me?"

"I'll be right with you, madam, after I finish with the Reddings. Why don't you sit in one of these comfortable chairs?" He gestured for her to sit in a cushioned chair. He should've asked Zeke to stay.

The woman ignored his suggestion, crossed her arms, and tapped her shoe. She didn't seem happy.

He took a deep breath. "Mr. and Mrs. Redding, right this way." He motioned them to the spindle chair. "Do you like this one? It's cherry."

Helen tapped a finger to her lip. "I'll need a moment to decide." She sat in the chair and wiggled to get comfortable.

"Sir! I don't have much time." The woman huffed and stared at him.

A short, round man came in using a handsome carved cane. He scowled and waved the cane in Andrew's direction. "Where are the bread boxes?"

Andrew's head began to ache. "In the far corner of the store on the right on the second shelf."

Helen stood. "Do you like the chair, Christopher?"

The woman in the velvet coat marched to the door and slammed it behind her.

"You need a salesman, Andrew." Christopher met his gaze and then examined the chair. "We'll take it."

"I can't find the bread boxes. Why can't you show them to me?" The man with the cane scowled.

"I'll be there right after I finish with the Reddings."
Andrew accepted their money. "Danki for kumming in.
Would you like me to carry the chair to your wagon?"

Mr. Redding picked the chair up and carried it to the
door. "No. I can strap it to the wagon, and we brought a
quilt to cover it. We're all set. Thank you."

Mrs. Redding thanked him and left with her husband.

Andrew bustled to the man with the cane. It was unusual for any store to have several customers at once like
this in a town this size. Why today? He wilkomed the business, but he needed an assistant. "You found the bread
boxes."

The man tapped the rolltop hardwood bread box. "I
like this fancy one. I'm buying it for my lady friend for
Christmas."

Andrew carried the box to the counter, accepted payment, and carried it to the man's buggy parked in front of
the store. "Danki for kumming in." He returned to the shop
and plopped on the stool behind the checkout counter.

A young couple strolled into the store. She gazed at her
husband with adoration and had her gloved hand hooked
through his.

"How may I help you?" Andrew approached the Englischers.

The young man wore a double-breasted black wool coat
and good-looking leather boots. "We'd like a coat tree and
two quilt racks."

"Theodore, we don't have to buy two quilt racks." She
batted her eyelashes at her husband.

"Go wait at the door."

Her cheeks reddened. She bowed her head and bustled
to the door. She rubbed her coat sleeves and shifted from
one foot to the other.

The man glared at her and then returned his attention to the furniture. "I'll take one quilt rack and the coat tree." The man glanced at the woman.

She didn't make eye contact.

Andrew accepted payment and helped the customer carry them to his wagon.

The man grabbed the woman's arm and jerked her into the wagon. "Keep your mouth shut."

Andrew thanked them.

They didn't respond, and the man drove away.

He went back inside. He didn't like the man's rude attitude toward his fraa. He'd never treat a woman the way the man had treated her. He respected Maryann, and her happiness was of utmost importance to him. He would expect they'd have differences, but he wouldn't dismiss her concerns. They'd discuss them and arrive at a mutual solution.

He locked the door to the shop at five. Store owners waved, and he smiled back at them. Buggies and wagons left the livery and drove onto the main road, peddlers packed up their goods, and couples headed for the corner restaurant in town for supper, taking big steps to avoid the dirty snow puddles.

He retrieved his horse from the livery and headed to Matt Yoder's haus. He hoped this man would make a favorable impression on him and agree to work in the store. The sun shone bright and had turned the snow to gray and dirty slush. His horse's hooves pounded what was left of the snow. He turned onto the long lane to the Yoders' farm. The two-story white haus, big barn, and tall silo were impressive. He parked his buggy and said a prayer asking God for His will about Matt Yoder being the right person for the job. He hopped down from the buggy, hurried to the door, and knocked.

A man about his age, with light brown hair and an average build, answered the door.

Andrew couldn't help but stare at the two-inch scar on the man's cheek. He tipped his hat. "I'm Andrew Wittmer. Are you Matt Yoder?"

"I am. What can I do for you?" Matt opened the door. "Please kumme in." Matt gestured to a high-backed maple chair with a brown seat and back cushion.

Andrew hung his coat on the knotty-pine coat tree. He noted the excellent workmanship. "Nice place you have."

"My parents passed last year, and I hired some friends to help me run the place, along with the men who worked for my daed. I don't have any openings at the moment."

This wasn't good news. Matt wouldn't have time to devote to the furniture store. He had to try. "I'm not seeking a job. My uncle owns Wittmer's Furniture Store. He's ill, and I'll be running it. Luke's friend, Zeke Miller, referred me to you. He said you were a handcrafter. I'm desperate for help. I prefer a man who can sell and build furniture. Any chance I can talk you into working for me?"

Matt slapped his legs, eyes wide. "I'd love to."

Andrew's jaw dropped. "I didn't expect you to accept. You have such a large property."

"I'd much rather build furniture than farm. I trust the men I have working for me to take care of the livestock. We've got two hundred twenty acres. We harvest enough crops and breed enough cattle to bring in more than enough money to pay them an excellent wage. Farming isn't what I enjoy. To get paid to handcraft and do what I love would be great. What are your expectations?"

Andrew discussed his wages and schedule. He cocked his head. "Are you comfortable as a salesman?"

"I will sell to customers, but I'd much rather build furniture." He sighed. "Are you aware of my past in this area? You may find some Amish who may refuse to shop in your store if I work for you."

"Zeke mentioned you jilted Annalynn Burkholder at the altar. It's none of my business why you made this decision. I'd still like to hire you." Amish should forgive those who recommitted their lives to God and Amish life. But each community had their share of gossips and those who liked to judge others. He remembered Ellie and Maryann had been prey to the gossips upon their return to the Amish life in Charm.

"It's true. I walked away from Annalynn on our wedding day. I fled to Lexington, Kentucky, and worked in a hardware store, but I remained true to God and Amish traditions. I had good reason not to marry her, but I'd rather not say why. I had to get away from Millersburg. I came back when a friend wrote and told me Daed had died. I needed to take over the farm. Mamm had already passed five years ago. Friends of the Burkholders give me the cold shoulder."

"None of this matters to me. You said you had good reason, and I believe you. I'd be grateful if you'd take the job." Andrew stood and held out his hand. He liked Matt. He'd been honest. This was going much better than he'd expected. He just hoped their business wouldn't suffer due to Matt's past with Annalynn.

Matt pointed to the scar on his face. "I didn't get this from a fight. A boy threw a rock at me in school and gave me this scar. I'm not a troublemaker." He smiled and shook Andrew's hand. "When do I start?"

"Did the boy get in trouble?"

"Yes. He got sent home. He apologized the next day. He didn't mean to hit me. He was teasing and his aim was better than he thought." Matt grinned.

"How's tomorrow morning at seven sound for your first day?" Andrew held his breath.

"I'll be there. Would you like to stay for supper? I've got leftover fried chicken." Matt nodded to the kitchen.

Andrew exhaled. "I'd love to, but I didn't tell my aunt and uncle I planned to visit you. I'm living with them, and I shouldn't be late. They'll worry. Maybe next time." Andrew lifted his coat off the tree, shrugged into it, and put on his hat. "You will make my life much easier, Matt. I'm grateful."

"Your visit is a wilkom surprise. We'll both benefit."

Andrew bid Matt farewell and left.

He snapped his fingers. He forgot the lemon drops. The general store stayed open until seven. He turned his buggy around, returned to town, jumped out, and ran inside the general store. The store was ready to close. He bought four small bags of lemon drops. He didn't want to disappoint Levi, and he wanted to bring a treat to his aunt and uncle. He'd give them each a separate bag. He'd enjoy the bag he'd bought for himself, too.

Andrew used his lantern he kept in the buggy to light his way as he drove to his uncle and aunt's home and met Levi outside the barn. He handed Levi the reins and a bag of candy. "Enjoy."

Levi grinned. "These are my favorite. Danki. I'll share them with my fraa."

Andrew swallowed his chuckle. Levi's eyes had twinkled, but the man had another front tooth missing since the last time he'd seen him. He wasn't sure if the candy was a good idea for his new acquaintance. He could be contributing to this man losing his teeth. He tipped his hat to Levi. He carried his bag of candy and the two other bags for his aunt and uncle and headed for the haus. Today had been challenging, but he felt good about hiring Matt. They'd need another employee to help out, but he would worry about that problem later.

Chapter Six

Maryann mopped the wet spot left from customers' snowy boots. She gasped as the door flew open and Joel rushed inside around noon Tuesday. "Maryann, Ellie, and I stopped to check on our parents, and we found Mamm wailing in pain. Ellie's there with Betsy. Mamm begged me to fetch you."

Her stomach churned as she removed her apron and hung it on the wall hook. With each episode, she feared it would be Mamm's last. She dashed to the back room. "Magdelena and Rachael, Mamm needs me. I'll be gone for the rest of the day. Would one of you oversee the counter? Danki."

"Go and don't worry. We'll take care of the customers and the baking."

Rachael limped to the front. "I'll take care of the customers."

Magdelena stopped stirring her oatmeal cookie batter. "Please give your mamm our best."

Maryann thanked them and followed Joel out the door and to the buggy. "I'm worried about Mamm." She wished they knew more about these headaches. It was scary not to understand what damage they could cause.

"Over the last several days, Mamm's painful headaches have become worse. Mamm's fragile and too much for the rest of us to handle. She responds best to you. You being in Charm is a must."

Maryann's stomach churned. She stayed quiet during the drive to their haus.

Joel pulled the buggy close to the front of the haus.

Maryann charged inside and followed Mamm's loud sobs to her parents' bedroom. Her daed and Ellie sat in chairs on opposite sides of the bed, trying to soothe Mamm.

Maryann knelt beside the bed. "Mamm, please stop crying. I'm not going anywhere."

Mamm uncovered her face, and her hands squeezed Maryann's. "My head throbs. I'm worried about you leaving us again. I need you."

Daed held a rag. "This is a fresh cold rag." He passed it to Mamm.

Maryann's stomach clenched. "Mamm, please stop fretting. I'm not leaving. I'm canceling the wedding and staying in Charm."

"I'm sorry to ask this of you, but I must. I can't bear to lose you again." She covered her face again and wept.

Betsy cried and held her arms out to Maryann.

Maryann kissed her forehead and wiped her dochder's cheeks as Ellie held Betsy. "It's all right, little one."

Ellie put Betsy on her other hip. "I'll take Betsy to our haus. It's best if I watch her for you."

"Danki." Maryann studied Mamm.

She had a vacant stare, groaned, and buried her face in her hands and wept.

"You all go about your day. I'll stay until she falls asleep."

Joel glanced at her. "We'll pack a bag for Betsy and return her tomorrow."

"Danki." Maryann rose and kissed Betsy's cheek.

She waved to Ellie, who was carrying Betsy, as they left the room with Daed. She stayed next to Mamm until she was certain Mamm had fallen asleep. She tiptoed out of the room and sank into a chair in the living room. Daed had apparently gone to the barn. The haus was quiet, and she leaned her head back. Right or wrong, fair or unfair, she was making the right decision to remain in Charm. She let tears drip onto her blouse. She'd never love any man like she loved Andrew. He was honest and trustworthy and he loved God and her and Betsy. She couldn't ask for a better provider or upstanding man. It would take a long time for her heart to get over him.

Daed joined her. "Is she asleep?"

She nodded. "This episode frightens me. She's in excruciating pain."

"Joel and Ellie stopped by later this morning, greeted me, and then went in the haus to check on Mamm. Joel came to the barn and told me Mamm was in pain and crying out for you. Then he collected you from the bakery. Ellie said she found Betsy in her playpen. I checked on Naomi, and she was in agony. She said she wished God would take her home."

Maryann covered her open mouth. "What can we do?"

"There's nothing more we can do. It's hard to watch her suffer." Daed's shoulders slumped.

Maryann's hands trembled. "I can't imagine what she's going through." She stared at her hands. "I could never leave her. I wouldn't be at peace knowing she needs me."

Maryann opened a drawer in the side table and pulled out a handkerchief. She recognized it as the one Mamm had given her for her tenth birthday. She'd always kept it in this drawer, and when she'd left home, she'd wished she'd taken it with her. She wrung it in her hands. "Daed, I ache for Mamm, and I ache knowing Andrew and I won't be together. I want Mamm to get better and for Andrew to move back to Charm. It's unlikely either of these things will happen."

"We must leave everything in God's hands." Daed covered her hand with his. "I'm sorry you're in this position."

"Andrew reminds me of you. Maybe that's why I fell in love with him. You have been patient and loved Mamm through her breakdowns. I admire and love you, Daed."

Daed hugged her. "I love you, dochder." He rose. "I was reinforcing the latch on one of the stalls before it becomes a problem. I should finish the job." He glanced over his shoulder. "I wish things for you and Andrew had turned out differently. You're making a big sacrifice for us. I'm grateful to you for it." He gave her a weak smile.

"I love you, Daed." She nudged his arm. "Are you hungry? Would you like me to fix you fried or scrambled eggs?"

He shook his head. "Danki, but I fixed a big breakfast before your mamm got sick. I'm still full. I'll be outside if you need me."

Maryann nodded and watched him leave. She sighed. She'd put off writing Andrew long enough. She pulled paper and a pencil out of the small desk drawer and wrote a letter to Andrew.

Dear Andrew,

I miss you, and I love you. I pray your uncle is better and the store is everything you imagined. Mamm has taken a turn for the worse. It's with a heavy heart that I write this letter to say I mustn't marry you. You have your obligation to your uncle, and I have mine to Mamm and my family. She's better with Betsy and me in Charm. It isn't fair, but nothing makes sense when you're dealing with someone who isn't right in the head.

I understand your uncle and his fraa need you. I'm glad you have the store you've always wanted. We must take care of our sick loved ones. It's the right thing to do. I pray you'll be healthy and happy and succeed in Millersburg. I don't understand why this is happening, but I trust God is in control.

I'll love you always, Maryann.

She folded the letter and slid it in the envelope. She wrote the address on the front and sealed the flap. She stared at Andrew's name. Young when she married Gerald, she'd been immature and reckless. Wiser today, she had no doubt she had chosen a respectable and caring man to marry. She'd never regret their courtship. She wasn't sure if her heart would open to another man.

Mamm shrieked from the bedroom. "Maryann! Maryann!"

She ran to her. "I'm right next to you. Please rest." Maryann held up her letter. "I'll mail this to Andrew tomorrow.

I've told him the wedding is canceled. I'm staying in Charm."

Mamm sat up and pulled Maryann to her. She held Maryann's face close to hers.

Maryann coaxed Mamm to lie down and rest, and then she padded to the kitchen. Mamm had had mood changes since she was old enough to remember. She'd never understood it, and she still found them a mystery. She'd sometimes thought Mamm had pretended to have extreme episodes, but the change in her behavior and body language told her otherwise. You couldn't fake the severe headaches and mood changes. She shouldn't have left Betsy with her. She'd ask Hannah—or Esther, Hannah's mamm—to watch her.

Maryann poured herself a cup of coffee and sat on a chair. It was past her noon dinnertime, and she should have a sandwich or something, but she wasn't hungry. But she couldn't afford to get sick, so she dragged her feet to the stove, fried an egg in the iron skillet, cut open a biscuit, and placed the egg between the layers.

She prayed and thanked God for the food and then choked it down with some coffee. She'd prepare leftover stew for supper later. She stared at the chair across from her where Andrew had last sat when he'd kumme to supper. She missed his handsome face and their conversations. What would he do when he received her letter? As Daed said, it was in God's hands.

Andrew met Matt at the shop Wednesday morning around seven, and he showed him how to record payments in the store's journal, and the list of consignors and percentages paid to each of them for their furniture when it sold. A couple came in shopping for a new bed and he had Matt show them the inventory. Within an hour, Matt had made the sale. They waited on a steady stream of customers. He reached under the counter, grabbed a clean flour sack, and opened it. "I've got meat spread sandwiches and a container of Aunt Dora's butter cookies for us."

Matt shook his head. He opened a basket. "I've got two jars of water, sliced ham, potato salad, and ginger cookies. Let's put it together and have ourselves a feast." He pulled two stools to the counter and cleared a space for them to have dinner.

They bowed their heads, and Andrew prayed and thanked God for the food.

Matt said, "I do have one condition to my employment."

"What?" Andrew held his sandwich. His heart raced. The request could end what he had assumed would be the beginning of a long working relationship and friendship.

"I don't want to end up running this place myself if you change your mind and make the decision to return to Charm." Matt gave him a serious stare.

"I'm staying." His heart clenched at the thought, but he ignored it. "My uncle is frail and my aunt needs support. He grows weaker each day. It won't be long before I'll be needed to move him from the chair or to bed." Andrew's heart ached over his uncle's health decline. He was grateful for this time with him while he was alert.

"Why aren't you married?" Matt unscrewed the lid off his mason jar.

"I will be May fourteenth. I'd invite you, but you'll have to run the store while I'm gone. We are in dire need of a salesman. We'd make enough money to pay him if we had more time to build pieces and collect one hundred percent of the profit on the sales. At present, our inventory is from consignors." Andrew spooned potato salad onto his plate. "Anybody kumme to mind?"

Matt chewed his cookie and stared at the ceiling. "Nope. Let's advertise the position in the general store."

"Zeke didn't have anyone apply from his posting there." Andrew lifted a ginger cookie out of Matt's container.

Matt rolled his eyes. "Have you read Zeke's note? It's laughable. 'Furniture store needs a clerk for long hours. Apply in store.'"

Andrew chuckled. "You're right. I'll write another one and take his down."

They finished their dinner, and Andrew dropped his empty containers in his bag.

Matt filled his basket with what he had left.

A tall and thin Amish man strolled in. Andrew guessed he'd be in his early forties. "Good afternoon. How may I help you today?"

"Afternoon. I'm James Glick. I'm new in town. Bought a small farm on First Street. I'm a widower, and I've got five boys who can take care of it. My oldest son is seventeen, and he's dependable and hardworking. The other four range in age from eight to fifteen. I could use extra money to make ends meet, and I'd like to find work. I noticed your posting in the general store. I'm not a handcrafter, but I can order supplies, wait on customers, and take care of whatever else is needed."

Andrew and Matt exchanged a satisfied glance and shrugged.

Andrew held out his hand. "I'm Andrew Wittmer, I was given the store days ago by my uncle Luke Wittmer." He gestured to Matt. "This is Matt Yoder. He accepted a job working in the store yesterday."

"Pleasure to meet you." Matt nodded.

"Are you willing to learn how to build furniture?" Andrew studied the tall and lanky man. It wouldn't be a bad idea to have this man wait on customers and order supplies while he and Matt built tables, chairs, desks, and other pieces.

James shook his head. "I don't have the talent." He squinted. "Is it a requirement?"

Andrew studied James. The man seemed sincere, and he had been honest about what he could do best. Why not give him a try? "No, you don't have to build furniture to work here." He discussed his wages and schedule and then showed him what he'd gone over with Matt earlier. "Are you comfortable with your responsibilities?"

James beamed. "Yes. Danki for this opportunity. I won't let you or Matt down." He shook Andrew's hand, and then Matt's. "I'll be here at six in the morning."

"For the next couple of days, six would be good until we work into a routine and you're more familiar with the store, and then you can kumme in at seven thirty."

"I'm happy to adjust my schedule to suit yours anytime. Danki again for giving me a chance." He nodded and had a lilt in his step as he walked to the door and left.

Matt chuckled. "You sure made his day."

"He made mine. You and I need uninterrupted time in the shop to increase the store's inventory and raise the profits." Andrew smiled. This day had brought unexpected blessings, and he was grateful for Matt and for meeting James. The last couple of hours, he'd been preoccupied with Matt, James, and the store. It had taken his mind off Maryann, and now his stomach clenched. She'd be disappointed when he wrote and told her his uncle's condition wasn't good and that he was needed in Millersburg to watch over his aunt and uncle and to save the business.

Matt glanced at the clock on the desk. "Do you want to stay tonight and start on a project? I can stay a couple of hours."

Andrew yawned. "I'm exhausted. This has been a busy day. I'd do better with a good night's sleep and kumming in early tomorrow. Danki for the offer." He and Matt walked out of the store, and he locked the door. Andrew waved to Matt as their paths parted. He was happy to reconnect with his aunt and uncle and to have free rein to run such a large store. It had special meaning coming from his uncle. He wanted to show his uncle he could make it a success again. To have Maryann with him would make all this perfect. But none of it would matter if he couldn't marry her. He'd face that dilemma when Maryann made her decision.

Andrew drove to his uncle and aunt's home and went inside the haus.

His uncle was coughing, and Dora was holding warm tea to his lips. He rushed over and knelt beside them.

Dora gave him a weak smile. "Luke's had a rough day. His cough has gotten worse, and he's a bit weaker than usual. He did have a little breakfast, and soup for supper. Maybe tomorrow will be better."

Uncle Luke sipped the tea, shook his head, and stopped coughing. "Danki, sweetheart." He spoke just above a whisper. "Andrew, tell me about the store."

Andrew dragged a chair closer to his uncle. He'd have to listen close to understand him. He shared his meeting and hiring Matt and James, the schedules and wages he'd agreed upon with them, and what pieces he'd like to build to sell. He watched his uncle's eyes dance and his thin lips spread into a grin. It made his day. "With Matt's help, I'm sure we can make potato boxes, sewing boxes, and other small pieces to put on the floor to sell in no time. Then we'll concentrate on handcrafting larger pieces."

"Andrew, I don't expect to get better. I'm not interested in going to the hospital. I'm comfortable at home, and I'm ready to go whenever the Lord is ready to take me. You living with us gives Dora and me the support we need. You're like a son to us. We have friends who drop off food and check on us, but it's not the same as having you with us. And the store would fail without you. A small percentage is all we need to live on, and the crops and cows we breed and sell will provide the rest."

"I'll do whatever you need, and the store's profits will soar soon." He had taken several special orders for small pieces he and Matt could make in a day. The customers hadn't flinched at the modest price increase, and they were content to return to pick up their purchases on the days he'd scheduled. The store would keep a hundred percent of the profit on any items they made themselves.

"You mentioned hiring Matt last night, and I was too tired to have much of a discussion. Did Matt say anything to you about jilting Annalynn at the altar?" His uncle pulled the quilt on his lap up to his chest.

Andrew cleared his throat. "Yes, but he didn't give details. He did say he had a good reason, but I didn't want to pry. Maybe he'll tell me more when we are better acquainted. Do you have any idea why he jilted her?"

"No, but there are gossips who keep the story alive. Friends of the Burkholders are upset. She's being courted by another Amish man, Elias Ropp."

"I hope not." Matt may have had a legitimate reason not

to wed Annalynn. He was sure time would make this less of a problem.

"I'm glad you're giving him a chance to show you his character. Aside from his not marrying Annalynn, he had a good reputation."

Andrew breathed a sigh of relief. For a moment, he was afraid his uncle was having second thoughts about him hiring Matt. He had a good impression of Matt, and he'd been glad to find him. "He loves to build furniture, and I'm hoping we make a good team."

"I trust your judgment. You're in charge." With his trembling hand, his uncle lifted a handkerchief to his mouth and coughed. He rested his head against the chair and closed his eyes. "Do you mind if I rest a while?"

Andrew patted his uncle's knee. "You call if you need me. I'm headed to the kitchen for supper."

Aunt Dora stood over the stove. "Sit. I've got liver and onions for supper and a vanilla cake for dessert." Gray wisps of hair had escaped her kapp, and she was rounder than he remembered. She had a sparkle in her eyes and deep dimples in her cheeks when she smiled, which was most of the time. "Is Luke resting?" She set a plate of food in front of him and sat.

He sat next to her at the table. "Yes, we had a pleasant conversation. His mind is sharp and he has wise advice." He bowed his head and whispered a prayer of thanks for the food. He raised his head and put his napkin on his lap.

She covered his hand. "We love you like our own son, and I'm grateful you're willing to help us in our time of need. I don't know what more I'll face with my precious Luke. I may need your assistance to lift him from place to place. Right now, he's shuffling his feet and using a cane to get where he wants to go."

"I'm happy to help." He gestured to a basket on the chair in the corner of the kitchen. "What are you making?" He grinned.

Dora had made him shirts as gifts in the past, and she'd done an excellent job on them. He could understand why she'd had a good home business doing alterations for the Englischers for many years.

"I've stopped sewing for Englischers, since Luke became sick. I'm stitching a pinwheel quilt in light and dark blues for his Christmas present. He loves those colors." She rose and returned with a pitcher of water and filled his half-empty glass. "How will you exchange presents with Maryann? Can she kumme here? We'd be glad to have her and her family or whoever she chooses for a traveling companion."

"You're sweet, Dora. With it being December, the weather is unpredictable for traveling. I'd like to have her visit, but I'd rather she be safe and enjoy Christmas with her family in Charm. I'm sure it's important for her to stay with her mamm." He pushed his empty plate aside and accepted the plate from Dora with his slice of cake on it. "Maryann's a widow, and she has a beautiful little girl, Betsy. She's about fourteen months old."

Dora's eyes opened wide. "What a joy it will be to have Maryann and Betsy living with us. Or do you suppose she may not kumme due to her mamm's sickness? Does she have family who can take care of her mamm?"

Andrew tensed. He wanted Naomi to get better, and he wanted to marry Maryann. "She has a bruder, Joel, and schweschder-in-law, Ellie, and Shem, her daed. They've wilkomed me and made me a part of their family, and Naomi has too. Naomi has a strong attachment to Maryann, and her emotional ups and downs and severe headaches might get worse if Maryann moves here. Her relocation would make it hard for her family."

Dora gave him a sympathetic smile. "I can understand why she might have allegiance to her family, considering the condition of her mamm. We're the reason you're not with her. This is awful."

Andrew took her hand in his. "Aunt Dora, please don't fret. Maryann and I have faith that God has a plan for us. We may have to accept that we are not meant to marry. It would break my heart, but we love our families, and we aren't the type of people to abandon them. I'm in Millersburg to stay. You and Luke are like my parents. I want to help you and Uncle Luke."

Dora rested her head on his shoulder a moment. "I'll pray for you and Maryann." She gathered the dirty dishes. "Luke has been a little better since you've moved in. His mood has lifted, and he makes an effort to take a couple more bites of his food than usual. You've unburdened us by taking care of the store and being with us when we aren't sure what we're facing with Luke's health. You've always been dependable and caring, like your uncle Luke."

"And you." Andrew grinned.

She blushed. "You're too kind. Now, go check on Luke while I finish cleaning this kitchen."

Andrew tiptoed to the living room, and sat in the chair across from his uncle, and stared at the soft glow of the wood burning in the fireplace. His uncle sat, asleep in the chair. The man was skin and bones, and his face was ashen. Andrew smiled. In the past, he and his uncle had fished together numerous times, and they'd had the best time catching mostly bluegills and catfish. His favorite part was Dora frying up their catch for supper. He'd enjoyed Luke's deep belly laugh and corny jokes, and he'd appreciated his openness, honesty, and excellent advice.

He shifted on the thick, soft cushion to get comfortable. Maryann flashed in his mind. She might be finished with supper and putting Betsy to bed. Betsy was a happy boppli. She'd brought joy into his life, like her mamm. He moved to the desk to write her a letter. He held the pencil and stared at the white sheet of paper.

Dear Maryann,

I love and miss you and Betsy. You, Betsy, and your family fill my thoughts often. My uncle is seriously ill, and the once-successful store he owns is in dire need of my help. I'm living with them, and it's for the best. My uncle can still advise me on the store, and I can help Dora with his care. They both like knowing they aren't alone in all this. They're like parents to me, and I must make Millersburg my home and stay and help them.

I hired Matt Yoder to help me build furniture and James Glick to manage the sales floor. They don't want to own or manage the store. The space is large and more inventory is needed. We do have consignors who make quality pieces, which has kept the doors open. It's important for Matt and me to handcraft and sell our pieces from the workshop to make the store a success again. The man managing the store previous to me kept it open and not much more. I am impressed with what my uncle has built. It is larger than what I'd planned to buy.

*I'll write a letter to Toby soon asking him to sell
my place. I must sell it in order to buy a haus in
Millersburg. I would've liked you to help me
choose the right property, but I want to have it
bought and ready for you and Betsy after we
marry. I pray Naomi is better and you and Betsy
will make your home in Millersburg with me after
our wedding in May. I realize this is one of the
hardest decisions of our lives. If you choose not to
leave Charm, I will be sad but I'll understand. I
pray for you and Betsy and your family and our
circumstances often. Hug little Betsy for me and
give your family my best.*

Love, Andrew.

He read and reread the letter. He'd wait to write Toby
about selling his haus. He had time. Maryann would be
disappointed to learn he was needed in Millersburg, as she
was in Charm. He would've given up the store and returned if it wasn't for his uncle's health and needed
income. And he didn't have the heart to ask his uncle to
try and sell it again. No one would want it until it was profitable. He folded the paper, tucked it in the envelope, and
sealed it.

Dora entered and placed a hand on his back. "Writing
a letter to Maryann?"

"I am." He rolled his shoulders back to alleviate the
tenseness. He didn't want Dora ridden with guilt over him
and Maryann.

She kept her voice low. "I don't want to wake Luke.
Let's go to the kitchen." She sat across from him at the

table. "I don't want you to stay with us if it means you'll lose Maryann. We'll manage."

Andrew shook his head. "I'm not budging, and put that notion out of your head. It's my choice to live in Millersburg and help you. I don't want to miss any more time with you or Uncle Luke."

"All right. May I ask how Maryann became a widow?" Aunt Dora leaned back.

"Her husband was an Englischer. She left home to marry him. After he died, she returned to her Amish lifestyle and the church. She'd never abandoned her faith in God." He didn't want to get into Gerald's gambling and foolish decisions he'd made or how the man died.

"If she could leave her mamm then, why not now?"

"While she was gone, her mamm's condition became difficult for the family. She has more frequent, excruciating headaches. The family is afraid they'll grow more severe if Maryann leaves at this time."

"I'm sorry, Andrew. I wish there was something I could do."

"We all face difficulties in our lives, and Maryann and I must trust God to know what is best for us." Andrew stretched his arms and yawned. "Danki for supper. I'm going to bed. If you need me for Uncle Luke, just holler."

"Will do. Love you, dear Andrew."

He kissed her cheek. "It's good to be with you again, Aunt Dora. I love you, too." He snuck past a sleeping Uncle Luke and to his room and shut the door. He dressed for bed and covered himself with the sheet and heavy blue and white star quilt. Christmas was fast approaching. He should craft something special for his aunt and uncle. But what?

He hoped Maryann, Betsy, and her family would like their gifts. Betsy would be the center of attention, and it would be fun to watch her big eyes widen and her little mouth spread in grins as she opened her presents. Kinner made Christmas exciting. Celebrating Jesus Christ's birthday at Christmas was an important and special time. The holiday wouldn't be the same without them. He couldn't wait to get a letter from her. *Or maybe I can wait.* The day he received it could be the best or worst day of the year.

Chapter Seven

Andrew woke and chuckled. *Here it is, Christmas morning.* He'd written a letter to Maryann a week and a half ago. He wondered if she'd gotten his letter. It may take a couple more days for her to receive it. He was like a little boy wondering what Maryann had made or bought for him. He'd been tempted to peek inside the package she'd given him when he left Charm, to save for Christmas. He grinned. He fought his curiosity and managed to keep his promise not to open it until today. He'd put it to the side of the hearth, along with the gifts Dora had there. He studied the wrapped gifts Maryann had given him for his aunt and uncle, before he left Charm. She was thoughtful to think of them.

He inhaled the scent of cinnamon. Was Aunt Dora making her special rolls with nuts and delicious vanilla frosting? He stretched, pulled back the covers, swung his legs to the side of the bed, and stood. He padded to the kitchen. Dora was frying eggs in the iron skillet, and Uncle Luke had a blanket wrapped around his shoulders and a lap quilt on his legs.

"Merry Christmas."

"This day is brighter because you're sharing it with us," Uncle Luke whispered and then sputtered a weak cough.

Dora served them eggs, bacon, and cinnamon rolls. "I can make more eggs, so don't be shy if these aren't enough."

Andrew, Aunt Dora, and Uncle Luke bowed their heads, and Andrew prayed to God and thanked Him for the food.

Aunt Dora sat close to Uncle Luke. She slathered butter on his bread for him.

Andrew was pleased his uncle had chewed and swallowed a couple of bites of eggs. He devoured his food and chose another roll out of the basket. The last weeks had gone fast at the store. He and Matt had gone in early and stayed later to build several pieces of furniture to sell along with the pieces their consigners had provided. He'd bought gifts for his family. "The holiday was profitable for the store. We're back to making a profit instead of just kumming out even."

"Remind me what Matt is doing for Christmas since he doesn't have family." Aunt Dora wiped crumbs from Luke's mouth. "I would've been glad to have him join us."

"I invited him, but he has asked the men who work for him to join him on the farm, along with the families, for a big supper in the evening, and he gives them a little bonus money for a present. He likes to cook and bake. We've become good friends in such a short time."

Uncle Luke shook his head to the piece of roll Dora offered. "I'm finished, sweet fraa. Danki." He glanced at Andrew. "I suppose James has his five boys to share the day."

"Yes. Matt and I surprised him with a bonus to help with Christmas presents. His cheeks turned red and he stuttered when we handed it to him. He has been a tremendous salesman. The customers love him."

Andrew helped Dora with the dishes, and then they gathered in the living room around the orange-hued flames in the fireplace.

Uncle Luke handed Andrew his Holy Bible and asked him to read the story of Jesus Christ's birth.

Andrew flipped the pages to the story and read it aloud, and then each of them offered a prayer of requests, praise, and thanksgiving to God. He set the Holy Bible on the end table and rose to put on his coat. He held up a finger. "I'll be right back. I've got a surprise for both of you."

He dashed out the door to the barn. Snowflakes decorated his hat and coat. He was thankful for the snow on Christmas. It topped off the day, making the fire in the fireplace cozy and warm in the living room and the bright white covering on the ground outside beautiful. He found the presents he'd hidden and carried them inside. He set the quilt rack in front of Dora and then the footstool under Luke's legs.

Dora ran her hand across the rack. "This holds four quilts. Andrew, it's beautiful. I love it! Danki."

Luke tapped the stool with his cane. "This is the perfect height for my chair. I can stretch my legs and rest my feet comfortably. Danki."

"I'm glad you both are pleased. I noticed you needed another rack to display your pretty quilts and Uncle Luke didn't have a footstool. I wanted to give you presents you could use and enjoy."

Dora bustled to the small pile of presents. "Open your gift."

He unwrapped the brown paper and lifted a handsome brown scarf Dora had crocheted for him. "This will kumme in handy. Danki." He kissed her cheek.

Uncle Luke gestured to another present. "Unwrap the one from me."

Andrew tore the brown paper. He opened the wooden box and gasped. "Was this knife Daed's?"

"Yes. I want you to have it. I forgot I had it until a few months ago. I meant to give it to you before now, but this is as good a time as any. It had been Grossdaadi's, and he gave it to your daed as a Christmas present long ago. Then he gave it to me as a congratulations gift."

Andrew lifted the hunting knife out of the brown leather sheath. "Danki. This means a lot to me. I'll take good care of it."

Dora passed Andrew his gift from Maryann. "I've been anxious for you to open this one."

He ripped the paper and pulled out a white cotton shirt with a note. "I'll read this later." He left it folded and set it aside. He'd be anxious to read what she had to say.

Dora peeled the wrapping back from her blue and white tea towels and oven mitt. "These are beautiful and I need them. How sweet of Maryann to think of us."

Andrew put Maryann's package for his uncle in Luke's lap.

Uncle Luke unwrapped the patchwork lap quilt she'd made him. He spread it on his lap and legs. "This warms my legs. What a thoughtful gift. I hope we get to meet Maryann and everything works out for you two. These gifts she sent are perfect. I'm sorry we've disrupted your lives and plans for the future."

"It's not your fault, and you've given me a store. I couldn't be more grateful for it and to be with you and Dora. If it's God's will for us to wed, we will." He didn't want them to fret about this, and it was Christmas. "How about some hot chocolate? I might snatch a couple of orange-slice candies you have in the bowl by your table."

Dora popped out of her chair. She passed him the bowl. "Take a couple."

He did and plopped one in his mouth.

She returned the bowl to the table. "I've got some cocoa warming on the stove. I'll check if it's ready." She left the living room.

Andrew gathered the brown paper and dropped it on the logs in the fireplace. He could envision Betsy playing with her new toys and Maryann and her family sharing Christmas dinner around their big oak table. He missed them so much.

His uncle had his eyes closed and he snored. His color looked better today and he hadn't coughed near as much. Maybe he was a little better. He might have been wrong about his time left on earth.

Dora returned with the hot chocolate. She whispered, "If you'd like to take this to your room and nap, I'll understand. I may close my eyes a few minutes after I enjoy mine."

Andrew was relieved to have time alone. "Uncle Luke has the right idea. My eyelids are getting heavy." He took Maryann's note and went to his room. He sat on the bed, sipped his hot chocolate, and read it.

My dearest Andrew,

I guessed at your measurements for your shirt. If it doesn't fit, I'll alter it or make you a new one. I wrote this note before you left for Millersburg to go along with your gifts to open for Christmas. When you open this, we will have been apart for

*weeks. I'll miss you each day you're gone and can't
wait until we're together again.*

Love, Maryann.

Andrew read and reread the note. He wondered what
had happened since he'd been gone from Charm, or since
she'd written this note. He was still in Charm when she
wrote it and handed him this present to take with him. How
was Naomi? He prayed her health would improve. Maybe
Maryann had written him. He'd been anxious to receive a
letter from her, but working at the store had kept him busy.
He often lost track of time and didn't get to the post office
before it closed. He'd check the post office soon.

Maryann yawned and stretched later Christmas Day.
Daed dozed in his favorite high-backed chair covered with
a patchwork quilt, and Betsy was asleep in her playpen.
Mamm was having a bad day, with a severe headache hit-
ting right after she woke up this Christmas morning. She'd
had to stay in bed, away from noise and light. Maryann
had cooked a big Christmas breakfast and cleaned the
kitchen. Joel and Ellie had gone home.

She loved the cedar chest Andrew had made to set on
her dresser. The aroma of the wood, and the space to store
letters and keepsakes, were perfect. Betsy kept her Amish
doll with her most of the day, and Joel and Ellie were
happy with their new bread box. Daed liked the new potato
box, and he had commented Mamm would be thrilled
since their old one was falling apart.

Maryann hugged herself. Had Andrew and his aunt and
uncle had a chance to open the gifts she'd sent them? She

hoped they liked their presents. She had looked forward to future holidays with Andrew. She frowned and pressed a hand to her heart. She dreaded him reading the letter she'd mailed explaining why she must cancel the wedding.

Daed raised his head and rubbed his eyes. "Is your mamm resting or asleep?"

"She was in a lot of pain this morning. More than usual. We should check on her."

She followed Daed to the bedroom, and walked with him to the side of the bed. She shivered and lit the lantern. She gasped. Mamm's eyes were wide and lifeless.

Daed checked Mamm's wrist for a pulse. "She's gone." He touched Mamm's cheek with the back of his hand and then he shut her eyes. He pushed the covers back. He cried out. "No! Please! No!"

Maryann froze. She pressed a hand to her aching heart. Mamm had gone home to Heaven. She sat, numb, next to Daed, who slumped over Mamm and sobbed. She rested her head on his back and hugged him as tears streamed down her face and dampened his shirt.

Moments later, he sobered and rose, and she helped him stand. He held her. "The only way we'll get through this is if we remind ourselves she's with God in Heaven and happy and healthy." He stepped back and stared at her through watery eyes. "I'll miss her every day." He wiped his damp face with his sleeve.

Maryann stared at Mamm. Her death didn't seem real. Daed's words echoed in the room, but she couldn't grasp her mamm had passed away. Her daed would be lost without the love of his life. She thought her heart would burst with grief over losing Mamm and with empathy for Daed. She sat on the edge of the bed next to Mamm and grasped her hand. It was stiff and cold. She jerked her hand back as if she'd been burned.

"Kumme with me to the living room, sweetheart." Daed ushered her out of the room.

They held each other again and cried.

Daed stepped back. "I need to tell Ellie and Joel and Bishop Fisher." He headed for his hat and coat. "I'll go now." His knees buckled and he slumped in the chair. "I can't believe she's really gone."

Maryann knelt and put her hand on his arm. "Would you like me to notify Ellie, Joel, and the bishop?"

Daed shook his head. "You stay with Betsy. I'll go." He stood and pulled on his black hat and heavy coat.

Maryann left the door cracked open and watched him walk through the light-falling snow and disappear into the barn.

She stood over the playpen and studied Betsy. Mamm, with her mood changes and overprotective ways, had been different than her friends' mamms. Regret washed over her. She could empathize with Mamm's heartbreak when she'd left to marry Gerald. She couldn't imagine the pain she'd have if Betsy did that to her. Her throat constricted. They'd had happy and difficult times together before and after she left Charm.

She glanced at her childhood Bible storybooks. Mamm had brushed her hair, read her stories, said prayers with her, and tucked her into bed until she was around thirteen. She'd made her favorite meal for birthdays and taught her to clean, sew, knit, bake, and cook. Then there had been the screaming arguments when she'd wanted to do things with her friends. Mamm had suffocated and pressured her to stay close to her and be the perfect dochder. She was grateful they'd had time to reconcile, enjoy Betsy together, and create new and happy memories until her severe headaches took their toll.

The loss left a deep hole in her chest. She wanted more time. A day, an hour, minutes. To tell Mamm she loved her and to thank her for all she had done. Had she expressed her gratitude? Did Mamm know how much she regretted leaving and hurting her? She dropped her head in her hands. Would she ever get rid of this overwhelming grief?

She needed Andrew. He'd hold her and tell her everything would be all right. He'd provide the strength she needed. She had Daed, Joel, and Ellie, and her friends, but she still needed the love of her life. He'd be distraught about Mamm. He'd become a part of their family.

She reminded herself over and over, Mamm was in Heaven with God and would have no more pain and suffering. She wished her own pain would go away. She walked down the hall and reached for the doorknob to her parents' bedroom to gaze at Mamm again. *No, I can't do it*. She dropped her hand and walked back to Betsy, and tears dampened her face. Mamm had enjoyed her granddochder and seemed the happiest when she was with Betsy.

Betsy rolled onto her stomach and raised herself up. "Mum." She held her arms up.

She lifted Betsy, grabbed her doll, and sat in the rocker. Maryann had understood Mamm wanting to protect her, even if it was too much. She'd do anything for Betsy. She hugged her dochder and took her to the changing table in Betsy's room, "You need a diaper change."

Betsy rubbed her nose with the back of her little hand, and she lay on the changing table. "Mimi?"

Maryann pinched her eyes closed, then opened them. She struggled to keep the sob in her throat from escaping.

"Mimi's gone." She gazed at Betsy as she changed her. Her dochder wouldn't understand where Mimi had gone or remember this particular day, but her dochder did sense something was wrong with the absence of Mimi. They would all miss her.

Betsy frowned and wiped a tear from Maryann's cheek with her tiny forefinger. She cocked her head. "Mum?"

Maryann managed a weak smile. "I'm all right." She walked back to the living room and set Betsy in the playpen.

Betsy picked up the Amish doll Andrew had given her for Christmas and held it tight. Then she dropped the doll and flipped through the pages of her book about Jonah and the whale.

Daed returned with Bishop Fisher. Ellie and Joel came inside behind him.

Maryann hugged Joel, and Ellie wrapped her arms around them. They wept and then separated.

Daed wiped his wet cheeks. "Danki for kumming, Bishop."

The bishop nodded and asked them to bow their heads. He prayed to God to comfort the family.

Daed stood with his hands over his face. Maryann turned away. He'd lost his fraa and lifelong partner. He'd stood by her through all the happy and tumultuous times in their married life. She wanted to snatch the grief out of herself and him. It was too much for them to bear.

Daed said, "Bishop, I'd like to hold the viewing, funeral, and burial on Monday. Let's have the funeral around one. It's best for me if we don't prolong the services."

Bishop Fisher nodded. "I'll be happy to have the services as you wish. I'm sorry for your loss, and I'll pass the news on to friends and ask them to tell others. I'll be here early Monday." He prayed again aloud with the family and then bid them farewell.

Maryann listened to her family share their memories of Mamm. She couldn't grasp they were talking about Mamm in the past tense. She watched Betsy play in her playpen, and Betsy smiled at her. Her heart swelled. Such a small gesture, but one she needed most at the moment.

Daed shook his head. "I should've checked on her earlier."

Maryann grasped his wrist. "It was her time to go to Heaven. You shouldn't have any guilt over this. You were a good husband to her. You gave her the best life." She wept with him.

"Maryann's right, Daed. You set a good example for all of us in how we should treat others. Mamm was blessed to have you." Joel's lips quivered.

Ellie went to the kitchen and returned with warm coffee. She served them. "I'm glad Naomi and I had a chance to get past our differences and become friends. I'll miss her."

Maryann gazed at Ellie. She was fortunate to have such a caring schweschder-in-law. She was glad Mamm had given Ellie a chance and then came to love her. Ellie was good to Joel, and she looked forward to their boppli being born sometime early this summer.

Joel offered his hand to Ellie. "We should go." He hugged his daed and then Maryann. He kissed Betsy's forehead. His lips trembled. "I'll be back tomorrow with benches, and we'll move the furniture out of the way and prepare for guests on Monday." He hung his head and held Ellie's hand, walking to the door.

"Won't the bishop need the benches for Sunday service?" Ellie glanced at Joel and then waved at Betsy.

Betsy grinned, plopped down, and picked up her doll.

He shook his head. "These are extra benches."

Maryann and her daed bid them farewell.

Daed turned to Maryann and put his hands on her shoulders. "I love you, Maryann. I'm glad you're here. You were the sunshine in your mamm's darkness."

Maryann's lips quivered. "We had our struggles, but we made it through them. I'll miss her smile, the touch of her hand on mine, and the memories we've shared."

His shoulders slumped. He went to his granddochder, bent over the playpen, and kissed Betsy on her forehead.

She patted his cheeks with her hands. "Pop. Pop."

He stood ramrod straight, eyes wide. "She called me Pop. Did you hear her? Leave it to the innocence of a boppli to make you smile amidst sadness." Daed picked Betsy up and hugged her.

"I've pointed to you and called you Pop whenever I thought of it, hoping she'd say it to you. She's often sprinkled a moment of joy in my life when I've really needed it."

"She's been the bright light for all of us since you came back. Naomi and I commented often how much she reminds us of you in appearance and ways she does things. You're precise with making your bed, folding your clothes, and with anything you arrange or assemble. Betsy lines up her toys, can't stand to have food on her clothes for too long, and wants her diaper changed as soon as she's wet. Spitting image of you. Your mamm would find me and tell me each day something Betsy did to remind her of you when you were little." He shrugged. "Something else I'll miss." He rested his forehead to Betsy's and then put her back in the playpen.

"Mimi?" Betsy raised her brows.

"Mimi's in Heaven, little one." Maryann rested her

head on Daed's shoulder. "I wish Mamm hadn't died on Christmas." Maryann pressed a hand to her heart.

"She was in such pain. For her, going home to meet Jesus face-to-face may have been the best gift she could've received today." Daed walked toward the door. "Selfishly, I'd do anything to have her back."

Maryann woke Friday morning, the day after Christmas, and found Daed was already in the barn. She checked on Betsy and found her sound asleep. She glanced out the window. Joel and Ellie were arriving in their buggy.

She greeted and hugged Joel first. They cried in each other's arms. Ellie wrapped her arms around them both.

They parted and found seats in the living room. Joel took Ellie's coat and hung it with his on the coat tree. "Daed's taking care of the horses. I sensed he wanted time alone when he didn't accept my offer to help." He raked fingers through his hair. "I'm shocked and numb. My mind can't accept Mamm is really gone." He shook his head.

Ellie sat next to him on the settee. She put a hand on his leg. "It's going to take time to sink in." She shifted in her chair to face Maryann. "I'm sure friends will bring food when they attend the viewing. Do you want to go to the bakery with me and tell the girls? We can bring back some cookies. I'm sure you'd rather they heard the news from you. We can stop by Liza and Hannah's places and tell them on the way."

"My mind is in a fog. I'm grateful to you for providing me with some direction. I'll feed and dress Betsy, and then we can go to Liza's first." Maryann rose, knees shaking.

Joel held out his hand. "Do you mind leaving Betsy with Daed and me?"

"Betsy will be good for them," Ellie prodded.

"Danki, bruder." Maryann shrugged into her coat and hat, hugged Joel, and said goodbye. She went to the barn with Ellie. "Ellie and I will stop by Hannah's, then Liza's and the bakery, and then kumme back. We won't be too long. Joel wanted Betsy with him. Do you mind?"

"No. We need her right now."

Daed looked as if he'd aged ten years in the hours since Mamm had passed away. He must feel lost without her. She and Ellie bid him farewell and drove to Hannah's.

Hannah wilkomed them inside. "Ellie and Maryann, what a nice surprise. Kumme on in and get warm by the fire. Liza came to visit me, too. She's in the living room. Where's Betsy?"

"How convenient Liza is with you. We were going to stop by her place next, and this will save us a trip." Ellie smiled.

"Go lie down, Sunny." Hannah pointed to the old tattered quilt in the corner.

Sunny's tail wagged as the pup scampered to the corner and obeyed.

Liza rose and hugged them. "When I came to Hannah's to visit, I didn't expect I'd get to visit with the two of you. What a wilkom surprise." She tilted her head. "You're not your usual jolly selves. What's wrong?"

"We left Betsy with Joel and Daed." Ellie gestured to Maryann. "I'll let Maryann tell you why we have long faces."

Maryann twisted her handkerchief in her hands. She explained the reason for their visit.

Hannah and Liza's faces drained of color. Hannah crossed the room to Maryann and held her hand. "What can I do for you? I can't believe Naomi is gone."

Liza looked at Ellie. "How are Joel and Shem holding up?" She dabbed her wet eyes with the back of her hand.

Ellie rested her hands on her protruding stomach. "Joel is doing better than I would've expected. He's shaken and not himself, but he's being strong for Shem and Maryann."

Maryann dabbed her wet nose with the handkerchief. "I must go and tell Rachael and Magdelena about Mamm." She stared and fumbled her hands. She couldn't sit still or get comfortable. She remembered going through the motions and not feeling like herself when Gerald died. There was no way to bypass the agony of the death of a loved one. And the next couple of days would be the most difficult while trying to plan for the services and greet their friends. She couldn't think straight.

Liza knelt next to Maryann. "Yes, they should know about your mamm. Would you like Hannah and me to wash and dress your mamm for the services?"

Hannah squeezed Maryann's hand. "Let us help you."

Maryann sucked in a breath. The act of doing this would be too much. It would rip her heart in two. She'd never get through it. "Please, would you?"

Hannah nodded.

Liza patted her arm. "Of course. When should we kumme to your haus?"

"Tomorrow, please, in case we receive mourners this weekend. There will also be time for a viewing before the funeral which will be at one in the afternoon with the burial to follow. Our family doesn't want to prolong the viewing and services."

Liza said, "Hannah and I will kumme Saturday around nine in the morning. We'll bring food. Don't worry about a thing. Do you have a dress for your mamm?"

Maryann gripped her handkerchief and held it to her

chest. "I do. The one she wore when she and Daed married won't fit. She has a fairly new one I'd like to have you dress her in. I'll lay it out for you."

Hannah wiped a tear from her cheek. "I wish I could erase the loss and anguish you are experiencing. I feel helpless."

"Your outpouring of love is all I need. I find comfort in your words and friendship."

"I should take you home. You're still in shock. You need to rest." Ellie escorted Maryann to the door. She glanced over her shoulder to Liza and Hannah. "I'm not sure I should've brought her out today. I remember when Mamm died. I was a mess. I'm still guilt-ridden over what I put you and Daed through."

Liza, Ellie's stepmamm, placed a hand on her back. "You were a challenge to win over since you were still mourning and bitter about your mamm's death, but it was worth it to have such a precious dochder as you. I'm proud of the woman you've become. And you're right. Maryann has been out enough today. Take good care of our girl, and I'll be at Maryann's with Hannah to help on Saturday. I'll go to the bakery before we arrive at your haus and put a sign on the door saying we're closed on Monday and the bakery will reopen on Tuesday. I want the girls free to attend the services and help with whatever you need."

"Danki, Liza." Maryann gave her a thankful smile.

Hannah hugged them goodbye. "Timothy will be at your haus early with me to help with setting up the benches, guiding guests where to park their buggies, and whatever you'd like him to do."

Sunny got up and ambled over to Hannah.

"Danki." Maryann petted the dog, bid them farewell, and left with Ellie.

Maryann rode with Ellie to the bakery, and they told Magdelena and Rachael.

The girls expressed their sympathies and hugged Maryann and Ellie.

Toby entered the bakery. "I ran into the bishop on the way here. Ellie and Maryann, I'm sorry for your loss." He glanced at Maryann. "Andrew would want to know about Naomi. Do you mind if I make the trip to Millersburg and tell him? I can make the trip up and back in a day. It should only take about two-and-a-half to three hours. I'll ask Timothy to take care of the livestock, and I'll leave in about an hour. Andrew may want to leave right away. I'm sure he can find someone to manage things for him."

"Toby, I'd appreciate it." Maryann gave him a grateful smile. "I feel bad putting this on Andrew right now. He's got a lot on his mind, and his uncle needs him."

Ellie said, "You need him, and he'd be upset if you didn't tell him."

"Yes, and he loved Mamm too. He will want to attend the services." She'd love to have him next to her. He had suffered tragedy with his parents. He'd empathize and give her strength just by his presence.

Andrew's eyes widened. "Toby!" He rushed to him. "Is everyone all right in Charm?" He was sure Toby wouldn't have traveled to Millersburg this time of day if something wasn't wrong. It was two in the afternoon.

Toby frowned. "It's Maryann's mamm, Naomi. She died on Christmas. I was sure you'd want to be informed, and I spoke to Maryann and offered to travel to Millersburg and tell you."

Matt and James approached them.

Andrew introduced them to Toby and told them why he was there.

James shook Toby's hand. He clapped a hand onto Andrew's arm. "You go to Charm. Maryann needs your support."

Matt nodded. "We can take care of the store. I'm sorry for your and the family's loss. Toby, we've heard a lot of good things about you from Andrew. It's a pleasure to meet you."

"I wish it were under better circumstances and I could stay and chat." Toby sighed.

Andrew glanced from Matt to James. "He's right. I should get going. I'll go to my aunt and uncle's haus, pack a bag, and be on my way. I'll return in a couple of days." He and Toby bid them farewell, went to his aunt and uncle's, had dinner with them, and headed to Charm.

He followed Toby's buggy. His heart ached for Maryann and her family. God would give them comfort and peace. Grief was painful, and it took time to ease. The loss of his parents had been agonizing. A day didn't go by without them kumming to mind. He'd always miss them.

They arrived close to three hours later in Charm. He pulled alongside Toby's buggy. "I'll head to Maryann's, and then I'll be home later tonight. Danki, Toby, for relaying the news about Naomi."

"It was important. You'd do the same for me. I'll check on the livestock at your place, and then I'll be over early tomorrow morning. Give Maryann and her family my best."

"Will do." Andrew waved goodbye and traveled to Maryann's haus. He met her daed and Joel outside the barn. "I'm sorry about Naomi." He waved to Timothy and friends unloading benches from a wagon to set up in the haus for the services.

Shem shook Andrew's hand. "I'm going through the motions of doing what has to be done. It's hard to grasp she's no longer with me." He took Andrew's reins. "Let us take care of your horse. Maryann will be delighted you're here."

Joel greeted him. "Danki for kumming. Good to have you with us."

"How's Ellie?" He hoped this wouldn't put too much of a strain on her. She was carrying their first child.

"I took her home. She's tired, and guests kept us busy, bringing food and expressing their condolences. Word spread fast once Bishop Fisher asked the women to let everyone know about Mamm. Go on inside. We don't want to keep you any longer from Maryann and Betsy."

Andrew thanked them and crossed the yard. He went inside and found them in Betsy's room. "How are my girls?"

"Andrew!" Maryann picked up Betsy.

Betsy held her arms out to him.

He took her and kissed her temple. "I've missed you." He grinned at Maryann. "And you."

He pulled her to him with his free arm and then let her go. "I'm sorry about Naomi. I'm shocked."

Betsy hugged his neck, then rested her head on his shoulder.

"Danki for kumming. We're all dazed and hurting."

He rubbed the little one's back. "I wish I could wipe your pain away. Losing a loved one is one of the hardest things to go through."

Betsy whined and held tight to Andrew's neck.

"Somebody missed you besides me." Maryann gave him a loving smile.

"I'm glad." Andrew kissed Betsy's hair. "How are you holding up?"

"I can't bring myself to wash and dress Mamm. Liza and Hannah are going to do it for me. It's difficult to accept she's gone. My mind says she's in Heaven, free of pain. My heart wants to tell her I love her one more time."

He gazed into her tired eyes. "You can lean on me for everything."

She gazed at him. "Having you here will provide a lot of comfort."

"I wouldn't have it any other way. I love you and Betsy. Being apart from you and this little one has been one of the hardest things I've ever done."

"Yes. I've thought of you each day and wondered how you are and how your uncle is doing."

Andrew sighed. "My uncle is weak and frail. He was a robust man with more spunk than me. It's heartbreaking to watch his health decline. We have good conversations. His mind hasn't been affected by whatever is making him ill. The doctor isn't sure what's to blame for his condition."

"I'm sorry." She gestured to the door. "Did you speak to the family when you arrived?"

He nodded. "Your daed, Joel, Timothy, and friends were unloading benches. I expressed my sympathies and came inside to find you. I ache for all of you. I remember my parents' funerals like it was yesterday. The pain has gotten better, but there are times when something will spark a memory of a special time with them and my eyes get watery, missing them. Knowing they're in Heaven gives me comfort. I wish I could say something to erase your and your family's pain. We both know it isn't possible. I wish it were under better circumstances, but I'm glad to be with you, Betsy, and your family."

Maryann twisted her hands. "We should talk."

He traced her cheek with his forefinger. "You're going through one of the hardest times in your life. We can discuss our future after the services."

Maryann acted nervous. Had she made the decision to stay in Charm and not marry him? His heart thumped fast in his chest. Maybe she thought it best to stay with her family. He had to exercise patience. This wasn't the time to question her about it.

Joel came inside Betsy's room. "Andrew, would you mind giving me a hand?" He looked at Betsy resting on Andrew's shoulder. "She's happy to have you with us. I am too, and I'm sure lots of friends will say the same." He winked.

Andrew handed Betsy to Maryann. "I don't mind. It's good to be here, but I wish it were not because of Naomi's passing." He nodded to Maryann and then followed Joel outside. An hour later, he bid friends farewell, had supper with Maryann and her family, and went home. He scanned the property. He didn't want to sell it. This place had been perfect for him, and it would be more than sufficient for him, Maryann, and Betsy.

He didn't see Toby's buggy. His friend had gone home. Tomorrow morning, he'd wake early and have breakfast with him before going to Maryann's haus. He checked the livestock. Toby had done a superb job taking care of everything. He'd missed his friend and being home in Charm. Being away from Maryann and Betsy had been more difficult than he'd imagined. What would Maryann say to him when they had time to discuss their plans? Would he leave without a promise of a future with her when he returned to Millersburg? She might be obligated to take care of Shem and not want to leave him alone. He could understand, but he didn't want to consider the possibility.

Chapter Eight

Saturday, Maryann, Andrew, and her family greeted friends who had brought food and expressed their condolences. She listened to the swirl of conversations around her, with Betsy balanced on her right hip, while Mamm, dressed in her blue dress and kapp, lay lifeless in the pine box on a long table. Maryann had been relieved and grateful to Liza and Hannah for preparing the body. She was too grief-stricken to do it. She swallowed around the lump in her throat and greeted the mourners, but she was going through the motions.

Sunday, she attended the regular church service and stared at Bishop Fisher while he gave his message. She found comfort in the verses the bishop shared about God's love and how He didn't forsake us. She had faith God would get her and her family through this difficult time. Friends came and went to visit them after church and until later that evening.

The days were a blur. Numb, she didn't feel like herself. She loved Andrew for standing next to her. He conversed with their visitors and helped with Betsy. She had to tell him about the letter she'd written to cancel their wedding.

The letter would be waiting for him at the post office in Millersburg when he returned there. She enjoyed him and let herself depend on his strength, understanding, encouragement, and love. Her family needed her, but how could she let him go? She wished she could recapture the letter, rip it in two, and throw it away. What would she do now? She couldn't leave Daed alone.

Monday, she couldn't imagine what this would've been like without him. He stood next to her.

"I'll get you some warm cocoa. Ellie has it warming on the stove. You haven't had anything all morning." Andrew gave her a loving gaze.

"Danki." She watched him walk away from her. None of this seemed real. She expected to inhale the aroma of Mamm's delicious cinnamon rolls from the kitchen and find her bringing in a plate of them to serve to their guests. The woman in the coffin seemed like a stranger. Maryann couldn't breathe. She had to have a minute to herself. She rushed to her room and stared out the window at the sea of buggies and wagons parked on the far right side of their property.

Liza and Hannah came alongside her. "Maryann, are you all right?"

Betsy outstretched her arms to Hannah.

Hannah took Betsy.

Betsy whined and rested her head on Hannah's shoulder.

Maryann walked into Liza's arms and found solace as her friend held her. Liza's arms felt warm and comforting. Just what she needed. She wept.

Hannah used her free hand and rubbed Maryann's back. "Get it all out. We're here for you. Anything you need."

Liza handed Maryann a clean handkerchief from under her sleeve. "I brought two. Keep it."

Hannah shifted Betsy to her other hip. "Ellie, Magdelena, Rachael, and my mamm are serving the mourners. Joel is with your daed. There's no rush for you to tend to guests. May I get anything for you?"

"No, danki. Andrew went to get me warm cocoa. He's been wonderful. Warm cocoa does sound good. Not much of anything does." She dabbed her eyes with the handkerchief. "You both have been understanding and compassionate. I don't have to hold back anything from you. I'm beyond grateful. I expect Mamm to walk in the room any minute. It's hard to accept she's left this earth. I'm comforted she's in Heaven with God, but I want her back. One more day. One more hour." She blew her nose. "She and I had our trials, but we loved each other. I never should've left the first time."

Hannah jiggled Betsy. "Andrew is one of the best men I've met. I'm thrilled he's back in Charm with you for Naomi's services." She reached for Maryann's hand. "You've made new memories with your mamm. And if you hadn't left, you wouldn't have Betsy. She's brought joy to all of us. Concentrate on the good times you've had with your mamm since you returned. You brought her a lot of joy."

Liza nudged her arm. "Listen to Hannah. You thrilled your mamm when you returned with your precious dochder. Hold on to those times. God forgave you, and you should forgive yourself for the past. Your mamm forgave you. She wrapped her arms around you, and she never wanted to let you go. You did all you could for her. Andrew is attentive and caring toward you and Betsy. Maybe the two of you can find a way to marry, since your mamm has passed and you no longer need to care for her. I never agreed with your family asking you to stay in the first place."

"Andrew and I have much to discuss. I'm not sure what my family's expectations are of me. I do have to consider Andrew and our love for each other." She managed a weak smile. "You both provide me with a healthy perspective. You're both blessings I treasure. I should pull myself together and mingle with our friends. Danki for cheering me up today. I needed it."

Betsy held her arms out to Maryann. "Mum, Mum."

Maryann took her from Hannah.

Liza said, "You can always count on us."

Maryann returned to the living room. Andrew handed Maryann the mug and took Betsy.

Maryann squared her shoulders and sucked in a deep breath. She glanced at the mantel clock and took her seat next to Daed. Ellie and Joel sat on the other side of him. Andrew and Betsy sat next to her. Bishop Fisher had taken his place in front of the rows of benches the men had put in place after moving their furniture to the shed. She folded her hands in her lap and waited for the bishop to begin. She prayed for strength to get through the kumming hours and days.

Bishop Fisher held his open Holy Bible. "We're gathered in the Wengers' home to celebrate Naomi's moving from this earth to her heavenly home with God. She's no longer in pain, and she has a new healthy body. We'll miss her, but we can find comfort in knowing she's in God's arms. She believed He gave His son, Jesus Christ, as the ultimate sacrifice for her wrongs. She asked Him to take over her life, and she loved God with all her heart." The bishop read scriptures, delivered his message on Heaven, led them in a hymn, and offered a prayer. He dismissed them to follow him to the burial site.

Maryann froze. Her daed's and Joel's shoulders slumped, and their sorrowful faces brought tears to her eyes. Ellie held on to Joel's arm, and Maryann was thankful they'd found each other. Ellie had been good for all of them. She was glad Mamm had accepted Ellie and they'd shared good memories before she passed away. She struggled not to cry again.

Andrew passed Betsy to her. "I'll pull the buggy to the front of the haus for you."

She nodded.

Toby approached her and offered his condolences. "Do you mind if Rachael and I look after Betsy while you go to the burial site?"

Betsy held her arms out to Toby, and he scooped her up.

Maryann nodded. "She sure likes you. Danki, Toby. I really appreciate it."

Toby placed a happy Betsy on his hip.

Betsy flung her hands into his hair and pulled a handful. She giggled.

Toby removed her little fingers from his hair. "No, little one." He smiled at Maryann. "Rachael and I can take care of her. We'll stay with her while you go with your family." Toby gave her a sympathetic gaze.

Rachael gave Maryann a reassuring gaze. "Don't worry about her. We'll be fine. I'll clean up while you're gone. Toby loves kinner, and he and Betsy have become fast friends. She's the best medicine for all of us. I can't imagine what you're going through, losing your mamm. I'm thankful Andrew is in town. Maybe you and he can resume planning for your wedding. You two are meant to be together. I love you, Maryann. He's the one for you and Betsy. I'm sure of it." She hugged her.

Maryann cried in her arms and then gently pulled away. "I love having him with Betsy and me. I'm hoping we can plan a future together. I don't want to let him go." She glanced out the window at Andrew in the buggy. "I should leave. Danki."

She couldn't stop quivering. Her mind was muddled, and her body was weak. She'd had trouble kumming to grips with Gerald's death, but Mamm's was more difficult. Mamm had had an obsession to hold on to her too tight during their life together, but Maryann had no doubt how much Mamm had loved her. Among their trying times, they'd sewed, cooked, baked, and laughed together more often than not. Mamm had held her when she'd been sad more times than she could count. She'd rejoiced with her too. She'd been a wonderful grossmudder to Betsy. Thank goodness they'd had time together.

She climbed into the buggy and sat next to Andrew. She patted his arm. "I'm blessed to have you in my life. I'm glad Mamm got to meet and talk with you before she died."

He gave her a weak grin and shrugged. "I'm thankful for our time together and my time with her."

She rode with Andrew to the burial site, with her family following in their buggy. They arrived, crossed the yard as a family, and stood in front of the big open hole in the ground. She stood next to Daed, with Andrew on her other side. She whispered to Daed, "You gave her a good life."

Daed stared at the pine box holding his fraa as the men were taking it out of the wagon. "Our good times outweighed the bad ones. I remember the day I met her. She was a little sassy, with a glint in her eyes. I was drawn to her, and our connection grew from the minute we were introduced by your grossmudder, who you never got to know. My mamm was a happy soul. She loved everyone until they gave her a reason not to. She loved your mamm. I'm lost without her. We had a routine. This morning, kumming back from the barn, I remembered something I wanted to tell her. It will take me a while to realize she's no longer with us." He bowed his head and shut his eyes tight. Tears dripped onto his cheeks.

Maryann hooked her arm through his and then she exchanged an endearing gaze with Joel and then Ellie. She watched as the men carried the box and used ropes to lower it into the open spot. She'd disliked this part the most at Gerald's funeral, and today, for Mamm's, it was final. It forced her brain to understand Mamm wasn't kumming back. The bishop offered a short message, led them in a hymn, and offered a prayer to God. He dismissed them, and she forced her legs to walk to the buggy with Andrew. She got in and hugged herself tight to stop the shaking, but to no avail. She watched her daed, Joel, and Ellie get in their buggy.

Andrew drove her home in silence. He glanced at her and gave her a loving smile now and then. He pulled in front of the haus. "You go inside. I'll tie the horse to the hitching post."

"Danki." Maryann glanced at the gray clouds. She was comfortable in her cape against the cool breeze. The absence of sunshine and the dull weather matched her gloomy mood.

Ellie and Joel caught up to her, and they went inside.

Benches had been pushed aside, and Rachael and Toby were on the floor with Betsy, stacking her blocks. She pulled herself up on the coffee table.

Joel and Ellie greeted Toby and Rachael and sat on one of the benches.

"Danki for watching Betsy." Maryann glanced from Rachael to Toby and pressed a hand to her heart. "I'm not myself today, and you've both been wonderful with Betsy. You helped me a lot."

Andrew entered the haus and greeted them. "Isn't Betsy such a joy to be around?"

Rachael patted Betsy's back. "She's a doll. We had fun with her. We'll leave you to have time with your family and Andrew."

Toby and Rachael bid them farewell and left.

Daed came inside the haus. His face was pale and solemn. "I'll be in the backyard for a couple of minutes. I need a little time alone." He dragged his feet out of the room.

Joel tapped her on the shoulder. "I can't believe she's not in another room folding clothes or cooking in the kitchen." Tears trickled down his cheek.

She put Betsy in her playpen. She wrapped her arms around her bruder, her head on his chest, and wept with him. She raised her head and wiped her face. "I'm numb."

"Me too." He stared at his shoes then glanced around the room. "Daed looks lost without her."

"He's grief-stricken, like us, but worse. It will take a while before he's comfortable with a new routine. She was a big part of our lives. The ache of losing her will not go away. I pray it gets easier with time. My heart breaks for him."

"I'm so sorry you're having to go through this." Andrew gave them an empathetic shake of his head.

Ellie rose. "Let's have some coffee in the kitchen. Maybe Daed will have some when he kummes back in."

Maryann followed Andrew, Joel, and Ellie to the kitchen. Daed came in and joined them. "Good idea. I could use a cup of hot coffee."

Ellie bustled to the stove. "I'll serve warm coffee. Rachael left some on the stove." She poured them each a cup and served it to them.

"Andrew, when do you have to leave?" Maryann picked up Betsy from the playpen and held the child on her lap. She didn't want to say goodbye to him.

"I should leave by ten in the morning."

"I'll stay home tomorrow until Andrew leaves. Do you think Hannah would watch Betsy while I work at the bakery?" Maryann stared at her coffee.

Ellie grinned. "Hannah mentioned to me she'd like to watch Betsy for you. She was planning on asking you."

"I'll visit her after Andrew leaves. If she's in agreement to start watching Betsy tomorrow, I'll leave Betsy with her and head to the bakery from her haus."

Daed cleared his throat. He'd sat staring at his mug during their conversation. "You and Andrew should keep your wedding date. There's no longer any reason for you not to move with him to Millersburg. It was never right of us to ask you to stay, even with Naomi alive. We all consider Andrew family now."

Maryann's heart thumped fast. Daed was right. She could visit her family. Joel and Ellie would look after Daed. She'd miss them. She gazed at Andrew. Her place was with him. "What do you say?"

"I'd marry you today if we could. I'm elated." He gestured to Daed. "Danki. I consider this family mine too.

Having you give your blessing at a time like this means a lot. You are a kind and thoughtful man. I promise I'll take good care of Maryann and Betsy."

Daed nodded. "I have no doubt. I apologize for pressuring Maryann into staying with us. It was wrong."

"No need for an apology, Daed. I'm glad I had this time with Mamm." Maryann patted his hand.

Joel glanced from Maryann to Andrew. "Ellie and I are sorry for asking Maryann to stay in Charm. It was unkind and selfish of us. I wouldn't have wanted anyone to put that on me when I wanted to marry Ellie. I hope you'll both forgive us."

"No apology necessary on my account. You were in a tough spot with Naomi," Andrew assured him.

"I accept your apology, and you must promise to visit us. You'll have to put up with me until after the wedding." She smiled at them. "Andrew, why don't you and I take a walk outside?" She followed him to the living room and grabbed her cape and his coat.

Her family had told them to take their time, and they'd watch Betsy.

"Andrew, I can't believe it. We'll be together after the wedding, in Millersburg."

He squinted. "I'm puzzled. Had you made up your mind not to marry me? Had your family talked you into staying in Charm before Naomi passed?"

Her cheeks heated. "I wrote you a letter. It will be waiting for you at the post office n Millersburg when you return. I wrote and told you I had to stay in Charm with Mamm. She had gotten worse, and I couldn't leave her or my family alone to care for her."

"Now I understand why your family was apologizing to

us. I didn't want to raise questions on this already difficult day for them. I figured I'd ask you more about it later."

"With Mamm's passing, there isn't any reason not to marry and move with you. I hadn't had time to digest this. Daed must've assumed I'd told you about the letter."

He beamed. "It doesn't matter. I'll throw it away. You and I are getting married May fourteenth. You'll love Aunt Dora and Uncle Luke. If my haus doesn't sell before our wedding, we may live with them until it does. They have a big haus."

"Will they mind having a boppli living with them?"

"They will love Betsy. Aunt Dora and Uncle Luke can't wait to meet you both." He pulled her behind the barn and kissed her gently on the lips. "I love you, and I can't wait to call you my fraa and Betsy my dochder."

"I love you, and having you with me and Betsy today meant so much. Danki. Tell me about the shop and the men you hired."

Andrew told her about Matt and James. "The three of us have become good friends. We make a good team. You'll like them."

"If you like them, I'm sure I will like them."

"When will you return to Charm again?" Maryann gazed into his brown eyes.

"I'll try to visit again, but the store and my uncle's health may keep me from it. I'll definitely come back sometime the first week of April for our counseling sessions, and then I won't leave until after we're married. If my haus is sold, I'll stay with Joel and Ellie if they'll have me."

Maryann pulled her cape tighter around her. "They would love to have you." She gazed at him. "Where will Toby work if you sell your place?"

"I'd like to ask Liza and Jacob to hire him. They have been so good to us with Liza owning the bakery and letting me work there. They have such a big farm and employ more employees than most Amish. We're close with them. What do you think?" Andrew stopped with her.

"It's a great idea." Maryann shouldn't have been surprised. She should've known Andrew would have a plan for Toby. This was perfect. Liza and Jacob had a big place and employed a staff to take care of it. She was sure they would be grateful to have Toby.

"I'd better get you back inside. I should head over there and talk to Liza and Jacob before I go to my haus, and you should get some rest. I'll kumme back in the morning." He kissed her cheek.

They walked back inside. Maryann fixed a light supper for all of them with the food friends had brought over. After they all finished their supper, Andrew, Joel, and Ellie bid her, Betsy, and Daed farewell.

Daed faced her. "I'm thankful Andrew came here. Are you happy your wedding is back on?"

"Yes. Danki." Maryann rested her head on his chest.

"He's the best man I could ever ask for in a son-in-law. I was a fool to ask you to let him go for us. I want you to enjoy a long marriage with him, like I did with your mamm." He motioned to the hallway. "I'm going to bed and read to try and get sleepy."

"Good night. I love you." Maryann held Betsy and took her to her room. She changed her for bed and set her in the crib. She sang her to sleep and then went to her room.

She picked up a star-patterned quilt Mamm had made her a long time ago. She hugged it to her neck. She removed her kapp and the pins in her hair. Her locks fell along her back, and she combed her fingers through it.

Mamm used to brush her hair, fix her favorite meals, and dote on her. It had been excessive, and she had clung to Maryann in an unhealthy way at times, but Maryann had loved her. The bad times had drifted from her mind and the happy moments had taken over.

Her time with Andrew had been precious. He'd again been caring and supportive of her. He'd made a sorrowful time bearable, being by her side. She was grieving Mamm's death and, at the same time, looking forward to her life with Andrew. She couldn't wait until Andrew and she would be together. She couldn't imagine anything would stand in their way. But then she hadn't expected the illnesses of their loved ones to interfere. Life was unpredictable, and anything could happen. She said a prayer, hoping nothing would stop them from getting married.

Chapter Nine

Andrew drove to Liza and Jacob's Monday evening.

Liza answered the door. "Andrew, please kumme in. Is everything all right?"

Andrew took off his hat and stepped inside. "Yes, I've got a favor to ask of you and Jacob."

Jacob came from the kitchen. "Greetings, Andrew. I overheard part of what you said to Liza. Something about a favor? How can we help?"

Andrew had a special place in his heart for this couple. They were generous and kind. He admired Liza for being such a good stepmamm to Ellie after Ellie had expressed her grief over her mamm's death in a rebellious and angry way. He admired Liza and Jacob for adopting young Peter when his mamm died. Peter's daed was gone and his mamm had asked Ellie to care for Peter when she was working. After she became ill, she'd left a letter in case of her death out in the open on her dresser asking Jacob to adopt Peter if she should pass away. She loved that Ellie had been like a big sister to Peter. Jacob hadn't hesitated and adopted the child. Liza had treated Peter like her own child after she and Jacob had married. If he hadn't known the circumstances, he would've thought they were the natural parents to both Ellie and Peter. They owned a large farm, and they were often giving jobs to Amish men who fell on hard times. "Toby Schlabach has been working for me, and I'll soon be selling my place to move to Millersburg to take over my uncle's furniture store. Maryann and Betsy will join me after we marry in May."

Jacob nodded. "We'd be glad to hire Toby when your place sells. Tell him he has a job waiting for him."

Liza stood. "Would you like hot chocolate, tea, or coffee? I should've asked you the minute you came in. I apologize."

"No, danki. I appreciate your giving Toby a job. It means a lot to me, as well as your friendship." Andrew stood.

"Happy to help." Jacob stood and opened the door for Andrew.

Liza put a hand to her heart. "We are sorry for Maryann's mamm's death. How is she and her family?"

"They are grieving, but they find peace knowing Naomi is no longer suffering and is in Heaven. I'm hoping her working at the bakery, and our upcoming wedding, and getting ready to move to Millersburg after we wed, will help bring her some joy amidst her sadness."

"I'm sad you will relocate to Millersburg, but I'm happy you, Maryann, and Betsy will be together."

"Danki. Leaving Charm will be hard for us, but we'll visit."

Jacob said, "We'll miss all of you, but we wish you the very best."

"Danki for everything, and take care." Andrew bid them farewell, retrieved his buggy, and drove home. It was past time for Toby to be working at his place, but his buggy was still in front of the barn.

He pulled up, got out of the buggy, and opened the doors. "Toby, I'm glad you're still here."

"Why? Is something wrong?"

Andrew shook his head. "No, I have good news."

"What is it?" Toby walked over to Andrew.

"I'd like you to put my place up for sale. Maryann and Betsy will join me in Millersburg after the wedding in May. I stopped by Liza and Jacob's place and asked them if they'd hire you. They said yes, and that you'd have a job waiting for you when my place sells."

"Danki, Andrew. You're a good friend. I really appreciate it."

"You've been such a good friend to me. It's the least I can do."

"I believe your place will sell this summer. Buyers tend to look then, and it makes for an easier move when the weather is warm." Toby kicked a small rock. "I'm sorry about Maryann's mamm's passing, but I'm glad your wedding is back on. Does her family approve?"

"Shem and the family apologized to Maryann and me for asking her to stay in Charm when Naomi was alive. Maryann had written me a letter saying she had to cancel the wedding when Naomi was still alive. Now, they have remorse for asking her to stay, and they are encouraging her to marry me. She's agreed. I'm relieved and glad." He stared at the ground. "I have deep empathy for the family. It tears your heart out to lose loved ones. It's a hard thing to accept."

"I'm thrilled for you and Maryann. You two are meant for each other. Naomi is singing God's praises in Heaven. She's pain-free. You're right, though. I am relieved each day Daed is with us. It's hard to tell how long we have with him. He's been ill for a long time now. I don't want to lose him. Am I being selfish?"

"No. God will take him home when He's ready. You enjoy each day with your daed, and there's nothing wrong with that. We'd all give anything for one more day with a loved one we've lost." He admired Toby for his devotion to his daed and family. He prayed Toby would open his heart to a girl one day and find happiness in marriage. He was afraid Toby would let his pride get in the way because he didn't think he made enough money to support a fraa and his family. He was sure the right woman would help him. He wanted to lighten Toby's mood. "Where's Pepper?"

Toby grinned. "Daed and Pepper are close. I'm sure Pepper is asleep at Daed's feet as we speak."

"Pepper's in the right place then." He grinned. "Liza and Jacob are looking forward to having you work for them."

Toby's eyes widened. "Andrew, danki for everything you've done for me."

"You're my friend. I wouldn't leave you without working something out. You'll make about the same money as you did with me. It should be plenty if you want to consider a girl."

"I will need years to save enough before I can support a fraa. My family is my priority."

Andrew didn't want to pressure him. Toby had stiffened and turned from him. He was sure his friend didn't want to discuss it. "Do you want to kumme in for a few minutes?"

"No, I should head home and check on Daed. Good to have you home. Will you be here in the morning?" Toby faced him.

"I will, and then I'll drive over to Maryann's and say

goodbye before traveling to Millersburg. I'll be back in April and stay until right after the wedding."

"Danki again for talking to Liza and Jacob for me." Toby had his horse harnessed to the buggy, and he got in.

"My pleasure." He watched Toby drive down the lane. He wanted more for Toby. He'd have to let Toby decide his own future, and Andrew would support him, no matter.

On Tuesday morning, Andrew had his bag ready and put it in the wagon. He'd have one last visit this morning with Maryann and Betsy before he left for Millersburg. He didn't want to leave Maryann, and especially right after Naomi's services. But he had to get back to his aunt and uncle and the store. He looked forward to their wedding in May, and then they'd make a new home together in Millersburg. He hoped she would like it.

Toby came out of the barn. "You heading out?"

"I am. Danki again for telling me about Naomi. Write me if we get any interest on the haus, or if you need anything." He got in his buggy.

"Travel safe. I look forward to your return." Toby waved.

Andrew drove to Maryann's. He didn't want to leave without seeing her and Betsy one more time. He arrived at her haus and went to the porch and knocked on the door.

Maryann answered the door holding Betsy. "You're in time for a nice hot breakfast."

"Dada." Betsy held out her arms to him.

He took Betsy from Maryann. He'd grown to love this little one so much. He really did feel like she was his dochder already. "It's going to be difficult leaving my girls." He took Betsy's hand and kissed the back of it.

Betsy patted Andrew's cheeks and giggled.

He followed Maryann to the kitchen and put Betsy in her wooden high chair. Leaving Maryann and Betsy would be one of the hardest things he had ever done. Andrew would miss having meals and special times like these with Maryann and her family while he was away.

Shem rose from the table and shook Andrew's hand. "I'm glad you stopped by before leaving Charm. Sit and have pancakes and eggs with us."

Andrew sat and took a deep breath. "I love the aroma of hot maple syrup and warm bread."

Maryann served them hot coffee, pancakes, and eggs. She set a basket of fresh bread and a small pitcher of warm maple syrup on the table. She gave Betsy a plate with a cut-up pancake and scrambled eggs, and then she sat. "The bread is still warm from the oven."

Shem said a prayer for the food. "I love pancakes. Don't you, Betsy?"

She held a piece up to Shem. "Pa-akes good."

They nodded in agreement.

Andrew said, "I visited Liza and Jacob, and they've agreed to hire Toby when my place sells."

Maryann grinned. "That's wonderful. Did you tell Toby?"

"He was still at my place when I went home after my visit with them, and I told him. He's thankful and happy about it. It's a big relief for me. I didn't want him to worry about where he'd find work. He's a good friend, and he's been an excellent worker."

Shem shook his head. "I'm happy you'll be together, but I sure am going to miss my girls."

"We'll visit each other, and I'll write you. And we'll still be here until May." Maryann exchanged a loving smile with her daed.

A half hour later, Andrew finished his breakfast and carried his dishes to the sink. "May I help you with the dishes before I leave?" He didn't want to head to Millersburg, but he needed to check on his uncle and the store.

Maryann shook her head. "I'll take care of them. You have a lot to tend to in Millersburg."

Andrew bid Shem farewell, and he kissed Betsy's forehead.

Maryann walked him to the door. She put on her cape and went outside with him to his buggy. "I don't want to say goodbye."

He pulled her to him and kissed her gently on the lips. "I love you, sweetheart. I'll count the days until we're together again."

"I love you, too. Travel safe."

Andrew stepped into the buggy, waved to her, and headed for Millersburg. He'd stop at his Uncle Luke's and Aunt Dora's, and then he'd go to the store. He prayed everything had gone smooth while he was away.

Andrew sipped his coffee on the porch Friday morning. The air was crisp and cold. There must have been three inches of snowfall from last night. Was it really January second, 1914? He shook his head and went back inside the haus. Time had passed fast since he'd returned from Naomi's funeral in Charm. He was glad he'd had a chance to get acquainted with her before she died. He said a silent prayer for Maryann and her family. It would be a while before they would begin to heal from their grief.

He smiled. Aunt Dora and Uncle Luke were thrilled Maryann and Betsy would be living in Millersburg with them after the wedding. Matt and James were anxious to meet her and congratulated him. He drove to work, went to the post office, collected his mail, shuffled through it, and stared at the envelope from Maryann. He ripped it open and shivered in the cold to read it. He stopped and held it. He should throw it away. It was no longer relevant. His curiosity got the better of him.

He read the letter she'd written to him before he'd gone to Naomi's funeral and they'd had a chance to reconcile. He ripped the letter in shreds and discarded it. He couldn't wait to marry her. She was special, with her loving and caring traits.

The snow crunched under his boots as he trudged from the post office to the furniture store. Matt and James would be in any minute.

Matt entered and brushed snow off his coat. "Good morning. It's brisk and the snowfall from last night was about four inches, and it's still snowing. It's going to take half the day for me to thaw out." He cocked his head. "What's wrong? You're not listening to me. Your mind is elsewhere."

"I received a letter from Maryann. She wrote it before her mamm passed, telling me she had to stay in Charm. I'm glad her writing me to cancel the wedding is no longer relevant." Andrew frowned and shrugged.

"Tear it up and throw it away. You're getting married. Concentrate on the positive. She sounds like the perfect woman for you. I can't wait to meet her."

"It's in the trash." Andrew nodded.

James shivered and closed the door behind him. "Is everything all right? You two look like you're in a serious discussion."

Andrew told him about Maryann's letter.

James hung his heavy brown wool jacket and hat on the

knotty-pine coat tree. "Toss it. You'll be a married man after May fourteenth. You and Maryann did go through a rough time. It had to be difficult to think you and she might not work out. I can't imagine if my fraa, Roseanna, and I had faced a similar situation. I miss her. She was the love of my life. The day our last son was born was the day I lost her during childbirth two years ago. We were thrilled to have another boppli. The shock of her death over-whelmed me. My boys keep me going."

Matt shuffled his feet. "I found the woman for me, but I was wrong. She betrayed me the night before our wedding."

James clapped a hand on Matt's shoulder. "The gossips have made you the villain. Why haven't you told them your reason for not marrying her?"

Andrew had been curious why Matt had left this girl at the altar. He would've asked the same question. He was glad James beat him to it.

"The Burkholders and Ropps have been close friends for years. Elias had left Amish life and returned. He was at Annalynn's haus often. I began to wonder if they were more than friends when I found them alone in the sitting room more than once."

"Did you ask Annalynn about Elias?" Andrew asked.

"I did. She said they were friends. But I caught them kissing outside of her family's barn. I'm positive they were sure they were hidden when I drove by. I waited until he left, and then I confronted Annalynn."

"What did she say?" James dragged a stool over and sat.

"She said he forced her to kiss him, but she didn't appear to mind, and she stayed in his arms. She said she loved me and not him. What really bothered me was when she said he didn't have any money and he would never be a man she could depend on. I couldn't help but think she was marrying me for security but she was in love with him. She begged me to forgive her and marry her."

Andrew dropped his jaw. "Why didn't you call off the wedding right then, instead of walking away from her at the altar?"

"I should have told her I wouldn't marry her before the wedding." He raked fingers through his thick brown hair. "She gazed at me with her deep blue eyes, and I didn't want to let her go. I stayed awake most of the night contemplating what to do. Then, at the altar, she glanced at him and he smiled back at her. I had clarity at that moment, and I had to face the truth. She loved him and not me. I was heartbroken, and I had to get away from her. Away from them. Now, I'm thankful I didn't marry her and then find out."

"Why wouldn't she call off the wedding and let Elias court her?" James asked.

"She wanted security and money more than she wanted love. As I look back on our time together, I was sure I had loved her more. I'm sure she found me comfortable, reliable, and a man she could count on for the long haul. Not the kind of relationship I want with a fraa. Elias is intriguing, lazy, and unreliable. I doubt they'll last." Matt sighed and shook his head.

Andrew sat on a stool next to James. "It didn't take me long to fall in love with Maryann. I had no doubt she was the one for me early on in our courtship."

At that moment, two young women sashayed into the store wearing black velvet capes and fancy hats. The tall one smiled wide at James. "I'm Alexandra Parker, and this is my sister, Nannette. We're visiting our aunt, and we'd like to buy her a sewing box."

James blushed. "We have two types." He walked over to the section of sewing boxes. He opened the first one and pulled out a tray and then closed the lid. Then he pulled out one of six drawers visible in the other. "Do you prefer the lift-out tray or individual small drawers?"

Alexandra stood close to him. "I'd like the one with individual drawers. It's quite unique." She batted her eyelashes. "Please show us the features of each."

Nannette scowled. "Alexandra, take the sewing box from the nice man and quit flirting with him. You're impossible."

"What's your name?" Undaunted by her schweschder's scolding, she gazed at James.

"James."

"Nannette, James doesn't mind. Do you?" She grinned.

He cleared his throat. "Madam, please follow me." He walked past Matt and Andrew and went behind the counter, carrying her selection. He accepted the money from Alexandra.

She accepted her purchase from him, strolled to the door, let her schweschder go ahead of her, and then gave James one last smile and shut the door behind her.

Andrew and Matt burst out laughing.

James wrinkled his nose. "She was bold. I wasn't sure what she was going to do next. I'm glad she's gone."

Andrew headed to the workshop. "You handled yourself well."

Matt nodded and followed Andrew.

"Do you have your eye on another woman in town, Matt?" Andrew removed the lid off a can and dipped his brush in the white paint.

"I'd like to marry and have kinner. I'm skeptical about women after what happened to me with Annalynn. Your

Maryann is the type of woman I'd like to find." Matt opened a box of nails.

"You will when the time is right." Maryann was beautiful inside and out. He prayed nothing would stand in their way of having a future together. He went to the counter, pulled out a sheet of paper, and wrote to Maryann.

Maryann stomped the dirty slush from her boots and walked into the post office. She read the date on the newspaper the postman had on the counter. *January nineteenth.* She sighed. It had been three weeks and a day since Mamm's funeral. She and Daed had settled into a routine, but she missed Mamm. She waited until it was her turn in line. "Do you have any mail for me?"

The postmaster smiled. "I do have a letter for you." He passed it to her.

"Danki." She smiled, hurried to the bakery, unlocked the door, and stepped inside. Hannah was taking excellent care of Betsy while she was working at the bakery. Maryann'd managed the haus and Betsy and working at the bakery without a hitch. Ellie assured her she'd take good care of Daed when she moved to Millersburg. "Good morning."

Rachael limped to her. "What do you have in your hand? The smile on your face makes me guess it's a letter from Andrew."

"Is she right?" Magdelena clutched a dish towel to her chest.

Maryann blushed and nodded. "He wrote me a letter. I'm saving it to read later."

"I'm glad he was here for you during Naomi's funeral." She grimaced. "How's your daed adjusting?" Magdelena leaned against the wall.

"He stares off, and I'm certain he's remembering her. It breaks my heart. I make breakfast and supper, and he takes care of his dinner. He takes more time in the evenings to play with Betsy or read her a story. He's always been helpful around the haus. More than is needed. He's the best."

Rachael hooked her arm through Magdelena's. "We should give Maryann privacy to read her letter."

"You're right." Magdelena went with Rachael to the kitchen.

Maryann unfolded the letter. She pressed the paper to her chest.

Dear Maryann,

I miss you and Betsy. My family and friends are anxious to meet you both. I can't wait to begin our life together. I pray you and your daed have worked into a comfortable routine and your pain and sorrow over losing Naomi is getting better each day. You have your memories, and they'll help ease the ache in your heart. She'll never be forgotten by any of us. Give my love to your family and hug Betsy for me.

Love, Andrew.

She kissed the paper. He was sweet to write such an endearing note. She was counting the days until he'd be in Charm again.

Toby opened the door and came into the bakery. "Maryann, have you received a letter from Andrew this week? How's he doing?"

She held up the paper. "I did. He's good. How are you?"

"I'm grateful to Andrew for asking Liza and Jacob to

employ me after you and he move. They came to visit me last night and officially offered me a job whenever I'm ready after Andrew's haus sells."

"I'm glad you have a job lined up." Maryann removed a tray of cookies from the shelf. "Which would you like?"

Toby scanned the assortment of cookies. "Two ginger cookies, please." He paid her.

She handed his purchase to him. "Did you want to say hello to Rachael?"

"Sure." He shrugged. "I'll go to the kitchen." He was gone for a couple of minutes, returned, bid her farewell, and walked out the door.

Maryann skipped to the back room. "I have an idea."

"What is it?" Magdelena sprinkled sugar on her cookies.

"Magdelena, you and Toby would be a good match. What do you think?"

Rachael washed her hands. "I've asked my bruder about Magdelena."

Magdelena blushed. "What did he say?"

Maryann nudged Rachael. "Tell us."

"He likes Magdelena, but he isn't ready. My bruder has to have what he considers the right amount of money to provide for her before he'll court anyone. He's right. We are living on what he and I make. He's also focused on Daed, and I understand. We worry how long we'll have him with us. They're best friends. Do you understand, Magdelena?"

Magdelena nodded. "His loyalty to his family is a trait I admire. I do understand. Maybe someday he'll be ready."

"I'll be curious to watch what happens with you two in the future." Maryann had noticed he couldn't take his eyes off Magdelena when they were all together in the bakery or at after-church meals. She was convinced he'd show he was interested in her someday soon.

Rachael squeezed Magdelena's arm. "He doesn't notice that Maryann or I are in the room when you're with us."

"He doesn't talk to me much." Magdelena shrugged.

"He will approach you when the time is right." Rachael squeezed Magdelena's arm.

Maryann wouldn't pursue this conversation. She'd respect Toby's position. It wasn't her place to meddle. She wondered if Magdelena would wait on Toby. Amish men had approached her beautiful friend, but Magdelena had found something wrong with each of them. Maybe she had her sights on Toby more than Maryann realized.

Maryann waited on customers and the girls baked breads and pastries the rest of the afternoon until closing time. She took off her apron and hung it on the wall hook. "Time to go, ladies." She gathered her things and followed the girls to the livery, scanning the town on the way. She'd be making a new life in a new town in a couple of months. Would she like it as well as Charm?

Rachael carried a tray of molasses cookies to the counter Monday morning. "I can't believe we're halfway through February. It's the sixteenth." She grimaced. "I haven't had a chance to tell you about Pepper."

Maryann frowned. "Is Pepper all right?" She pressed a hand to her heart, hoping nothing bad had happened to the dog.

"Yes. The pup has become a part of our family. Pepper and Daed have become close. He doesn't leave Daed's side very often. And he sleeps at the end of Daed's bed through the night. Mamm enjoys Pepper too. She's happy the pet has lifted Daed's mood."

"I'm thrilled the dog has become a part of your family. Pets can be a comfort." Maryann brushed a spot of flour from her sleeve, relieved Andrew's pet was bringing cheer to Toby's family.

"We love the mutt." Rachael glanced at the counter shelves. "I should finish the sugar cookies I started and get them ready to sell." Rachael grinned and headed to the kitchen.

A woman with a stained coat, matted hair, and a tattered scarf around her neck came inside the bakery. Her body odor was hard to endure. She scowled and glared at Maryann. "Give me a vanilla cake with buttercream frosting, a dozen oatmeal cookies, and three apple fry pies."

A big brusque man wearing gloves with holes, and a tattered coat, was at the woman's heels. He also had a bad odor. "Nadine, I told you to wait in the buggy. I said I'd get the desserts."

The heavyset Englisch woman scoffed at him, and stomped out.

The man squinted and slapped his gloved hand on the counter. "Give me whatever she ordered, now!"

Maryann shivered. The back door slammed shut. She glanced out the window, and she saw Magdelena was running across the street.

She hurried to put the cake in a box and passed it to him. He towered over the counter. His eyes narrowed. "Give me some of them maple sugar cookies."

"How many?" Maryann's hand shook.

"All of them!" He slapped the counter again. "And hurry." The man grabbed the bag and ran into the sheriff kumming in the door with Magdelena behind him.

The sheriff had his coat pulled back and his hand resting on his Browning pistol, still in its holster. He narrowed his eyes. "Did you pay for those?"

The man scowled, dug in his pocket, and threw money on the counter.

"Did he pay you enough, Maryann?" The sheriff blocked the man from leaving.

She glanced at the coins. It wasn't near enough to cover the cost, but she didn't care. The couple looked desperate and hungry. She nodded. "Please don't arrest him. I'm sure he didn't mean any harm."

The sheriff still didn't move. "Thank the lady."

The man mumbled, "Thank you."

"Where are you from?" The sheriff glared at him.

"Akron," the man snarled.

"Get out of this town and don't kumme back. You got it?" The sheriff stood inches from the man's face.

"Got it."

The sheriff opened the door, with Magdelena still behind him.

The man ran outside.

The sheriff pinched his nose shut and then dropped his hand. "He could use manners and a bath. Are you girls all right?"

Rachael limped to the front. "Magdelena and I peeked around the door, and before I could say anything, Magdelena flew out the back door. I figured she went for the sheriff, and she was right to get help. The man was rude and angry. I stayed back and held a frying pan, just in case. We're not supposed to cause physical harm, but I wasn't going to let the man hurt my friend."

Maryann blew out a breath. "I doubt he'd have harmed us. Their coats and hats hadn't been washed for a while, and they had holes in them. They seem poor, and they were probably hungry. I'd have helped them out if they'd asked."

Magdelena huffed. "There's no sense in the way they acted."

The sheriff stepped outside and then came back in the bakery. "They're gone. I'm sure we won't encounter them again. I got the same impression. They could've asked for help instead of trying to steal. We don't tolerate stealing."

"Danki, Sheriff." Maryann had encountered her share of bullies in the past when she was in Massillon and married to Gerald. She'd gotten comfortable in peaceful Charm. She was grateful it was unusual for troublemakers to visit their town.

She served customers the rest of the afternoon then closed the shop, bid the girls farewell, and drove to Hannah's to collect Betsy. She parked her buggy and trudged through the dirty slush of snow to the door and knocked.

Hannah had Betsy balanced on her hip. "We've had a wonderful day."

Betsy held her arms out. "Mum."

Maryann stepped inside the haus and took Betsy in her arms. She kissed her dochder's cheek. "How's my girl?"

Betsy grinned and put her little arms around her neck.

"Let me take your cape. Have a warm glass of hot chocolate with me." Hannah held out her hand.

Maryann put Betsy down and took off her cape and handed it to Hannah. "Where's Timothy?"

Hannah put the cape on the maple coat tree beside the door. "He's at his parents' haus helping his daed put up a shelf in the main bedroom."

Betsy stood, wobbled, and then toddled across the room to an Amish doll on the chair.

Maryann and Hannah gasped, their mouths open.

"Are those her first steps?" Maryann hoped she'd not missed Betsy walking for the first time. She had expected Betsy to walk before now. She was sixteen months old. This was such a relief and so exciting.

Hannah nodded. "Yes, and she didn't hesitate. How wonderful!"

Maryann held her arms out. "Kumme to Mum, Betsy."

Grinning, Betsy walked into her arms.

"Good girl." Maryann chuckled. "You may want to stop watching Betsy now she's walking. You may have to chase her from room to room."

Hannah pointed to the playpen. "That will be her safe place when I'm out of breath from trying to keep up with her." She sat back. "You must be thrilled about your wedding in May."

"I am, but I'm sad about leaving Daed. Joel has Ellie, and they'll have a new boppli to keep them busy. I worry about Daed being alone." Maryann sucked in her bottom lip. He'd been through so much with Mamm. She enjoyed their time together, and he and Betsy had grown close. He'd go through another change when they left.

"Your daed's haus isn't far from Joel and Ellie's. He'll enjoy their boppli and adjust to living alone. He understands you and Betsy belong with Andrew."

"Danki, Hannah. You're right, and God will take care of all of us." She would write to him often. Her heart sank. It wouldn't be the same. She'd miss him. "God took care of us at the bakery today." She recounted about the man and woman who attempted to steal from them.

"Magdelena reacted fast. I'm glad Sheriff Williams's office is close. What a shock. We don't have danger too often in Charm. I hope we don't again, and I'm relieved you girls are unharmed."

"It was a shock, but it doesn't deter me from working at the bakery. It's a wonderful place to bake with friends and serve customers." She'd miss everything about Charm.

Maryann met Rachael and Magdelena at the livery early in the morning. They crossed the road.

The newsboy waved a paper above his head. "It's February twenty-third! Find out the latest news!"

Maryann couldn't believe another week had passed. She shouldn't be glad time was passing fast for her. She grinned. She was closer to having Andrew in Charm. She and the girls crossed the road to the store and unlocked the door, and they went inside the bakery. They removed their capes and hung them up.

Maryann glanced at Rachael. "You've been quiet this morning." She faced her. "Have you been crying? What's the matter?"

Rachael's lips quivered. "Pepper was killed by a coyote."

Magdelena nodded. "We rode together today. She told me when I got in the buggy. It's sad."

"Oh no! How awful. How did it happen?" Maryann motioned for them to sit at one of the café tables. She handed Rachael a handkerchief.

Rachael dabbed her eyes. "Pepper leaves Daed's room and goes to Toby when he needs to go outside. Toby let him out, and he went to get a glass of water. He opened the door to let Pepper back in, and he wasn't in sight. He came upon a coyote running away from what was left of Pepper's dead body. Toby, I, and our parents are sick about it. Pepper was such a sweet pet. We fell in love with him right after Toby brought the dog to us. Daed's mood lifted, and they became fast friends."

Magdelena squeezed Rachael's arm. "I'm sorry this happened. Do you want another dog? Our dog had puppies six months ago, and we have one left, a male, to give away. He's a good pet."

Maryann got up and poured them each a mug of coffee and served them. "What do you think, Rachael?"

"I'll take him. Daed was happier with Pepper around. A new pet would be good, and sooner than later. Danki, Magdelena."

"Anything for you. I'll bring him to your haus tonight, right after I get home and before supper." Magdelena rose and put on her apron.

Maryann tied the ribbons on her apron behind her. "Did you name the dog?"

"He's got patches of dark and light brown hair, so we named him Patches."

"I like the name." Rachael limped to the doorway between the kitchen and café. "Maryann, will you consider a pet for Betsy after you move to Millersburg?"

"I wonder how she'd do with one. My parents introduced me to a puppy when I was about three, and I didn't want anything to do with the dog. Then when I got older, I wanted one, and Mamm wouldn't let me have a pet. I might wait until she's around eight. Andrew may have another idea of what kind of pet to get her." She and Andrew would be making decisions together after they were married, and she was anxious to have his help.

Maryann and the girls baked until it was time to open for customers. She let her favorite customers, Sheriff

Williams and Dr. Harrison, inside. "You're here earlier than usual."

Sheriff Williams yawned. "We were at the Ziegler family's home at four this morning. Norm and his eldest son, George, scuffled. His middle son, Bud, came and got us. I broke up the fight, and Dr. Harrison stitched cuts on their foreheads. George is a no-good son who should have moved out and be making a decent living for himself. He's lazy and a freeloader."

Maryann poured coffee and served them. She pointed to two warm peach-jam pastries. "Would you each like one?"

The men nodded.

She set them on plates and then put the plates on the counter. "How old is George?" She shouldn't get involved, but curiosity got the best of her.

Dr. Harrison huffed. "He's twenty-five, and I agree with the sheriff. He should no longer be living at home. If he'd change his belligerent and obnoxious ways, he might find a good woman to marry. He's not bad looking."

"He'd have to find steady work. I wouldn't wish that man on any woman."

Maryann thought about her first marriage. They could've been describing Gerald when he'd started gambling with the hopes of making fast money. He'd become frustrated and short-tempered. She didn't want anything to do with her past life or any of Gerald's gambling partners. She'd started life fresh after moving back to Charm, and she wanted to keep it that way. Andrew was dependable. He wasn't afraid of hard work, and she loved his positive disposition. They were happy, and they had a bright future ahead.

* * *

Later in the afternoon, Liza entered the bakery with Charity and Peter.

Charity skipped inside the bakery, with Peter following. "Maryann!" She hugged Maryann's legs. "Is my schweschder in the kitchen?"

Maryann pointed to the kitchen. She enjoyed watching little Charity, six, and Peter, seven, interact. They had a close friendship. "Magdelena's baking goodies. You can give her a hug."

She grinned. Magdelena's little schweschder, Charity, and Peter, Ellie's little adopted bruder, had been close since the day they met. She'd be curious as to whether their friendship would blossom into something more as they grew and became adults.

"Maryann, it sure smells good in here." Peter ogled the desserts on the shelves.

"I'm sure Magdelena has treats for you in the back." Maryann gestured to the kitchen.

Charity waved to Peter. "Kumme with me."

Peter hurried to catch up with Charity.

Maryann poured hot chocolate in two mugs and passed one to Liza. "Magdelena has told me those two have been friends since the day they met."

Liza took a seat at the counter. "They are inseparable and adorable. They don't fuss, and they don't grumble when I give them chores to do. They're doing well in school. They're both good with Lorianne, which is a big help to me. She's pulling herself up to stand wherever she can find a chair or table. Hannah said Betsy started walking."

"She is a handful. She keeps Daed and me on our toes before she goes to bed. She loves to run from us in the haus. I'm grateful to Hannah for caring for Betsy for me."

"Esther begs me to keep Lorianne. My schweschder has Lorianne more than I do. She came and got her yesterday, and she wanted to keep her overnight and today." She grinned. "She wanted more kinner besides Hannah, and now she's happy to have Lorianne anytime I'll let her. Kinner have brought joy to all our lives." She sipped her hot chocolate and set her mug on the table. "The news of your wedding being back on has spread throughout the community. I'm thrilled for you and Andrew, but I'll miss you."

"Esther did an excellent job raising Hannah, and I treasure both their friendships. Betsy took to Hannah right away. I never worry about my dochder when she's watching her." She gazed at Liza. "Danki for the job at the bakery, and for not being upset I'm leaving it." Maryann stood and lifted the glass dome lid on a plate of butter cookies. She took two and handed one to Liza.

"I'm grateful for the time you've spent here. It's wonderful you'll marry Andrew and create a life with him. It will be exciting to pick out a haus, make new friends, and have Andrew with you each day." Liza patted her hand.

"I am happy, too, but I'll be homesick for all of you. It won't be easy living with his aunt and uncle until we have our own place." She winced. "Betsy might be an annoyance for them."

Liza batted the air. "Andrew loves his aunt and uncle, or he wouldn't have wanted to stay and help them. If they're anything like him, they'll love you and Betsy. It may be helpful to stay with them for a bit while they introduce you to friends and the bishop."

"You're right. Andrew has nothing but good things to say about them." She hoped Andrew's haus would sell before the wedding so they could purchase a haus in Millersburg soon after they moved there. She didn't want to get in his aunt's way. She'd do all she could to help his aunt and uncle, whether they lived with them or not.

Charity and Peter bustled to the table with cookie crumbs on their mouths.

"Magdelena and Rachael gave us iced sugar cookies. They were yummy." Charity beamed.

Peter picked up Liza's cloth napkin and wiped his mouth and then Charity's. "She had her cookie and half of mine."

Charity's face reddened. "You said you didn't want all of it."

Peter shrugged. "I knew you wanted more, so I gave it to you."

Magdelena and Rachael came out from the kitchen.

Magdelena motioned to the kinner. "Charity and Peter, Maryann and Andrew are getting married in May. Won't it be fun to go to the wedding?"

Charity glanced at Peter and blushed. "Peter's going to marry me when we get big."

Liza glanced at Peter. "Is this so, Peter?"

He stared at his shoes and shrugged. "Yes, but I'll have to build us a haus first unless maybe we can live with you and Daed."

Charity gave him a shy grin. "Or we can live at my haus. Right, Magdelena?"

Maryann pressed her lips against a laugh. These kinner were precious.

"Of course you can." Magdelena put a hand on Charity's shoulder.

Rachael wiped flour from her hands with a big smile

on her face. "I'm glad you came in today. It's fun to have kinner here."

Maryann swallowed the chuckle struggling to get out. This was adorable. She wondered if they would wed when they reached adulthood. They had much life to live before they were old enough to make that decision. She considered how her life would've been different if she had grown up with Andrew and married him first.

Liza stood. "We have a long time to make those decisions." She ushered them to the door. "Danki for the treats. I enjoyed our visit. I need to stop at the general store before we leave. Then on my way home, I'll stop at my schweschder, Esther's haus, and pick up Lorianne. We should get going."

Rachael hooked her arm through Magdelena's. "We better finish our yeast rolls."

Maryann and the girls watched them leave, and then the girls returned to the kitchen. Ellie and Peter were blessed to have Liza for a mamm. She was wise, generous, and loving. It was no wonder Esther, Liza's schweschder, had the same traits. Maryann and Ellie had become close, and she was glad to have her for a schweschder-in-law. She'd miss being involved in their lives and watching their kinner grow. These women were family and precious to her. Would she build close friendships with women in Millersburg like she had in Charm?

Andrew sat by the fireplace and enjoyed the orange hue of the small flames with Uncle Luke Tuesday evening. "Matt and James have been wilkom additions to the store. They're hard workers, dependable, and trustworthy. We've formed a friendship. God sent me two good men when I needed them most." Andrew let out a satisfied sigh. "And I'll have a fraa for you to meet in May. Everything is kumming together for me."

Uncle Luke rested his head against the back of the high-backed chair. "I'm relieved there's nothing keeping you and Maryann apart any longer. I was burdened for you losing her on account of you being here for us and managing the store. I didn't want our situation to cause trouble for you."

"If Maryann had decided not to marry me, I wouldn't want you to have any guilt about asking for my help. We're family. I trusted God with His plan for my life, and so did Maryann. We believed if it's God's will we should be together, He would intervene. I'm sorry Naomi has passed away, but I'm relieved she's no longer in pain and is now in Heaven. I can't wait for you to meet Maryann and Betsy."

"Assure her we're eager to have her in the family. Your aunt Dora is counting the days until she'll have them in this haus. Any news on the sale of your haus in Charm?"

Andrew shook his head. "Nothing. Winter's a bad time to sell. If couples marry or new Amish move, they try to travel and relocate in the spring, summer, or fall. I expect there to be some interest when the weather breaks. We can rent in the boarding haus in town if it's too much to have us living with you."

"Don't be silly. Little Betsy will liven the place up, and we'll love having you three with us."

Andrew whistled on his way from the livery to the store Monday. *March second.* It was still cold outside, and he was ready for some warmer temperatures. Maybe April would bring them warmer weather. He was happy with the furniture he and Matt had added to the sales floor, and the consignors had brought in more pieces. He'd been counting the days until he'd return to Charm. Matt and James were comfortable with their roles in managing the store. He was ready for the snow to end and warmer temperatures to begin. He was a little later than usual arriving at the shop, due to Uncle Luke requiring help getting from the bed to his favorite high-backed chair. At noon, he'd go home and check on him.

A beautiful Amish woman headed for the shop.

Andrew opened the door for her. He tipped his hat and followed her inside.

Matt gasped. "Annalynn."

Andrew straightened. Matt's open mouth and stiff stance told him this was a surprise. "Good morning, madam. I'm Andrew Wittmer, the new manager for the store. Are you shopping for anything in particular?"

She was a pretty Amish lady. "I'm Annalynn Burkholder, now Ropp. It's a pleasure to meet you. Matt and I are old friends. Do you mind if he waits on me?" She strolled over to him. "I'm interested in a quilt rack."

Matt blushed. "We have several. I suggest the cherry one."

She gazed at him. "How are you, Matt?"

Two Amish women came in and asked James to show them desks. He led the two women to the area of the store where desks were on display.

The two women glanced back and forth from each other to Matt and Annalynn.

Andrew stepped behind the counter and flipped through the sales journal. He was itching to finish the headboard to the bedroom set he was building, but he wanted to remain available for the customers, since Matt and James were busy. He glanced at the two women stealing glances at Matt and Annalynn. The two women must know them and wonder why they were talking. He hoped they wouldn't spread gossip about them. He couldn't help but overhear Matt and Annalynn's conversation.

"I have to talk to you." Annalynn gazed at him.

Matt pulled her aside to a corner away from customers. "If it's about why I haven't said anything to you, we both know why. I caught you and Elias kissing the night before our wedding. You said he forced the kiss on you, but I knew you weren't telling the truth. You stayed in his arms willingly. I tried to make sense of it, since I loved you so much. But I couldn't marry you when the time came for us to say our vows, and I had to face the fact I was fooling myself to dismiss what I'd seen. How long had you been meeting him behind my back?"

"No good will kumme from going into the past. I'm sorry, Matt. I really am. I'm ashamed of my behavior. I hope you can forgive me. It's taken this year to muster the courage to approach you. You and I have been in Sunday services, social events, and passed each other in town without saying a word. It's time we put this behind us."

Matt uncrossed his arms and relaxed. "You're right. Yes. Let's put this behind us. There's no reason we can't be civil. I forgive you."

She pointed. "Danki. I'm relieved we can quit avoiding each other. Maybe things between us won't be awkward now we've cleared the air." She smiled. "I really do want to purchase the quilt rack."

He accepted her payment. "Danki for kumming to me. I appreciate it. Yes, we can both relax around each other now. I'll take the rack to your buggy for you." He picked it up and carried it outside the store and then returned minutes later.

"Is everything all right, Matt?" He was glad Matt and Annalynn had had a chance to talk. It was better they not avoid each other and wonder what the other was thinking. Forgiveness lifted heavy burdens. Annalynn was bold to confront him. She reminded him of Ellie, Maryann's schweschder-in-law. She was more direct than most Amish women, but he respected and liked her. He always knew where he stood with Ellie, and she'd been a tough one to win over her approval. But she'd given her blessing when he'd proposed to Maryann.

Matt came behind the counter and faced him. "She shocked me. I've avoided her when I've seen her. I wasn't sure what to expect. I'm glad we have forgiven each other. It will ease the tension between us." He sighed. "I did notice the two women who came into the store whispering about us. I recognize them. I'm sure they were wondering what Annalynn and I would have to say to each other. Thank goodness they're two of the kindest women in town. They've not shunned me since I've been back."

"Ignore the busybodies, and it's good these ladies are not unkind. Hopefully, they'll keep to themselves seeing the two of you speaking. I'm glad for you, Matt. Maryann and I were distraught over having to cancel our wedding plans. We didn't have anything to forgive on either end. I can't imagine your situation. I'm not sure I'd have been as forgiving if I'd experienced what you did with Annalynn. I hope I would do what you did today."

"I'm a patient man, but I began to think I'd never let go of my frustration and disappointment in losing Annalynn to Elias. I've asked God to take away the bitterness and let me get over her. As time passed, God answered my prayers. It became easier to forgive and let go of all the animosity I had toward her. I admire her for approaching me and getting things out in the open. Now we can greet each other and be amicable."

Andrew and Matt made room on the floor to bring out pieces they'd finished in the backroom workshop. A confident, slender woman with auburn hair peeking out of her kapp entered the store and went to James. She handed him a bag. Andrew recognized Lena Ramer from Sunday services. He hadn't had a conversation with her, and he wondered if she and James were friends. He hadn't mentioned her. Andrew exchanged a puzzled look with Matt.

Lena smiled at James. "I made you butter cookies, and I'd like to invite you to supper at my family's home tomorrow night. We've greeted each other at the services, but we've not had a chance to talk." She smiled at him.

Andrew didn't dare look at Matt or he'd let out a chuckle at James's shocked face. He would like for James to meet a sweet Amish girl.

James blushed as he accepted the bag. "Danki."

She passed him a note. "This is my address. Arrive at six sharp tomorrow night." She gave him a warm smile. "Goodbye, gentlemen." She strolled to the door and left.

James blew out a breath. "She's direct, for an Amish woman. She's greeted me at the Sunday service and then she asked me where I'd lived before I moved to Millersburg and how my fraa died. I found her questions too personal for our first meeting. I don't want to go to supper at her haus. I should've declined the invitation, but I was too shocked to think straight. What should I do?"

Matt clapped a hand to his shoulder. "It's too late to tell her no. You should go enjoy her company and then tell her you aren't ready to court any woman."

James shrugged. "I wouldn't mind meeting a woman I'm attracted to. I liked being married, and I miss having a woman in the haus. The boys take good care of themselves, but it wouldn't hurt to have a stepmamm to care for them. Just not a forward woman like her."

Andrew tapped his forefinger on the counter. "I suggest you be honest. After supper, tell her she's a kind woman but you wouldn't want to mislead her into thinking your friendship would develop into a courtship."

"Courting again after having been married will be difficult. Finding the right woman is important, and I didn't realize I was so picky. Roseanna was perfect for me. She didn't raise her voice when she was frustrated. She was calm and explained what she wanted from me. We didn't go to bed angry. We were up late a number of times until we both came to an agreement on our differences of opinion." He grinned.

"What are you going to do?" Matt squinted.

"I'll go, and then do as Andrew suggested."

Matt cringed. "Her confident approach with you tells me she won't take your news well."

Andrew headed to the workshop and glanced over his shoulder. "Maybe you'll learn more about her during supper and you'll change your mind."

James cocked his head. "Did you have an instant connection to Maryann when you first saw her?"

Andrew stopped walking. "I did, and I haven't had a doubt about her since then. I doubt men and women who marry would all say they experienced the same. You might be surprised by the end of your evening with Lena."

James groaned. "I wish I felt the same, but I don't think so." He opened the bag, took out a cookie, and bit off a bite. He smiled. "These are delicious."

Andrew and Matt stifled grins and went to the workshop.

Andrew picked up a piece of sandpaper. "I don't envy James. I do pray he finds a good woman."

"You're blessed to have found Maryann. I pray I find the right woman for me someday."

"I'd like you and James to find the right Amish women to court. You and James need to open yourselves up to the idea. You both are rigid and closed off to the women after church. You only talk to the men." Andrew had observed women greeting the two men at after church dinners and the men didn't move away from their buddies to consider having a chat with any of the women. He didn't have any trouble when he'd introduced himself to Maryann the first time. He didn't understand why they couldn't make more of an effort to find the right girl.

"You're right. I'll be more observant. Maybe a nice girl will catch my eye." Matt winked at Andrew.

"Good." Andrew sanded the chair's spindle until it was smooth. He couldn't wait to have Maryann living in the same haus with him, planning their future, and talking about when to have kinner. He missed her sweet face each day. Maybe she could play matchmaker for James and Matt if they hadn't found girls on their own by the time she arrived.

Chapter Ten

Maryann opened the door Tuesday evening and found Magdelena with Rachael, who was holding a dog with dark and light brown patches of fur. She grinned and let them in the haus. "Is this the puppy Magdelena is giving you and your family, Rachael?"

"Isn't he adorable? This is Patches." Rachael handed Maryann the dog.

"He is a cutie. Kumme in and visit." She knelt by Betsy with Patches in her arms. "Meet Patches."

Betsy, giggling, patted the dog's head. "Oggie."

Patches licked Betsy's arm and wiggled in Maryann's arms, trying to get down and play with Betsy.

Magdelena chuckled. "Betsy and Patches connected right away." She sat next to Maryann and Betsy on the cotton braided rug.

Rachael sat in a chair close to them. "She brought him over after work. We skipped supper to bring him to meet you and Betsy."

Magdelena reached over and scratched the dog's ears. "We were sure Betsy would love him. Patches is sweet and loving. We don't have to worry about him growling or biting her."

"Has Toby met her?" Maryann nuzzled her face in the dog's neck. "You are a beauty."

Magdelena blushed. "He was outside when I drove up, so I had him hold the dog for me while I got out of the buggy. He's thrilled to have a pet again. He couldn't wait for his family to meet the dog, so we went inside. His daed smiled wide when he held Patches. The pup has met with everyone's approval."

Maryann gestured to her friends. "Why don't you both stay for supper? I've got chicken and dumplings on the stove. The food was done right before I answered the door. Don't hesitate. I have more than enough for all of us. It will be fun, and Daed would enjoy your company."

Betsy giggled. She pulled her hand back and forth and giggled each time the dog licked her fingers.

Rachael shrugged. "I'm sure my family has had supper without me by now." She took Patches from Maryann.

"Mine too." Magdelena headed to the kitchen. "I can't pass up chicken and dumplings."

Maryann stood and picked up Betsy. "Should we let the dog down?"

"He'll be fine. The dog did his business right before we came inside. He hasn't chewed on furniture or caused any damage at home. We've trained him to behave." Magdelena washed her hands in the kitchen.

Maryann put Betsy in her high chair and then got a wet rag and washed her hands.

Rachael put the dog on the floor and used the lye soap to wash her hands.

Daed entered the kitchen. "Wilkom, ladies. Who do we have here?" He bent to pet the dog.

Rachael said, "After Pepper died, we wanted another dog. Magdelena gave us Patches from her litter."

Daed chuckled. "He's a handsome dog."

Betsy wiggled in the high chair with excitement. "Oggie."

"She's not afraid of him. That's good." Maryann chuckled.

Maryann transferred the pot of chicken and dumplings onto a large potholder Mamm had used for such things. Memories of Mamm's slender fingers placing the holder on the table flashed in her mind. Her shout to tell them supper's ready, and her table set with the same utensils and dishware they'd used for years. *Oh, how I miss her.* "Daed, would you offer the prayer for the food?"

Daed prayed to God and offered his thanks for the food. "Dig in." He grinned.

Betsy grabbed the spoon and then set it down and switched to using her fingers.

"I'm too tired to argue with you, little one. Go ahead and use your fingers." Maryann frowned.

Patches rested between Betsy and Rachael's chairs.

Rachael cut her slice of white bread in half. "I miss Pepper. Having Patches will lift our moods. The first night Pepper stayed with us, he burrowed underneath a pile of dirty clothes Toby left on the floor. Toby scooped them up to throw them in the basket and out jumped Pepper. Toby yelped and almost lost his footing. I was kumming to announce supper when it happened. We laughed, and Pepper hid for a good hour. He was more frightened than Toby. I'm sure Patches will entertain us, too."

"You can count on dogs and kinner to make you laugh." Magdelena smiled. "Charity insisted she had to make butter cookies. They were going on a picnic, and they were Peter's favorite. I told her not to leave the cookies on the table. She did, and went to her room to play. Bandit devoured them. I scolded her, and she blamed it on the dog. She was furious and told Bandit no supper for him." Magdelena shook her head. "She blames the dog for everything she does wrong."

Maryann watched Daed laugh with the girls. She loved them for keeping Daed entertained and cheering him. He hadn't had this good a time since Mamm died.

She, Magdelena, and Rachael had become close, and she'd miss these times with them. She hoped they'd visit her in Millersburg.

The girls helped her wash and dry the dishes and then bid her family farewell.

Betsy wrinkled her nose and whined when the girls and Patches left. "Oggie."

"Patches was cute. Maybe we'll invite him back soon." Maryann put an Amish doll in her dochder's hands while she changed her for bed.

"I'll read her a story and put her to sleep for you. You relax and get some rest." Daed reached for his grand-dochder.

"Danki, Daed." Maryann loved him for supporting her, Andrew's, and Betsy's relocation. She was happy Ellie would give him another grandchild soon. He'd miss Betsy, but having a new boppli in the family would help make their departure easier for him.

Maryann rolled back her shoulders and relaxed Wednesday evening. Today had been an exceptionally good day. She loved kneading dough for bread, and she'd had more time without customers to help the girls bake. She'd craved a gingerbread cake and made three extras before they opened. She and the girls split one and displayed the other three. She chuckled. It was a surprise when the sheriff bought two and Dr. Harrison paid for the other.

She'd enjoyed the bakery, but she was glad to be home.

She checked on a sleeping Betsy and then walked into the living room. She looked out the window. Who was the man with Toby? This was an odd time for Toby to visit. She opened the door. "Good evening."

Toby took off his hat and stood next to the man at her door. "Maryann, I have someone you'll want to meet." He put his hand on the man's back. "This is Andrew's bruder, Gabe Wittmer. Do you mind if we kumme in? I could've brought him to the bakery, but we'd have a more uninterrupted visit at your home."

Andrew has a bruder? She wrinkled her forehead. "Yes, please, kumme in." She studied Gabe. He had Andrew's attractive big brown eyes and thick brown hair. Same straight nose and structured jawline.

Gabe grinned and stepped inside. "Danki. It's a pleasure to meet you."

Daed joined her and shook Gabe's hand. "I'm Maryann's daed, Shem Wenger. Please take a seat."

Maryann studied the man. He had a kind face, and his demeanor was friendly and not overbearing or intrusive. There was nothing threatening about him. Why had Andrew not mentioned Gabe? "May I offer you a piece of butterscotch pie or something to drink?"

"No, danki, on the pie or drink." Gabe cleared his throat. "Toby said Andrew didn't tell him about me. I was a surprise to him when I showed up looking for Andrew. Had my bruder told you about me?"

She shook her head. She didn't want to hurt his feelings.

He'd sucked in his lip and his disappointed eyes told her he hoped she'd say yes.

She wouldn't lie to him. "No, and I don't understand why. Do you have any idea?"

Gabe wore Englischer clothes. Why had he left Amish life? She had left once. She understood you didn't mention loved ones who had left, but why would Andrew be uncomfortable telling *her* about Gabe? She'd left and returned. And they were getting married. Her heart plummeted to find out he'd kept this from her. His openness and honesty were what she loved most about their courtship. Secrets her husband kept were what destroyed her first marriage before Gerald died.

"After our parents passed away, I left to explore the outside world. Maybe that's why. Andrew said he'd leave a forwarding address with the postmaster so I could always find him if I wanted to return to Amish life. He was upset I left, but we'd been close as kinner. I traveled and wrote letters, but I got caught up in my own world and stopped writing. I have no good excuse for it." He hung his head.

Toby nodded to Gabe. "You should tell her the rest of your story."

"Maryann, when Toby told me your last name, I realized you must be Gerald Harding's widow. He'd mentioned you and your dochder once in conversation."

"How did you meet Gerald?" Maryann's heart thudded. She gripped her skirt.

"I was in Massillon for a short time. He sat at the same gambling table with me twice. We were casual acquaintances, nothing more." He winced. "I was there the day the hot-tempered man murdered your husband. I reported him to the sheriff. My conscience wouldn't let me turn a blind eye. I was sure the man didn't know it was me who turned him in because there were a lot of witnesses in the place. But I didn't want to take any chances. I left town. I'm sorry for your loss."

Daed took a deep breath. "This is shocking news."

"My husband made bad choices, but he didn't deserve to die. I appreciate you telling the sheriff the culprit's name. I'm sure it wasn't an easy decision. Was Andrew aware of this?" Maryann's head began to ache.

"It was all in the last letter I wrote to him. I disappointed him by leaving. I wanted him to be proud of me for doing the right thing. Imagine my surprise when Toby told me who you were and your relationship to my bruder. Knowing you had left Amish life and returned made it easier to meet you concerning my circumstances."

Toby set his hat in his lap and sat back.

"What are your plans, Gabe?" Daed met his gaze.

"I'm anxious to reunite with Andrew in Millersburg. I'd like to settle near my bruder and reestablish a family relationship. I've asked God to forgive me, and I'll do the same with the bishop and church. I'm returning to Amish life. Living in the outside world isn't for me."

"What wonderful news." She had much to learn about Gabe, but he made a good impression. She was baffled why Andrew wouldn't want to share memories about his bruder with her. She wouldn't have cared Gabe left, except she'd have prayed for his return.

"Andrew will be relieved you're safe and changing your life." Daed relaxed and settled back.

"I'm excited to tell him. We have lost time to make up. I won't leave again. I've missed him, and I'm hoping to work with him. Toby told me he's with Aunt Dora and

Uncle Luke and why. I'm worried about Uncle Luke. I hope I can have time with him before he leaves this earth. They're important to me. I'm anxious to be with family again." He gave her a sheepish grin. "I understand we'll be family soon. Congratulations on your upcoming wedding."

She beamed. "Yes. Danki. I look forward to getting better acquainted. And you'll meet my dochder, Betsy. I'd get her up and introduce her, but I'm afraid she might not be in the best humor. She's just started walking and wears herself out during the day. This is her bedtime."

"I love kinner. We'll have plenty of time to spend together when you move to Millersburg. I look forward to it."

Toby traced the brim of his hat and stood. "Gabe, we should be going. I need to take you to Andrew's to stay for the night, and I'll head home to check on Daed. Do you mind waiting for me at the buggy for a minute?"

"No, I don't mind waiting. It's been a pleasure to meet you, Maryann and Mr. Wenger."

"Call me Shem." He shook Gabe's hand. "Give Andrew our best tomorrow."

Maryann nodded. "Danki for kumming, Gabe. Have a safe trip to Millersburg tomorrow."

He smiled, opened the door, and stepped outside.

Toby frowned and addressed them. "I hope I did the right thing bringing Gabe to you. I was unsure if Andrew told you about him or not. I felt sure you'd want to meet him, whether he did or didn't tell you. I don't want to upset Andrew. Maybe I should've waited and let him tell you about Gabe in his own time."

Maryann gave him a reassuring smile. "Danki for bringing him to us. Gabe seems like a good man. I'd be disappointed to find out he was in town and we didn't get to meet. We're all puzzled Andrew never mentioned him. He'll be surprised we found out about his return before he did. We'll all be curious to find out why he never told us about Gabe."

Toby nodded. "He arrived, expecting to find Andrew, and introduced himself, and we've talked nonstop most of the afternoon. He's easygoing, confident in a good way, and really ready to commit to Amish life. I've enjoyed his company. I don't want to keep him waiting." He smiled and tipped his hat. "Good night."

She waited until their buggy disappeared down the lane and then shut the door.

Daed sat on the edge of his chair. "I'm surprised Andrew kept Gabe from you, considering your history."

"I'm confused and disappointed. Why would Andrew keep Gabe from me? I'm thrilled to meet Gabe, but it concerns me Andrew would keep him or anything from me. I made it clear from the beginning how important it is for us to be open and honest. No secrets." Her stomach churned. She'd been certain they'd shared everything about their past lives. She didn't like discovering she'd been wrong. Andrew should've known from her past history she would've given his bruder the benefit of forgiveness.

"You and he have a lot to discuss. I'm sure he'll have a reasonable explanation." Daed held her hand.

"Will he? Is he hiding anything else from me? I said I wouldn't marry a man who held back things from me. It's unsettling. And this was news I'd been happy and thankful to receive." Maryann got up and paced.

"Maybe it's because Gabe turned in Gerald's murderer."

"Gabe didn't really know Gerald. He was a gambler at

the time. I am glad Gabe had the courage to do what many men in that room probably didn't."

"Don't make any rash decisions. Give Andrew a chance to explain."

"The distance between us makes this more difficult to discuss. Letters take time. Will he return to Charm once he knows I've met Gabe? He should've told me about Gabe and his acquaintance with Gerald, there's no question. But this isn't just about Gabe. It's about him holding back important facts from me. Should I go there? I'd have to ask you or Joel to accompany me. I'm upset and not sure what to do."

Maryann entered the bakery Thursday morning to find Rachael and Magdelena at the counter. Each carried a tray of tarts and apple fritters drizzled with vanilla icing. "I'm sorry I'm late."

Rachael put down the tray and hugged her. "Toby told me about Gabe and that you weren't aware Andrew had a bruder. He really likes him. He's puzzled Andrew didn't mention him. Maybe a little hurt, too. He thought they were close friends. I told Magdelena this morning. Are you upset?"

"Yes, but not at Gabe. His acquaintance with Gerald doesn't matter to me, other than I'm grateful for what he did. It doesn't make sense. I would have understood better than most about Andrew having a bruder who left Amish life. We could've been talking about memories of them growing up, and so much more."

"You'll have plenty of time to share those things with

Andrew once you're married and living in Millersburg near Gabe." Rachael limped to her.

"We would if I end up going to Millersburg. Right now, I'm questioning our future together. I was certain he'd told me everything about himself and his family." She put her hand on Rachael's arm. "Your limp is more exaggerated today. Are you in pain?"

Rachael shook her head. "No, when I'm tired, my leg seems heavier. Since my accident with John a couple years ago, when the robbers chased us to rob us and the wagon fell over on my leg, the pain has lessened. It's mostly heavy and stiff. The pain of John dying in that accident hurts my heart more than the injury to my leg. Maryann, don't be too hard on Andrew. You and Andrew make such a good couple. I would not want you to sever ties with him over a misunderstanding."

"I'm sorry about what happened to you. I'll heed your advice." Maryann gave Rachael's arm a gentle squeeze. Magdelena stood in front of Maryann. "Wait a couple of days. Give Andrew a chance to kumme to Charm. I can't imagine he won't want to explain in person. He'll have an explanation. He loves you. He wouldn't do anything to jeopardize your future together."

Rachael motioned for them to sit at a café table. "You could write to Andrew and ask him why he kept something important from you."

Maryann wrung her hands. "I'd rather speak to him in person."

"Don't overreact. Do what Rachael suggested. Wait a couple of days. If he doesn't kumme to Charm, you can go there. Joel, Toby, or your daed will go with you. Hannah would watch Betsy, and we'll manage the store."

She couldn't damp down the frustration rising. Why had he made this choice? It unnerved her and shook the foundation of the trust she thought they had. "All right. I'll wait."

Andrew grinned at James later Thursday morning. "I've been waiting for you to tell us about your supper with Lena. Don't keep us in suspense. How was it?"

James blushed and shuffled his feet. "Interesting."

"We're going to need more." Matt chuckled.

"She asked me lots of questions, and it overwhelmed me for a couple of minutes. Then she softened her voice and relaxed, and I had a pleasant time with her."

"What questions did she ask?" Andrew wrinkled his forehead.

James scratched his neck and then stared at the floor. "Was I happy in my marriage? My boys' names and ages. Do I want to remarry? Do I want more kinner?"

"She doesn't waste time." Matt cocked his head. "Is she a widow or has she never married?"

"She's an only child, and she's not been married."

"Were her parents with you at supper?" Andrew leaned back on the counter.

It wouldn't be proper for them to dine alone, but they were adults. James's shyness about answering their questions about Lena gave the impression he might like her. The woman had been direct and determined when she asked him to supper. Maybe she had showed him a different and softer side.

"Her parents were kind and quiet. Lena did most of the talking. I told her I had a happy marriage, I'm open to marrying again, and I would consider another child. As I said it, I surprised myself. It wouldn't be fair to a childless woman to say no to more kinner."

"Sounds like you like Lena." Matt winked at James.

"She's kumming to our haus for supper tomorrow night. Jonathan is my oldest, and he likes to cook. He's making vegetable soup and ham sandwiches. She's bringing sugar cookies. I do like her. She struck me as bold when she asked me to supper at our first meeting. When I went to supper at her parents' home, I found her caring and kind. And she makes me laugh." He held up his palms. "She shocked me in a good way."

Andrew grinned. "I hope this works out for you and Lena." He couldn't wait for Maryann and Betsy to join him so he could have suppers with them.

"I hope it works out for you, too." Matt patted James's back.

"Danki." James beamed.

A woman bustled to them. "I'm in need of a dining room set. I'd prefer cherry."

James gestured to the right side of the store. "We have two sets in cherry right in the far corner of the store, if you'd please follow me."

Andrew and Matt slipped into the workshop. "James has a lilt to his step. This is going to be fun to watch."

"I'm jealous. You both have found your true loves. I'm still waiting on the right girl."

"I have no doubt you'll find the perfect one for you when the time is right." Andrew clapped a hand on Matt's shoulder.

* * *

Later in the morning, Andrew studied the dresser he'd finished for Gertie and Fred Nolan. "I was afraid I wouldn't get this done in time. The Nolans were insistent on picking this piece up today."

Matt whistled. "You did a nice job. Cherrywood was an excellent selection for it. They'll be pleased. I'll help you carry it out to the front. We can put it aside for them."

"Danki." Andrew and Matt picked up the dresser and carried it to the front. They put it down and Andrew's mouth gaped open.

"Gabe!" He ran and embraced him.

Gabe wrapped his arms around him. "Good to see you, bruder."

Andrew separated from him. His bruder was safe and appeared healthy. Would he stay? Where had he been? "Matt, James, this is my bruder, Gabe. It's been a long time since we've been together."

"Pleasure to meet you." Matt shook his hand.

James smiled. "You two resemble each other. Same hair, eyes, and mischievous grin."

Matt said, "I'm sure you have a lot to talk about. We'll give you privacy." He went to the counter with James.

Andrew gestured to the workshop, and they sat on stools. "I have a mountain of questions. I don't know where to start. Are you passing through or back for good?" It was a relief Gabe was safe and he appeared healthy and happy. Memories of their childhood skipped through Andrew's mind. They'd been close, and he'd missed him. He'd never stopped praying for him, and he'd finally accepted Gabe might not write or visit him again.

"I'm staying with you. I'm through with the outside

world. I'm committed to God and Amish life." Gabe grinned wide.

"I'm thrilled you're going to stay. Did you get the forwarding address I left with the postmaster for you?"

"I could tell you'd moved from our home when I passed by. Another family had hung their name outside. I got your forwarding address to Charm from the postmaster. I arrived and met Toby. He told me you moved to Millersburg and why. I stayed at your place last night, got up this morning, and drove straight to the shop. I wanted to speak to you first, before Aunt Dora and Uncle Luke."

Andrew sucked in a breath. "Toby must've been surprised to meet you." He should've told Toby about Gabe. He might be hurt to find out this way.

"Yes, he said you hadn't mentioned me. From the way he praised you, I got the impression you'd become friends. Why didn't you tell him about me?"

He read the disappointment in Gabe's face. "I now regret not telling him."

"And Maryann." Gabe raised his gaze to meet Andrew's.

"You met Maryann?" He gulped air. What must she think? He wouldn't have liked it if she'd kept information like this from him. Gabe's last letter to him about what happened with him and Gerald flashed in his mind. He hadn't expected Gabe to return. He couldn't stand what Gerald had put Maryann through with his bad decisions. Gabe's interaction with the man wasn't worth mentioning. He cringed. With Gabe's return, he regretted this. He'd sure made a mess of things.

"Toby told me about her. I said I'd met her late husband and I wanted to meet her. He took me there." He sighed. "She was taken aback, not having been told about me. She and her daed wilkomed me and were warm and friendly. I like them. She's upset and rightfully so. You'll need to explain to her why you didn't mention me. Why didn't you?"

Andrew sighed and shook his head. "I'm sorry. It was wrong of me. I didn't expect you'd return. Your letters had stopped. I had no idea where you were or what you were up to. I'm protective of her. If I brought you up, I'd have had to bring up Gerald. It didn't seem relevant to bring up the past and your minor interaction with her late husband. She's been through enough. It had nothing to do with us. I wanted a fresh start. I chose to practice the Amish way and not mention you."

"You should've been honest with her from the start. I don't want a fraa who wouldn't share everything with me, let alone something like this. Secrets are destructive."

"In hindsight, I agree with you. Maybe I was protecting myself. It hurt to talk about you and not know if I would ever see you again. I made it easier on me. Now she'll question if I'll keep other secrets, and she made it clear we were to share everything. I'm in trouble with her for sure." He'd assumed Gabe was lost to him in the outside world. He'd accepted his bruder had chosen a life without him. It hurt for a long time. Maybe it had been easier to bury the hurt and not talk about him.

Gabe gazed at him. "This decision could cost you. I'm sorry I am the reason for this secret, but she's got to wonder what else you're holding back."

"Nothing! This is it. I'll go to Charm and explain. I didn't mean to hurt her or you." Andrew wished he could turn back the clock. He'd been upfront with her about everything. He was ashamed he'd given up on Gabe and for disappointing Maryann.

"It sounds like as long as I was out of sight, I was out of mind." Gabe stared at his bruder.

Andrew shook his head. "Not true. I told you I prayed for you each day." He should've had more faith Gabe would change his life.

"I don't mean to be so hard on you. I want you happy, and with Maryann. She's someone I'd like to have for a schweschder-in-law from the little time I spent with her. I'm sorry I caused you trouble by exploring my selfish desires and leaving Amish life. I left you alone to fend for yourself on the farm. Forgive me?"

"Yes. I forgive you. Forgive me?" He would've been crushed to learn Gabe had kept him a secret from the woman he loved, if the situation had been reversed.

"Of course. Would you like me to go with you to visit Maryann, for support? We got along well."

"No. This is bigger than me not telling her about you. I have to convince her she can trust me to not keep things from her in the future. To her, the most important thing in a marriage is honesty and full disclosure. I'm worried I've destroyed this for her. I pray she'll forgive me and believe I won't do this again." He rubbed the tension in his neck. "I'll leave early tomorrow."

"I pray you and Maryann can work through this."

"Me too." He patted Gabe on the back. "On a more pleasant note, we'll have to get Aunt Dora to sew you some Amish clothes. Until then, you're wilkom to wear mine. They should fit."

Andrew's stomach whirled with regret. Maryann might never trust him again. He hoped things would go as well with her as they had with Gabe. "Aunt Dora and Uncle Luke will be ecstatic when we walk inside the haus together. You'll be an instant shot of joy for Uncle Luke, in spite of his pain." His eyes dampened. "Wilkom home, bruder. I couldn't be happier to have you back."

Gabe shook his head. "How are they doing?"

"Uncle Luke isn't the robust man you remember. He's skin and bones, has a gray pallor, and has a raspy voice. I miss his pleasant voice." He frowned. "He says the doctor isn't sure what's wrong. His mind's sharp, and Aunt Dora is sweet and helpful, as always. You'll boost their moods."

"Do you think it'll be all right if I live there with all of you?"

"Yes. There's plenty of room. Aunt Dora will insist you stay with us. You remember. They have a big haus, and it has four bedrooms." Andrew studied Gabe. "How are your handcrafting skills?"

"Improved. I've built pieces for furniture stores while I've been away, including special pieces for friends who paid me. I'd love to work in this shop."

Andrew grinned. "Wonderful! Do you mind starting work tomorrow? You can build furniture with Matt. We're working as hard as we can to fill the store with more of our products and fewer consigned pieces. You'll be a big help to us."

"Do you plan to no longer take items from consignors in the future?"

"We won't take in as much from them, but we'll accept their products. I want to help them out. They've been loyal to the store."

Gabe nodded. "Good. I appreciated being a consignor to shops during my time away. And it produces goodwill in the community. You take all the time you need in Charm. The outcome from your trip will determine your future. I'll help with the store and Uncle Luke."

"Danki, bruder." Andrew's chest ached.

He wasn't sure they could recover from his mistake. Maryann had every right to question him, given what he'd done. He hadn't intended to hurt her. Could he convince her to trust him again?

Chapter Eleven

Maryann yawned and stretched her arms at the bakery early Friday morning. She hadn't slept much last night.

Dr. Harrison and the sheriff slid onto their usual stools at the counter. You could set your clock by their morning arrival.

Dr. Harrison quirked his brow. "Do you have hot tea?"

"Yes. Would you like honey in it?" She poured him a cup.

"A teaspoon, please."

She drizzled the spoonful in his tea.

"What about you, Sheriff?"

He grinned and peered over his paper. "I won't be as much trouble as my friend." He rolled his eyes at Dr. Harrison. "I'll take coffee."

Dr. Harrison shot him a disgusted glance. "You often have a laundry list of requests for your dessert. A drizzle, not a lot, of icing on your pastries. Warm, not too hot, cocoa. Should I go on?"

"Please don't. I still say I'm not as bad as you." The sheriff guffawed. "I'll have two raspberry jam pastries."

She smacked her hand on the counter and grinned. "I don't mind special requests."

"Thank you, Maryann." He wrinkled his nose at Dr. Harrison and then faced her.

"I'll take the same." Dr. Harrison lifted his paper. He pointed to an article for the sheriff. "This is tragic. Yesterday, seventeen soldiers with the Austria-Hungary Empire were killed during maneuvers on Ortler."

"Where is Ortler? What happened?" Sheriff Williams squinted. "I can't read it from over here."

"An avalanche. Ortler is the highest mountain in the Eastern Alps. I'd have never made it doing this maneuver. I wouldn't like climbing mountains. The weather would be a challenge in itself."

Maryann's heart hurt for the soldiers' families and for the men in charge who would have to notify them. She liked it when there was cheerful and interesting news, but not news like this. The two friends took her mind off her displeasure with Andrew as they teased, laughed, and discussed world events until they left.

She grabbed a rag and washed crumbs from the counter. Andrew and Gabe would reunite today. She liked Gabe, and he had some of the same mannerisms as Andrew, especially his kind, wide smile. Gabe impressed her. He'd exposed Gerald's murderer and might have saved other lives from such a dangerous man by putting him behind bars. She prayed his transition back to Amish life would be easy. She was sure Andrew and his family would support him, like her family had with her.

Rachael and Magdelena walked in the front door. Magdelena held up a bag. "We're back. We brought you a treat from the general store."

Maryann loved them for trying to cheer her. "Peppermint candy?"

"Yes." Rachael took the bag and opened it. She held a

piece in her fingers. "Open your mouth, and I'll set one on your tongue."

Maryann opened her mouth, and Rachael set a peppermint on her tongue. "Danki."

The door opened, and Andrew entered. Maryann gasped.

Magdelena and Rachael greeted him and scampered to the kitchen.

"Andrew, I'm shocked and glad you're here." Maryann wanted to run into his arms, but the other part of her wanted to shout at him.

"I'd like to explain about Gabe and convince you I'll not hold anything back from you again. I realize the bakery isn't the ideal place for our conversation. I planned to wait until you were home, but I couldn't let another minute go by without talking to you face-to-face."

"We don't have customers right now. Let's go to the storeroom. I'll ask Rachael to manage the counter." She went to the kitchen. "Rachael, Andrew and I are going to talk in the storeroom. Do you mind moving to the front for a couple of minutes?"

"Sure." Rachael bustled to the front.

Maryann and Andrew went to the storeroom. She left the door open.

Andrew faced her. "I'm sorry. I should've told you about Gabe."

Maryann toyed with the corner of her apron. Those brown eyes of his were hard to resist. She'd missed him. The sound of his voice made her heart skip a beat. She loved him more than she cared to admit at the moment. "I bared my soul to you. I assumed you did the same. I said no secrets. I trusted you didn't keep any. There was no need for you to withhold anything from me. Let alone Gabe. I treasured this about us. I emphasized the importance of honesty between us. You communicated with me better than any man I've ever known. Why did you keep this from me?"

"I didn't expect this day to kumme. I was foolish. If I mentioned Gabe, I had to tell you about his connection to Gerald. My fresh start in Charm included one with you. I regret the decision I made. I understand why you're upset with me. Please remember I love you and I'll not keep things from you again. Please, Maryann, don't let this ruin our future."

Maryann met his gaze and then wrenched her gaze from his. "I was convinced you and I understood each other about having clear communication. I had no idea you would keep anything from me. It hurts. If you'd have told me about Gabe and Gerald's acquaintance and what happened, I'd have been surprised but thankful to Gabe. Your bruder's return is a joyous occasion. We should be celebrating together instead of having this conversation. This is what secrets do. They tear couples apart."

Andrew nodded and clutched his hat to his chest. His eyes were filled with regret. "You're right. What can I say or do?"

"I was secure with you. I was convinced you and I had a unique bond. It's no longer true. I want to forgive you and let it go, but I can't. This sick feeling inside won't subside. It's finding out you withheld significant information from me that I can't get past." Tears dampened her cheeks.

"Do you have other important information you've neglected to mention?" She didn't know if her heart could handle it if he did. More than anything, she wanted to get past her endless trust issues. This was Andrew, not Gerald. Her past with Gerald was hurting her ability to move on with her life and her relationship with Andrew.

"No, and moving forward, I'll not keep things from you. Please believe me."

"I forgive you, but I need time. I don't know how to get over this." She fought the sob in her throat and swallowed. No matter how much she loved him, she wasn't sure she wouldn't always wonder if he was holding things back from her. She sighed. Would her future always be ruled by her past with Gerald? What if they ran into financial or other problems? Would he rationalize not telling her things that might upset her?

"What can I do to convince you I'm sincere?" His pleading eyes gazed into hers.

"I want to fix this, but I'm not sure how to get past it." She swallowed the bile rising in her throat.

Andrew covered her hand. "I'm truly sorry. We must overcome this. I love you."

"I have no doubt your apology is sincere. I'm miserable letting you go. But I vowed not to marry another man who didn't treat me as a partner. You should've trusted me enough to know telling me Gabe's story wouldn't have mattered."

"I do trust you. You are my partner. Can you admit you love me?" Andrew pleaded. "At least give me that much hope."

"Yes. I love you. If I didn't, I wouldn't be upset. Love isn't enough. I learned this lesson when I married Gerald. You had me convinced we'd built a firm foundation for a marriage and future, until this. Please give me time."

"I'll leave, but I urge you to reconsider your decision. We grew a friendship, which blossomed into a long-lasting love and respect for each other. I promise you we can have the future you desire." He walked to the door and glanced over his shoulder. "I love you, Maryann. I always will."

* * *

Andrew willed his knees not to buckle as he left. Maryann had been through her share of heartache, and he had been a fool to assume she'd pardon him after one conversation. She might never agree to marry him, and he'd never forgive himself for making such a bad decision.

He got in his buggy and headed for his home in Charm. He should check on Toby. He stared at the road ahead. He'd do anything to earn back Maryann's trust. He'd never keep anything from her again. He wasn't sure he'd get the chance to show her this. He drove down the lane and waved to Toby kumming out the front door.

Toby and a black-and-white fluffy dog met him in front of the barn.

He pulled the buggy next to them and jumped out. "Toby, you have a new friend."

"Andrew! Great to have you in Charm. Greetings." Toby slapped him on the shoulder. "Meet Patches."

Andrew petted the dog. "Where's Pepper?"

Toby frowned. "A coyote attacked and killed him."

"Oh no! I'm sorry to hear this."

"Danki. Magdelena's dog had a litter, and she gave one to our family. Patches reminds me of Pepper with his sweet disposition. Easy to train, he's a good pup. Patches took to my parents and Rachael right away."

"I'm glad Magdelena gave you Patches."

Toby cocked his head. "You must be happy to have Gabe home."

"I'm thrilled, and so are Aunt Dora and Uncle Luke."

"Why didn't you tell any of us you had a bruder?"

Andrew ached at the sincerity and disappointment in Toby's eyes. He'd never considered the negative impact his keeping this inside would have on Gabe, Toby, Maryann, and his friends. He was sick he'd disappointed all of them. What a hard lesson to learn. "Let's go inside, and I'll explain. It's chilly." Andrew crossed the yard and went inside the haus to the warm kitchen.

"I've got coffee on the stove." Toby removed two mugs from a stand on the counter and poured coffee in them. He passed one to Andrew and sat across from him at the table.

Patches settled at Toby's feet.

"I doubted Gabe would return to Amish life. He's adventuresome. He makes friends easily, and he's responsible and hardworking. He could make a living and survive in the outside world. I worried he'd be drawn to the greed, conveniences, and unacceptable things we Amish avoid. He stopped sending letters before I moved to Charm, and I'd given up on ever seeing him again. I didn't want to explain about him."

"I'm your friend. You couldn't tell me?"

"I apologize, Toby. You're right. I regret not telling you, Maryann, and her family. You're my close friend. Please don't hold this against me. I used bad judgment. Gabe sharing a gambling table with Gerald has nothing to do with me. It wasn't a subject I cared to address with Maryann, since I thought she'd put the past behind her. I didn't omit my having a bruder to deceive anyone. I just wanted a fresh start."

"A bruder is important information to keep to yourself." Toby frowned.

"I realize this was wrong of me and to keep it from Maryann was wrong. Not talking about Gabe has gotten me into more trouble than I could've imagined. I thought I was doing the right thing, following Amish tradition in not speaking about those who have left our community to live in the outside world. But not telling those I love and care about is another matter."

Toby scratched Patches behind his ears. "I can respect your position."

Andrew sipped his coffee and held his mug. "Danki. Your friendship means a lot to me."

"I would assume you went straight to the bakery when you got to town. Did you and Maryann have a chance to talk? The bakery might not have been the best place." Toby winced.

"I did go straight to the bakery. We had some privacy, and I explained the best I could about why I chose not to mention Gabe and his connection to Gerald, and I apologized. She is upset I kept an important fact like this from her. She doubts me. She wants a partner who will be upfront and honest. I would never withhold anything like this again from her, and this is all I have withheld from her. I pleaded with her to forgive me and to give me another chance."

Toby leaned forward. "What did she say?"

Andrew slumped in his seat. "She needs time. She isn't sure she can't let this go. I'm sick about it. There's nothing more I can say or do. I've ruined any chance of a future with her. I'd give anything to fix it." He would take a long time to heal from this heartbreak, and he was sure this would always be his biggest regret.

"You must give Maryann time. You withheld information about someone near and dear to you. It's a big part of your life you didn't share with her. She assumed she was the most important person in your life. Trust and communication make for a happy and healthy marriage. My parents have it. I want it when I marry." Toby gave him a sympathetic smile. "She'll want to forgive you. Will she in the end? I'm not sure. Pray about it. God will intervene if it's His will you and she should wed." Toby gave him a sympathetic nod.

"For not having time to consider a woman, you are a wise man. Sounds like your parents set a good example for you. My parents did for Gabe and me, and I didn't follow it. The cost of this mistake is immeasurable. I pray I don't lose her for good." Andrew rubbed the ache in his neck. He couldn't get her utter disappointment in him out of his mind. It shattered his soul.

"I, Maryann, her family, and our friends care about you. It hurt you didn't tell me, but I accept why. For Maryann, it's a much harder decision. She isn't going to overlook this overnight."

"Should I go to Shem and ask for his help? Should I apologize to him?" Andrew didn't want Shem upset with him. He'd admit his mistake and make it clear he didn't mean any harm.

"Maybe you should talk to him. Go there before Maryann is off work." Toby heaved a big sigh. "I'm sorry you're going through this. I wish there was something I could do to help you."

"Your understanding and advice are much appreciated." He scanned the room. "Have you had any offers on the haus?" He'd liked the layout, and before his uncle had contacted him, he'd envisioned his life with Maryann and kinner in the future filling the house with laughter, love, and overcoming struggles together. He'd hoped to have a new life in Millersburg with her and Betsy in a similar haus. She didn't leave him with any hope for this.

"No. I'll let you know right away when I do get an offer."

Andrew rose and pushed his seat back. "Danki for your

understanding and for your help with this place. I'm glad you and Gabe had a chance to meet. He had nothing but good things to say about you. I should head over to Shem's and then travel back to Millersburg."

Toby slapped him on the back. "Gabe seems like an upstanding man. I enjoyed having some time with him." He smiled. "I'll pray for you, my friend, and travel safe."

Andrew reached in a satchel on the chair and removed an envelope. He passed it to Toby. "This is for you. Again, danki for everything."

Toby nodded. "You're wilkom. Let me know if there's anything I can do, and danki for this." He flashed an encouraging smile and squeezed Andrew's shoulder.

Andrew left and drove his buggy to Shem's. He knocked on the door.

Shem widened his eyes. "Andrew! Kumme in."

"Shem, happy to see you." Andrew sat on the settee. "A lot has happened while I've been away, and I owe you an explanation." Andrew took off his hat and enjoyed the warmth kumming from the wood burning in the fireplace.

"I met Gabe. He's a delightful fellow. I'm baffled why you wouldn't tell us about him." Shem tilted his head. "Have you talked to Maryann? She's owed the explanation from you." Shem settled back in the chair and crossed his legs.

Andrew fidgeted with his hat. "Yes, I've told her. I made an error in judgment. She said we should share everything. I didn't. She's having a hard time forgiving me."

"We all make mistakes. She loves you. Be patient." Shem folded his hands on his lap.

"Will you talk to her on my behalf? She respects you."

Shem scratched the back of his neck. "You've opened up an old wound from her past. Gerald kept important information from her and left her out of decisions. She longed for a partnership like she was sure she had with you." He rubbed his palms together. "I believe you're truly remorseful for this. I'll talk to her. I can't promise you anything."

Andrew shook his hand. "Understood. Danki. Again, I apologize for the upheaval I've caused. I love your dochder."

"I can tell, and I pray I'll be attending your wedding in May." Shem patted his arm.

Andrew's heart sank as he left Charm and began the drive to Millersburg. He wondered what Ellie and Joel and her friends would say. He worried some might encourage her to cancel their wedding plans. He'd compromised his integrity. One bad decision had caused serious damage.

Almost three hours later, he arrived and shivered against the cold from the still wintery weather they were having in March. He took his horse to the livery and paid the livery owner to give his horse food and water. Then he went to the furniture store and walked inside. Gabe was engaged in conversation with a couple. James accepted payment for two nightstands from an older gentleman.

Andrew smiled. "I'll help you out with these."

The gray-haired man twisted his mustache. "Thank you, kind sir."

James picked up the other piece. "I'll carry this one." He nodded to Andrew. "Good to have you back."

"Danki." Andrew carried the furniture to the patron's wagon and lifted it into the back. He assisted James in adding the second one. They spread an old tattered quilt over the pieces and used rope to tie them in place.

The man waved his hand. "Thank you again."

They watched the man leave.

James opened the door for him. "I didn't expect you to return. You left early and in a hurry. Is everything all right?"

He shook his head. "I'm in huge trouble with Maryann." He told him about his not mentioning Gabe, and her reaction to his apology and explanation.

"I'm sorry, Andrew. I'll remember you and Maryann in my prayers."

"I appreciate it."

Gabe bid farewell to his customers and approached Andrew and James. "You didn't have to rush back. Your droopy eyes and shoulders tell me things didn't go well."

Matt met them in front of the counter. "You're back. What didn't go well?"

Andrew explained what happened in Charm.

"I'm sorry." Gabe shook his head.

"She's disappointed and hurt, and I understand why. I must accept the consequences of my poor decision. If Maryann severs ties with me for good, I don't imagine I'll get over her. She's the one for me, and she has been since the day I met her. I pray she forgives me and gives me another chance." Andrew pressed his palms together.

"Don't be hard on yourself, and don't speculate. Maryann may kumme around." Matt gave him an encouraging nod.

James pointed to the oak wall clock. "Andrew needs some rest. It's past time to lock up and go home, gentlemen."

Andrew yawned and stretched his arms. "I've traveled six hours today. I'm exhausted."

Gabe grabbed his coat and shrugged it on. "I'll pray for you and Maryann. Get a good night's sleep."

Andrew walked out with Gabe and his friends, locked the door, and went to his buggy. He bid Matt and James farewell, followed Gabe home, went inside, and told his aunt and uncle what had taken place when he confessed the truth to Maryann and begged for her forgiveness.

Uncle Luke sat in his chair. His favorite tattered quilt covered and overpowered his small body. "Have faith. You never expected Gabe to show up. Miracles happen. I couldn't be happier having the two of you here and working in the store."

Aunt Dora put her hands to her cheeks. "Listen to your uncle Luke. Don't give up. God always has a plan, but we may not know what it is. Have faith." She squeezed Andrew's hand. "I wish it wasn't so complicated for you and Maryann. Your uncle and I are here for you, and we're thrilled you're both with us. We never imagined we'd be so blessed. I've got supper ready. Let's go to the table."

Aunt Dora served them chicken pot pie, biscuits, and apple butter.

Andrew and his family bowed their heads, thanked God for providing them with food to eat, and turned to Gabe. "How do you like working at the store?"

"I love it. Matt and James are pleasant fellows, and I enjoy their company." Gabe snapped his suspenders. "Danki for the clothes. They fit."

"I thought I recognized those clothes. They look good on you." Andrew snatched a biscuit.

Aunt Dora dipped her biscuit in the apple butter on her plate. "I hope you don't mind. I had washed those, and instead of putting them in your clothespress, I passed them to Gabe."

"I don't mind. Help yourself to any of my clothes." Andrew smiled.

"I'll make more clothes for you over the next couple of days." Aunt Dora put another biscuit on Andrew's plate.

Andrew enjoyed having his family together. He struggled not to let his mind wander to Maryann and what she might be thinking. Would Shem encourage her to give him a chance, or wait? He forked a bite of his serving of chicken pot pie. His impatience and worry consumed him.

Gabe polished off half of his pot pie. "I lived in Lexington, Kentucky, for a couple of months. I met Sally Butterfield. We went on picnics and buggy rides each day for two weeks. I fell in love with her after our first day together. She has golden blond hair and the bluest eyes." He sighed.

"What happened?" Aunt Dora held her biscuit in midair.

"She broke my heart." He heaved another big sigh.

"How?" Uncle Luke's hand quivered as he lifted his fork to his mouth.

"I went to pick her up for a dance in town, and she wasn't there. I'd had a friend teach me a few steps, and I had practiced at home to impress her. Her daed said she was already at the dance with another chap. I walked into the hall, and she ignored me. When the music ended, I approached her and the man. I asked if we could have a word in private."

"What did she say?" Aunt Dora's eyes widened.

"She motioned to the side of the room. She told her beau she'd be back in a couple of minutes. She explained they had been engaged but he had left town. He had returned and begged her forgiveness. He'd proposed again, and she'd accepted. She said his family owned a big horse farm and he had a lot more financial security to offer. She said she loved me, but not as much as she loved him and his money. I left town the next day and went to Massillon."

"What a story!" Dora reared back and gasped. "Did you meet another girl while you were gone?"

"No. Sally caused me to question my judgment about Englisch women. Her greed was an unwilkom revelation. Later, I started to consider returning to Amish life. I would've closed that door if I'd married an Englischer. I avoided women showing me attention. I didn't want to put my heart out there, but I'm ready now if the right one kummes along. I'm hoping I meet a sweet Amish girl like Maryann. I want a woman to take my breath away and make me forget all about Sally." He gave a weak grin to Andrew. "I'm not a stranger to heartbreak. I can empathize with you."

Uncle Luke put down his fork. "Dora and I hit it off from the get-go. She's my first and only love. I pray you both find a woman like her. We've had our ups and downs, but nothing we couldn't get past. We made a pact not to go to bed angry."

Dora pressed both hands to her chest. "It's true. I've loved him most of my life. Grew up together and never considered another man. Best decision I ever made. We did stay up late some nights until we settled an argument or two. But I wouldn't change a thing."

Andrew wanted their kind of love. He prayed Maryann would get past that he'd let her down. He longed for a future with her and Betsy.

Gabe assisted Uncle Luke to his chair.

Andrew carried the dishes to the sink for Aunt Dora. "I'll wash."

"No. You've had a long, rough day. Go to your room, shut your eyes, and get some sleep."

He wouldn't argue. He couldn't wait to rest, although sleep might be a challenge. He padded through the living room. "Good night, Uncle Luke and Gabe. I'm turning in early." He went to his bedroom.

Gabe pushed Andrew's bedroom door open. "Can we talk a minute?"

"Sure." Andrew sat on the side of the bed.

Gabe pulled a chair in front of him and sat. "Should I go talk to her?"

Andrew shook his head. "I appreciate your willingness to intervene. Let's give her time."

"The offer stands. If you change your mind, I'll go."

"Danki. Not right now." He didn't want to talk or think about all he'd lost with Maryann. He needed to change the subject. He slapped Gabe's knee. "Isn't the store a great place?"

"I love it. The store is big, the workshop is organized, and the counter is just the right size. Matt and James are likeable and hard workers." Gabe gazed at him.

"Yes, the store is making a profit, and we'll make more money with your extra set of hands building furniture. We've got the space, and it will be wonderful to fill it." He never expected he'd be discussing the store with Gabe. His stomach danced with happiness at having him in this haus, working at the store, and having this conversation. He could use the help. The more hands to build furniture to sell, the more profit they'd make for the store rather than depending on consigners for a good bit of their stock.

Gabe winced. "Aunt Dora said I've got to have a sit-down with Bishop Detweiler. I'm nervous about it."

"Would you like me to go with you?" Andrew didn't want anything to get in the way of Gabe's staying in Millersburg and following through on his commitment to God and Amish life. He wanted to support and encourage him. He wished he knew the bishop better. Aunt Dora and

Uncle Luke praised him, so he was sure Gabe's meeting with him would go well.

"No, you have enough on your plate. I'll make a better impression if I go alone." Gabe stood. "I'm ready to call it a day, and you must be tired from traveling. Good night. Get some sleep."

"Danki. See you in the morning." He waited until Gabe left and then fell on his back onto the bed and stared at the ceiling. Having Gabe back had opened one door, and then another door closed—Maryann rejecting him. Were he and Maryann supposed to wed? He believed so. He prayed for God to forgive him and to intervene on his behalf with Maryann. He gripped the coverlet. He hoped Maryann would find it in her heart to forgive him.

Andrew sat at the breakfast table and glanced at Uncle Luke Saturday morning. His uncle had dark circles under his eyes, and he'd pushed his full plate of food aside. His health seemed to be failing, and it was a constant concern to him, his aunt, and Gabe.

Gabe scooped out a spoonful of peach jam. "I'm going to the bishop's haus today and tell him why I'm back. I suspect he'll want to meet with me in private for a series of sessions to make sure I'm committed to God and Amish life. I'll do what he asks." He cleared his throat. "Then I've got to make a trip. I've got my bag packed. I'll be gone for a couple of days. Please don't ask me any questions. There's no need for concern. I'll tell you all about it when I return."

Aunt Dora squeezed Gabe's arm. "Bishop Detweiler is a wise and understanding man. You'll like him. Please be careful as you travel. We'll look forward to your return."

Uncle Luke waved a trembling hand. "Please take care of yourself."

Andrew cupped his warm mug of coffee. "Let me kumme with you."

Gabe shook his head. "No, it's something I must take care of. I'm not in trouble. I'll tell you more when I return." He kissed Dora on the cheek, patted Uncle Luke on the shoulder, and nodded to Andrew. "I'll be back soon." He pushed the door open and shut it behind him.

Uncle Luke wiped a tear. "I'm grateful to God for bringing my nephews to us before I leave this earth. It's been a precious time to have you both with me. An unexpected blessing."

Andrew's uncle had been supportive, caring, and an excellent example for him. He didn't want to lose him. "We're blessed to have you in our lives." Andrew took his plate to the sink. "I'd better get to work." He bid them farewell, got his buggy ready, and drove to the shop. He crossed the road from the livery. What was Gabe up to? He'd noticed the worry in his family's faces. He shared their concern, but Gabe didn't need their permission. He was a grown man. Curious about his bruder's sudden trip, his questions would have to wait.

The newsboy raised the paper above his head. "Read all about it! The first scheduled airline may be going out of business! You don't want to miss this news about the St. Petersburg–Tampa Airboat Line! Buy your paper now!"

Andrew had overheard Englischers talking about this. The airline covered eighteen miles and it took twenty-three minutes between St. Petersburg, Florida, to Tampa. Much faster than traveling by train. His family had traveled by train to visit close friends when he was a boy, and he liked it. The train had been acceptable for a long-distance trip.

Would Maryann like to take a trip on a train someday? An airplane would be acceptable, but probably not affordable. He wondered what it would be like to travel by airplane.

Andrew worked throughout the day at the shop, but he couldn't take his mind off Gabe. He wondered how his meeting with the bishop had been. It was obvious from Gabe's demeanor he'd given up living in the outside world. The bishop had most likely assigned him scriptures to guide him back into Amish life.

He grinned. Gabe had asked him question after question about the business. He'd review the financial and supply records with Gabe and teach him all aspects of running the shop when he returned. They'd make a good team. He prayed Gabe was safe and hadn't had to visit someone from his past who would cause him trouble.

Chapter Twelve

Maryann mopped the floor in the kitchen Saturday evening. Betsy had spilled her small cup of milk. She poked her head into the living room. "Daed, would you like another cup of coffee? Is Betsy behaving?"

"No, dear, and Betsy and I are fine."

Betsy toddled to him and bounced her block on his leg. "Play? Pop. Pop."

"Not right now, sweetheart."

Betsy whimpered and rubbed her eyes. She tugged at her socks, pulled them off, and threw them. "No. No."

"She's acting cranky. I should put her to bed." Maryann crossed the room and scooped her up.

"No. No. Bed." Betsy shook her head and wiggled in Maryann's arms.

"Stop whining or I won't read you a story." Maryann squinted her eyes and pinched her lips.

Betsy rested her head against Maryann's shoulder and settled.

"She doesn't want to miss her bedtime story. That always seems to work." Daed chuckled.

Maryann leaned Betsy over to Daed. "Hug Pop good night."

Betsy hugged his neck and then whimpered in Maryann's arms.

Maryann took her to her bedroom. She changed her, rocked her, and read her a story. Then she sang to her until she fell asleep. She had her daed in Betsy's life, but Andrew and her daed would have been better. She still couldn't squelch the doubt and disappointment she wanted to shove out of her mind.

She rejoined her daed. "Betsy was fussy tonight."

"She has bad days sometimes, like the rest of us." Daed closed his Holy Bible.

Sometimes she wondered if Betsy sensed she was upset since Andrew left. Her dochder had adored him. Maybe she missed him, too. She stood. "Someone's at the door. It's an odd hour for company." She opened the door and gasped. "Gabe, is everything all right? Please kumme in."

He stepped inside. "I've got to talk to you." Gabe removed his hat and traced the rim.

She pointed to the chair. He wore Amish clothes.

Shem stood and offered his hand. "It's good to have you, Gabe. I hope everything is all right."

Gabe shook Daed's hand and sat on the settee. "I had to kumme and speak to Maryann on Andrew's behalf." He shifted his body to face her. "Andrew is miserable and full of remorse. As his bruder, it's difficult to watch him beat himself up over losing you. You and I agree he handled this all wrong, but he's remorseful. Please reconsider."

Maryann sat back in the chair. "Gabe, I appreciate you kumming on Andrew's behalf. I forgive him. I'm struggling to let go of the worry he'll keep things from me in the future. I'm afraid my past with Gerald has made me overprotective of myself. I'm trying to sort it out."

Gabe held out his palm. "You should believe him. He's proven to you he's a good man. He just used bad judgment, but he didn't do it to hurt you. Quite the opposite. He didn't want to dredge up the past." He inhaled a big breath. "Andrew isn't aware I'm in Charm. I told him I had to take a trip and I'd explain why when I returned."

"You're a good bruder. I'm glad you've reunited with Andrew. And I'm glad we met. It's been a blessing. Marriage is work. Trust, communication, commitment, and respect are important to help it to succeed. Andrew has made me doubt he can carry through with trust and communication. The sick feeling in my stomach won't leave, and my mind won't let me erase it. I want to overlook it, but I'm having a difficult time with it."

"You have every right to be upset. Time sometimes does heal wounds, but it can also be a detriment. The problem can grow and the water gets muddy when we let our past experiences affect our future. Don't confuse your frustration with Gerald and put it on Andrew. Consider why you fell in love with him. He still possesses those good traits. No one is perfect. But I can assure you, he desperately wants to win you back. He's learned a valuable lesson."

Shem nodded in agreement with Gabe. "Listen to the man, Maryann."

Maryann gave him an apologetic glance. "I promise you, Gabe. I'm praying about it. I do love Andrew."

Gabe clutched his hat. "Andrew and I were close while we grew up together. I was curious about automobiles, trains, the latest inventions, and world news. He had his nose in the Holy Bible more often than me, and he didn't waver from being committed to God and Amish life and hard work. He took care of me until I left. I may be prejudiced, being his bruder, but he's one of the best men I know. He's reliable and strives to do what's right. Don't rob yourself and Betsy of having a wonderful life with Andrew."

Shem studied him. "You're a loyal man to do this for him. I admire you for kumming here."

Maryann pressed a hand to her chest. "You warm my heart for what you're trying to do. Andrew is a wonderful man in many regards. But I'm afraid my past with Gerald has made me afraid to trust Andrew again. Maybe I'm being too hard on him. I may need to grow from this and realize I can't let my past dictate my future over one poor decision on Andrew's part."

"It's late and I've said what I came to say." Gabe took long strides to the door. He put on his hat. "Maryann, please don't let Andrew go, over one mistake. His love is fierce, his loyalty is like no other, and his devotion is immeasurable." He sighed. "I'm staying for the service tomorrow. I'll leave Monday."

Shem stood and nodded. "Gabe, I'll see you at the service. Kumme over and visit tomorrow. We'd love to have you." He yawned. "Time for me to go to bed." He padded down the hall and left them alone.

"Daed's right. It will be wonderful to have you at the service, and please follow us home afterward and visit. We enjoy your company."

"I'll take you up on your offer. I'd like to play with Betsy." He tipped his hat, went outside, and got in his buggy. Maryann watched him leave, then shut the door when his buggy turned down the lane. She sat in a chair and stared at the ceiling. She agreed with Gabe. All the things he said about Andrew were true. She couldn't have put it better before all this happened. Was she letting

Gerald's bad judgments keep her from trusting Andrew over one poor decision? She wanted to think she'd put the past behind her. Was she being fair to Andrew?

Maryann held Betsy on her lap during the Sunday service at the Masts' home. She smiled at Gabe and Toby. They seemed really comfortable with each other.

The bishop said, "In the Holy Bible in Luke, we are reminded God is merciful to us and we should be merciful to others. We tend to guard our hearts when someone has hurt us. We should forgive them, but we sometimes put a wall up or we sever ties with them to protect ourselves. It's easier than having to work at it. We say we forgive them, but we hold on to the transgression. We hurt God over and over by being too busy to pray or to read the Holy Bible or when He convicts us to do something and we ignore Him. He's there for us no matter. Are you robbing yourself of the joy of someone's friendship and love today over a mistake they've made and which you've placed too much importance on? If the situation were reversed, would they treat you as you have treated them?"

Maryann's heart pounded, and she slid down in her seat a couple of inches. Had Gabe, Daed, or her friends talked to the bishop? Had they prompted him to aim this message at her? She swallowed around the guilt in her throat. The bishop's message had pinpointed what was disturbing her. Had she been so busy blaming Andrew that she hadn't considered what was right and good about him? Had she let her past with Gerald cloud her judgment? *Yes.*

She was guilty of both. Andrew wasn't Gerald. He'd made a mistake. She was foolish if she didn't let it go and forget it. He'd accepted her past mistakes, her dochder, and her family without reservation. Other Amish men hadn't considered her before Andrew. She suspected it was due to her past. Andrew hadn't condemned her. He'd given her a chance. She had to let the past go and grow from this conflict she'd caused with Andrew. She loved him, and she wanted a lifetime with him.

She and Gabe joined Ellie, Joel, and her friends after the service.

Ellie asked him questions, and he answered them politely.

Joel pulled her to him. "Enough, Ellie."

Gabe batted the air. "It's all right. I don't mind Ellie's questions. We'll soon be family." He reached for Betsy. "I'm your Uncle Gabe."

Ellie grinned at Gabe. "Danki." She shrugged and smiled at Joel.

Betsy patted his cheeks. "Unkie."

"Yes, Unkie. I like it." Gabe tapped her button nose.

Maryann invited Gabe to join her, Daed, and Betsy at home. He followed them in his buggy. They arrived and went inside.

Gabe sat on the floor and played with Betsy and talked to her family for another hour. He cocked his head to Maryann. "Have you thought anymore about you and Andrew?"

Betsy toddled over to him and dropped in his lap. "Unkie."

"She and you have become fast friends."

He helped her clap her hands.

Betsy bounced and giggled. "Unkie. Unkie."

Maryann sat with them on the floor and grinned at Gabe's happy reaction.

"Betsy, I'm hoping Andrew and I will be holding you

more often if I can convince your mamm to let us." He gave Maryann an impish grin and turned back to Betsy. "You are adorable." He kissed her hair.

"If I didn't know better, I'd think you had talked to Bishop Fisher and requested a message on forgiveness and regrets." The bishop's message had resonated with her on the way home. She'd said a silent prayer and finally let go of the resentment and hurt. She'd been lost without this wonderful man she'd pledged to marry. She had crushed his heart and hers in the process. Andrew had been truly remorseful. For the first time, the sick feeling in her stomach left.

Gabe held Betsy and stacked her blocks.

She giggled and knocked them over.

"I have ginger cookies. Would you like a couple?" Maryann took Betsy and put her in the playpen with a small ball, her doll, and building blocks.

Betsy's lips quivered as she kept her eyes on Gabe. Then she picked up her doll and smiled.

"Nothing for me. Danki. I'm still full from the after-service dinner." He grinned. "Andrew is in love with you. You're in love with him. I will soon have a niece whom I will not give up. I'm not leaving until I convince you he had no ill intent when he made his decision to keep quiet about me. I also need a schweschder-in-law to keep me in line. So, I'm being selfish. I'm here on my account, too." He made a funny face and leaned toward Betsy, who stood in the playpen.

She patted his cheeks with her hands and cooed.

"I have Betsy's approval. She agrees with me. How about you?" Gabe gave his best puppy-dog eyes.

"I believe God sent you here and gave the bishop the

message today to cause me to reevaluate why I severed ties with Andrew. I don't want to be a prisoner of my past experiences. I can't let my life with Gerald and the disappointments I had with him rule my future with Andrew. I can see where I've grown from accepting this about myself, and it's allowing me to forgive Andrew. I've been too judgmental toward him. I can't let him go. I love him. And I would miss out on having a wonderful bruder-in-law and *unkie* for Betsy." She chuckled.

"Does this mean the wedding is back on?"

"Yes, the wedding is back on, if your bruder will have me."

Shem joined them a couple of minutes later, and Betsy lifted her arms to him. "Pop, Pop."

Shem lifted her out of the playpen and hugged her. "You are precious." He rocked Betsy in his arms. "You're both smiling. This talk must've gone much better than the previous one. I'm glad." He lifted his brows. "I don't suppose the bishop's message had anything to do with it?"

"Did you speak to him about me?" She motioned for them to sit.

"No. When God speaks to us through a message, we assume it's just for us. I would surmise others in the service benefited from it as well." Shem patted her hand.

Gabe winked at Betsy. "I'll be your uncle in a couple of months. What do you think about it?"

Betsy wiggled in Daed's arms and clapped her chubby little hands. He set her back in the playpen.

She plopped down and stacked her blocks.

"Is it true?" Shem smiled.

Maryann nodded.

"I'm happy you came. Danki, Gabe, for intervening. You're a good man." Shem patted his arm.

"Are you heading back to Millersburg in the early morning?" Maryann relaxed.

"Yes. I'll have breakfast with Toby and then leave."

Maryann tilted her head. "I've enjoyed our time together. I look forward to more like these."

He had shown how much he loved his bruder by kumming to Charm and pleading Andrew's case. She loved his devotion to Andrew. She'd look forward to talking with him more.

Shem gazed at him with a wide smile. "Now I will gain two good men in the family soon."

"Do I have your permission to tell Andrew you've changed your mind when I return to Millersburg, or should I annoy him until he visits you again in Charm?" He grinned.

"I'm anxious for him to know. You tell him as soon as you are back in Millersburg. I would like him to kumme to Charm in April as planned. I'd go with you, but it would be easier if Andrew came here, since I have Betsy. Is it possible, with regard to your uncle and the store?"

Shem put his hand on her arm. "I'm sure the bishop would shorten the counseling sessions and still marry you on May fourteenth, given his uncle's condition."

Gabe waved a hand. "I can take care of the store and my uncle while Andrew kummes to Charm to marry you. You'll love Aunt Dora and Uncle Luke. They have plenty of room in their big haus for you and Betsy until you and Andrew have time to sell his place and buy one in Millersburg."

She didn't miss the moment of sadness in Daed's eyes. She'd miss him, too. She considered Andrew. Would he be thrilled, or have misgivings about the way she'd treated him and doubted his integrity? Andrew didn't know Gabe had kumme to fix things between them. What if

Gabe didn't realize Andrew had changed his mind about her through all of this? She shuddered. "I'll be happy to move to Millersburg." She squeezed Daed's wrist. "I'll miss you. We'll visit."

"I'm thrilled for you. You've done a good thing, Gabe, bringing these two back together." Shem nodded.

"I have no doubt Andrew will be elated. I am, too." He gave her a mischievous grin. "I'm not sure I could've kept that secret."

They chuckled.

"How is your uncle's health?" Maryann asked.

"My uncle is a bag of bones. His hands tremble when he holds anything. He won't eat. I'm not sure how long he'll last. I'm glad I've gotten some time with him. He's always been wonderful to Andrew and me."

"I'm sure your uncle is thrilled to have you with him. Andrew, too." She rose. "I'll be right back." She padded to the kitchen, warmed coffee, and poured it into three mugs. She unwrapped ham and cheese slices and put ginger cookies on a plate, added folded cloth napkins and small plates, and set it all on a tray. She carried it to the living room. They each took a small plate and filled it. She left again and returned with the mugs of coffee on another tray.

Shem sipped his coffee. "Tell us about the furniture store in Millersburg."

"I can't resist." Gabe patted his stomach. "You're determined to make me gain some weight I don't need. I love the store. I'm fortunate Uncle Luke gave it over to Andrew and he's hired me. I'm anxious to learn everything about it. I love creating furniture, and being with family again makes my heart happy."

"What did you do for a living while you lived in the outside world?" Maryann brushed crumbs from her lap.

"I worked in furniture stores. I don't consider building pieces work. It's more like a hobby. Getting paid for doing it is a blessing." Gabe set his mug on the end table.

"Did you meet a girl of interest while you were away or since you've been home?" Maryann smiled.

"I did. I fell in love, but, in the end, she chose another man who had more money. I would like to marry and have kinner someday." Gabe picked up his mug and took another sip of coffee.

Betsy lay asleep in her playpen, her doll tucked under her little arm.

Shem had his head back against the chair, mouth open, eyes shut. He let out a snore.

Gabe and Maryann grinned.

Maryann shared stories with Gabe about the bakery, customers, friends and family, until time to go to bed. "Danki, Gabe, for kumming. You've changed my life for the better, and I'll not forget it. I've enjoyed our conversation, and I look forward to more."

"Already we've made memories, and we have a lot to look forward to. I should get back to Andrew's place and get some shut-eye before I have to travel tomorrow." He followed her to the door, kissed Betsy on the forehead, and bid them good night.

She woke Daed. "Time to go to bed."

He startled and roused. "Did Gabe leave?"

"Yes. He needs a good night's rest for traveling tomorrow."

Shem nodded. "Good night, sweet dochder."

"Good night, Daed."

He padded down the hall to his bedroom.

Then she carried Betsy to bed. She went to her room, and her heart soared. God had worked a miracle for her at the church service today and blessed her with a message and a new family member. She'd be a bride on May fourteenth. She couldn't wait to feast her eyes on Andrew soon. Today had been a remarkable one. One she would never forget. She prayed Andrew would be as elated as she was.

Andrew worked in the workshop with Matt Monday morning. How long would Gabe be gone? He didn't want his bruder to settle old debts or revisit his past for any reason. He should've inquired more about what he had to do. What did he travel for? He'd worried about Gabe's whereabouts and safety for a long time. Having him home had been such a relief. Now, he was back to wondering if Gabe was all right.

Matt clapped a hand on his shoulder. "You upset about Maryann? You've been staring out the window for a good minute or two. Is there anything I can do?"

"It's Gabe. He wouldn't tell me where he was off to or why. I could've gone with him. I'm frustrated I didn't insist on it." He'd been consumed with his problems with Maryann, but he didn't doubt Gabe would return. He wasn't sure if Gabe would be detained or hurt if he was settling an old gambling debt, trying to right his wrongs.

"We could go look for him." Matt put his hands on his hips.

"He didn't say where he was going. I'm sure he'll be home soon." Andrew picked up a piece of sandpaper. "Danki for offering, friend."

"Sure."

James poked his head in the door. "Lena brought sandwiches." He handed them each one.

"Does she have any available friends?" Matt chuckled.

"She takes good care of you. Feeds you and made you a shirt. Have you missed a day where you and she haven't been together?"

James beamed. "No, and my boys like her. She's been to my haus each day while I've been at work. She spoils the boys with cooking food for them and doing their household chores. She's cleaned, done laundry, and had supper ready when I kumme home. Is it too early to propose?"

Andrew choked on the bite of sandwich he'd taken, took a swig of water, and swallowed. "What! You've known her for a couple of weeks. You need more time."

Matt shrugged. "Love at first sight isn't a crime. Sounds like you and she are meant for each other. Ask her. If she doesn't need more time, then why not get married?"

"I'm not sure this is wise advice." Andrew stared at James.

Matt waved a forefinger at him. "You told me you didn't wait long to propose to Maryann."

Andrew moved his head from side to side. He'd had a deep connection he couldn't explain the moment he met her, and he'd never doubted she was the perfect girl for him. He'd give anything if he and she could plan for a future again. "Matt's got a point. You should go where your heart leads you."

"Danki. I'll talk to the boys tonight." James ducked his head back and out of sight.

"I'm jealous and happy for James." Andrew pictured Maryann and Betsy and his heart sank.

At closing time, Gabe hurried into the store and rushed into the workshop. "Andrew, I've got to talk to you!"

Andrew's heart thumped fast. "What is it? Are you in

trouble? Are you all right?" Andrew put a hand on Gabe's back. Relief washed through him. It had passed through his mind he wouldn't know where to find his bruder if he'd gone missing for days or weeks.

Matt stood next to Andrew. "Tell us whatever it is. We'll help you."

"No. I'm fine. I'm not in trouble or hurt. I went to Charm." Gabe dragged over a stool and sat.

"What! Why?"

"To talk to Maryann."

Matt whistled. "Without your bruder's permission?"

"Yes, if I said anything, he may have tried to stop me. It's partially my fault you and Maryann are apart, Andrew. I owed it to you to try and fix it."

"No. It's not your fault. You don't owe me a thing. What did you say? What did she say?" His stomach clenched. Had Gabe angered Maryann? This might have made their situation worse.

"She was as miserable as you. We visited each day I was there, and we had a pleasant time together. I met your friends and the rest of her family at the Sunday service. Ellie is a stitch. She's direct, funny, and outspoken. She doesn't hold back. She shot questions at me and didn't take a breath. She then showed her softer side, telling how much she cares for you and Maryann. I do like her."

"I'm glad you met my friends in Charm. Please, though, tell me about Maryann. How was she when you left?"

"Your wedding is back on. The bishop's message at the Sunday service had pricked her heart, and all our prayers have been answered. She gave me her blessing to tell you she'll marry you and move to Millersburg!"

Andrew dropped his jaw. "Did she say she'd marry me?"

Gabe nodded.

"What great news!" Matt exclaimed.

"I've got to go to her. Gabe, how did you do it?" Andrew's mind raced with questions of what to do next.

"With God's intervention, a well-delivered message from the bishop, and a reminder of your stellar traits, she searched her heart and really forgave you. She realizes the cost is too great to not give you another chance. She doesn't want a future without you."

"Danki for talking to her. I can't believe it. This is amazing news."

James snuck in the room.

They jerked when he spoke.

"What's going on back here? Gabe, where have you been?"

Gabe recounted his story to James.

"Congratulations, Andrew!" James grinned.

Matt chuckled. "Gabe, you and I better get busy. Everybody's getting married but us."

"Lena's got friends. I'll ask her to introduce you." James's eyes twinkled.

"Just kidding, James. I prefer to keep an eye out for the right one on my own."

"Me too." Gabe cocked his head. "Who else is getting married?"

James put a finger to his lips. "Don't say anything. I've got to talk to the boys first. I'm planning to propose to Lena soon."

"Are you out of your mind? Didn't you say you'd met her two weeks ago?" Gabe's eyes widened.

"That's what I said." Andrew threw up his hands.

"I told him if he's sure she's the one for him, I support his decision." Matt chewed on a toothpick.

"I might be asking her too soon, but I don't care. She's different from my first fraa, but I like her quirks and decisive attitude. I made all the decisions in my first marriage, and I'm not opposed to having a partner who shares her opinion on matters. She's smart, funny, and not as serious as she portrays. We got sleds out of the barn, and she joined right in. We all laughed and had a lot of fun together."

"You are smitten, my friend. It's all over your face," Matt said.

They laughed.

"A double wedding might be in order," Gabe teased.

"Lena would insist on her own day, I'm certain," James said. "Please don't take offense, but I prefer it that way, too."

"Gabe's jesting with you. You should have your own day, and I prefer for Maryann and me to have the same. That sounds good. I was afraid it wasn't ever going to happen. I've got a lot to do before I go to Charm. Do you men mind managing the store for April and part of May? I'd like it if you'd close the store for a couple of days and attend our wedding on May fourteenth." He would miss having his friends and Gabe there. Maybe he shouldn't expect it with his uncle being sick. Someone should stay back.

"I'd love to attend." Gabe bit his bottom lip. "I may need to stay in Millersburg. Uncle Luke and Aunt Dora may need me."

"I'll be there, unless you need me here." Matt grinned.

"I'd love to go to the wedding. But I will stay in Millersburg if you need me." James clapped a hand on Andrew's shoulder.

"Matt and James, we'd love to have you. Gabe, we'll assess how Uncle Luke is doing and then decide."

Gabe rose. "Time to call it a day, isn't it? I'm tired from the drive home."

Andrew said farewell to Matt and James and followed Gabe home. "I'll take care of the horses. You go inside. They'll be glad you're home safe. We'll tell them the wedding is back on, and I'll leave early in the morning to go to Maryann. I'll stay a day or two and then return and go back to Charm in April. I can't wait to celebrate with her."

Gabe nodded, handed him the reins, and strolled across the yard to go inside the haus.

Andrew finished securing the horses in the barn, and then he went inside. He glanced at Aunt Dora and Gabe visiting in the kitchen. He bent to greet Uncle Luke. Something wasn't right. Uncle Luke's lifeless eyes were wide open. His skin was gray, his head drooped, and his jaw was slack. He checked his uncle's pulse. No sign of life. His uncle had died. It couldn't have been long. The room was semi-dark, with the small fire in the fireplace providing a dim light. Aunt Dora and Gabe must've assumed their uncle was asleep. His heart sank. "Gabe, Aunt Dora, please kumme to the living room."

Aunt Dora hurried in with Gabe. "Your bruder told me the wedding is back on. I'm so happy for you!" She looked at Andrew and then to her husband. Her smile vanished, and she rushed to Uncle Luke. She knelt on the floor, laid her head in Uncle Luke's lap, and wept. "Oh no! He's gone."

Gabe wrapped his arms around her. "He's in Heaven

singing with the angels." His voice cracked. "And in no more pain."

Andrew let tears drip onto his cheeks. He sat in the chair close to them. He was grateful for the time he and Gabe had had with their uncle. It'd been apparent Uncle Luke had been on death's door last week. He'd struggled to move at all. He'd noticed the grimaces and winces as he'd sat in his chair throughout the evening, and he'd assumed it was pain. His uncle's suffering had ended, and he had moved to his home in Heaven. He'd miss him.

Minutes later, Gabe helped Dora to her feet and to a chair.

Aunt Dora dabbed her face with a thin, worn handkerchief. "I had a good life with your uncle. I'll miss him each day for the rest of my time on earth. It's like half of me went with him. We were best friends, soul mates, and very much in love." She wiped her wet eyes. "I don't want to prolong the services. Your uncle said it should be a celebration when he went to his home in Heaven. I agree, but I'll still wear black, and I'll dress him in white to follow Amish tradition." She stared at her husband.

Gabe's lips quivered. "I'm grateful for the time I had with him." He rose. "I built a pine box for this occasion while you were in Charm the first time, Andrew. I sensed it was kumming. I have it covered up in the barn. I'll bring it inside when you're ready, Aunt Dora."

Aunt Dora squeezed his hand and nodded.

Andrew gasped. "What a thoughtful thing to do." He'd been reminded of Gabe's compassionate heart since he'd returned. His bruder kept showing him how he'd matured.

"You and he have set a perfect example for Gabe and me." Andrew gazed at his aunt with loving eyes.

"We had such a good life together. I pray you boys will

share the same happiness with your fraas. Andrew, I'm happy for you. I'm glad things have worked out with Maryann." She grabbed his hand. "I'm thankful you and Gabe were with us before he passed. We have enjoyed you both so much."

Aunt Dora knelt again by her husband. "You boys living in this haus will make this easier for me. I'd rattle around in this haus not knowing what to do with myself." She wiped her tears with the back of her hand, got up, and pulled a drawer out of the desk in the corner. She handed Andrew papers. "He signed the store legally over to you a week ago. He told me to make sure I gave you this when he passed."

"Danki. We'll make sure you're always taken care of, Aunt Dora." Andrew hugged her.

Gabe circled his arms around them both.

Aunt Dora's lips quivered. "I'd like to open the haus for friends to visit Wednesday morning and have the service at one in the afternoon and the burial right after. I'll wash and dress him for the services, and you boys can put him in the pine box."

Gabe held her elbow. "Are you sure you want to do everything so close together?"

"I am. Your uncle and I discussed it. It's the way he wanted it. He didn't want to prolong the days before his burial. I'm sure he was thinking of me. He knew this would be agonizing for me." She dragged a chair over to Uncle Luke's and stroked his hand. "I love you, my dear, Luke." She wept.

Andrew and Gabe stayed silent for a couple of minutes, and then Andrew guided her to the bedroom. "Please lie down. You need to rest."

Aunt Dora argued with him for a couple of minutes and then relented.

He shut her bedroom door behind her, and then he walked to the front door and held it wide open for Gabe as he came in with a patchwork quilt from the barn. They carried Luke's body to the guest bedroom. Andrew faced Gabe. "You must be exhausted after traveling from Charm today. Your grief has added to it. I'll go let the bishop know to tell our friends and to prepare for the services."

"Yes. I am tired. Danki for offering to go speak to the bishop. I'll stay with Aunt Dora." Gabe rubbed his eyes.

Andrew bid him farewell and drove his buggy to the bishop's haus.

Bishop Detweiler answered his knock. "Andrew! Is everything all right?"

"Good evening, Bishop. Uncle Luke has passed away, and he's gone to Heaven. Aunt Dora doesn't want to prolong the visitation, funeral, and burial. She requests it all be done on Wednesday. She and my uncle discussed his wishes before he died, and these were his wishes."

"Luke's passing is a great loss. I'll be honored to oversee his service, and I'm happy he's no longer suffering. I'll tell friends to spread the word."

"Danki, Bishop." He nodded. "I have some good news." Andrew told him about his upcoming wedding in Charm. "You're wilkom to kumme."

"Congratulations! Danki for the invite. I may surprise you. I look forward to meeting Maryann and little Betsy, whether it be at the wedding or when you bring them to Millersburg."

Andrew chatted with him for a couple of minutes and headed home. He relived conversations he had enjoyed with his uncle and the memories they'd created. He regretted

Maryann hadn't met him. Luke would've loved her. This had been a happy and a grief-stricken day. He drove home, and Gabe was in the living room in front of the fireplace.

"Why don't you leave early tomorrow and tell Maryann? She'd want to support you. You can bring her to Millersburg and take her back to Charm after the funeral, and I'll stay with Aunt Dora and take care of things. Having Maryann and Betsy with us will give Dora joy during this difficult time. I'll tell Matt and James what happened in the morning. We'll close the store the day of the services."

"Danki, Gabe. I can't tell you how much I appreciate you pleading my case to Maryann."

"I love you, bruder. I always have and always will. Your happiness is important to me. Our family is growing smaller with the loss of Uncle Luke. I'm thankful Maryann's family will be an extension of ours after you marry. Betsy captured my heart. She calls me unkie. I love it."

Andrew chuckled. "I can't wait to hold her. She's precious. I love you, too, Gabe. Having you back in my life has been an answer to prayer, and a blessing." He covered his yawn. "I'm going to turn in. I'll leave early tomorrow morning for Charm. If Dora isn't up, please tell her I'll be back tomorrow night or early the next day."

Gabe nodded. "I will."

Andrew left Millersburg early Tuesday morning and went straight to the bakery in Charm. His stomach danced with excitement. He arrived close to eight, and he knocked on the door.

Maryann opened the door. "Andrew!"

He stepped inside. "I couldn't stand to wait until April to kumme. I'm relieved, happy, excited, and more, now that our wedding is on again. Maryann, I'm sorry for putting you through such heartache."

"I'm sorry for being hard on you. We don't need to mention it again." She poured him a cup of hot cocoa. "Betsy is wild about her unkie Gabe. I like him, too. How's your family?"

Andrew frowned. "Uncle Luke passed yesterday. I was sure you'd want to know. Are you interested in kumming to Millersburg with me for the service? You could meet Aunt Dora."

She covered her open mouth. "I'm sorry for your loss. Yes, of course, I'll kumme. We've had our share of tragedy this year. Rachael and Magdelena should arrive any minute. I came a little earlier than usual today. They can manage the bakery for a couple of days. I'll pack a bag for Betsy and me, and we'll go. I don't want to keep you from your family during a time like this, and I'd like to support you and help Aunt Dora."

He'd been sure she'd not hesitate to leave on the spot with him. Her loving face and attitude made his heart soar. He would miss Uncle Luke, and having her there with him would make it easier. "How are you and your family doing since Naomi's passing?"

"I'm still grieving her death, but it gets easier with time. I'll always think of her. You were here for me when she passed, and I want to do the same for you during this difficult time. We'll go to Hannah's and pick up Betsy. Then we'll go to my haus and tell Daed."

Rachael and Magdelena bustled in the door. They greeted Andrew.

Maryann told them what happened.

Magdelena took off her cape. "I'm sorry, Andrew. Maryann, go. We'll take care of the bakery."

Rachael hung her cape on the wall hook. "Yes, Andrew, I'm sorry about your uncle Luke, but, at the same time, we're happy your wedding is going forward."

"Danki." Andrew smiled.

He ushered Maryann outside and followed her to the livery to get her buggy, and then to Hannah's haus.

They crossed the yard, and Hannah opened the door with Betsy on her hip and Sunny wagging her tail and barking. "Betsy, Mamm and Dada are here." She wrinkled her nose. "Andrew, Maryann, is everything all right?"

Betsy clapped her hands. "Dada." She held her arms out to him.

"She called me Dada." Andrew took Betsy and hugged her. "I've missed you, little one. You made my day."

Maryann grinned. "You can thank Hannah for suggesting it. She's been fussy since you left. I would surmise she missed you a lot."

"Danki, Hannah. I'm happy to hear Betsy call me Dada early. I'm sorry. We've gotten sidetracked and didn't answer your question. My uncle Luke died yesterday, and I've kumme to take Maryann and Betsy to Millersburg. We've reconciled and I was hoping Maryann would want to attend the services and be with my family."

"Andrew, I'm sorry about your uncle's passing. Of course you would want Maryann and Betsy with you. Be careful traveling, and I'm happy you've worked out your differences." Hannah hugged Maryann and Betsy.

"Danki, Hannah. We should get started on our journey."

They bid Hannah goodbye.

"I'll pray you have safe travel." Hannah waved to them, and Sunny barked and stood next to her.

Andrew secured Betsy in Maryann's buggy, and then he followed them home. He explained to Shem about his uncle, while Maryann packed a bag, water, and snacks for them.

They got in the buggy, and bid Shem farewell.

Betsy fussed but soon fell asleep in Maryann's arms.

Andrew reached for Maryann's hand. "It's good to have you next to me. Danki for kumming."

"I would've been upset if you hadn't told me. This is a tragic time for you. I'll soon be a part of your family, and I want to be there for all of you. How's Aunt Dora holding up?"

"She's usually a cheerful and uplifting woman. It's difficult to watch her suffer over losing my uncle. She's lost her best friend and partner. She reminds us he's in Heaven, and I'm certain the thought is as much for her as it is for us to help ease our grief. It will be hard to walk past his favorite chair and not remember him in it and the conversations we've had. He was like a second daed to Gabe and me. Some of the best advice I've received has been from him after my daed passed away."

"I'm looking forward to meeting Aunt Dora, but I wish it were under happier circumstances."

"You and Betsy will be a bright spot in her grieving. I have no doubt you, Betsy, and Dora will get along from the minute you meet." He'd enjoy watching his soon-to-be dochder and Maryann and Dora get acquainted. "You'll meet James and Matt. I talk to them about you a lot." He told her about Matt and Annalynn.

"What a story! It's unusual for an Amish woman to take up with another man. Matt was right not to wed her. He's an honorable man to not tell what happened and allow gossips to misunderstand, and protect her reputation, especially when she was the one in the wrong."

"He made a noble choice. If he had told the truth,

Annalynn and her now husband would've been banned from the community. He was frustrated and disappointed with her, but he had loved her. I admire what he did. I pray he finds the right woman to marry one day. James and Lena have a strong connection. He didn't wait long at all to propose."

Maryann said, "I'm happy for them. Why not? If they love each other and they're ready, they should wed. His five sons need a mamm, as much as he needs a fraa. I can't wait to meet her."

"I assume she'll be at the service with James. She cooks meals for him and his sons, does their laundry, and packs dinners for him to take to work. He thought her bossy and forward when she first asked him to supper, but he changed his mind after they had an evening to talk. He got to know a softer side to her. They've been courting since then. He's a kind and gentle man. He said he enjoyed his first marriage and he's looking forward to his future with Lena."

"I can understand. I'm looking forward to my future with you." Maryann beamed. "This will give me a chance to get acquainted with your family and friends before I move to Millersburg."

Andrew prayed she'd like the town, his family, and his friends. He understood she'd miss her family and friends in Charm once she made her home in Millersburg permanent. He hoped his haus sold soon in Charm so he could buy a place here.

He shared some of his memories of Gabe, Aunt Dora, and Uncle Luke, and he appreciated Maryann giving him her attention. She didn't interrupt, and she always seemed genuine in her interest in what he had to say. He liked this trait in her. Some women didn't allow their husbands to get a word in with their constant talking.

They arrived in Millersburg Tuesday afternoon.

Andrew tied the reins to the hitching post. "I'll carry Betsy. I'm excited to introduce you to Aunt Dora."

Andrew took a sleeping Betsy from Maryann.

Betsy awoke and rubbed her eyes.

Aunt Dora opened the door and spread her arms in wilkom. "You must be Maryann and Betsy." Her puffy eyes gleamed.

"Meet my girls, Aunt Dora." Andrew grinned, as he bounced Betsy on his hip.

Betsy smiled at Aunt Dora.

Maryann gave her a loving smile. "It's a pleasure to meet you. I'm sorry it's under these circumstances. I'm ready to help you with whatever you need."

Aunt Dora hugged her. "I'm sorry it's not at a better time, but I'm glad you're here. Kumme in, and I'll show you to your room. Gabe had told me you might be kumming. He brought a crib, playpen, and high chair from the furniture store for Betsy. I told him he should wait until you came, but he wanted everything in place, just in case."

Andrew took Betsy's hand in his and kissed it. "You are a good girl. You slept all the way to Millersburg. You must be hungry." He took her to the kitchen and put her in the high chair. He made scrambled eggs and mashed them up for her. He put water in a small tin cup.

She picked it up and drank it all.

Maryann and Aunt Dora stepped into the kitchen.

"Betsy, we're going to stay with Aunt Dora." She watched him feed Betsy a small bite of egg. "Dada"—

she pointed to Andrew—"has taken good care of you and fixed you eggs."

"Dada." Betsy picked up a bit of egg with her fingers and held it out to him.

"I'll never tire of her calling me Dada." His eyes widened. "I love you, little one!"

Aunt Dora embraced him. "You are the sweetest little family. I can't wait for you to marry and move in with Gabe and me. You gave me a bit of joy when I needed it most, Andrew, bringing your girls to our home." She dropped a small amount of bacon grease in the iron skillet, cracked eggs open, and fried them. She served fried egg and bacon sandwiches, molasses cookies, and warm cocoa.

Gabe strode into the kitchen. "Maryann, it's a pleasure to have you with us." He tousled Betsy's curly blond hair. "And little Betsy, you are a doll." He bent and kissed her forehead.

"Unkie." She chuckled and patted her food-covered hands together. She picked up another handful of eggs and pushed them in her mouth.

"Betsy, use your spoon."

Betsy shook her head. "No. No."

Maryann filled her spoon and handed it to her.

"Don't worry. The mess will be easy to clean. Let her enjoy it." Aunt Dora patted Maryann's shoulder.

Gabe faced Andrew. "Our friends have arrived with benches. Want to help us move the furniture, and we'll carry them in and organize them in rows for the guests?"

"Sure." Andrew followed him outside.

Maryann woke early Wednesday morning. She had breakfast with the family while Betsy slept. She washed the dishes while Andrew helped Aunt Dora dress her husband for the service and burial. She liked Dora on sight. She was warm and inviting, and she admired Aunt Dora's strength under such tragic circumstances. It was clear why Andrew and Gabe loved her. She had a broad smile and dimples, and her eyes twinkled with kindness when she watched Betsy, but now the sadness of loss showed in her slumped shoulders and somber mood.

An hour later, Maryann found Aunt Dora at the stove. She watched her stir a pot of buttered noodles with onions and cheese mixed in. "What can I do?"

Aunt Dora gestured to dishes filled with food on the table. "Friends will bring casseroles, vegetables, and desserts. I probably don't need these noodles, but they go with most any food dish, and I'd rather have too much than not enough." She nodded to the cupboard beside her. "You can get plates and glasses out of the cupboard and set them on the end of the long table for me. You're such a dear. I'm anxious for you to make this your home."

"I hope we won't be an inconvenience for you when we move in. Having a boppli around can be a challenge." Maryann removed plates from the shelf.

Aunt Dora glanced over her shoulder at Maryann. "I'm easygoing." She gave her a reassuring smile. "I don't want you to worry about getting in the way. You and I will have no problem sharing this kitchen and chores."

Maryann circled her arm around Dora's shoulders. Dora reminded her of Liza. They were both compassionate toward others and put you at ease when you were with them. "Andrew's right. You are wilkoming and loving." She put a hand behind her ear. "Betsy's calling me. I'll get her up."

She hurried to the guest room, picked up Betsy, changed

her, took her to the kitchen, and put her in the high chair. She fixed her oatmeal.

Betsy grinned, cooed, and enjoyed her breakfast. "Down."

Maryann picked up Betsy, gave her a sponge bath, changed her diaper, and put her into a clean dress. She placed her in the playpen in the corner of the living room, away from where the men had lined up the benches.

Andrew motioned her over to him. "Meet James and Matt."

Maryann greeted the gentlemen. They wilkomed her and gave her approving smiles. She followed them over to Betsy, and Andrew introduced her. He told them she called him *Dada*. Pressing a hand to her heart, she smiled. He was overjoyed to share this with his friends. He would be a wonderful daed to Betsy.

She greeted guests later in the morning with Andrew and his family, and she took dishes to the kitchen and served hot coffee and water.

Andrew introduced her to Lena. He was then pulled away by another man.

Maryann folded her hands in front of her. "Congratulations. I understand you'll be getting married soon."

Lena shrugged. "I'm smitten with James. He's a gentle soul, and he puts up with my strong personality. I can be direct, and I should keep some opinions to myself. Other men were put off by my abruptness at times. I don't mean any harm. He looked past my faults and accepted me with all my flaws. I want a partner who will value my opinion. A man who won't try to change me. James is wonderful. He treats me like a partner, and a best friend. His sons are added blessings to my life. They are wonderful."

"Andrew considers him a good friend. I'm happy for you. Andrew and I are getting married May fourteenth in Charm. We'd love to have you, James, and his sons attend."

Lena reminded her of Ellie. She was bold and genuine and not haughty or uppity. Sincere and kind in her own way, Maryann sensed if she were Lena's friend, much like Ellie's, Lena would be loyal and protective of her.

Lena smiled. "I'd love to attend. We'll make every effort to kumme. I'd like to meet Betsy. Where is she?"

"Gabe has her." She smiled at Gabe. "She's being passed around to Andrew's family's friends." She and Lena threaded through the crowd to Gabe.

Gabe greeted them, holding Betsy on his hip.

Betsy cast her eyes toward Maryann and held up her arms. "Mum. Mum."

Gabe excused himself as a friend engaged him in conversation.

Maryann took Betsy. "Betsy, this is Lena."

Betsy grinned and clapped her hands. "Eena."

"She likes to clap her hands to make noise." Maryann kissed Betsy's cheek.

"She's beautiful, and she mirrors you." Lena gazed at them. "I'd like to have a couple of girls in the future. Don't get me wrong. I love the boys. They took to me right away. It may have been because I lightened their load of work by cooking meals and doing their laundry. I go over each day and do chores for them. I love being a part of their lives. It gave me a chance to get to know them. Andrew told James you'll be moving to Millersburg after the wedding. Consider me a friend, and I'll be glad to help you with whatever you need."

Maryann embraced Lena. "I'll be more comfortable

with the transition to Millersburg, having made a friend. Danki, Lena. When is your wedding?"

"Our wedding will be June first. I've been stitching shirts for the boys and James, and I'm making a wedding quilt for us. I didn't want to rush, and there are three other weddings kumming up in the next couple of weeks. I'm helping those brides, and I wanted to give them my full attention and not squeeze our wedding in there."

"You're a busy woman. They are blessed to have you for a friend. This way, you'll enjoy your wedding when June first arrives."

She and Lena, alongside Aunt Dora, greeted more guests offering their condolences to the family. She appreciated Lena staying to help them, and she was glad Betsy had taken to Lena. The woman glowed, having Betsy in her arms. She said a silent prayer to God that Lena and James would have some girls in their future. She regretted not meeting Luke. His friends had nothing but favorable remarks about him. They shared precious memories and made her remorseful for having not had time to get acquainted with him.

The bishop raised his hands. "Please take your seats. It's time for the service to begin." He waited for them to sit and then he offered a prayer to God.

Maryann sat with Betsy on her lap, blinking back tears. It wasn't long ago she'd sat on a similar bench and listened to her Bishop Fisher in Charm give Mamm's service. She offered a prayer for Andrew's family.

Andrew sat and scanned the sea of black hats and bonnets surrounding him on the benches filling the living room. He gazed over at the open pine box with Uncle Luke's shell of a body inside. He pictured his uncle running free in Heaven, wearing a big smile.

Bishop Detweiler spoke about his uncle and then about how short our life on earth was and that finding eternity in our forever home was in Heaven. His uncle had set a good example for him in every way. He had no doubt Uncle Luke would've been glad to know he and Maryann would enjoy a fulfilling and happy marriage supporting and encouraging each other the rest of their days.

The bishop shared Bible verses and spoke on life in Heaven for the rest of his message. Two hours later, he closed his Bible. "Let us bow our heads." He then offered another prayer to God. "Please now go to your buggies, and we'll proceed to the burial grounds located about a mile down the road on the left."

Andrew drove Gabe, Aunt Dora, Maryann, and Betsy to the cemetery.

Aunt Dora twisted a handkerchief in her hands. "I'm thankful you are all here with me."

Betsy patted Aunt Dora's cheek.

Aunt Dora took her hand and kissed it. "Especially this little one."

Andrew parked the buggy, and they walked to where the men had dug the hole for Uncle Luke's coffin. He stood on one side of Aunt Dora at the burial site and Gabe on the other as Bishop Detweiler said his final words. He stared at the pine box and then at the deep hole as four men lowered the box into the ground. He glanced at the gray clouds overhead and then at Aunt Dora. His sad mood and hers seemed to match the gloomy weather and slight coolness in the air.

Aunt Dora gave him a weak smile and pointed to the

sky. "He's above with our Heavenly Father. The bones in the box aren't him anymore."

Andrew was grateful to God He'd given his aunt peace for today. Her face was dry of tears, and she knew her husband had been ready to meet God for some time now. He'd known it, too. "We've got our memories."

"Yes, we do. It's all I need until I join him when my time kummes." Aunt Dora rested her head on his shoulder. "I doubt the ache of him being gone will ever leave, but I do have the assurance he's with God."

The bishop offered a prayer and dismissed them.

Andrew drove them home, and some of their friends followed.

Dora and Maryann served guests, and then the last one left. He and the family filled their plates with food and enjoyed a light supper.

Andrew grinned at Betsy while he ate with his family. The little one entertained them with her cute smiles, attempts to talk, and learning to use her spoon instead of her fingers as they reminisced about Uncle Luke.

Maryann finished her last bite of food and stood. She carried her dishes to the sink and brought back a damp cloth to clean up Betsy. "I'll take care of the kitchen."

Andrew carried his plate to the sink. "Maryann, I'll help you do the dishes." He glanced at his bruder and aunt. "Do you mind watching Betsy? She loves to play with her blocks. We'll join you in the living room as soon as we're finished."

Gabe lifted Betsy. "Kumme on, my sweet girl. I'll help you build a haus with your blocks." He swooped Betsy up and tickled her tummy.

She giggled.

Andrew noticed a faint smile on his aunt's lips as they

headed for the living room. He and Maryann cleaned the dishes, put them away, and wiped off the table. They went to the living room, where Betsy was asleep on her blanket and his aunt had nodded off but woke up as they approached her.

Aunt Dora picked up the tattered quilt Uncle Luke had used to keep warm in his favorite chair. "If you all don't mind, I'll retire to bed."

"You go right ahead." Andrew sat in the rocker.

Maryann lifted a sleeping Betsy. "She's enjoyed your Aunt Dora, Lena, and friends."

Andrew approached them and stroked Betsy's cheek. "She's a happy child. She brings joy to many people."

Gabe sat across from him. "She loves me best."

They laughed.

"I'll put her to bed and return." Maryann carried her out of the room.

Gabe said, "Maryann fits right in. It's like she and Betsy have lived here all along. You picked a good woman. I'd like to find one like her."

"You will."

"Uncle Luke made Aunt Dora happy. I'd like to support my fraa like he did."

"Me too." Andrew sighed. "He had more patience with Englischers than Daed. I was there a time or two when he chided Daed for being curt with them. Uncle Luke had more patience than any man I know." Andrew rolled his tired shoulders back. "He had a lot of Englisch friends who bought furniture from him."

"The store provides quality furniture. Honest and a great conversationalist, Uncle Luke didn't discriminate. He liked everybody." Gabe chuckled. "I remember Daed telling him he shouldn't be so open with the Englischers, and he told Daed he should be more receptive to them. Daed changed the subject to planting corn."

"They were blessed to have each other, and we are too." Andrew slapped his bruder's knee.

"I agree. I'm sorry I robbed us of time."

"Let's leave the past in the past. We're making new memories and holding on to the good ones." Andrew closed his eyes for a moment. "Daed used to say, 'Yesterday is gone, concentrate on today.'"

"I remember." Gabe straightened in his seat. "An idea occurred to me earlier today."

"What?"

"What was keeping you in this town has changed. You wouldn't have to stay in Millersburg. You, Maryann, and Betsy can stay in Charm. You've grown roots in Charm, and Maryann would be thrilled to stay there. You can open a store there. When I was in town, there was a For Sale sign in the window of Mr. Kline's furniture store. I forgot to mention it to you."

Andrew stood and paced. "I do love Charm. If Mr. Kline would sell his shop to me, I would be content with the space." He stopped and wrinkled his nose. "But what about you and Aunt Dora? The store?" Andrew blinked and blinked again. What a wonderful idea if it could work. Maryann would be pleased, and they could be a part of her family's lives. Gabe could take care of Dora.

Gabe motioned for Andrew to sit. "We'll make the drive now and then to stay with you. Little Betsy stole my heart. I've got to visit her once in a while. Aunt Dora will kumme with me. I would enjoy taking over the store."

"I could offer Toby a job at the store. He loves hand-crafting." Andrew's heart raced.

"Toby has a heavy load to carry with his daed being

sick. Their farm is small, and he and Rachael are responsible for their monetary needs. He told me you asked Liza and Jacob to hire him, and he was grateful, but I'm sure he'd rather work with you. He's excited about building things. I sensed he was sad he wouldn't have time to do it anymore, once your place sold. He enjoyed it more with you there."

"This could work. Toby would be doing me a favor if he ran the farm and worked in the shop part-time. Having a friendship with him makes him a good choice. I don't have to find a stranger who might not work out." He raked fingers through his hair. "I hope Toby hasn't sold my haus in the last couple of days. It's got plenty of room for Maryann and me to raise a family, and for you and Aunt Dora to stay with us when you visit."

Maryann strode into the room. "What's this about keeping your haus?"

Andrew recounted their conversation. "What are your thoughts?" He was grateful she was with him and they could have this conversation face-to-face and not through letters.

"I'd be thrilled. I'd have my job at the bakery, my friends, and my family. What about Aunt Dora?" Maryann winced.

Gabe smiled. "We can visit, and you can kumme to Millersburg. Aunt Dora would want you and Andrew to live where you'll be happy. If Uncle Luke could yell down from Heaven right this minute, he'd tell you to go to Charm."

Gabe was right. Uncle Luke would tell him to do what was best for him and Maryann and Betsy. "The more we talk about it, the more I'd like to go through with this plan." He'd miss Gabe. They'd just reunited, and he'd looked forward to being close again. Having him home, he realized time hadn't destroyed their close relationship. He did miss Maryann's family, and he loved the town and his friends in Charm. It would be the right decision.

"I'll do whatever you want to do." Maryann studied him. He gazed at her. Her eyes were hopeful and excited.

"I'll take you home, and I'll talk to Mr. Kline. Let's pray and ask for God's guidance. He'll open doors for us if it's meant we're to live in Charm."

"Gabe, you're a good bruder to suggest this. I appreciate you putting our happiness before yours. I'm sure you were looking forward to spending more time with Andrew." She shifted her gaze to Andrew. "Your openness to this change is admirable. You could stay with your family, but you're choosing to make Betsy and me happy. I can't thank you enough." She locked gazes with him for a moment.

"I'm being a little selfish. Our haus is waiting for us, if Toby hasn't sold it. I could have a store there, and I'm close to your family and friends. It's not a hardship for me to return. I love Charm. More importantly, I love you and Betsy. Let's pray it works." He gave her a warm smile. "You should get to sleep. We've got to get you and Betsy home tomorrow, and I have stops to make before I leave Charm to kumme back to Millersburg."

Maryann nodded. "Good night, gentlemen." She padded down the hall.

"Gabe, danki. It's generous of you to offer to take over the store and watch after Aunt Dora."

"I pray Mr. Kline sells you his store. Maryann's eyes had hope in them, and her smile widened when you told her. She's being a supportive partner, but her heart is really in Charm."

"I'm excited about it. I'll meet with Toby and then Mr. Kline tomorrow."

"The space next to his, which looks larger, is for sale, too. You should expand and buy both."

"Great idea. Again, danki." Andrew bid him good night and went to his room, his mind whirling with all the things he had to do in Charm. He shouldn't have mentioned the idea to Maryann until he had more information about his haus and store. He hoped he wouldn't have to disappoint her.

Chapter Thirteen

Early Thursday morning at breakfast, Andrew told Dora his plan.

She touched his hand. "I want for you to have the strong marriage your uncle and I had, whether it be in Millersburg or Charm or wherever. You have my blessing. The door is always open for you, Maryann, and Betsy, in our home."

Gabe smiled. "You still have me."

"I love spoiling you, and I'm thrilled you're here." Aunt Dora managed a weak smile and then it faded. "I'm not myself. You'll have to excuse me. It's going to take time to adjust to Luke not being with me. I miss him so much I ache inside."

Maryann bounced Betsy on her hip. "We understand. I remember Mamm each day."

"My parents pop in my mind often. Memories are a gift to hang on to." Andrew gave her a loving smile.

Gabe nodded.

"We should get going. I'd like to talk to Mr. Kline and Toby before I return." Andrew stood.

"Stay as long as you need." Gabe cupped a hand on his shoulder.

"I packed our things. I'll grab our bag." Maryann carried Betsy to the room they'd been staying in, and then returned with her dochder and her bag.

Andrew took the bag from her and slung it over his shoulder. He and Maryann bid his family goodbye and got in his buggy.

Betsy clutched her doll and babbled to it.

Andrew drove toward Charm. "Uncle's funeral brought friends and family together, and you had the opportunity to meet them. A sad occasion where good things happened. I wish I could erase Aunt Dora's pain. It's hard to watch loved ones grieve. You and I have firsthand experience. The pain eases, but it never fully goes away."

"No. I shed tears at moments of remembering Mamm's hugs, finding something she made for me, or the fun we had making cookies and laughing at the mess we made. How tired we were after cleaning it up. Funerals do bring loved ones and friends together to share special memories. It adds a sprinkle of happiness to the sorrowful day."

"Aunt Dora is holding up well. I didn't want to tell her our possible change in plans today, but I thought it best to prepare her." He'd been blessed to make close friends in both Millersburg and Charm. He'd prayed early this morning that God would open doors for them in Charm if it was meant for them to stay there.

Betsy wiggled on Maryann's lap and fussed, and then she fell asleep.

"Your aunt is one of the kindest women I've met. I am confident we could get along fine until we found a haus, if Millersburg is where we make our home. I enjoyed meeting your friends. I really like Lena. She told me her wedding date is June first."

"They must've just set the date. Good for them. We'll kumme to their wedding."

"I'd love to. I plan to write letters to her if we stay in Charm."

"We'll have to schedule visits so we don't get busy and neglect Gabe and Dora and our friends." Andrew was glad their wedding and James's would bring his family and friends together again.

Close to three hours later, Andrew pulled the buggy in front of Maryann's haus, and they went inside.

Maryann yawned.

Shem got out of his chair. "This haus was too quiet with my girls gone. Greetings, Andrew."

Betsy held her arms out to Shem. "Pop! Pop!"

"Someone missed you!" Maryann grinned and passed her to Shem.

Andrew sat and told Maryann's daed his plan.

"I want what is best for your family, but I would be delighted if you choose to stay in Charm. This is wonderful news."

"It's not a done deal. I have to speak with Mr. Kline first." Should he have waited until after he spoke with Mr. Kline to tell Shem what he had planned? The man's eagerness and relief were evident on his face.

He stayed and chatted with Shem, Maryann, and held Betsy another hour. "I've changed my mind. I'll talk with Mr. Kline first and then Toby."

He bid them farewell and drove to Mr. Kline's furniture store. He went inside and greeted Mr. Kline. "Do you have a couple of minutes to discuss the sale of your store?"

Mr. Kline gestured to a young man standing next to him. "This is Kenneth Smithers. He's agreed to work for me part-time until I sell the store. He'll be moving to Canton, Ohio, next month. His friend is opening a store there, and he'll work for him."

"Nice to meet you." Andrew shook Kenneth's hand.

"I'll oversee the store while you two talk." Kenneth nodded to them and moved away.

"Danki." Mr. Kline opened a door, ushered Andrew into a small office, and sat in a chair behind a worn maple desk. "Have a seat." The man moved slowly, his shoulders slumped, and he had dark circles under his tired eyes.

Andrew sat on the other side of the desk in a matching chair missing two of its spindles and in need of a good staining. "I'm surprised you're selling your store."

"My bruder has bought a large farm in Mt. Hope. He's offered us a home on his property. I've been more tired than usual, and I've been having a harder time catching my breath. The doctor doesn't know why. Each day, I feel worse. My fraa and I are getting older, and it's best we be near family. We'll go as soon as I sell this place. Are you interested? I also own the space next door. I bought it with plans to expand my business before I got sick. Then I received my bruder's offer."

"I'm interested in both, and your present inventory." Andrew's pulse increased. It would be a relief not having to barter with two owners. Andrew couldn't help but note the irony of both his uncle's business and this one needing to have new owners for health reasons.

They discussed the price and bartered back and forth, and Andrew accepted Mr. Kline's final offer. "When would you like me to take ownership?"

"How's Tuesday, April first?" Mr. Kline gazed at him.

"Perfect." Andrew's heart raced with excitement. Maryann and her family would be pleased. He'd have time to get the store in order before the wedding. This had worked out well. Gabe would be happy to have a store of his own to manage.

Andrew drove to Maryann's haus and told her and Shem the good news.

"I'm thrilled! It means so much to me to stay in Charm." She gently squeezed his hand. "You're wonderful, Andrew, for working this out for us." She froze. "I'm sorry. I'm being selfish. Of course, you must have some remorse about leaving Gabe, Aunt Dora, the store there, James, and Matt."

"I would've liked managing the store with Gabe, but it's best he's in charge of his store and I have mine. It's what we've both aspired to have one day. He'll stay with Aunt Dora until he finds a fraa."

"You must tell Toby. He'll be delighted we're staying in Charm."

Shem beamed. "I'm so happy about this. Ellie and Joel will be, too. Danki, Andrew."

"My pleasure, Shem." Andrew smiled.

Maryann shooed them into the kitchen. "I kept supper warm." She had the table set, and she served them vegetable soup, slices of cheddar cheese, and crackers. Then she brought over meat spread sandwiches. She had water in glasses already in front of them.

Andrew dipped his spoon in the soup. "I should've stopped to tell Toby what's happened and ask about the haus, but I couldn't wait. I'll go there after we're finished."

Shem asked Andrew questions about his plans for the store, and Maryann listened intently.

Betsy ate mashed potatoes while they talked.

Andrew wiped his mouth. "Betsy, have any of those peas made it into your mouth? At least you ate the mashed potatoes."

"No. No. Dada." She smashed a tiny handful to her lips.

"A portion must be inside her. She's not a skinny boppli. She's got two more teeth kumming in. She wants to chew on her round-headed clothespin all the time."

"Orsie." Betsy patted her table. She cocked her head and held up her food covered hands. "Unkie go?"

Andrew chuckled. "Gabe would be over the moon to know she'd asked about him right now."

"Uncle Gabe is at his haus. You'll see him again." Maryann wet a rag and washed Betsy's face and hands, and then the tray. She removed the dirty dishes and gave Betsy her clothespin and horse. "You can keep me company while I do the dishes."

"Toby will have had supper with his family by now. I'll go discuss our change in plans with him." He kissed the back of Betsy's hand. "Be good."

She waved. "Bye, Dada."

He said goodbye to them and drove to Toby's haus. He shivered against the cool wind. He was looking forward to the trees growing their green leaves, and flowers blooming.

Toby answered the door with Patches beside him. "Andrew, kumme in. Have you had supper?"

"I did, danki." He greeted Rachael and Eleanor and petted the dog. "He's cute. I'm sorry about Pepper."

"Patches is a good pet, like Pepper. It was tragic what happened to Pepper. I think of our pup often." Toby scratched the dog's ear. "Have a seat. I'm sorry about your uncle Luke."

Eleanor had dark circles under her eyes. "Yes, I'm sorry

for your loss." She smiled. "Danki for all you've done for Toby and our family. My husband is sleeping or I know he'd want to danki."

"I understand. How is he?" Andrew took off his coat and handed it to Toby and then sat.

"He has good days and bad. Today was a better one. He ate and drank more than he has for a while, and he slept better last night." She gave him a weak smile.

Rachael left and returned with butter cookies and warm cocoa. "Andrew, please accept my heartfelt sympathy regarding your uncle."

"Danki, Rachael."

Each of them took a cookie and mug.

Andrew sipped the warm cocoa. "I've made big changes. I've bought Mr. Kline's store and the space next to it."

Toby's eyes widened. "You did?"

Rachael pressed a hand to her throat. "You and Maryann will be staying in Charm?"

Eleanor settled back. "This is wonderful news. My kinner have been dreading losing you and Maryann to Millersburg."

"Yes, Maryann and I will move into my present haus after we're married." He winced. "You haven't sold it, have you? I should've checked with you about the haus before I talked to Mr. Kline, but if I couldn't buy the store, it wouldn't have mattered."

"I haven't sold your haus. It's in good shape and ready for you. I didn't have one offer. I'm sure it's because God had this plan in mind for you. Tell us more."

"Gabe will take over my uncle's store. With Gabe's return and Uncle Luke passing away, I no longer need to stay there. Gabe will take care of Aunt Dora, and I'll pass ownership of the store to him. Maryann can still work at the bakery, and I'll need some help when you're not busy managing my place, Toby."

Toby grinned. "I'd be happy to work for you at both places." He frowned. "Will I be letting Liza and Jacob down?"

Andrew shook his head. He respected Toby for caring what his friends thought. "They would've loved to have you, but they'll be happy for you and me."

Toby's eyes shone with excitement. They would have fun working together again.

"I must agree. I love them both." Eleanor set her mug on the small table next to her chair.

"I'll tell them about our change in plans tomorrow." Toby finished the last piece of his cookie. "Will you expand the two spaces and make it one big store?"

"Yes. I'm taking down the dividing wall. I'll add a workshop in the back, like my uncle had in his store in Millersburg, so we can build pieces when business is slow, or early in the morning." Andrew drank his remaining cocoa. He rose. "I'll go back and settle things in Millersburg for a week or so, and then I'll return to Charm for good. Danki, Toby, for all you've done for me. I'm happy we'll be working together again. I'll teach you more about crafting fine furniture." He put on his coat.

"I look forward to it. I'm thankful for all this. What a pleasant surprise." Toby walked him to the door.

Andrew bid them farewell, and he headed to his home in Charm. He was glad he'd brought his savings with him in case he and Mr. Kline worked out a deal. He prayed and thanked God for working things out for him with

Maryann, the store, his bruder, and Toby, and for his haus not selling. God was good.

Friday morning, Maryann went to the bakery. She had prayed and thanked God for allowing her the opportunity to stay in Charm. She noticed Daed had a lilt in his step at breakfast and seemed more chipper. She was sure their good news was responsible for this. Rachael and Magdelena had unlocked the door.

She went to the kitchen and greeted them with a happy smile.

Rachael clapped flour from her hands. "I told Magdelena you are staying on at the bakery."

"I'm relieved and so happy!" Magdelena faced her.

"Me too. I was prepared to make the best of the situation if we moved to Millersburg, but I'm delighted we don't have to go. I do regret Andrew and Gabe won't be in the same town and us not being close to Aunt Dora. But Andrew is comfortable with Gabe taking over the store and living with her. Oh, how I would've missed you both." She breathed in the aroma of fresh white bread. "You must have put some loaves in the oven."

"I did." Magdelena sniffed in the scent. "There's nothing like fresh warm bread." She checked the shelves of goodies. "We need more tarts. Maryann, is Andrew still in town?"

"He's meeting with Mr. Kline again today. He'll stay the week and head to Millersburg on Friday. He'll return to Charm the first of April, when he'll get the keys to the store. He's excited." Maryann baked with the girls until time to open. She turned the sign and opened the door for two women wanting to kumme inside. Maryann smiled. "Wilkom."

The two Englischers greeted her and then continued their conversation. "You should forgive your sweet husband. He didn't tell you about his scheming sister for a reason. He didn't want her near you, and rightfully so. She's ruined lives with her lying tongue spreading untruths about family members. She's spoiled, deceitful, and a terrible human being."

The young woman stomped her foot and glared at the pretty older lady. "Mother, I don't care. He tells me everything. Why not this?"

Maryann made more coffee while the two women talked. She wasn't sure what she should do. She didn't want to interrupt them.

"He's given you no reason to suspect he's anything other than the upstanding man he's shown you. You're punishing him for what your last no-good fiancé did to you. Your wonderful husband didn't lie, cheat, or steal from you. He was protecting you. He can't help it his rotten sister showed up in town after all these years. He was sure she was never coming back or had died. She hadn't bothered to write or attend their mother's funeral."

Maryann was glad the young woman's mamm was giving her wise advice. She hoped the young woman would listen to her.

The young woman dipped her chin to her chest. "I love him, but I'm scared to trust him. I know in my heart he had good reasons not to tell me about her. Why can't I get past this?"

"You're letting what happened to you before threaten to destroy your marriage, and the situation isn't the same.

Please reconsider and resume your happy life with him. You'll regret it the rest of your life if you choose not to. You'll forget all about this in no time."

The young woman pressed her hands to her chest. "You've made some valid points. I don't want to lose him. I should talk to him."

The door opened. A handsome young man barged in. "Lori."

Maryann glanced at him. She hoped this young couple could work out their differences.

The young woman gasped. "Trenton, did you follow me?"

"I did. Please come home. It's been a month. I need to know where we stand. I miss you." He held his dapper brown hat.

Tears stained her cheeks. "I've missed you. Mother's been defending you, and what she says makes sense. I've been too hard on you. Can you forgive me? I've been awful to you."

"I should've told you about my sister. I had hoped she was out of my life for good. She's always been mean to me and my siblings. I don't want her near you."

"I'm sorry she's been trouble for you. I'll honor your wishes. I don't want anything to do with her, based on what you've told me." She blushed and glanced at Maryann. "I apologize. We've made a spectacle of ourselves in your bakery. Please forgive us."

Trenton nodded. "Yes. I'm sorry."

"No need to apologize." Maryann gazed at them. She could relate to their disagreement. She'd been too hard on Andrew, and she almost destroyed their future. She was glad this couple had resolved their differences, just as she and Andrew had. "Would you like anything from the shelves?"

Lori's mother stepped to the counter. "We must celebrate. We'll take the vanilla cake with white icing. Trenton and Lori, I'll split it with you. White cake is my favorite. I find any excuse to have some."

They laughed.

Maryann accepted payment, passed them the wrapped dessert, and watched them leave. She was happy for them.

The door opened, and she smiled. *Andrew.* She moved to face him. "Did you finalize the deal and pay Mr. Kline?"

He beamed. "I did. I gave him half the money, and I'll give him the other half the day he gives me the keys. With the space next door, the shop is larger than my uncle's in Millersburg. I am excited to get it organized. While I was there, two men already dropped in and asked to consign pieces with Mr. Kline. He introduced them to me, and we came to an agreement."

"How wonderful. Oh, Andrew, we've got a lot to look forward to. Our wedding, Betsy and me moving into your haus, and beginning our future together as a married couple." She couldn't wait to put her touches on his haus and make it theirs.

Magdelena and Rachael came from the kitchen to greet Andrew.

Magdelena passed him a custard tart. "These are fresh. I'm sorry about your uncle Luke." She poured him a cup of coffee. "Congratulations on your new store and choosing to make your life here in Charm."

"Danki." He accepted the stoneware cup.

Magdelena glanced at Rachael. "We should give these two some privacy." She hooked her arm through Rachael's.

"Kumme on. We've got pies, cookies, and bread to bake. Have a safe trip to Millersburg, Andrew."

Rachael nodded. "Yes, drive careful."

The girls went to the kitchen.

Andrew brushed her hand with his. "It won't be long before you'll be Mrs. Wittmer."

"And you'll become a husband and a daed on the same day." She chuckled.

"I can't wait. I like that Betsy's already calling me Dada." He gazed into her eyes.

He held her hand for a moment. "I have a question for you."

"What?" Maryann raised her brows.

"How many kinner do you hope God blesses us with?" He gave her an impish grin.

"I'm not sure." She had Betsy. She hadn't considered how many.

He teased. "I hope we have fourteen. We'll call all the boys, Noah. And we'll call all the girls, Betsy. It will make it easier on us when we call them all for chores and meals!"

"Oh my goodness! We'll need a four-story haus!" She laughed and held her stomach.

"We have a lot to look forward to in our future. It will be fun to watch Betsy grow and to create wonderful memories together."

A woman and two small kinner entered.

"I'll be right with you." Maryann said goodbye to Andrew and gave him a warm smile.

He grinned back at her and put his hand on the door. "I'll be at your haus in time for supper."

Maryann watched him leave. Soon, she'd be Mrs. Wittmer. She grinned. The name had a nice ring to it.

* * *

Andrew got in his buggy in Charm Friday morning to head to Millersburg. He had enjoyed the suppers at Mary-ann's and the time they'd spent together this past week, but it was time for him to return to Millersburg and tie up loose ends. It had been hard to say goodbye to Maryann and Betsy. He couldn't wait for his permanent return to Charm after their wedding. Only an hour into the journey, the cold wind and rain blew against the curtain used to cover the door opening on his buggy, and he tugged the wool blanket over his legs and pulled his scarf higher to cover his nose. He shivered. The next two hours, he squinted at the road and wished visibility wasn't so poor.

He was within ten minutes of Aunt Dora's. Thank goodness, his journey would be over soon. He slowed and noticed an empty buggy ahead to the side of the road. It had a broken wheel and the horse was nowhere to be found. Another buggy and mare was parked on the road. It was Gabe's mare. The mare had patches of brown and black fur. Who had been in the broken buggy? "Giddy-up! Go!" He hurried to help them and jumped out. "Gabe! Gabe!"

"Andrew?" Gabe yelled. "I'm over here!"

"Yes, it's me. I'm kumming." Andrew inched sideways down the slight hill. Two young Amish women stood, one on either side of Gabe, holding on to his arms.

"Andrew, can you hold on to one of the women? I can't take them both at the same time, and I'm afraid to let go of either of them as they may fall. One girl has a turned ankle and the other cut her leg."

"I'll make my way to you." Andrew made his way to them in the rain. The ditch wasn't bad to climb, and they weren't far from the road. He did a double take. The women were twins. He held out his hand to the nearest girl. "Take my hand or my arm. We'll walk up the hill together. Hold on to my arm as we take steps."

She worried her brows and grabbed on to his arm and then let go of Gabe's.

The other girl held on to Gabe's arm, and he helped her climb up the hill to his buggy.

Andrew said, "I'm Andrew Wittmer, Gabe's bruder."

The girl shivered. "I'm Gracie Miller." She removed a handkerchief from under the cuff of her sleeve and tied it around her cut.

"I'm Katie, her schweschder." She held on to Gabe's arm and didn't put weight on her injured ankle.

Gabe inspected their wagon. "I'll take you both home."

The girls nodded, and Gabe helped them into his buggy.

Andrew pointed to the buggy. "Let's push their buggy a little more off to the side of the road."

Gabe nodded, and they got the buggy off the road.

"Do you need me to follow you to their haus? We could pick up their daed and I could help you and him replace the wheel."

Gabe said, "No, I'll be fine. I'll help their daed retrieve the buggy and horse." He smiled. "You arrived at the right time. I was relieved you stopped."

"Happy to help. Talk to you later." Andrew waited until Gabe's buggy disappeared down the road. Gabe had had a big smile on his face as he helped the twin girls into his buggy. He'd be curious to find out if his bruder had an interest in either of them. He didn't recognize them from Sunday services or around town.

He traveled to Aunt Dora's haus, parked his buggy, unharnessed his mare, put her in the stall, and offered the animal food and water. Then he closed the barn door. He crossed the yard and went inside. "Aunt Dora, I'm home."

"Andrew, I'm in the kitchen." Aunt Dora stirred a big kettle of ham and beans. She put her big wooden spoon down and wrapped her arms around him. "How was your trip?"

"It couldn't have gone any better." He recounted his meeting with Mr. Kline and told her he was giving Gabe the store in Millersburg.

"I'm happy for you and Maryann and little Betsy. Your uncle would be pleased you've bought a store and will raise your family near Maryann's, especially since Gabe can take over this one. You each need your own store. Gabe, being younger, may have had trouble working with you. He looks up to you, but he likes to create his own path."

"I agree with you. We'll have a better relationship this way."

"Where is your bruder? He should've been home from the shop by now. I'm surprised you didn't pass him on your way home." She picked up her spoon and stirred the noodles.

"I did run into him. Two girls had a wheel break on their buggy, and they ended up down the ditch in all the commotion. Gabe was helping them up from the ditch when I came upon them. He was having trouble handling both of them. One had a cut on her leg, and the other girl had twisted her ankle. I assisted the one girl, and he held on to the other. He took them home. They were twins. I don't remember seeing them in town or at the services."

"Maybe they are new in town. I'm anxious to find out from Gabe what he learned about them. I'm relieved they're unharmed. Buggy accidents can be tragic, and this weather adds more danger."

She set the table. "Let's go ahead and have supper. We'll save a plate for your bruder." She poured water in two glasses and set a basket of rolls and a small dish of grape jam on the table.

Two hours later, the front door opened. "I'm home." Gabe waved at them, then removed his coat and hat and hung them next to Andrew's on the knotty-pine coat tree. He walked to the kitchen.

"There's a plate for you on the stove." Aunt Dora ushered him to the table and dished out a serving of food and then poured him a glass of water. "Andrew told me about the girls and their buggy. Are they all right?"

Andrew sat. "And did their mare return?"

Gabe patted his stomach. "Danki for keeping a plate for me, Aunt Dora. But I'm too full from having supper with the twins. To answer your questions, the twins were rattled from the fall. One twisted her ankle, and the other one had a cut on her leg. But no serious injuries. The horse had returned home on its own when we arrived. Their worried parents were ready to get in their buggy and search for the girls when we pulled up. Mr. and Mrs. Miller invited me inside for supper. Mr. Miller and I went outside after we finished supper. He had a spare wheel. We tied his horse to the back of the buggy, and then we returned to the scene of the accident and replaced the broken wheel and fixed the harness. He went home, and I came here. Everything's taken care of." He drank a third of his water. "They are beautiful girls. Coal black hair and dark eyes." He grinned. "I've got my eye on one of them."

Andrew wrinkled his forehead. "How in the world would you know which one you would like to consider?"

"Gracie has about a one-inch scar above her right eyebrow. She's the one." Gabe winked.

Aunt Dora sipped her water. "Why her and not the other girl?"

"She has a sweet, soft voice, and she's a bit shy. Katie is more direct, and you wouldn't use *subtle* to describe her. She's nice, but she's like a bull in a china shop. She snatched her hat off her head and threw her coat on the coat tree. Gracie took her time removing her cape and hat, and she hung them with care."

"Tell us about their parents." Andrew was intrigued with Gabe's assessment of the girls. He was happy Gabe was interested in one of them. He'd like him to marry and have kinner.

"They're from Lancaster, Pennsylvania. They wanted a fresh start in a new place. They lost a son in a hunting accident. It's a tragic story."

"You're not wasting any time getting to know Gracie, accepting their invitation to supper," Andrew teased. Gabe had found a girl who interested him. He would have the means to build a haus or buy one, and he'd have a steady income to provide for a family.

Dora waggled a forefinger at him. "I'd like you to invite the Miller family over for supper one night. Andrew and I would like to get better acquainted with them. We'll schedule it before Andrew leaves for Charm."

"I don't want to schedule anything with them yet. I might learn something about her I may not like. I'm not always right about my first impressions." Gabe gave her a lopsided grin.

Andrew and Matt carried a hutch to the front and set it in the corner of the store among kitchen tables and chairs.

James was assisting a couple searching for chairs.

The Miller twins entered the shop. Gracie carried a covered plate and stepped to Gabe. "I baked you a sugar milk pie to danki for rescuing us. You're kumming to supper tonight. Right?"

He nodded and accepted the pie. "I'll be there."

"Kumme at six." She gave him a shy smile.

Katie strolled over to Andrew and Matt. "I made maple sugar cookies to danki for walking me up the hill yesterday." She faced Matt and smiled. "I'm Katie Miller. I'm new in town."

"I'm Matt Yoder. It's a pleasure to meet you. Wilkom to Millersburg. Andrew and Gabe told James and me about your accident yesterday. I'm glad you're both all right."

Andrew stepped back to leave them alone. He doubted they'd noticed. They only had eyes for each other.

Gracie and Gabe approached Matt and Katie. Gabe nudged Matt's arm. "Looks like you've met Katie."

Katie straightened her shoulders. "Yes, we've met. Andrew, Matt, and Gabe, you should all kumme to supper."

Andrew studied the two couples. He'd leave them to get better acquainted. "I'll stay home with Aunt Dora this evening, but, Gabe and Matt, you two should go."

Katie stood next to Gracie, who let her schweschder do all the talking. "We'll expect you at six." She gave Matt directions.

Andrew understood what Gabe meant when he said Katie was direct. Gracie had a soft, pleasant voice and was a bit timid. She seemed content to let Katie take over.

The girls chatted for a couple of minutes and then bid them farewell.

Andrew bumped Gabe's shoulder. "You and Matt didn't hesitate to accept their invitation."

Matt whistled. "I'd be foolish not to want to get better

acquainted with Katie. She's a spitfire and gorgeous. I like a girl to challenge me, as long as she isn't too overbearing." He punched Gabe lightly. "Gabe, you said they were pretty. You failed to say they are gorgeous."

On April first, Andrew handed Gabe the deed to the furniture store. "You'll make it a big success. You've got two good men to help you."

"I'll make you proud, bruder." Gabe clapped a hand on his arm. "You enjoy setting up your store with Toby."

"We will." He hugged Aunt Dora. "Keep my bruder out of trouble. Danki for everything."

"He might have to keep me out of trouble." She chuckled. "Give Maryann and Betsy our love. We'll look forward to attending your wedding."

Andrew bid them farewell, went to his buggy, threw his bag in the back, and drove to Charm. Big gray clouds threatened to burst with rain. The cool air was refreshing, and the roads were clear. Maybe the temperatures would rise from now on.

He arrived and went straight to the bakery. "Maryann, I'm back."

"Andrew, I'm glad you're here. Your timing is good. The bishop stopped by for Danish pastries, and he's asking if we still want to meet on Tuesdays at six."

"Greetings, Bishop." He shook the man's hand. "Tuesdays at six are fine with me."

"I'm happy you're staying in Charm. I would've been sad to have you move away." He picked up the bag Maryann had filled for him. "I'll have coffee ready. Great to have you back, Andrew." He held up his bag as he left the bakery. "Danki, Maryann."

Maryann passed Andrew a cup of tea. "You saved us a trip from having to visit and ask the bishop when we should have our sessions. I'd forgotten what he'd told us."

"A lot has happened the last couple of weeks since I was last here. It's understandable. How is everything?" Andrew wanted to take her in his arms and hold her. She had a lilt in her step, and her eyes glowed with love for him.

"The community is buzzing about our wedding. We're the next big event for everyone to attend." She beamed. "Kumme for supper. Betsy will be delighted to hug her dada. She's been a little grumpy. I'm sure it's because she misses you. How are Gabe and Aunt Dora?"

Andrew told her about Gabe and Matt going to supper with the twins. "They're both smitten with these women. It's humorous to watch when the girls bring them food or invite them to go for buggy rides or socials."

"I'm tickled for them. I hope I get to meet the twins sometime." Maryann served him a piece of sour cream cake.

"The rate they're going, we'll be attending their weddings before the year ends." He chuckled and accepted the cake. "James and Lena's wedding is next. She sends you her best." Andrew sipped his tea. He finished his dessert fast. He got up and went to the open doorway of the kitchen. "Greetings, girls."

They smiled. "We're excited about your wedding! Glad you're back in town!"

"Danki, I wish it was tomorrow!"

Rachael shook her head. "We need more time to stitch presents. We've got special gifts for you. You're going to have to wait."

"I'll wait then. I am eager to find out what you're making for us." He grinned and told them goodbye.

"Maryann, I should go to Mr. Kline's and collect my keys and pay him the other half of the money I owe him. Then I'll go home and work with Toby. I'll kumme over at six."

"Sounds good." Maryann gave him a loving smile, and he departed.

He crossed the road to Mr. Kline's store and went inside. The man had lost at least twenty pounds, and his face was drawn. Andrew was shocked and saddened to see the downturn in his health in such a short time. "Greetings."

Mr. Kline shuffled to him. "You buying my store has been a blessing. I'm not sure how much longer this old body of mine is going to last. I've deteriorated a lot since you were last here." He passed Andrew the keys.

Andrew passed him an envelope. "This is the remaining balance. I'm sorry you're ill. Is there anything I can do for you?"

"You're doing it by taking this place off my hands. I loved having this shop for the last thirty years. In the last year, it's been a burden. I don't have the energy to run it. After today, I can pack up and move near my bruder. It will be a wilkom relief. The gossips have been spreading your wedding date around town. I'm sorry I'll miss it."

"I understand. You should go while you're able to travel." He chatted with the kind man for another twenty minutes, and then he locked the store, left with Mr. Kline, and retrieved his buggy and went home.

He opened the workshop and found Toby and Patches. "What are you working on?"

Toby threw an old blanket over the wooden piece. "It's a gift for you and Maryann. All hands off."

"I won't peek." Andrew was touched Toby was making something for him and Maryann.

Andrew jingled the keys. "We have the store. We can start arranging it anytime."

Toby grabbed a pencil and paper. He showed Andrew his jotted notes. "I've been in there. We've got some work to do before you open. I'll help you knock out the wall, and we'll paint the inside. We should expand the workshop. It's going to look great."

Andrew threw up his hands and wrinkled his forehead. He loved to tease Toby. "You've made me tired with your list. I'm not sure you'll have time to complete it before we open." He loved Toby's enthusiasm and his willingness to help.

Toby dragged two stools together. "How are things in Millersburg?"

Andrew sat on one of the stools. "Gabe is excited to run the store. I'm thankful he, James, and Matt get along well. They've become fast friends. I'll miss working with them, but I'm ready to venture out on my own with this store in Charm." He told Toby about the twins.

Toby chuckled. "I picture Gabe as a charmer. These boys might be getting married not long after you and Maryann."

"They're funny to watch with these girls. They're two flirts. More confident than they should be, even though the twins seem to enjoy their teasing and compliments. I'm happy for them. Time will tell if a future is in sight for them. I hope they take their time and don't make any rash decisions." He shifted on his stool to get comfortable. "How's your daed's condition?"

"Daed is about the same. He's sitting in his chair and has his wits about him, and we're enjoying his company. He's had a better appetite the last couple of weeks. Patches keeps him entertained." He traced the rim of his mug. "I ran into

Liza and Jacob in town. I thanked them for offering to hire me. They assured me they are happy I am staying on to manage your place and work at the shop when things are slow."

"They go out of the way to help others. They're two of my favorite people in Charm. Liza's brought a lot of happiness to Charm and the women who've worked in her bakery. Maryann has told me how Liza ran it when her late husband, Paul, was alive. It gave her peace amidst her life of turmoil. Now she's married to Jacob and happy to be home with him and let us manage the bakery. Maryann said all the girls who've worked there have become close. Little Peter being adopted by Liza and Jacob was a blessing for them and him. You'd never know Liza didn't birth him." Andrew said goodbye to Toby and then drove to Maryann's haus. They'd encountered some major issues during their journey, but they'd found their way, and their future held a lot of promise. He'd count the days until he said, "I do."

May fourteenth, Maryann stood facing Andrew. Her special day was finally here. She'd be Mrs. Wittmer today. She'd fidgeted during Bishop Fisher's message and the songs they'd sung without music. They'd enjoyed their sessions with the bishop in April, and they'd been in agreement about communication, finances, and raising a family. She was ready to promise her love to Andrew before their friends and family. To be his fraa forever.

The bishop said a few words about them, prayed, and then directed them to say their vows. Her voice cracked while saying hers, and she was sure she heard his crack, too.

The bishop put a hand on each of their shoulders. "I pronounce you Mr. and Mrs. Andrew Wittmer."

Her heart soared, and they both laughed as Betsy giggled and clapped her hands while in Hannah's arms.

Betsy reached for her. "Mum. Mum."

"You stay with Hannah, little one." Maryann was delighted Aunt Dora, Gabe and Gracie, James and Lena and their boys, as well as Matt and Katie had traveled to attend their wedding. The Miller twins and Lena had stayed at her haus, and she liked them. She'd invited Hannah, Ellie, Magdelena, and Rachael over one night, and they'd all chatted and shared stories.

She and Andrew had received gifts the week before the wedding: tea towels, kitchen utensils, dishes, rugs, and new gardening tools.

They went to their friends and family together and thanked them for their gifts and for kumming to their wedding. They bid their friends and family farewell as the crowd departed.

Andrew held her hands. "Toby constructed an extra square counter for the middle of our kitchen. You're going to love having the extra counter space. He showed it to me yesterday, and it's in the kitchen, ready to use."

"What a wonderful gift!" Maryann smiled.

Andrew grinned. "Gabe brought over a brand-new bedroom suite, and it's all set up, and I put sheets on the bed. Matt and James gave us a much-needed end table for the corner chair in the living room. We'll enjoy having somewhere to set things while sitting there."

"Our family and friends have been generous. We're fortunate to have them in our lives." She stroked the top of his hand. "I love the hope chest you gave me. It's the perfect gift."

"I like the beautiful quilt you made for us. The pocket stitched on it with your sweet note tucked inside was a nice touch. I intend to keep it as my keepsake. I'll pull it out and read it on our anniversary." Andrew pulled her to her feet. "Mrs. Wittmer, is this day meeting your expectations?"

She had hoped to find the right husband for her, and a good daed for Betsy. She'd received more than she could've ever hoped or wished for from God. She was glad she'd not let what happened in the past destroy her future with Andrew. Andrew had shown her true love, and she was ready to embark on their future together. God had blessed her by bringing Andrew into her life. He far exceeded her expectations. "Yes, my hope and prayer to find the right husband for me and the right dada for Betsy was answered when you came along, my dear husband." She hugged him. "I couldn't be happier or more in love."

Epilogue

Maryann rocked on the new wooden swing Andrew had put up for them on the porch of their new home. "It's June fifteenth. We've been married a month, and I love our life together. The sunshine and longer days are a wilkom change from the cold."

Andrew sat next to her. "I adore Betsy and the joy she brings, but I do look forward to this time together after she's gone to bed." He gave her a loving smile and a wink.

"I do, too." Her face warmed with love for him. "I'm happy we're settled in Charm, although I am thankful for the friends we've made in Millersburg. Do you have any regrets about not moving there? I've gotten to stay close to family and friends, but you're separated from Aunt Dora and Gabe."

"I missed Gabe while we were apart, but I'm thankful he returned to Amish life. We haven't had much time together since his return, but we'll visit them. He's happy running his furniture store, and he's smitten with Gracie. Aunt Dora is thrilled he's living with her. It's a blessing we each have our own shops." He kissed her forehead. "I don't regret anything, as long as I'm with you and Betsy."

"I'm relieved you are happy here. It was wonderful Gracie came to the wedding with Gabe and Aunt Dora. They seem happy together. I might have a schweschder-in-law soon." She hoped the couple would marry. Gracie was kind and shy, and Gabe was the opposite of shy. They seemed to bring out the best in each other the way she and Andrew continued to do.

Maryann rested her head on his shoulder. "Yes, Gabe will be a good daed, like you. He plays with Betsy and holds her. Speaking of kinner, Ellie's boppli, Emma, is two weeks old today. Don't you think she looks like Ellie? I loved holding her in my arms."

"Emma is a beauty. Are you hoping we'll have a boppli soon? I am anxious for Betsy to have siblings. The more the merrier." He squeezed her hand.

Maryann said, "Emma does make me want a boppli sooner than later. It's all in God's timing. I'm ready." She pushed the swing with her foot. "We need to keep Hannah and Timothy in our prayers. Hannah expected to be with child before now. She's worried."

"Yes, we do. Like you said, it's all in God's timing. I'm surprised you aren't playing matchmaker for Magdelena and Toby. Although, I'm not sure when Toby will be ready, since he's busy taking care of his sick daed and providing financially for the family. I've offered him money, but he wants to save his earnings and not owe anyone. He won't accept it as a gift."

"Magdelena doesn't need my help. She's determined to change Toby's mind. She's ready to court him. She finds excuses to take meals to his family, and she'll bake his favorite butterscotch pie and take it to him. Rachael told Magdelena her bruder isn't ready to court her, but he's interested in her. Magdelena says they can court as long as he needs to take care of his daed and save money. Rachael told her Toby doesn't have time to court with all the work he does. What's your opinion?" She liked discussing their friends, future plans, and their day. His opinion most often was like hers, and he was patient and wise. She'd learned to appreciate this about Andrew.

"I admire and respect Toby for his hard work and devotion to his family. I trust he'll court Magdelena when he's ready."

Maryann lifted her head and gazed into his eyes. "Have you noticed how Toby smiles and seems happy when he's talking to her? He doesn't take his eyes off her."

Andrew chuckled. "I couldn't take my eyes off you when we met. That's where our story began, and look at us now. In all seriousness, let's keep those two in our prayers. We'll ask God to intervene for them."

Maryann kissed him. "You're right. Look at us. Miracles do happen."

GLOSSARY
PENNSYLVANIA DUTCH/GERMAN

baby	*boppli*
brother	*bruder*
children	*kinner*
come	*kumme*
covering for Amish woman's hair	*kapp*
dad, father	*daed*
daughter	*dochder*
grandmother	*grossmudder*
grandfather	*grossdaadi*
house	*haus*
mother, mom	*mamm*
non-Amish male or female	*Englischer*
sister	*schweschder*
thank you	*danki*
welcome	*wilkom*
wife	*fraa*

Recipes

MARYANN'S APPLE FRY PIES

Ingredients

Filling:

    2 large apples, peeled, cored, and diced
    ½ cup brown sugar
    1 teaspoon vanilla
    ¾ teaspoon cinnamon
    1½ teaspoons cider
    1 teaspoon cornstarch

Dough:

    2 cups flour, sifted
    4 Tablespoons butter
    2 egg yolks
    ⅓ cup hot milk
    ¼ teaspoon salt
    2½ cups vegetable oil for frying

Glaze:

    2 Tablespoons milk
    ¼ cup powdered sugar
    ¾ teaspoon vanilla

Directions

Filling:

Combine apples, brown sugar, cinnamon, and vanilla in a small saucepan. Cook on medium heat until juices start to form, three to four minutes. Make a slurry by whisking together the cider and cornstarch. Stir this into the pan, turn the heat up to high, and cook, stirring until mixture is thickened. Remove from heat and set aside.

Dough:

Cut the butter into cubes, then use a pastry cutter to work it into the flour. Continue to cut in the butter until it's in small pea-sized lumps. In a small bowl, beat the egg yolks and salt together. Slowly pour in hot milk, stirring constantly. Pour the milk mixture into the flour mixture. Stir together until the dough forms. Turn the dough out onto parchment or wax paper and knead it until it smooths out.

Divide the dough into six pieces and roll them each into a ball. Use a rolling pin to roll them out to about six-inch circles. Fill each circle with two tablespoons of apple mixture. Fold the dough in half over the filling and pinch the edges together to seal. You can flute the edges or use a fork to crimp them. Wet edges with small amount of water to help seal if necessary.

Heat the oil in a deep saucepan.

Place the pies in the hot oil one at a time and fry until golden brown on both sides. Remove from the oil with a slotted spoon and place on paper towels to dry.

Glaze:

Whisk together in a small bowl the powdered sugar, vanilla, and milk until smooth. Glaze the pies while they're still warm. Drizzle or brush the glaze on one side; then let it dry, flip them over and glaze the other side. If you love glaze and want two coatings, wait for the first one to dry.

Pies uncovered are fresh for two days. For glaze to remain hard, do not put them in a bag or container. Just leave them uncovered.

MARYANN'S CUSTARD PIE

Ingredients

1 unbaked pie shell, store bought or your favorite
   piecrust recipe
3 large eggs
¾ cup sugar
½ teaspoon salt
¼ teaspoon nutmeg
2⅔ cups milk
1¼ teaspoon vanilla extract

Directions

Preheat oven to 350 degrees.

In a small bowl, beat eggs and set aside.

In a large bowl, mix together sugar, salt, nutmeg, vanilla, and milk.

Add eggs to mixture. Mix well and pour into the unbaked pie shell.

Bake for 45–50 minutes. Remove from oven and cool.

Sprinkle the top with nutmeg. Keep any remaining pie refrigerated after serving.

MARYANN'S HOT CHOCOLATE RECIPE

<u>Ingredients</u>

10 cups of dry milk powder
5 cups powdered sugar
2 cups unsweetened cocoa powder
2 cups powdered non-dairy creamer

<u>Directions</u>

In a large bowl, combine and stir all the above ingredients. Makes about 16 cups.

For one serving: Place six tablespoons of mixture in the bottom of a cup or mug. Add ¾ cup of desired temperature of warm to hot water and stir until the mixture is dissolved.

Add whipped cream or marshmallows if desired. Store mixture in sealed airtight container.

MARYANN'S VANILLA CAKE RECIPE

<u>Ingredients</u>

Cake:

    1¾ sticks unsalted butter, softened
    1¾ cups sugar
    2½ cups flour
    2 teaspoons baking powder
    ¼ teaspoon salt
    6 large egg whites
    1¼ cup milk

Icing:

    1½ cups powdered sugar
    ½ teaspoon vanilla
    2 Tablespoons milk

<u>Cake Directions</u>

Prepare 2 (9-inch) pans, 1½ inches deep; or 1 (13 by 9) pan, 2 inches deep, buttered and dusted with flour.

Set rack in the oven to the middle and preheat oven to 350 degrees.

In a large mixing bowl, cream together the sugar and butter until fluffy.

In a separate large bowl, stir together flour, baking powder, and salt. Set aside.

In a small bowl, combine egg whites, milk, and vanilla extract.

Add one-third of the flour mixture to the butter mixture.

Then add half the milk mixture. Repeat these steps until you have all the batter in one bowl.

Mix and scrape the bowl often. Pour batter into prepared pan.

Bake cake(s) for 25 minutes or until an inserted toothpick in the center of the cake comes out clean.

Remove pan from the oven. Let it cool for five minutes. Then turn the cake out of the pan onto a wire rack to cool completely.

Icing Directions

Mix the icing ingredients together until desired thickness and spread the icing on your cake.

Connect with U S

Visit us online at
KensingtonBooks.com
to read more from your favorite authors, see books
by series, view reading group guides, and more.

for sneak peeks, chances to win books and prize packs,
and to share your thoughts with other readers.

facebook.com/kensingtonpublishing
twitter.com/kensingtonbooks

Tell us what you think!

To share your thoughts, submit a review,
or sign up for our eNewsletters, please visit:
KensingtonBooks.com/TellUs.

Books by Bestselling Author
Fern Michaels

___	**The Jury**	0-8217-7878-1	$6.99US/$9.99CAN
___	**Sweet Revenge**	0-8217-7879-X	$6.99US/$9.99CAN
___	**Lethal Justice**	0-8217-7880-3	$6.99US/$9.99CAN
___	**Free Fall**	0-8217-7881-1	$6.99US/$9.99CAN
___	**Fool Me Once**	0-8217-8071-9	$7.99US/$10.99CAN
___	**Vegas Rich**	0-8217-8112-X	$7.99US/$10.99CAN
___	**Hide and Seek**	1-4201-0184-6	$6.99US/$9.99CAN
___	**Hokus Pokus**	1-4201-0185-4	$6.99US/$9.99CAN
___	**Fast Track**	1-4201-0186-2	$6.99US/$9.99CAN
___	**Collateral Damage**	1-4201-0187-0	$6.99US/$9.99CAN
___	**Final Justice**	1-4201-0188-9	$6.99US/$9.99CAN
___	**Up Close and Personal**	0-8217-7956-7	$7.99US/$9.99CAN
___	**Under the Radar**	1-4201-0683-X	$6.99US/$9.99CAN
___	**Razor Sharp**	1-4201-0684-8	$7.99US/$10.99CAN
___	**Yesterday**	1-4201-1494-8	$5.99US/$6.99CAN
___	**Vanishing Act**	1-4201-0685-6	$7.99US/$10.99CAN
___	**Sara's Song**	1-4201-1493-X	$5.99US/$6.99CAN
___	**Deadly Deals**	1-4201-0686-4	$7.99US/$10.99CAN
___	**Game Over**	1-4201-0687-2	$7.99US/$10.99CAN
___	**Sins of Omission**	1-4201-1153-1	$7.99US/$10.99CAN
___	**Sins of the Flesh**	1-4201-1154-X	$7.99US/$10.99CAN
___	**Cross Roads**	1-4201-1192-2	$7.99US/$10.99CAN

Romantic Suspense from
Lisa Jackson

Absolute Fear	0-8217-7936-2	$7.99US/$9.99CAN
Afraid to Die	1-4201-1850-1	$7.99US/$9.99CAN
Almost Dead	0-8217-7579-0	$7.99US/$10.99CAN
Born to Die	1-4201-0278-8	$7.99US/$9.99CAN
Chosen to Die	1-4201-0277-X	$7.99US/$10.99CAN
Cold Blooded	1-4201-2581-8	$7.99US/$8.99CAN
Deep Freeze	0-8217-7296-1	$7.99US/$10.99CAN
Devious	1-4201-0275-3	$7.99US/$9.99CAN
Fatal Burn	0-8217-7577-4	$7.99US/$10.99CAN
Final Scream	0-8217-7712-2	$7.99US/$10.99CAN
Hot Blooded	1-4201-0678-3	$7.99US/$9.49CAN
If She Only Knew	1-4201-3241-5	$7.99US/$9.99CAN
Left to Die	1-4201-0276-1	$7.99US/$10.99CAN
Lost Souls	0-8217-7938-9	$7.99US/$10.99CAN
Malice	0-8217-7940-0	$7.99US/$10.99CAN
The Morning After	1-4201-3370-5	$7.99US/$9.99CAN
The Night Before	1-4201-3371-3	$7.99US/$9.99CAN
Ready to Die	1-4201-1851-X	$7.99US/$9.99CAN
Running Scared	1-4201-0182-X	$7.99US/$10.99CAN
See How She Dies	1-4201-2584-2	$7.99US/$8.99CAN
Shiver	0-8217-7578-2	$7.99US/$10.99CAN
Tell Me	1-4201-1854-4	$7.99US/$9.99CAN
Twice Kissed	0-8217-7944-3	$7.99US/$9.99CAN
Unspoken	1-4201-0093-9	$7.99US/$9.99CAN
Whispers	1-4201-5158-4	$7.99US/$9.99CAN
Wicked Game	1-4201-0338-5	$7.99US/$9.99CAN
Wicked Lies	1-4201-0339-3	$7.99US/$9.99CAN
Without Mercy	1-4201-0274-5	$7.99US/$10.99CAN
You Don't Want to Know	1-4201-1853-6	$7.99US/$9.99CAN

Available Wherever Books Are Sold!
Visit our website at **www.kensingtonbooks.com**

More by Bestselling Author
Hannah Howell